Louise Jensen began writing after an accident left her with a disability, enforcing a complete lifestyle change. She has sold over 1.5 million copies of her international number 1 psychological thrillers, which all contain complex characters and unexpected twists. She's been nominated for several awards including the Goodreads Debut, the *Guardian's* 'Not the Booker', a CWA Dagger and best Polish Thriller. Her novels have also been translated into twenty-five languages and optioned for TV.

As well as regularly returning to the number 1 spot in the Kindle charts, Louise's books have been featured on the *USA Today* and *Wall Street Journal* bestseller lists. Louise also writes emotional book-club fiction as Amelia Henley.

When she's not writing, she finds inspiration during country walks with her dog.

Also by Louise Jensen

The Fall
All For You
The Stolen Sisters
The Family
The Gift
The Sister
The Surrogate
The Date

Writing as Amelia Henley

From Now On
The Art of Loving You
The Life We Almost Had

THE
INTRUDERS

THE MILLION-COPY BESTSELLING AUTHOR
LOUISE JENSEN

ONE PLACE. MANY STORIES

HQ
An imprint of HarperCollins*Publishers* Ltd
1 London Bridge Street
London SE1 9GF

www.harpercollins.co.uk

HarperCollins*Publishers*
Macken House, 39/40 Mayor Street Upper,
Dublin 1, D01 C9W8, Ireland

This edition 2024

5

First published in Great Britain by
HQ, an imprint of HarperCollins*Publishers* Ltd 2024

ISBN: 9780008508548
CA/ANZ: 9780008508555

This book contains FSC™ certified paper and other controlled sources to ensure responsible forest management.

For more information visit: www.harpercollins.co.uk/green

This book is set in 10.5/15 pt. Sabon by Type-it AS, Norway

Printed and Bound in the UK using 100% Renewable Electricity at CPI Group (UK) Ltd, Croydon, CR0 4YY

For Sarah Wade,
with much love.

NOW

I *didn't mean to hurt anyone but it's irreplaceable and after it was taken I was desperate to get it back.*

Now that I have it again, I'll do anything to keep it.
Anything.
After you've heard my story, I think you'll understand.
I think, perhaps, you'd do the same.

Prologue

Somebody's trying to break into the house.

It's almost inaudible, the sound of the front door handle being lowered, slowly, slowly, but on her way back from the fridge with a bottle of wine, Marina hears the squeak.

Sees the movement.

Her heart pounds painfully in her chest.

Think.

Her husband is upstairs taking a shower – all of her family are upstairs. Their youngest child already in bed, the eldest supposedly reading.

Marina's eyes are locked on the handle but it doesn't move again – had she imagined it? There's a raging storm battering the house.

Could the ferocious wind have rattled the door? She checks that it is locked.

The grandfather clock shows it's only just gone 8.15 but the nights are already lengthening. From the record player in the drawing room, Flanagan and Allen sing 'Run, Rabbit, Run'.

She's playing the song, not because she likes it, but to remind herself.

Run.

Run.

Run.

She shivers. It's cold in this part of the house. She thinks of the fire she has lit as she peers out of the window. Outside, the sky is inky black, the moon casting a creamy light. In the darkness the window is a mirror; all she can see is her own worried face peeking back at her.

Rain lashes against the leaded pane, a cold breeze pushing through the cracks in the frames. The beech tree creaks and bends, a branch tap-tap-taps against the glass.

Let me in.

Let me in.

Let me in.

She is just berating her overactive imagination, allowing herself to relax, heading back to the battered leather armchair that moulds around her body, when she hears the crunch of gravel from the courtyard.

A throaty cough.

Oh, god.

This is not solely a storm or a tree or anything innocuous.

Somebody is out there.

There's a sudden whip of lightning. Startled by the flash she whimpers, her fingers tightening around the neck of the wine bottle, the source of her nightly pleasure has now become a weapon.

Thunder rumbles, low and loud.

Remembering the back door she hurries through the kitchen to double check it's locked, feet cold against the flagstone floor. She grinds to a halt, horrified.

A face outside the kitchen window.

Eyes staring in.

Hot breath misting the glass.

She presses herself against the wall, trying to make herself invisible. The lingering scent of mince and onions from the children's dinner turns her stomach.

The shadow lifts. The figure gone.

Hurry.

Marina rushes back to the entrance hall, picks up the phone with a shaking hand. Her fingers are trembling so violently she has to jab at the numbers several times until she gets it right.

999.

As soon as she is connected she whispers urgently, stating her name, that she lives in Newington House. That she is scared.

Somebody is trying to break in.

She garbles that she is downstairs, by the front door. That, no, she is not safe.

When she had first moved here she had loved the solitude; there aren't any neighbours for miles. It's so beautiful when the buttery sun melts over the woodland. Peaceful. Often the only sound is the rustling of leaves, the birds singing loud and clear, the bubbling of the brook.

Now she feels too isolated.

Aside from her family, there's nobody to hear her scream.

'Mrs Madley, help is on the way,' the operator says in a calm voice. 'Who else is in the house with you?'

'My family.' She runs through them even though it is painful to think of her youngest child starfished in the cot bed that has been passed down through generations, in the pale yellow nursery where cheerful ducks march endlessly around the border.

The eldest child, a teenager, concentrating on her book, forehead creased as she absorbs herself in a world which, right

4

now, is very preferable to this one. Why oh why couldn't she be out with some unsuitable boy tonight?

Her husband, shampooing his hair. Apple-scented suds frothing down the drain.

'How long will the police take to get here?' Marina asks. What should she do in the meantime?

There are precious things under this roof that she needs to protect.

The shatter of glass from the kitchen.

A creak.

The back door opening?

The phone thuds from her hand. Dizziness engulfs her. Ridiculously she is still clutching the bottle of wine. Her mouth hanging open as she draws in shallow breaths, sweat trickling from her upper lip into her mouth.

Think.

She hears the sound of a low voice muttering, the dull thud of footsteps, slow, leaden.

Somebody is inside the house.

Terror beats at her chest with clenched fists.

Run.

She darts into the great hall. Eyes wildly seeking refuge. The oak panelling Marina had once thought so elegant now dark and oppressive, closing in on her. The beamed ceiling pressing down.

She could try and find somewhere to hide but upstairs...

She has to warn her family, *has* to.

She raises the bottle. Can she really smash it into somebody's face?

Yes.

Yes, she can do whatever it takes, her fight or flight response has kicked in, and she is not running away.

But she has never, ever, felt so scared.

From upstairs, the groan of a floorboard. One of the children moving around their room.

Don't come downstairs.

Don't come downstairs.

Don't come downstairs.

She sprints, her socked feet slip-sliding. Has almost made it to the bottom of the stairs in the corner of the room, when an arm snakes around her neck, a hand clamps across her mouth. The wine bottle smashes as it hits the floor, liquid splattering her legs.

She writhes and kicks and tries to bite the fingers that smell of nicotine and that's when she notices.

There is somebody approaching her.

Two.

There are two people in her house. Possibly more.

Hysteria rises.

The intruder is wearing a mask, a sheep's head, and she has never seen anything more terrifying.

Tears leak from her eyes as she watches helplessly as he takes the stairs two at a time. She's still fighting to be free.

Her family.

Marina is bundled roughly away from the stairs, into the drawing room. Shards of glass from the broken bottle pierce the tender skin on the soles of her feet leaving a trail of bloodied footprints behind her. She tries to resist, knocking over a side table with her elbow as she scrabbles for traction on the oak floors. A china bowl smashes on the ground, the scent of floral potpourri cloying. It had always been her favourite but after tonight she would forever associate the smell with this.

If there is an after.

She feels a momentary rise of hope that her husband might have heard the bowl smash but this is dashed when she hears the water gurgling in the ancient pipes.

He's still in the shower.

She imagines him naked, vulnerable, unable to protect them.

She wants to weep.

The intruder throws her onto the green velvet sofa. She scurries into the corner and folds in on herself, crossing her arms over her chest both forming a barrier and trying to hold herself together.

'Help,' she screams.

There's the stinging crack of a hand across her cheek. She begins to cry.

'Please, don't hurt me. I can give you money.'

'Money is not what I'm here for.' The voice is sharp from behind the mask.

Terror is a heavy pressure building in her lungs.

Breathe.

She can't.

Think.

'Please. Take what you want. Those candleholders are solid silver. You could sell them. I've got jewellery upstairs.'

'This is not a robbery.'

'But there are antiques, you could—'

'I am not here for money.'

What do these people want?

But when she learns what it is, she shakes her head, shocked, confused. The intruder advances towards her, eyes blank behind the sheep mask. She cowers. Her cheek still throbbing with pain, fearing there is more to come.

Marina is shaking so violently her teeth rattle together.

'I called the police, they're on their way. If you leave now you can get away. I won't tell them anything. I haven't seen your face.'

Almost in slow motion, bathed in the orangey glow from the crackling fire, the intruder slowly lifts off the mask.

And grins.

And that's when Marina knows with certainty, she is going to die tonight.

There's a chilling scream from somewhere above her.

Her eldest.

'No. She's just a child, a teenager!' What is the man upstairs doing to her? She staggers to her feet. Charges towards the door. Feet stinging. Feels a burning pain in her skull. Instantly there are fingers wrapped around her hair, she feels a clump being yanked from her scalp.

'Please,' she begs. Her arms above her head, hands holding the intruder's wrists, digging her nails sharply into skin, clawing at it.

'Bitch.'

She is roughly pushed away, landing heavily onto her hands and knees. A foot stamps on her back so she's sprawled flat on the floor, clutching the edges of the rug. Rockets of pain shoot through her spine.

'Please,' she begins to crawl. Begging, not just for her life, but for her family's.

Reverberating through the house, her husband's roars of pain.

'Please!' Somehow she staggers to her feet. Hands held out in front of her. 'Please stop.' Every cell in her body buzzing with panic. Willing for someone to save her. For the sound of sirens. For anything.

Lightning whips. Thunder grumbles.

'Mummy?' The sound of a small voice. 'I'm scared.'

The intruder releases her. Stalks towards her youngest child, her baby. Freshly bathed, in hedgehog pyjamas.

Innocent.

'No.' She leaps onto the intruder's back. 'No!'

The breath leaves her body in one violent rush as she's tossed onto the floor as though she weighs nothing. As though she is nothing. Fuelled by a primal instinct she scrambles to her feet. Propels herself forward again.

She doesn't see the knife.

Doesn't feel it pierce her body.

She crumples. Hands automatically seeking out the wound, feeling the warmth of the blood flow through her splayed fingers. Smells the metallic tang.

She stares in horror as the intruder grabs for her child. She wills herself to move, but she can't. She cannot give what has been demanded but she cannot bear what she is seeing. What she is hearing.

'Please,' she begs, no longer sure what she is begging for.

Now, finally, she hears the sirens. Through the glass, the flash of blue lights.

It has felt like hours but can only have been minutes.

The record player whirrs and clicks as it restarts the record.

Run.

Run.

Run.

She closes her eyes.

PART ONE

Chapter One

Cass

The blindfold is tight. The knot against the back of my head uncomfortable.

I've never felt so small, so vulnerable. My anxiety is through the roof as I lick my dry lips and wait.

And wait.

Finally, the opening of the car door. A hand on my elbow.

I unfold myself from the passenger seat, stumble on my pins and needles feet.

'I've got you.' James steadies me. 'We're not going far, you won't need your coat.'

My heart rate begins to slow as cool air caresses my cheeks. The outside bringing a sense of space that chases away the feeling of being trapped.

That all too familiar feeling that causes panic to rise in my throat.

'Can I take this off now?' My fingers flutter to one of James's work ties binding my eyes.

'Not yet. I want it to be a surprise.'

The excitement in James's voice is palpable. I don't ruin

things by telling him that anywhere we are right now is likely to be a surprise – unlike him I didn't grow up in the south, almost everywhere is unfamiliar.

Stripped of my sight my other senses are heightened. I use them to search for clues. I can't hear any traffic so we must be somewhere remote, although from what I've seen of the area where James grew up, everywhere is remote. It's impossible to reach anywhere without driving past acres of green fields first.

The birdsong is loud and there's the rustle of leaves so we must be surrounded by trees. I inhale; the early morning rain has intensified the smell of grass. I can taste the freshness on my tongue – there's no pollution here.

The ground underfoot crunches before hardening. Gravel and concrete.

It isn't so much where we are that I'm desperate to know, but why we're here? Why the secrecy? Images of an ice bucket propping up a bottle of Champagne, a board of pungent cheeses and a punnet of strawberries come to me. A red tartan picnic blanket. James on one knee. A glittering ring...

But surely not today, autumn nipping at the tip of my nose, my cheeks. It's too cold.

Too soon?

Although I've never been as certain about anything as I am about James, we've only been together six months. It's both no time at all and a lifetime. I can't imagine being with anyone else.

Despite what my father might want.

'Almost there,' James says.

I refocus. Wanting to solve the puzzle. I've identified sounds, taste, touch and smells but now there's something else.

A feeling.

A slow crawl of trepidation from the tips of my toes to the top of my scalp.

I stop abruptly. 'James,' my tone is urgent now, 'I don't like this anymore...'

'Relax, Cass. We're here.'

He fumbles to untie the blindfold and then I'm blinking in the unaccustomed brightness. Curved around me is a horseshoe-shaped manor house. With its wings stretching either side of me I feel like the house is holding me.

Gripping me.

Despite the low temperature a flush of heat rushes through me. I push up the sleeves of my jumper. Stepping back, my eyes scan the black and white Tudor timber work above the entrance. The iron 'Newington House' sign, blistered with rust.

Ivy clings to the stone building. There's a sense of someone watching me through the small leaded windows.

This is not a tourist attraction. That much is clear from the unkempt courtyard. The tangle of weeds and nettles.

A crow lands in the tree to my left; he screeches and it sounds like a warning.

My mind is crowded with questions but before I can ask any of them the front door slowly swings open.

A middle-aged woman steps outside. 'Hello again, James.' She smiles warmly at him before she turns to me. 'You must be Cassandra?'

'It's Cassie but most people call me Cass. And you're...?'

'Fran.' She must register my blank look because she elaborates. 'Frances Phillips. I've come to show you around.'

She glances down, her gaze lingering on the zigzag scar on my arm before she looks into my eyes with such intensity I feel all my secrets are exposed.

'Cass.' She's still holding my hand. Her attention flickers back to my arm once more and I feel judged somehow. I want to cover up my scar. To tell her that my dad didn't mean to hurt me, that he loves me, but that would be ridiculous. I don't really know what she's thinking, I'm oversensitive because of the way I left things with my father.

He is over two hundred miles away and I can still feel his fury.

'Fran?' James cuts through my thoughts. Obviously, her thoughts too because her hand suddenly drops mine. She's flustered as she invites us inside.

I hang back because although I can't quite decipher it, I've some deep-rooted instinct telling me that if I step over the threshold, my life will be irrevocably altered and I'm not sure I'm ready for that. But James has a light touch on my lower back, gently propelling me forward.

The entrance hall is dark, oppressive. Low-beamed ceilings and oak panelling make the space feel smaller but really, it's almost the same size as the cramped lounge in my father's flat. On the wall, a fox's head. His beady eyes follow me as I take in the grandfather clock, its hands suspended at half past eight. A shoe rack nestles against a dusty pew. There's a single pair of sunshine-yellow wellington boots. The contrast of the bright, modern footwear against the dated interior is unsettling.

'Come through.' Fran's heels click over the black and grey flagstones. We follow her, James ducking through the doorway, into a larger, grander, space.

The floor is now oak, but both the panelling on the walls and the beams on the ceiling remain the constant. Solemn portraits in gilded frames hang suspended from a picture rail.

Cobwebs stretch between the wall lights like paper chains at Christmas except this is not a family home. It is filthy and unloved and there's a coldness to the air that chills me to the bone. A mustiness that fills my nostrils.

'I'm so glad you're here, Cass,' Fran says softly, with such sincerity for a moment I am glad I'm here too, even if I don't understand why. 'Both of you.'

I stand awkwardly, not sure what I should be doing, saying. James, on the other hand, is like an excited puppy. Rushing to all corners. Trailing his fingers over the intricate carvings on the largest inglenook fireplace I have ever seen.

'I have to be honest' – I pull an apologetic face – 'I've no idea where I am or what I'm doing here.'

Fran throws a confused glance at James. 'You're here about the vacancy? We were all so impressed with your application—'

'Can you please give us a moment?' James dazzles her with his winning smile. Fran glows under its radiance. She's obviously already fond of him.

Who *is* she?

'Of course. I'll be in the drawing room.'

The drawing room!

'Okay.' I'm feeling, not exactly duped, but confused. 'What's going on?'

'This property has been empty for years,' James tells me.

'No shit?' I've only been here for a couple of minutes but already I'm dying for a shower to wash away the grime.

'It was sold to a development company almost thirty years ago. They didn't maintain it because the plan was always to knock it down and build on the land but they never did. It isn't easy to get permission to demolish a Grade I listed building unless there's no viable option and there's nothing wrong with this, structurally. I think they wanted—'

'James.' I can't work out what this has to do with me, with us, and I want him to get to the point. Being blindfolded for the journey has left me feeling queasy.

'Sorry. The development company went bankrupt.' James looks remarkably pleased at this. 'So, it went to auction and Richardson's Retreats snapped it up. They have plans for an exclusive retreat but in the meantime they want to hire a caretaker to keep an eye on the place.'

'And you've applied for the job?' I'm hurt that I didn't know this. That he's apparently planning a future without me in it.

He reads me. 'I've applied for *us*. They want a couple. I guess couples are less likely to have wild parties. Take advantage.'

'For us?' It's too much to take in. Part of me is annoyed that James has dropped this on me without giving me time to formulate my thoughts but then his spontaneity and zest for life is precisely why I adore him.

'I can still keep my job in pharmaceuticals. It's not like I'm on the road that much. They literally just want a presence here so vandals don't break in, that sort of thing. You can set up a studio. Paint.'

'But...' I've so many questions, so many doubts, I don't know where to start. 'This is so far away from home. From my dad.'

'I know.' He's suddenly serious as he encloses my hands in his. 'And I don't want to put you on the spot. I know we haven't been together that long, Cass, but when I think of my future all I see is you.'

'Same.' I grin.

'I hoped if you saw this place, you'd be wowed.'

'I'm... something.' Could I ever feel at home here? It's a world away from where I've come from.

The shabby flat I share with Dad.

That cupboard.

The sense of feeling trapped. Stuck. Screaming and screaming – *help, help, help* – until Dad lifted me out. My arms around his neck.

I shake the thought away. Focus on James telling me all of the things I want to hear.

'Look, Cass. I want to be with you, live with you, but I can't ask you to move into my place even if the landlord wasn't selling it. I've got the smallest room as it is and my housemates are, well, you've met them.'

He pulls a face and he's right. They're idiots. At thirty-four and with a good career, James should perhaps have his own place and I haven't questioned too deeply why he doesn't because at thirty-three I still live at home and the last thing I want to talk about is why.

'I wish we could afford to buy a place together, but we can't. We could look at renting, though it doesn't have to be here, of course. I could move to yours.'

'But it's miles away. You love your job and the head office is here.'

'I love you more. And...' he tries to lighten his voice, 'your dad could always move in. It's big enough.'

'He wouldn't go for that,' I say. We both know that what he wouldn't go for is me living with James. He has never liked him. Half the time I think he doesn't like me either. It's just his way.

'But it's...' I look around helplessly, lower my voice. 'How can we possibly live here—'

'Come with me.' Fran beckons us from a doorway. We pass

through to the next room. It's smaller. Cleaner. Cosier with the large faded red Persian rug in the centre of the room. A green velvet sofa and a squashy leather armchair face the roaring fire. James holds his hands in front of the flames to warm them but I am wary. Scared almost. Perhaps because I've never come into contact with a real fire before, only radiators.

'It may seem overwhelming,' Fran says, 'but really, this is small for a manor house. As well as the great hall and this drawing room there's the dining room, kitchen, off the kitchen is the housekeeper's room that was last used as a study, three bedrooms, a bathroom, a library and a chapel.'

'A chapel?'

'It's not as fancy as it sounds. It was once a bedroom. We've cleaned the rooms we think you'll use. Obviously it's draughty, as old houses are, but there is heating and you can light fires. There's even a TV in that cabinet.' She pointed at the corner and laughed. 'All the mod cons. Can I show you around?'

I nod, not sold on the idea by any stretch but certainly intrigued.

We traipse back into the great hall, to the staircase in the corner.

It's made of stone. Less to hoover, I think.

Stop it.

I haven't agreed to anything yet. But my posture has changed, my spine straighter as I imagine being a lady of the house in times of old, feeling quite at home. James flashes me a smile, knowing I am falling for the house the way I fell for him. I try to neutralize my expression but I can feel my mouth stretch wider, turning up at the corners.

Stop it.

When we reach the landing he bows deeply from the waist and kisses my hand. 'My lady.' He gestures for me to go first.

'My lord.' I drop into a curtsy.

We turn left and then right, walking down a long landing. From out of the window, across the courtyard, I can see the opposite side of the house. We reach the far end and pause in front of the door. 'This is the master.' Fran stands aside so James and I can enter first. I drink in the tapestry on the wall, the oak four-poster bed. Again, a fire burns in the grate. The smell of smoke merges with the lingering smell of cleaning products. Fran has really made an effort.

We move to the next room.

'The nursery,' James says before he opens the door.

He's right.

'Have you been here before?' This room is cold. Untouched. Faded yellow ducks march around the walls, the dusty wooden cot bed pushed against the wall, long enough for a small child. A mobile hangs above by the window, cows and pigs and chickens spinning slow circles.

'No.' He frowns. 'Lucky guess. It makes sense to have the nursery next to the master bedroom, doesn't it?' His breath mists in front of him as he speaks.

I rub my arms, it's freezing.

'Let's go back down to the kitchen,' Fran says, perhaps sensing I am changing my mind.

She hurries us back the way we came, past the front door and into the kitchen.

I don't know what I'd been expecting, a cauldron above a fire perhaps, but it's bright with its cream walls and, not exactly modern with its Eighties country pine cabinets but at least I'd be able to cook when we move in.

If.

I wander over to the window and gaze out onto the tangle of wildflowers, imagine painting them. The textures and the colours, the vibrancy.

'What do you think?' James slips his arms around my waist and nuzzles my neck. 'If we lived here we could save everything we earn for a deposit on our own place.'

'Let's have a coffee and a chat.' Fran opens the cupboards and pulls out mugs.

A thought occurs to me.

'Why didn't the family take any of their possessions when they moved out?'

Fran and James exchange a glance. Again, unease feathers down my spine.

'What?' I cross my arms.

'There is something...' James begins, just as Fran says, 'Full disclosure.'

I wait.

Fran swallows hard and I know that whatever is coming is worse than the things I am imagining. 'The Madley family, three of them were killed. Both parents and their—'

'Killed?' I repeat but she can't look me in the eye. 'Do you mean... murdered?'

There's a beat, her brow creases, she bites her lip and I don't know whether her expression is one of sympathy for the Madley family or worry that we won't want the job anymore. How many other candidates might she have lost when she revealed the tragic history?

'There was a break-in,' James says gently. He's having problems meeting my eye too and I realize he dropped this information on me so I couldn't google the house beforehand.

I'd never have come.

'So they were murdered? What sort of person kills a baby during a robbery?' I feel sick to my stomach thinking of the nursery upstairs.

'The child who died was a teenager. The youngest was a toddler. I haven't been able to find much but they survived, apparently,' Fran says, as though that makes it better and it does, marginally, until I think of those small yellow wellington boots by the front door, forever waiting to be worn.

I turn to James. 'Did you think I wouldn't find out?' I am incredulous. I can't believe he brought me here. Expects me to live here.

'I was going to tell you but I thought if you knew you wouldn't want to come and look.'

'Of course I wouldn't. A family were slaughtered here.' What was wrong with him? Earlier I'd been so certain I knew him well enough after six months to want to spend the rest of my life with him. Now he feels like a stranger.

'I'm sorry. I didn't know how you'd feel about the history. Some people wouldn't mind, it's not as though it affects the present. I want to live with you, Cass. It doesn't have to be here. We can walk away now.'

'It's horrible,' Fran says quietly. 'But opening a retreat here will give the house a second chance. A fresh start. Everyone deserves a fresh start, don't they, Cass?' She looks at me so imploringly.

Have I overreacted? Can I live with the history of the house?

There's an appeal to living here. No distractions.

No Dad.

No Leon.

It's far enough away that he can never find me.

I could actually focus on my work rather than jumping every time I hear a sound. Each time somebody knocks on the door.

But still, people were *killed* here.

Murdered.

Again, I think of Leon.

Don't I have blood on my hands too?

Chapter Two

Cass

*B*lood on your hands.
Blood on your hands.
Blood on your hands.

The train wheels churn out the rhythm while I think of Leon during the long journey back home. Think about the house. The Madley family who aren't here anymore and the people who are. James. My dad.

I think of my mother, imagine her really softly brushing the hair out of my eyes, telling me to follow my heart. I was so young I can't quite remember her. When I try, my mind conjures amorphous memories. Sounds. Smells. Music and laughter and then... nothing. My dad comforting me but also, something else.

Pain in my arm.

A zigzag angry scar.

My father apologizing over and over.

Once, at primary school, one of the boys was bragging he had watched his dad's copy of *A Nightmare on Elm Street*. He had laughed at me, pointed at my arm and called me 'Freddy Krueger'. Looking back through adult eyes I can see it was a gross exaggeration but he was showing off. The only one in our year who claimed he had seen the film, we were all far too young. Impressed by his knowledge of the horror genre the rest of the boys had joined in with the chanting 'Freddy, Freddy', and although I'd held it together in the playground, the second I got home I had burst into tears. Dad had found me in the bathroom, scrubbing and scrubbing at my arm with the nailbrush, trying desperately to wash away the puckered skin.

Gently he had taken the brush off me and dabbed me dry with a soft, white towel.

'You can't wash away a scar,' he said. 'It's part of who you are.'

'What happened to me?' I'd never thought to question it before because he was right. It was as much a part of me as my nose or my ears. And it never hurt, until that day.

'It was my fault,' Dad said.

'Why?'

'I dropped a whisky bottle and you cut yourself on a shard of glass.'

He used to drink a lot. That, I remember clearly. His sour breath. Bloodshot eyes. I think that must have started after my mother died. We never talk about her. He can't.

Or won't.

I wonder when he turned from being my hero to the one I sometimes feared? My memory told me that he had saved me on more than one occasion as I'd banged on the door of the cupboard with my small fists, terrified.

Trapped.

But sometimes, I wonder if he had put me there too.

Locked me in. But why would he? He isn't an abusive man, despite how it might sound.

I remember the sense of relief though, of safety, when he

had leaned in and lifted me out. My arms tightly around his neck. I wouldn't let him go, not for a long time.

Am I ready to let him go now?

Will he let me go?

He relies on me and I'm worried that if I'm not around he'll start drinking again and that never ends well. Is it selfish to want my own life?

Follow your heart, my mum would say.

Wouldn't she?

The ringing of my mobile drags me back to the present.

'Hey, you.'

'Hey.' I stuff my air buds in my ears and settle back to talk to James properly.

'I'm missing you.'

'I've only been gone four hours.' But I smile, the feeling mutual.

'How's the journey?' he asks but what he's really asking is if I've made a decision and I'm not quite sure I have yet.

'It's okay. Had a dry egg sandwich.' I'd saved the crusts in a napkin, and when I'd changed trains I had fed the pigeons who stalked the station platform. 'And my coffee was cold but the giant chocolate chip cookie was amazing so I had a second to make up for the sandwich.'

'You should have a third to make up for the coffee.'

'That's why I love you.'

'That's why you should live with me.'

There's a beat.

'I've read the contract twice now. It's a great opportunity,' he says gently. 'I know the money isn't amazing but with the bonkers price of everything these days it'll be great to not have to pay rent, the bills.'

'And there's no small print? No catches?'

'No. It's like Fran explained. Now Richardson's own the property they want a presence there to protect the place.'

'I don't know what good I'd be if anyone tried to break in.'

'I don't think that's likely. The way the house is shielded from the road, you'd have to know it was there. It hasn't even appeared on any urban explorer videos that I can see. If it was plastered all over the internet I'd be thinking differently. I wouldn't want to leave you there alone if I thought there was a risk.'

'You've really looked into this.'

'Yeah.'

'So we literally just have to live there. No maintenance or gardening.'

'No. Richardson's will be doing their own renovations when they've drawn up the plans and got the relevant permissions. I've looked into that too. Getting permission to change even the interior of a listed building is quite a process. There's the inventory, of course.'

'I've been trying to block that bit out.' Fran had explained the company wants a list of everything in the house so they can decide what to restore and put back in and what they might sell. 'I don't know how to describe half of that stuff, "creepy painting one", "creepy painting two".'

'Fran isn't expecting you to identify and value everything. You aren't presenting the *Antiques Roadshow*. She said you can number things and take photos of anything you're unsure of.'

Right now I'm unsure of everything.

'So. I've been thinking about my mother.' I don't ease in to the change of subject. I don't need to. James understands. He's lost his mother too. It was the first common ground we found. When you're a grown-up you're supposed to be able

28

to cope, aren't you? But it was at that time when everything had escalated with Leon and I wasn't coping. Not with him.

Not with anything.

Anyway, the only reason I'd gone out that night was because my old college friend Shobna was getting married.

'It's my hen do, Cass. You can't miss it.'

Shobna was one of those people with bucketloads of friends. She'd scarcely notice whether I was there or not but she had been so good to me when I had badly needed a friend and so I had gone along to the bar hoping it might make me feel less lonely. Less sad. Less guilty because what I wanted to feel was... more.

Complete.

Instead, I had leaned against a pillar, gripping a glass of Prosecco, uncomfortable in my black dress that clung tightly around my stomach and hips – I am not one of those women who lose weight when they're stressed. Shobna and her friends had danced with abandon in their short sparkly dresses, arms above their heads, hair flying wild around their faces. Shobna's mum had stood on a table, wearing a bright pink silk 'Mother of the bride to be' sash and made a heartfelt speech.

'Here.' Someone offered a tissue and it was then I realized I was crying. I dabbed at my cheeks, embarrassed.

'Sorry,' I said to the man standing in front of me. 'Weddings always make me emotional.'

'Love is a powerful thing,' he said, rolling up the sleeves on his white shirt.

'I think that's what it is.' I drained my drink, my fourth. My head spun and my lips were loose. 'Seeing how much Shobna's mum loves her, it made me... sad, I guess. Sorry. I'm not usually the type to offload on a random stranger.'

'Can this random stranger buy you a drink? I'm here on business and I don't know anyone.'

I hesitated.

'I'm James, if it helps. Not a stranger anymore.' He offered his hand and I took it and it felt so natural it was as though he had held it before.

Soon, we were in a table by the window, fresh drinks in front of us, looking out at the city lights twinkling below us.

'So, random stranger—' he began.

'Cass.'

'Cass. Why does love make you sad?'

'Not love exactly. More a lack of it. Sorry, I'm coming across as very tragic.'

'You're coming across as someone who apologizes a lot. You should never apologize for the way you feel.'

I thought of the million apologies I had made since Leon.

James didn't rush me, he didn't seem remotely uncomfortable with my display of emotion and so I told him how seeing Shobna's mum here for her special night highlighted the fact that my own mother is never, would never be, by my side when I needed her.

'She was decorating my nursery. Dad had painted it mint green before I was born because they didn't know what sex I'd be but when I arrived Mum wanted it to be pink. She fell off a ladder, hit her head. It was instant, apparently.'

'That must be so tough, not having any real memories of her.'

'Yes. I have some grainy Polaroids taken at the hospital of her holding me, and this pendant she always wore.' I fiddle with the silver swan around my neck. 'But that's it really. I have to imagine what she was like because Dad can't bear to talk about her.'

'Perhaps he feels guilty? Like he should have been the one up the ladder.'

'I think so. When I was young I believed it was because he loved her so much that the very thought of her caused him so much pain, and it probably was that, to a degree, but he must blame himself too. Our relationship has always been complicated.'

'My relationship with my dad is fractious. It was as if he never wanted me. I always seemed to irritate him whatever I did.' James opened up to me. 'My mum, she was wonderful though… she died, last year.' A look of utter pain etched into his face. I knew that look, had worn it myself.

'Oh god, I'm so sorry.'

Instinctively, I took his hand again. It wasn't as though my loss was recent like his but still it hurt. Would probably always hurt. My mother had left a gaping hole in my life, in my heart, that I just couldn't fill.

We talked long into the night. Not superficial-we've-just-met chat but real I-want-to-know-you-properly conversations. We discovered that we had a lot more than deceased mothers in common: strained relationships with our fathers. We shared a love of art. A mutual loathing of opera. But it was more than that, more than the superficial, even then. I really believed something had brought us together. That the one in a million chance encounter perhaps hadn't been random at all. We had both lost something but we had found each other. Been given an opportunity to form a new family and although we are living miles apart, that is what we've become over the past few months.

I want to build on that.

Suddenly, I am certain.

'I think in a way my mum – our mums – brought us together and I think that maybe that was for a reason. I don't want to be so far away from you anymore. So yes,' I say now urgently into my phone, as the train rushes past a row of neat terraces.

'Yes?' James questions.

'Yes to the house.' I feel my words lift, light as a balloon, knowing I'm not just saying yes to the house. I'm saying yes to James, to everything, all of it.

Our future.

It is dark by the time the train approaches my station. I wait by the door, suitcase between my legs, swaying with the gentle movements. The train slows, stops. The doors hiss open. The fumes noxious. I'm the only one who alights, the station quiet. Bright lights creating dark shadows. There's a figure with his back to me. He turns, slowly.

Leon?

My hand tightens around the handle of my case, but it isn't him. Ridiculous to think it could be, but I still walk briskly to the taxi rank. Don't let myself relax until I am safely inside a cab. If anything, the scare has cemented my decision. Set it in stone.

I'm leaving.

My stomach churns. I feel sick again. It isn't because of the cloying traffic-light air freshener dangling from the rear-view mirror. It's the thought of telling Dad.

What am I going to say?

Help-help-help.

Sometimes, inside my own head, I still think I can hear myself screaming. Desperate for Dad to rescue me from that cupboard. Dependent. But, if I'm honest, I think that's the way he likes me because it's kept me close and I've relished always having that safety net because I've made mistakes.

Leon.

I close my eyes and think of my future. Of Newington House. But all I can imagine is blood and the screaming in my head morphs into the terrified screams of that poor family. By the time we pull up outside my flat – Dad's flat – I am shaking, slicked in a thin layer of sweat. But ready. Ready to be the hero of my own story. Despite what Dad might say.

What he might do when I tell him my news.

I shudder.

It's been many years since I've been shut in that cupboard but I still fear it.

Deep down, I still fear him.

Chapter Three

Cass

'The Madley family were murdered there.' Dad pales, covers his heart with his hand. I can feel my own breaking. Why had I been so transparent when I told him? A triple murder is hardly likely to convince him that it's a good idea I move to Newington House, is it, and more than anything I'd like him to be happy for me.

'It was a long time ago,' I say. 'The...' I hesitate. Not wanting to say the word 'murderers' but recognizing that 'killers' didn't sound any better. 'The intruders responsible were caught.'

I had googled the house as soon as I'd got onto the train. There weren't many results, which surprised me, but then it was over thirty years ago. Not everything ends up on the internet. The newspaper report I read, though, said that there had been two perpetrators – one had been found dead in the house and the other had been arrested and later sentenced.

The police officer who attended the scene said it was one of the most horrific scenes he'd ever come across and didn't believe it was 'indicative of a robbery'.

From there I'd trawled the internet for some reassurance that tragedies didn't always mean negative energy, ghosts. Forums seemed to be split 50-50 with half not believing in spirits and the others convinced that almost everywhere was haunted.

I don't know what I believe in, except love. I believe in love.

I want to be with James.

'Dad, this isn't something I've agreed to lightly. As soon as I heard the history of the house, I wanted to leave but whatever happened there is in the past and it has no bearing on my future. Bad things happen every day. We don't know anything about the former tenants of this flat but—'

The smoke alarm begins to trill.

From the oven, the smell of caught pastry. I'm touched he's taken the time to cook for me, my favourite leek and potato pie. He's shaky as he pulls himself to his feet and flaps a red and white chequered tea-towel at the smoke alarm.

I feel a swell of love for him. Growing up, our relationship was one big contradiction. On one hand there was his drinking, his mood swings. My confusion that one minute he'd be nurturing and kind, and the next he'd be distant, angry. My bewilderment that each time he lifted me out of the cupboard he'd stroke my hair and tell me I'd put myself there although I had no recollection of it. But then, there were all the times he'd sit on the edge of my bed and make me giggle, making up stories of the animals who lived in the forest, putting on different voices for Faulkner the fox and Bartholomew the badger. On sports day he'd stand at the finishing line, cheering loudly as I ran towards him, balancing an egg on a spoon. He'd always enter the fathers' race. He never won.

Perhaps when I move, when there's a distance between us and we aren't living on top of each other, our relationship will be on more of an even keel. But still I'm wary as I watch him trying to silence the smoke alarm, trying to second guess what he's thinking.

I should have waited until we were sitting around the table, Dad making his usual jokes about how restaurants would charge more for the lumps in his mashed potato and me laughing it'd be worth every penny. I shouldn't have blurted out the news almost the minute I walked in but I am cold and tired and scared that if I wait, if I sit on my familiar chair with the wobbly leg, and use the same fork I have always used with the bent middle prong, that moving will seem too overwhelming. Too enormous. That I will resign myself to staying here where everything is exactly as it always has been.

Safe.

I glance at the cupboard in the hallway. Feel the jolt of panic as the sense of being trapped seeps through me.

Safe?

But my demons are here and I know who they are, where they are. What if I get new ones when I move into that big old house with its dark, dark history?

The beeping noise stops and Dad turns to me. His face displays it all – shock, fear, anger – but then it settles on such an unbearable sadness I stand and rub his upper arms with my hands. They're thinner then they used to be. He's ageing. Should I really be leaving him?

'It's so far away, Cass,' he says in such a small voice.

'It's just a train ride.' I force a smile because I've just got off that train and I know it's three changes and five hours and it's exhausted me. It isn't a journey a sixty-year-old with angina should be undertaking regularly.

'Are you leaving because of me?' His voice cracks. I've never heard him sound so vulnerable and it tears me apart. I cross to the oven and pull open the door. Flap away the smoke with one hand, while I slide the dish onto the worktop. The pie is home-made. He's rolled our initials out of the leftover pastry just like he used to, glazed them with milk and they sit on the top, shiny and fat.

Sing a song of sixpence.

The nursery rhyme from my childhood.

I imagine those four and twenty blackbirds fighting to be free under the crust. Wings beating furiously. Beaks pecking. Suddenly everything seems so fragile.

I feel so fragile.

I want to travel back in time. Back to popcorn in front of *Beauty and the Beast*, being carried to the park on Dad's shoulders. Sunday afternoons building model aeroplanes out of Airfix, him instructing me on where to dab the glue, how to apply the paint in a thin layer because sometimes his hands shook so much. The good times must have outweighed the bad because, in spite of everything, he was there for me.

Always there.

My childhood hadn't been all princesses and castles, glitter and sparkles, there had been dragons and monsters too, a blackness under the surface, a bleakness, but mostly we were happy then. Mostly, we're happy now.

Or we were.

Before Leon.

'I'm leaving because...' I take a deep juddering breath because here, with my feet firmly on the brown swirl carpet, surrounded by the walls and shelves lined with framed photos of my milestones – in a hospital cot, hours old, woollen hat falling across one eye; first bath, the rubber duck almost as large as I was; first tentative steps, arms spread for balance; first day at school, hair already escaping from my plaits – I am not sure I want to leave at all. 'Because I love James.' And there it is, the wedge between us, the one thing I am certain of. 'He's a good man, Dad.'

'If he's a good man, he wouldn't be dragging you to the middle of nowhere.' Dad's fists clench by his sides, the muscle in his jaw tics. His burst of anger reminiscent of the one he displayed when I had left this time for the weekend. When I leave every time for the weekend. I shrink back in my seat.

'I'm sorry.' He takes a moment. Splays out his hands. 'Can't you both live here?' He looks around the too cramped space. 'Well perhaps not here but locally? I could help you with rent.'

'Dad, you can't.' He's become more and more frugal over the years, taking 'make do and mend' to a whole new level. He works so hard. Despite his drinking, he's managed to hold down a job as a GP, but money seems to slip through his fingers. It doesn't go on booze anymore but it shouldn't go on me either. 'And… what would I do? Get another job that… that…' I lower my head. I can't talk about Leon. I just can't. 'At Newington I'd have the time to paint. The space. A chance to explore whether I can make it as an artist. And I'd get paid for it. It's a great opportunity.'

'It isn't your home,' he says firmly.

'This will always be home,' I say gently but that isn't true. Home is where the heart is and my heart is with James.

When there is nothing left to say we pick at the pie that is cold and unappealing in silence. Later, in bed, through the thin walls I hear the sound of crying and I want to go in and comfort him the way he would comfort me when I was a child, but if I do that, if I sit on his bed and take his hand in mine, I might make a promise that will be impossible to keep. So instead I pull the soft feather pillow over my head, and breathe in the smell of summer meadow fabric conditioner and I tell myself that I can always come back here if things don't work out. Of course, I didn't know then that I wouldn't be able to.

It had been a strained week before I find myself saying goodbye to my home. Goodbye to Dad.

Hours later, my eyes prick with tiredness as I stack my suitcases into the rack by the door after another change. It's the last leg of an exhausting and uncomfortable journey. The waistband of my jeans is digging in me and I can't wait to take them off and put on my comfy pyjamas. I really shouldn't have bought yet another giant cookie. The train leaves the station, gathering speed. Each turn of its wheels taking me towards James but further from Dad and although the screaming pain in my shoulders is from hefting my luggage all day, it could easily be because I'm being torn in two.

I miss you.

I miss you.

I miss you.

The train hisses out the rhythm, my body swaying along as I head towards an empty seat. There are only two other people in the carriage. A middle-aged man, folding his scarf into a pillow before settling his head against the window, and an elderly lady with a mop of unruly white hair. I make eye contact as I pass her. She pats the seat next to her and smiles.

I hesitate. I'm exhausted, emotional, not in the mood for conversations with a stranger, but there's a loneliness about her which amplifies the guilt I'm feeling about Dad.

Who will he talk to without me?

I sit next to her and introduce myself. She tells me her name is Peggy and she's been to visit her grandchildren. I ask if she has any photos of them, not because I want to see them, but because I can tell how much they mean to her.

'I don't but they are on the Facebook. Do you have a computer? I could give you their names?' She looks so hopeful.

'I've got my MacBook right here.' I tap my tote bag, stifle a yawn. 'Shall I go and get us some coffee and you can show me?'

'Oh, that's kind of you. You must let me pay.' Her hands shake as she unzips her purse.

'Please don't worry. I can pay on my phone.' I stand and reach for my bag.

'I'd like to treat you.' She pushes coins into my hand before I can pick up my tote. 'And a pack of shortbread if there is any.'

The buffet car is at the other end of the train and by the time I'm making my way back to my carriage we've pulled into a station and when we leave again I stumble, spilling coffee over myself. Still, for Peggy's sake I force a smile as I enter our carriage but when I reach our seats, she isn't there. Confused, I look around. The man is still in the same spot. My suitcases are by the door but Peggy has gone, and so has my bag.

'Excuse me,' I ask the man. 'Have you seen the old lady that was sitting here?'

'She got off at the last stop.'

'Did you notice if she had a bag with her?'

'A large, brown leather one, I think. Are you okay?'

'She's stolen my bag, my phone, my laptop.' But more than that, she's stolen my trust.

Tears sting the back of my eyes.

The man looks at me with pity. 'I'm Robin. Do you need anything?'

I sit down on the seat opposite him, shaken, 'do you want this?' I push one of the coffees across the table. 'If I could borrow your phone and ring my boyfriend please?' I'd told James I'd meet him at the house but without money for a taxi I need him to pick me up. But when Robin hands me his mobile I realize I don't know James's number from memory.

'I'm Cass, by the way.' I'm at a loss. 'I don't know who to call. I need to cancel my bank card but I don't know the number.'

Robin googles my bank and I contact them on his phone and explain the situation.

'At least Peggy can't go on a spending spree at my expense,' I say after I've hung up.

'What station are you getting off at?' Robin asks and when I tell him, he tells me that's where he's heading too. 'It's where I grew up,' he explains. 'My dad's died and I'm going to sort his house out.'

'I'm so sorry.' Suddenly my own problems seem minor.

'It's...' He tails off, shrugging. 'It's early days. That's why I'm oversharing. It really hasn't sunk in yet. I didn't spend as much time with him as I should have done. Bloody selfish really because I work from home and can be based anywhere.'

I reach across the table and give his hand a brief squeeze before I slide the shortbread towards him, aware that this could be me one day. Telling a stranger I didn't spend enough time with my own dad.

Am I doing the right thing?

'Sorry if I've made you uncomfortable,' Robin says.

'You haven't. It just made me think about my own father. I'm moving away. Today, actually. Now. Or I'm trying to at least. I don't even have the address of where I'm going. It was in my bag. You might know it. It's quite large. Newington House?'

'The Madley murder house?' Robin gasps. 'Sorry, I only

know it because I grew up in the area. You do know, don't you, about—'

'Yes. Do you think I'm awful for moving in?'

'I think what happened there was...' He shakes his head. 'I don't think you're awful. When a property gets to a certain age it's bound to have experienced loss, tragedy in some shape or form.'

'You don't think Peggy stealing my bag is a sign that I should go home? Fate?'

'I don't believe in fate,' Robin says.

'I believe in everything. Dad told me once that coincidences mean we're on the right path. I read a book where there was an eight-year-old called Sally Ashley who let go of her kite which had her phone number on. It landed in a different county, in the garden of another eight-year-old girl called Sally Ashley.'

'That's crazy.'

'I know, right? And there was a pair of twins, separated at birth, who reunited after forty years. Both were called Vanessa, both married men called Stan and divorced them. Both had second husbands named Frank and daughters named Helen, cats called Smoky and both were HR managers.'

'That's... mind-blowing. Okay, I concede, coincidences are a thing but I don't think you getting your bag stolen is an omen. Look, I know where Newington is and I can drop you off on my way to Dad's.'

'Thanks.'

We chatted for the rest of the journey. I felt I'd found a friend in my hour of need.

I trusted him, confided in him, the odd circumstances we'd found ourselves in made me open up. Tell him things I hadn't told James.

There were things I *really* should have told James about myself.

Perhaps if I had, everything might not have ended the way it did.

With another tragedy.

Ladybird, ladybird, fly away home.

Chapter Four

James

There are things James hasn't told Cass that he probably should have, but he hadn't meant to – doesn't want to – hurt anyone.

His mobile rings again and once more he checks the screen wanting it to be Cass – she hasn't replied to him for hours – but it isn't. It's Angelica, for the fourth time.

He answers, not because he wants to talk to her, but because she isn't going to stop calling until he does.

'James.' She's crying and all at once James feels terrible. Something must have happened.

'What's wrong? Are your parents okay?' After the sudden passing of his mother he carries a low-level fear of death that he hadn't had before she had died. An uncomfortable awareness of his own mortality. The fragility of everyone around him.

'They're both fine.' She reassures him of this first because she knows how hard he'd been hit by the loss of his mum because she had been the one to hold him when he cried. The one to thread her fingers through his as the dark, polished coffin with the shiny brass handles was slowly lowered into the damp ground. She had made him chicken soup, not the chicken soup of his childhood with noodles and sweetcorn and the distinct spicy tang, but she'd done her best to replicate it. Then he'd repaid her love, her loyalty, by leaving her. It doesn't matter how often he tells himself that their relationship had been over months before it actually ended. That he'd been on his way to tell Angelica that they were through when the hospital had called about his mum. Guilt still squirms in the pit of his belly whenever he thinks about the way Angelica's eyes had lit up when he said he had something important to say. How she had briefly glanced to her empty ring finger before gazing up at him with such hope.

'I was in Boots,' she says now, taking a shaky breath while James's mind conjures up the worst reasons she might be in a chemist. She's sick. Dying. 'Buying a lip balm, you know the one you like?' He doesn't reply, invaded by the unwelcome memory of her mouth pressed against his, sticky and tasting of peppermint. 'And I bumped into Chris.'

'Right.' James knows what his flatmate must have said, what's coming.

'He said you're moving out today? That you're moving into that... that murder house, with *some woman*?'

Only Angelica could make 'some woman' sound more repulsive than the word 'murder'.

'Yes, I am.' He doesn't offer any sort of explanation because, with her, he has already used all of his apologies.

'What's she got that I haven't?'

'It isn't like—'

'Is she pretty?'

His silence causes more guilt to turn over in James's stomach. Is he being disloyal to Cass by not telling Angelica that Cass is the most beautiful woman he has ever seen? It seems cruel if he does though.

'Does she look like me?'

'Angelica, please. I'm sorry I've hurt you but—'

'You're making a mistake, rushing into it. You've known her five minutes, James.'

'Six months.'

'Six months?' A beat. 'That means that—'

'I'm sorry.' He isn't proud there was a crossover, even if it was only a few days.

'You fucking should be. Anyway, six months isn't long enough to get to know someone properly. You can't have got over us yet. We were together for three years. *Three*.'

'I know.' He doesn't know what to say. Is it worse to tell Angelica he loves Cass, that this isn't a whim, or to let her think this is a rebound? But if he does that then she might carry the hope they'll get back together. Either way, he can't magic away the pain she feels.

'I want you to be happy,' he says, because this much is true.

'No you don't. And I don't want you to be happy either.' She cuts the call and he knows he hasn't heard the last of her.

He pulls up outside Newington House. Fran's car is already there.

'Welcome.' She beams, the lines around her eyes crinkling. 'I'm so glad you're here.'

He grins back, thoughts of Angelica fading away. There's something reassuring about Fran, comfortable. It is all going to be okay.

James opens his boot and she peers inside.

'Is this everything?'

'Yeah.' He doesn't have much. His clothes. Some photos of his mum. When he separated from Angelica he pretty much left everything behind.

They carry his possessions into the house. He gazes around with wonder.

'I can't believe we're going to live here.'

'What time is Cass arriving?'

'I'm not sure. She hasn't texted me to confirm. She shouldn't be too far away but she might have missed her connection. I've got a meeting in an hour. I'm a little worried, actually. She has the key you couriered to her but it won't be nice arriving after a long journey to an empty house.'

'I can wait for her, make her a cup of tea. I've stocked up on some basics for you.'

'Thanks. I hadn't even thought about shopping. I'll pick up a takeaway on the way home.' Between them they carry his things up the stairs. The air is noticeably cooler. The window on the landing is open. The smell of lemon cleaning products is overpowering but still it's freezing.

James latches it shut.

In the master bedroom James hefts his case onto the bed. The bed the Madleys' slept in.

The bed...

'Fran. Were they...' For some reason, James lowers his voice. 'Did they die in here?'

'I don't think you should dwell—'

'But did they?' He turns to her, desperate for answers.

'No details were ever released other than the basics.'

'It's like they just stepped out and could be back any moment.' On the dressing table, a silver brush. Dark strands of hair entwined in the bristles.

The personal touches he'd thought of as charming when he'd first visited now seem creepy. He picks up the brush, turns it over his hand. The handle is cold, untouched for many years.

He places it in the drawer. 'I'm amazed that urban explorers haven't broken in and stolen everything.'

'You can't see the house from the road and it isn't known because it hasn't got a significant history, I mean in terms of royal visits or anything,' she quickly adds. 'I think, over the years, it's just been forgotten. The tragedy happened in the time before everything was logged online. I'm sure if it took place now and the house was left empty, it would be on YouTube in an instant.'

'Probably. It's amazing. The National Trust didn't want it?'

'The National Trust are gifted many of their properties and probably couldn't afford to buy it, even if they wanted it. The government won't fund a purchase unless there is a good reason. If Henry the Eighth or Queen Victoria had slept here then things would probably be different. You'd be surprised at how many smaller manor houses have become derelict because nobody has put money into them. We're lucky the building company didn't auction off the contents.'

'Isn't it too small for a retreat?' James hadn't asked before because all he had been thinking of was himself and Cass.

'It will be an exclusive retreat. We're hoping to convert the barns into accommodation. The house will be mainly for dining and therapy sessions.'

'Like massage?'

'Talking therapies. For trauma.'

It seems apt. Trauma is ingrained in the very fabric of this house.

James gives an almost imperceptible shake of his head. Thinking of the house as a living, breathing thing that can feel.

Remember.

Goosebumps spring up on his arm.

Someone's walked over your grave, his mum would have said.

'I've got to get to my meeting,' he says. He's early but he's craving fresh air, space. Not this oppressive room with the carnivorous fireplace that looks as though it could swallow you up. 'I'll just use the bathroom.'

'I'll go and wait for Cass in the kitchen,' Fran says.

After James has used the toilet he washes his hands, the water gurgling as it runs through the pipes. It sounds like a groan, as though the house is in pain.

Hurriedly he heads back to the bedroom to pick up his brief-case.

The brush is on the dressing table again. James shoves it back into the drawer, hoping they won't have problems with Fran rearranging things. He and Cass might only be employees but this will be their home, however temporarily.

He heads down the landing.

The window is open again. James appreciates Fran trying to air the house but shuts it nevertheless.

By the front door he pauses. Looks at those small yellow wellington boots in the shoe rack. He really should put them out of sight but he doesn't have the heart.

As he gazes at them he feels eyes on him.

Beady, amber eyes.

He grimaces.

That bloody taxidermy fox's head can definitely go.

He had told Cass that the past of the house didn't affect the present because all he could think of was the fact they'd be paid for living rent-free. Be able to save up. But now he's at Newington, with its low ceilings and dark furniture and troubled history, it doesn't exactly seem like the answer to his dreams, more like the start of a nightmare.

From a glass casket on top of the dresser a badger bares his teeth in a forever scream.

Like something out of a horror film.

James has just slid into the Audi his mum gifted him on his thirtieth birthday, when the phone rings.

It isn't Cass as he'd hoped, but her father.

'Hello, Adrian.' James is wary. Knowing that his potential future father-in-law doesn't much like him and that was before he moved his daughter over two hundred miles away from him.

'James.' Adrian falls silent but James can hear the scrape of a chair, the flare of a lighter. Adrian drawing deeply on a cigarette. For a doctor he isn't very healthy but then for a pharmaceutical rep neither is James, eating too many Big Macs when he's out on the road.

'Before you move in with Cass,' Adrian pauses, 'there is something you need to know.'

James doesn't think there is anything that can change the way he feels about Cass but as Adrian continues to speak James realizes that Angelica is right. Six months really isn't long enough to get to know someone.

He might be keeping secrets, but Cass's are worse.

Chapter Five

Cass

I don't know what's worse. Pulling up outside Newington House and realizing from the absence of his car that James isn't here, or that Fran is. All I want to do is shower and unpack but now, first, I'll have to tell her that the paperwork and the key she sent me has been stolen.

'Thanks for everything.' I give Robin a quick hug. 'I'll be in touch.' He has written down his phone number for me.

By the time the cab has disappeared from view Fran has joined me outside.

'Cass.' She opens her arms and I step into them. She hugs, not in the brief way you do when you don't really know someone, but tightly as though she's trying to tell me something but I don't know what it is.

'Is everything okay?' I step back. 'Where's James?'

'He's in a meeting. He wasn't sure what train you were on. He's been trying to contact you. We've both been worried.'

'Sorry.' I don't tell her what's happened, partly because I want to tell James before anyone else and partly because, if I'm being honest, I feel like a fool trusting a stranger with my bag just because she looked like a sweet old lady.

She lifts my case laden with brushes and palettes and oils, my hopes and my dreams, as though it weighs nothing at all.

As we step inside it's as though a cloud has passed over the sun and I blink in the gloom. It's colder in here than it was outside.

My stomach flips as my eyes are drawn to those small yellow wellingtons and when I pull my gaze away it lands upon the fox's head. I'm definitely going to throw a tea towel over it as soon as Fran has left. I love animals so much I turned vegetarian several years ago. If I don't eat dead creatures, I certainly don't want to look at them.

It's warmer here, a fire burning. She invites me to sit and I sink onto a pine chair with spindly legs. Exhausted from the early start, the journey, I let her take charge. She fills the kettle, drops teabags into mugs, slices me a thick slab of coffee cake. I wonder if this is what it would have been like growing up with a mother, not that Fran is old enough to be mine but someone looking after me at the end of a bad day isn't something I'm used to.

While my fork scrapes the buttery icing from the plate I scan the kitchen. From what I remember it's definitely the most modern room in the house but still some of the original features have been preserved.

'What are those grinders on the beams?' I ask Fran.

'One was for salt and the other for sugar, they both used to come in blocks.'

'Perhaps they can be the first things I list on the inventory.'

I'd been trying not to give the daunting task too much thought. Instead, I'd been too busy romanticizing our new roses-around-the-door life. Picturing how I'd pass my time creating art, my hair bundled on the top of my head, wearing

James's oversized shirts. He'd arrive home at the end of the day, tenderly wipe a streak of paint from my cheek. Tell me it was adorable how I'd lost track of time, hadn't cooked any dinner. He'd unbutton the shirt, slip it from my shoulders and...

Stop it.

My imagination has veered into terrible rom-com territory, either that or a porn film, depending on what happens after my shirt – his shirt – is puddled on the floor.

'Great. I've begun a list to start you off so you have some idea how much detail we need.' She pushes papers across the table towards me. 'If you come across anything you think I need to know about, can you call me straight away?'

'Okay.'

'The main thing is to maintain physical presence here both to let in any tradesmen that might need access to quote and to put off any' – she frowns – 'explorers.'

We both know what she means and it's a stark reminder that this is not a roses-around-the-door-house.

I stifle a yawn.

'I'll leave you to settle in before James gets home.'

Home!

Fran fumbles in her bag, pulls out her car keys. Her steps are light as her heels tap-tap-tap across the flagstone floor towards the front door. 'Cass' – she turns, face solemn – 'if you notice anything out of the ordinary can you give me a ring? You've got my mobile number.'

'Out of the ordinary?'

'Yes. Older places can be full of surprises. This is the first time I've been allocated my own project and I... It hasn't been easy for someone like me to be given such a position.'

'Like you?'

'A woman. Biological clock ticking. Some of the men at Richardson's think I should never have been promoted. Convinced I'll be disappearing to have a baby before it's too late on that front.'

I nod, sympathetically. I know all about male entitlement in the workplace.

Leon.

'Of course. I'll come to you first with anything.' Our eyes meet and something unspoken passes between us.

As she drives away I can still feel the bond between us.

The front door is heavy. It's the first time I've closed it. I can't help smiling. However temporary, for now this is my home.

Our home.

I glance at the grandfather clock. It says 8.30 but when I check my watch it's only two-thirty. I open the door to the clock and find the key and then I wind it. It tick-tick-ticks, moving time forwards. In a few hours James will be back and there are a million things I want to do first.

Revitalized at the thought of our first evening here I pick up my case and head into the great hall. Although Fran keeps saying this is a small manor house, to me, growing up in a flat in a crowded city, the space seems vast. I know from all the googling I've done this week that it will have been in this room that social events took place, local disputes would have been heard. What did they argue over?

Did an argument lead to the murder of the Madleys?

The thought takes my breath away. I'd been trying my hardest not to think of the family before.

I drag my case up the stairs but I can't escape the presence of the Madleys. Everywhere there are portraits. Men and women posing in stiff, uncomfortable clothing, solemn expressions. Children with their arms looped around dogs, no expression in their eyes.

Cobwebs stretch between them.

My chest is tight, the feeling that I've made a huge mistake pressing down on me as I hurry across the landing.

In the bedroom, I breathe a little easier. James's luggage is already on the bed. A fire burning. It's clean. Warm.

I unzip my case and pull out the dress I want to wear tonight. Lift out my make-up bag and set it on the dressing table next to a silver brush. I pick it up, am about to put it in the drawer when I spot the long dark hair twisted among the bristles, waiting to decompose.

At the thought of decomposition I think about the rest of the Madleys. How fragile life is. How you can be here one minute and gone the next. Gently, I place the brush back where I found it. I don't want to hide their possessions away, pretend they never existed. I can live here alongside their memories.

Suddenly, I have an urge to explore the rest of the house. I know there is the nursery and the bathroom on this wing so I head back past the stairs to the other wing. The first room I reach is a bedroom with a single bed. It has a calming energy and I think here, I could paint. Unlike the rest of the house, which is stuck in time, here, torn posters hang from the wall; Guns N' Roses. Nirvana. Oasis. Bon Jovi. A small, faded, orange and yellow striped rug over the oak floorboards.

This must be where the teenage girl had lived – did she die in this room? I swallow a lump of sadness that has risen in my throat. It's all so tragic. I open the heavy wardrobe door. At the bottom is a doll, long dark hair matted, waxy, rigid arms raised towards me as though pleading to be picked up as she stares at me with unnaturally bright blue eyes. How long has it been since she was last played with? A childhood favourite the teenager couldn't bear to part with or a family heirloom?

Those eyes…

Hurriedly I shut the door but I can still feel it watching me.

Lonely.

That's the sense I get from it. Perhaps that was how the girl it belonged to felt? I gaze out across the garden. What had she thought when she looked at this very view? Did she notice the beauty, the tranquillity, or did she take it for granted? What was the last thing she saw? Was it the twisted face of her killer or was she staring out of the window? At the treetops? The sky?

Can I really stay here?

Fran had asked me to call her if I noticed anything out of the ordinary but *nothing* about this house is ordinary.

Older places can be full of surprises.

Full of ghosts.

I can almost hear them whispering to me but cannot make out what they are saying.

It's just the breeze.

I glance towards the wardrobe, imagining the doll tap-tap-tapping on the door to be free. Wondering why she's spent thirty years being shut in the dark. I can't stop obsessing. What can have happened to the Madley family? The teenage girl? The toddler? The parents? Who were they? What led to the terrible events that night? I close my eyes and ask for a sign and when I open them again there's a single white climbing rose swaying from the trellis in the breeze, directly in front of the window.

In the overgrown garden a swing moves back and forth in the breeze as though it's searching for a child to play with.

I open the window and reach for the flower, a thorn pricking my skin, a drop of blood rising to the surface.

Usually I don't mind the sight of blood but today it turns my stomach. It must be the stress of the move, the history of the house making me nauseous. I pull a tissue from my pocket and wrap it around my thumb.

When I turn back to the rose its petals are no longer pure white but decaying, curling at the edges. Am I so tired that I'm imagining things? I step closer to the flower; it's as though it's been dead for days but that's impossible, isn't it? Unless I'm going crazy. Just seconds ago it was living. Healthy.

Here one minute, gone the next.

Just like the Madley family.

What did happen to them? The girl whose bedroom I am in? Who were you?

Tell me.

Tell me.

Tell me.

An overwhelming sense of loss fills me as I stare at the flower. Whispering its name as though I can bring it back.

Out of the corner of my eye a shadow passes and I jump as I think I hear the same name whispered back to me.

Rose.

Chapter Six

Rose

'Rose!'

Her little brother called her name, squealing with laughter, pumping his chubby toddler arms by his sides, small legs covering such a short distance that Rose could easily have caught him, but she didn't. Enjoying the game although, at fifteen, feeling too old for it.

'Careful,' she called as he dodged a side table. 'You'll trip.'

'Just like Trip!' He brandished the green plastic T-rex he carried around in his fist. They had named him Trip because the proportions of the dinosaur made it appear as though he'd trip over at any moment.

'Just like Trip,' Rose laughed.

It pained her to remember now that when she had found out her mum was pregnant she had been horrified.

She had longed for a sibling to play with when she was three years old but not anymore, with a twelve-year age gap between them.

It was *embarrassing*.

For the next few months Rose adjusted to the thought of

no longer being an only child. Thought it might even be fun, having a sister to share secrets with.

She had felt the disappointment bitterly when her dad told her it was a boy. But when she held her brother for the first time she had fallen instantly in love. Gazing with wonder at his tiny fingers and toes. His paper-thin skin. He was strapped in a sling across her mother's chest like a baby kangaroo. Rose had affectionately called him 'Roo' and the nickname had stuck.

And just like that they had became a four.

She adored her little brother.

Now, the end of the school holidays loomed towards her and she couldn't bear the thought of saying goodbye.

When her father had first told her that after primary she would be going away for the next stage of her schooling she had been scared, confused, felt unloved, unwanted, but he'd shared his own experiences with her. Made it sound like the most exciting thing ever.

'You'll have such fun.' Mum placed a clutch of musty old books into her hand. 'I loved these when I was a child. They're all about a boarding school called Malory Towers.'

Rose had read one, her nerves calming as she read that despite their differences and challenges the pupils shared a sense of camaraderie.

But when Mum packed her off with a too-bright smile, eyes glazed with tears, she had realized that her school was nothing like the one depicted in those books. It didn't look like a castle. It wasn't surrounded by the sea. Dad was fond of saying that boarding school had been 'the making of him' but Rose felt it would be the breaking of her. The unfamiliar bed. Food she wasn't used to. Endless rules. But still she worked hard, wanting her father's approval until, eventually, she settled in. Her pillow no longer soaked by her tears each night. She had friends. But she'd give it up, she'd give them up in an instant if she could come home. She adored Roo and she wanted to be there for every single milestone.

'I don't want to go back to school and leave him,' Rose had said to her dad as she cradled a new born Roo on her lap while her mum took a bath.

Dad laughed.

Laughed.

And that sound was stinging and hurtful.

'We'll be okay without you, won't we, my son and heir?' Dad said as he lifted Roo and held him to his chest.

And that was when she began to question her place in the family. Noticing that Dad's tone was hard with her, but softer with her brother.

'But he is just a baby,' Mum reassured her when Rose raised her concerns but Rose knew, she *knew* that she was an outcast. She felt as though she was on the outside looking in, the stray cat with his nose pressed up against the window. Her dad feeding her scraps of love, as he fed the cat scraps of fish.

Still, she hadn't broached leaving boarding school since then but more and more she thought of Roo when she was away. She had missed his first words, first steps.

He was slowing now as she chased him, tiring. He climbed on the sofa and stuck his pudgy thumb in his mouth. Rose sang 'Twinkle, Twinkle, Little Star' until he fell asleep.

After covering him gently with a blanket she joined her mother in the kitchen. She was whisking eggs for an omelette. Rose picked up a knife and began chopping vegetables.

'Roo's asleep.'

'You've worn him out. He's been so excited about you coming home.'

'He's grown so much. He'd literally only just learned to walk and now he's running.'

'He's been running a while.'

'I'm missing it all.' Rose wiped her eyes with the back of her sleeve.

'Let me do the onions, you start on the mushrooms,' Mum said but it wasn't the onions bringing tears to Rose's eyes.

'Mum? I was thinking I could leave boarding school? Live here full time? Go to the village secondary?'

She held her breath while she waited for the reply.

Mum's hand stilled mid-air, knife poised.

'I think…' She cleared her throat. 'Boarding school can give you a far better education than anywhere local.' She went back to chopping and Rose felt the sharp point of the blade in her heart. She'd thought her mother would jump at the chance to have her here full-time. She felt unsure, uncertain. Now not entirely convinced that she belonged here in this large house where she sometimes felt like a visitor. But then she didn't completely belong at boarding school. She didn't belong anywhere.

'Rosy Posy.' Sensing her distress, Mum placed her hands on Rose's shoulders, her eyes, the same shade of green as her own, filled with emotion. 'I love you and I miss you when you're not here. I thought you were enjoying school now?'

'I don't hate it,' was the best that she could offer. Does anyone ever enjoy school?

'We just want you to have options. The local school is in special measures again. If you decide on university you need good grades.'

'Yeah, I know.'

'You know what else you need?' Mum turned up the volume on the radio. 'Love, love, love,' she sang, her voice soft, melodic. She took Rose by the hand and twirled her across the kitchen. They sang the Beatles' song together, slip-sliding in their socks, locked in a clumsy waltz. And in that moment Rose truly believed that all you *did* need was love.

She *was* lucky.

Her parents cared about her education. Encouraging her to plan for the future even though she was not yet sure what she wanted to do once she was grown up but knowing she wanted to do *something*.

Be someone.

To travel the world.

To fall in love.

To experience everything.

Her plans changed daily but she jotted them down in her journal. Lists of things she wanted to achieve by the time she was thirty after which she'd probably feel too old to do any of them. Although since becoming a big sister she had realized that she liked looking after things. She could become a nurse. A vet.

When the omelettes were ready Rose fetched her father and gently woke Roo and they sat around the table deciding whether to go to the park or go swimming that afternoon.

To outsiders looking in they looked like the perfect family. Proud parents, two perfect children, a beautiful home.

But they weren't.

Not then.

Not ever.

She had no idea that her plans for the future would never

come to fruition. That she would never get the opportunity to pass her exams, travel the world, fall in love.

Unlike the stories she read to Roo from his beloved *Roartastic Dinosaur Stories* book before bed, there would be no happily ever after for her.

For any of them.

Chapter Seven

James

James thought that moving into Newington House would give him – them – their happily ever after but during their first dinner he feels anything but happy, the phone call from Adrian, Cass's father, looping around his mind.

He picks at the chips he had bought on the way back from work. They were already cold by the time he got home. In the middle of a bustling town he was used to having an array of takeaways on their doorstep. Here, on the outskirts of a village, fast food isn't that fast after all.

Cass has served them on white china plates which have ivy creeping around the rim. James pulls at his collar as though the plant is wrapped around his neck when really he knows it is the things Adrian has told him that are pressing down on his lungs, making it harder to breathe.

'James?' There is a question in his name but James doesn't know how to say what he needs to say, ask what he wants to ask.

'I'm okay,' he says but he isn't. He isn't okay at all.

'We probably should have sat in the kitchen,' Cass says miserably. 'At least the food might be warm. It's such a trek to reach the dining room. Kirstie Allsopp would have something to say about the flow of this house.'

'Kirstie Allsopp has a lot to say about everything.' James attempts a smile.

'It seemed such a shame not to sit in here when it – the room – was waiting for someone to come.'

A shiver passes down James's spine. He knows what she means though. The table had been laid. Cutlery with bone handles, crystal glasses for water and wine, a silver salt and pepper pot. A candelabra in the centre with three candles, now lit and dripping wax. Orange flames flicker, casting shadows across the face he knows so well. On their very first meeting he had mapped her face in his mind, knowing every freckle, the curve of her mouth, the upturn of her nose. He had held her hand that night and it was so familiar, it was like he had held it before.

Now, after that devastating phone call from her father, it's as though she's a stranger.

She's making such an effort though and so should he.

'Do you want some more wine?' He sloshes the deep red liquid into his glass but all he can think of is blood.

This room. This table, waiting for a family that would never come.

He shivers again although behind him a fire roars.

'I'm impressed with your fire-making skills,' he says. This, along with the yellow wall lights and the free-standing lamps with the apricot shades, brings a warmth to the oak panelling. It's cosy in here.

'It was terrifying.' Cass shakes her head with a smile. 'Honestly, I was so nervous. It's the first time I've ever lit one but the radiators don't seem to do a lot.'

'We take so much for granted, don't we? Double glazing. Cavity wall insulation.'

'Spotify.'

A record player cracks and hisses and the turntable spins. Karen Carpenter singing 'We've Only Just Begun'.

'I was going to set up my Bluetooth speaker but I thought this was more authentic,' Cass says. She's trying so hard and all at once James feels that he is, perhaps, being overdramatic. It's been a long day. The call from Adrian, unexpected. The awkward conversation with Angelica. His surroundings new and strange. He is sitting on someone else's chair, using someone else's dinner service. He's bound to feel unsettled. Cass does too. He can see it in the way she swallows frequently. Her fingers fluttering to the silver swan around her neck. Seeking her mother's comfort.

He *does* know her.

Perhaps not everything but the essence of who she is. He knows that she always slows down when she sees a dog running free until she can spot their owner and is certain that the animal is safe. She eats her M&M's in a specific colour order, saving the orange ones until last. He loves that her favourite member of Destiny's Child isn't Beyoncé.

He's being overdramatic. He *knows* her.

He leans over and kisses her, her lips slick with oil, tasting vinegar on her tongue.

'Sorry I'm not the life and soul of the party.'

'This is your idea of a party?' She grins, reassured.

'Absolutely. With no other guests to mock me I might even dance.' He shoulder bops to the music, out of time.

She laughs. 'How much booze have you had?'

'More than you.' James picks up the bottle but she covers her glass with her hand.

'Not for me. I feel a bit sick.'

'Too much grease and excitement,' he says.

'It's been quite a day.'

'Yeah. I… I spoke to Angelica today.'

'Your ex?' Cass doesn't know much about her. She's never asked and fleetingly James wonders whether she hasn't asked any questions so she doesn't have to share her own past with him.

'Yeah. She'd bumped into Chris and he'd told her I'd moved here, with you.'

'Right. And…' She tails off. Obviously aware he is trying to tell her something but not sure what.

'She… she said that six months isn't long enough to get to know someone and it set me off thinking that there are some things that perhaps I haven't been entirely honest about.'

Cass touches her pendant again, her eyes lowered to the remains of her dinner. The beige vegetarian sausage wrapped in golden batter. James feels awful. It's been a lot for her today, saying goodbye to her father, the long journey.

But he can't get the conversation with Adrian out of his head. Was Adrian really telling the truth or was he trying to come between them? Because that's a possibility. He must be desperate for Cass to move back home.

'When I met you I said that I was single, and I was… kind of.'

'Kind of?' Cass crosses her arms over her chest, hugging herself.

'It had been over between Angelica and me for months but before I could break up with her… my mum died and she… I fell apart. You know I've always had a strained relationship with my dad? Angelica was the only one I could turn to. It

67

wasn't fair on her, I know that, but I needed her and then…
then I met you and I knew that night that I wanted to be
with you.'

'So I was an excuse—'

'Not an excuse.' James reaches for her hand but she doesn't
give it to him. 'Not a reason. It wouldn't have worked out with
Angelica.'

'So how much of an overlap was there?' Cass bites her lip,
trying not to cry.

'The minute I got home I told her. I packed my bags and
moved out that day. Left pretty much everything behind. A lot
of it was stuff my mum paid for but that's all it was. Stuff.'

'Was I a rebound?' Cass's eyes are wide, bright with tears.

'No. You? You are everything.' This time she lets him link
his fingers through hers.

'Does Angelica know you'd met me before you ended it with
her?'

'She figured it out today when I said I'd been with you for
six months.'

'That must have hurt her.'

'I didn't mean to keep it a secret, it's just… if I'd told you
then you might have thought that I wasn't ready but I am. I love
you, Cass. I want to share the rest of my life with you. Get to
know you properly.'

'You already know me.' She sniffs.

'Not everything. Exes, for example, we've never really talked
about them.' James approaches this cautiously.

'Has she told you about Leon?' her dad had asked and when
James said she hadn't, Adrian had clammed up, refusing to say
who he was or any more about him. But he'd said other things.

Worrying things.

'There's never been anyone I was really serious about.' Cass pushes her plate away. Reaches for her water glass.

'But there must be things you haven't shared that perhaps you should?' It's a clumsy question. Cass nods. James holds his breath. 'I was robbed today,' Cass says.

'What?'

James holds her hand tighter as she tells him about Peggy, the elderly woman, and he hates himself for not being there to protect her. For doubting her. If Cass hadn't tried to do a good turn for a lonely old woman, she'd never have had her bag taken.

She has a generous heart and that is all he needs to know.

'Do you think we should tell Fran? Peggy has the front door key.'

'I don't think getting the locks changed for a door like Newington is that simple. She was just an opportunist thief. It's not like she has the address, is it?'

'The contract was in the bag.'

'That was a pretty basic contract between us and Richardson's Retreats. The address of this property wasn't on it.'

'Good.' Cass looks relived. 'I'd hate to tell Fran I've messed up before I've even begun.'

After they've finished talking he blows the candles out and together they climb the creaking stairs. The landing is freezing. The window cracked open again. Cass must have been trying to get rid of the musty smell. He pulls it shut.

The bed is made up with fresh sheets. He climbs into it, realizing as he stretches out on his back that it isn't as long as the beds he is used to. The canopy over his head flutters when Cass knocks the post as she clambers in beside him.

They bury themselves under the layers, bodies pressed close together, sharing heat. He holds her tightly, feeling her relax as she warms up. He thinks he should perhaps kiss her but they are both exhausted and this is his very last thought.

His sleep is deep and dreamless and when he wakes, the morning light pooling on the wooden floor, Cass is still asleep.

He tiptoes across the room so he doesn't disturb her.

The landing is cold.

The window open again.

He closes it as silently as he can and pads down to the kitchen.

It's such a contrast to the flat he shared with Chris and Michael. There, the sink was often piled with dirty crockery. The milk bottle in the fridge usually empty. The radio always blaring.

It's quiet. Peaceful.

There is a jar of honey next to the butter. He smiles. He hasn't had his childhood favourite for years. He stands while he munches on his toast, gazing out of the window at— A shadow catches his eye, pulling his attention towards the laurel bush. The leaves are moving but he can't see what's causing them to tremble. There's no movement in the trees, no breeze.

And yet the swing is swaying even though nothing else is.

Had something kicked into it as it scurried past?

An animal? A squirrel? Something larger. Big enough for James to have noticed in his peripheral vision.

A hare?

A fox?

It's so isolated here it must be a haven for wildlife. There's no telling what's out there.

Who's out there.

He doesn't know where this thought comes from so he pushes it away. He won't think about the history of the house. He will think only of Cass and their future.

It's beautiful here, it really is.

A pigeon struts across the courtyard, iridescent feathers glistening under the low morning sun. Greens morphing into purples, greys.

James opens the window, tears his crusts into tiny pieces and tosses them outside for the birds before rinsing his plate and mug in the sink. Leaves a note for Cass.

Forming a routine in their new home. Their new life. Picturing the start of every day like this.

But life rarely works out as planned, does it?

James doesn't know yet that in a few days Cass will admit to something that will irrevocably change everything.

Set them spinning on a new, unexpected and terrifying path.

Chapter Eight

Rose

Everything was changing. The taxi dropped Rose off at home with a suitcase full of laundry and a heart full of joy. It was the school holidays, six whole weeks of freedom.

'Rose!'

The second she stepped into the hallway Roo cannonballed into her arms. She hoisted him onto her hip.

'You've got so heavy.'

'That's because I'm three. Can you play hide-and-seek with me today? Can you push me on the swing? Can you—'

'Slow down. First things first, did you miss me?' She rested her chin on his head, the smell of strawberry shampoo smelled like love. Like home.

'Yes. We made popcorn without you and it went pop. Pop. Pop.' For each 'pop' Roo clenched his small fist before springing his hand open, splaying his chubby fingers. 'I lost Trip the T-rex too. I miss him A LOT.'

'But you missed me more, right?'

'Yes. But I love him too. He had the loudest roar.'

'I'll tell you who has the loudest roar.' She gently dropped him onto the sofa, hands curled like claws. She tickled him in

72

the ribs. 'Me.' She bellowed as loudly as she could which was still barely audible over Roo's laughter.

'Rosy Posy.' Mum slipped her arms around her waist, resting her cheek against Rose's back. 'I've missed you.'

'More than dinosaurs?' Rose turned and hugged her mother tightly.

'Dinosaurs?'

'It doesn't matter. It's good to be home.' Rose drew back and looked at her mum, the face so familiar and yet not. She was pale, her smile not quite reaching her eyes. Threads of grey shining in her dark hair. It was as though she'd been away three years, not three months. 'Is something the matter?'

'No, of course not.'

'You look tired.'

'So would you be, looking after this monster.' Mum leaned over Roo and began to tickle him but her movements were slow, forced.

'Do you want some help with dinner?' Rose asked after her mum had straightened up.

'No, it's okay, thanks. You unpack. I don't need any help.'

It wasn't as though Rose had much to unpack. 'You know what you need?' She grinned.

'What?'

'Love, love, love.' Rose burst into the opening bars but Mum didn't join in. Instead, she raised a brief smile before she turned away.

Dinner was long. Formal. Quiet.

Dad was late home from work. Roo had already eaten and was playing in his room, overjoyed that Rose, while hiding under his bed during their game of hide-and-seek, had unearthed Trip the T-rex. Rose wished she'd eaten with her brother, pasta dripping with tomato sauce at the kitchen table, rather than roast lamb in the dining room. The tang of mint sharp in her mouth. It was supposed to be a special occasion, her first night home, but it didn't feel like a celebration at all. The atmosphere strained.

Nobody spoke. Rose peered at her parents from under her lashes, trying to gauge what was going on.

It wasn't until he had finished eating and laid down his knife and fork that her father finally looked at her properly. Spoke to her. 'Your end-of-term report isn't what I'd expect.' He removed his glasses and wiped them on his napkin before putting them back on again.

'I thought it was okay.'

'It isn't. You've slipped back a grade in science.'

'Oh. Well our teacher left and the new one—'

'Is extremely well qualified, the way you'd expect them to be.'

'Yeah – yes – but—'

'Butts are for goats. I'm not paying a fortune for you to fail. You might as well be at the local secondary.'

Dad didn't speak again, waiting until Mum cleared his empty plate away.

'Your GCSEs will be here before you know it, and it's imperative—'

'I know.' Rose twisted the corner of the tablecloth round and round her finger. 'I *am* trying.'

'Sometimes, Rose, working hard, it just isn't enough.' His tone was hard and angry.

She pulled the cotton tighter and tighter until her finger began to lose sensation. 'I'm sorry.'

'I'm trying too.' He swallowed hard, rested his elbows on the table, and dropped his head forward into his hands.

'I… I know, Dad. I'll study harder. I'll—'

'Rose,' Mum said, standing behind her, rubbing her shoulder, 'you may be excused. Roo's already in bed so don't disturb him.'

'Right. I'll go upstairs and read then.' Rose folded her napkin before standing, tucking her chair back under the table. At the door, she cast a glance back. Her mum leaning over Dad, her cheek pressed against his.

Rose was at home, with her family, but she felt utterly alone.

Rose was sprawled on top of her bed, trying to read – *Little Women*. Mum had told her that it was her favourite book but it frustrated her. It was slower paced than the stories she usually read. Would Jo March and Laurie ever get together? It was taking an age to find out.

What would she do if she ever met a boy she really liked? Where would she ever meet a boy she really liked? Her school was all girls. She was fifteen and had never been kissed. Not even close.

It was hard to focus on the novel because drifting up through the floorboards, Rose could hear the whisper shouts of her parents. It was ridiculous that when grown-ups tried to hide the fact they were arguing, it only made it more obvious. What were they fighting about? They so rarely did.

She couldn't focus, she'd read the same paragraph twice. It was too early to sleep. Too hot.

She placed the book on her bedside stand and stretched, her arms above her head, fingers linked, feeling the click in her shoulders. She crept down the hallway into Roo's room. He was fast asleep, flat on his back, taking up all the space. Soon he'd have grown out of his cot bed. Would need a proper single bed. He was growing up although he looked smaller somehow when he was asleep. No pyjama top on, bottoms scrunched up to his knees. She watched the outline of his ribcage rise and fall with his breath. She smoothed his fringe away from his forehead, it was damp with sweat. Then she moved Trip the T-rex from the pillow in case Roo rolled over onto him, standing the dinosaur on the bedside table.

She was bored. Restless. Longing to go outside but unsure where to go. It wasn't like she had any friends to catch up with. She had grown apart from the girls she had been to primary school with, didn't always recognize them when she saw them around with their heavy make-up and glossy hair. They thought she was a snob, as if she had chosen to go away to school and leave them.

Slowly, slowly, she crept downstairs, through the empty kitchen and out through the back door. She didn't say goodbye to her parents, let them think she was still reading. She set off down the hill. There was still some heat left in the sun that shimmered 'Look at me. I can give you a glorious summer.' The sky was the same blue as Mum's favourite vase. Rose breathed in deeply. The intoxicating scent of the white flowers hanging prettily from the lime trees.

She walked without purpose, meandering through the village, the smell of chips drifting from the local chippy tantalizing – she should have brought some money – cutting through the park she brought Roo to sometimes. Pushing him on the swing, his short legs bending and straightening as he swung, higher, higher, higher. Him saying it's faster than the one at home in their garden.

'Oi.' A voice broke her out of her thoughts. Sitting cross-legged on the grass a couple of boys, a similar age to her. One shouted, 'You got a fag?'

Rose felt the heat rise to her cheeks. 'No... I'm sorry. I don't smoke.' Four years at an all girls' school had made her self-conscious around boys.

'Right.' The boy's eyes travelled across her and Rose felt a different kind of heat. A pull towards him. 'What's your name?'

'Rose.' Her voice trembled.

'*Rose*. Very fucking posh,' the other said and Rose turned to walk away.

'Don't be a dick. It's a nice name.' The first boy patted the grass beside him. It was dry and brittle, yellowing with thirst, scratching at her bare legs when, after a moment's hesitation, she sat down. This was what she wanted, wasn't it? To make friends?

'I'm Gunner.'

'Gunner?'

'That's what me grandad's always called me. Said I was obsessed with guns and war when I was little.' Gunner thrust the bottle of cider he was holding towards her, his fingers stained with nicotine. 'And this is Kamal.'

'Nice to meet you.' She took the bottle, and tentatively took a sip. The liquid both sweet and sour in her throat. She began to cough.

Kamal snatched the bottle back. 'You *do* drink, don't you?'

Rose shrugged, wiping her mouth with the back of her hand.

'Where have you been?' Gunner asked but not unkindly.

'Boarding school.'

'You are a posh bird then?'

'Rich bird,' chipped in Kamal.

'No, we're not. Not really. Do you both go to the local secondary?'

'Sometimes.' Gunner and Kamal exchanged a look, laughed. 'But we're entrepreneurs, us. No need for a traditional education. School of life teaches us all we need to know. Where do you live when you're not at boarding school?'

Rose told them and Kamal whistled. 'Nice.'

He offered Gunner the bottle but Rose swiped it instead. This time taking a confident gulp. She'd show them she could be one of them.

Later, her head was muzzy. Gunner had asked her a lot of questions about herself, her family. Who she lived with, what their routine was. He was interested in her in a way that nobody had been before.

He fancied her!

She was aware of his hand on her leg, creeping higher up her thigh, but she didn't stop him because she liked it. She began to giggle. What would her dad think if he could see her now? With the 'common' boys. The ones he'd likely sent her to boarding school to avoid. Her giggle turned to a loud burp. The taste of cider filling her throat, sour now. Embarrassed, she stumbled to her feet. 'I've got to go.'

'See you again?' Gunner asked. 'Might have a business proposition for you. A chance to invest.'

'Oh, I don't really get an allowance. I don't have any money.'

'That's all right.' Kamal grinned. His incisors were pointed – *all the better to eat you with.* 'Perhaps we'll rob it off your parents. What do you think, Gunner? She's loaded.'

'You can't—'

'He's only kidding.' Gunner stood and cupped her worried face between his hands. She had never felt so... so special.

So wanted.

He rubbed his thumbs against her cheek and she had never experienced anything as erotic. And when he let her go, despite the warmth of the sun, her face was cold without his touch.

Their eyes met and in hers, she knew, was a pleading. There was so much she wanted in that moment and she didn't know how to convey it, what to do, but he read her, leaning forward. Gently, oh so gently, he gave Rose her very first kiss, his lips dry, moving against hers softly and then harder, his tongue wet in her mouth, hands tangled in her hair. Her body slumped against him and when he let her go she feared that she might fall. She was breathless. Panting. Wanting more. Aware of Kamal watching her and not caring anyway. She tilted her face towards Gunner's again. But instead of kissing her he pushed a pound coin into her hand. 'Stop at the shop and get some water. Sober yourself up before you go home. Promise me?'

She nodded, touched by how much he cared.

'See you soon, Rosie.' He patted her on her bottom as she walked away, too uncertain to ask him where she would see him again. If his kiss, *that kiss*, meant that she was his girlfriend now.

How she wanted to be.

Obediently, she did what he had said and went to the newsagent. She sat on the bench outside basking in the last vestiges of daylight, the bottle of water on her lap. She was reluctant to unscrew the cap, not wanting to take a sip and wash off the taste of his lips on hers.

Her first kiss!

Excitement ran through her as she remembered his tongue pushing into her mouth, his hands in her hair, on her bare leg. She closed her eyes and trailed her fingertips across her thigh, imagining it was Gunner's fingers she could feel.

She wanted, more than anything, to see him again. No, she *needed* to see him again. Suddenly she had that childish desire to be in bed, asleep, to make tomorrow come quicker, the way she had on Christmas Eve when she was small. The way Roo did now.

She ran, tossing the bottle of water into the bin as she passed.

Rose felt a flutter of nerves as she approached her house. Could she get back inside without her parents knowing she'd been out? Without them seeing how dishevelled she looked, smelling the whiff of alcohol on her breath? She touched her lips. How could they possibly look at her and not realize she had been kissed?

But when she slipped through the front door all of her worries vanished. The atmosphere was thick. Heavy.

Mum didn't call her name as she usually would. Rose knew instinctively that something was wrong. Very wrong.

Tonight had felt like the beginning of something, but instead it was an ending.

Chapter Nine

Cass

This really feels like the beginning of something. My brush swirls the red, into the blue, dabbing on orange and lavender with the lightest of touches.

I stand back and survey the painting on the canvas – the dawning of a new day – it seems apt.

My heart swells with happiness.

Once I'd finally found my brushes, which somehow I'd wrapped inside one of my jumpers in the drawer, I'd been engrossed.

It's been such a long time since I painted. It wasn't only the limited space in Dad's cramped flat that prevented me from trying but after everything with Leon, it was the absence of motivation, inspiration. I'd had a complete lack of interest in everything until I met James. Our relationship had been sudden and all-consuming and although since I met him I've experienced the unfurling of desire, passion, I hadn't made the time for art.

Now I have seemingly infinite time.

It's hard to believe we're earning money living here. Me being paid to paint, that was always my dream, but somehow it got lost along the way. I have never felt so lucky, so grateful, and for once I want to remain present. Make the most of every second instead of doing my usual thing of worrying when it will end. When the retreat will be granted the relevant planning permissions and we will have to leave. Already, I am attached to the house, at home, here in this room.

The girl's room.

There's a good energy here.

Again, I wonder about her. Who she was. I've googled her, of course, but cannot find anything about her online. It's hard to imagine growing up before the time of social media. If she'd lived I wonder what she'd think of the world today. Our addiction to technology. She loved to read, that much is apparent from the shelves crammed with books. Would that have changed if she were a teenager now? Would she read on her Kindle, or not at all?

What happened to her?

Rose.

It's the faintest of whispers. I hold my breath, listen intently, but there's nothing. Am I imagining things? I thought I'd heard the name last night but I put it down to an unfamiliar house, the noises older properties make.

If Rose is your name give me a sign.

Another noise.

This time it's my belly though. I had skipped breakfast, stomach swirling from too many chips and too much red wine last night and now, suddenly, I am ravenous.

In the kitchen I read the note that James left:

I can't text you until you replace your mobile so I thought I'd go old-fashioned. Fits with the house. I've left you my key in case you want to go out. Love you xxx

I like old-fashioned.

I've contacted my phone provider and reported my handset as stolen but I haven't ordered a replacement yet. It's been twenty-four hours without it and I'm definitely more relaxed. No longer feeling apprehensive checking my phone in case Leon has found out my new number and there's a string of text messages. Missed calls.

Leon.

I still feel sick whenever I think of him so I push him out of my head. This is a new start. A new me. I'm going to unpack.

It isn't until I'm filling the shelves in the medicine cabinet with my toiletries, holding an unopened box of tampons, that I begin to question whether the sickness I've been feeling lately is down to Leon, anxiety, or something else.

Someone else.

Once I step out of the courtyard I'm surrounded by overgrown hedges, a tangle of weeds. To my left were once formal gardens. There's a grey statue of a lady, her arms broken off, stretching her stumps towards me. A chipped fountain. A couple of inches of water in the bottom covered by thick green algae. Looking out of place, the swing. Its red plastic frame faded, chain rusted. Yellow seat grimy. A reminder that a family had lived here in modern times.

In front of me there's nothing but trees. I want to explore the grounds properly but for now I wind my way through the woods until I pick up the track with tyre marks. Fran was right, you'd never find the house if you didn't know it was here.

It's dark. Chilly. Twigs crack underfoot. Shadows loom and retreat as the wind blusters branches towards me. Leaves swirl around my feet. I hurry until I burst back into daylight. Space. Cows grazing in surrounding fields. Perhaps all this land might once have belonged to Newington.

The walk into the village seems endless. I'm not entirely convinced I'm heading in the right direction until I stumble across a small estate of new houses. Rows of red bricks, neatly manicured lawns, trimmed hedges and picket fences. The new-builds give way to the cottages, the Victorian terraces, the village as it was before it expanded. A church, its spire stretching tall and proud into the grey sky.

It's so quaint. The park, the green with the duck pond. There's a chip shop. That must be where James picked up our takeaway from last night. A greengrocer. Crates of shiny red apples and bright orange satsumas stacked outside. A Co-op and, just as I'd hoped, a chemist.

After I've made my purchase I head for the churchyard. The wooden gate creaks as I push it open. There's a sense of peace here. There are multiple moss-covered benches, some with brass plaques. It must be nice to have somewhere to come. To feel close to the one you've lost. Mum's ashes were scattered at the beach and although I still talk to her I'd have liked a physical place to visit. A place that felt like hers. I begin to scan the gravestones. Some are new. Names in cursive script etched onto shiny marble. Bouquets of pink roses, vases of cream carnations. The nearer I get to the church, the older the plots. If the Madleys died thirty years ago, surely this is where they are buried? Some headstones are too faded to read.

I find a simple wooden cross with a tarnished plaque. It's been vandalized, sprayed over. The name 'Madley' is barely visible along with partial letters which I'm sure form the words 'husband' and 'father'.

This must be him. Mr Madley. The date of death matches the murders.

I've found them!

Eagerly, I examine the other plots nearby. Nothing.

Mrs Madley and Rose are not here.

Where are they and why were they separated from Mr Madley, and by who? Surely a family that lived together, died together, would want to remain together?

What happened to them?

They remain elusive and out of reach and I try to put them out of my mind on the walk home but I can't.

All afternoon I rehearse what I'm going to say to James, running through conversations in my mind, filling in the parts he'll say.

I have no idea what he'll say.

I'm pregnant.

I'm too agitated to paint. I can feel the flow of adrenaline through my veins. Eager to learn more about the family, I explore the house, inventory in hand. I scan the list Fran has started. She'd begun in the basement. The items listed as either 'personal', 'non-valuables', 'antiques' or 'unsure'.

The drop in temperature is startling. I stand in the entrance to the basement, flick on the light switch.

Immediately I see a pale face staring back at me.

I scream.

Trying to take the stairs backwards, I stumble, landing

awkwardly, my ankle throbbing. When I look up again I realize I'd been looking into a mirror, the glass speckled, frame tarnished.

A nervous laugh escapes me. The sound echoing around the room. Part of me wants to head back into the warmth of the main house but my curiosity surrounding the Madley family is stronger than my fear.

Pulling myself back to my feet I hold my breath, partly not wanting to inhale the cold, damp air, but also because I'm listening for the sound of scuttling rats, claws scratching against the stone floor, spiders scurrying on tiny legs, but it's quiet.

The electric bulb suspended from a dusty cord throws out a weak light.

I walk towards the boxes, shrieking again when something tickles the back of my neck.

A cobweb.

I talk out loud to myself as I brush it off, reassuring myself I'm ridiculous. That there's nothing here that can hurt me, is there?

On the floor, a bear. I pick him up. His forlorn eyes plead with me not to leave him down here. Could I wash him for the baby? Even if he doesn't clean up properly, it might be a fun way to tell James he's about to become a father.

There's a red ribbon around his neck. A tarnished name tag. I can just about make out the writing: Mr Tatty.

'Did Mr Tatty belong to you, Rose?' I ask, holding the bear to my chest.

Instantly, there's a slamming. The door to the basement swinging shut.

A loud pop.

Glass showers down on me.

Blackness.

I scream.

The bulb has exploded, it crunches underfoot as I hurry towards the stairs, holding my arms out before me, bear still clutched in my hand. Feeling a damp wall where the staircase should be.

Rose.

There's a whisper. Panic builds. I can't find the way out. Clinging to the bear I try another direction. My hip catching on something hard.

A rocket of pain shoots through me, along with a sense of relief. It's the edge of the staircase.

I'm almost sobbing as I clutch the banisters and half-drag myself up the stairs, almost expecting the door at the top to be locked.

It isn't.

I'm free but am I safe? Safe is the last thing I feel.

Upstairs, I force myself to calm down. Inexplicably the landing window has come open again and the draught wafting around the house. Would that have been enough to push the heavy basement door shut? I'm doubtful. What about the bulb? The wiring in the house is ancient.

There are a multitude of rational explanations but I'm not convinced by any of them.

I am fine.

I am safe.

I am normal.

I haven't used my mantra once since I met James. Now it falls from my lips over and over.

I've only missed one dose of my medication, what might happen if I stop taking it completely? And I will stop taking it completely. With the baby, there isn't only me to think of now.

But I can't go back into the darkest depths of my mind.

Not again.

I sit the bear on the table in front of James. 'I found him earlier.'

James reaches out a hand and touches the bear's ears. He's still damp from where I washed him.

'If Fran's lot don't want him then I thought we could give him to someone.' I smile.

'Mr Tatty,' James says softly, picking him up.

My mouth dries, my pulse skyrocketing.

'What... what did you call him?'

'Mr Tatty.' James runs his fingers over the bear's ears.

'But... that *was* his name. It was on a tag around his neck but it was so tarnished I threw it away. You can't possibly have known that.' My voice is fast and high.

James frowns, turns the bear over in his hands.

There's a beat. 'Well he is rather ragged, it seems to fit. Lucky guess.'

My gaze travels from the bear to James, back to the bear again. James is right. The name does suit him but still, it's a coincidence. But then I think about the book of coincidences, the last one I read. A girl had lived in a house previously owned by Sylvia Bartlett; when she left home she bought her own house and that had also been owned by the same Sylvia Bartlett. Years later, she got a job 250 miles away, arranged to view a house and met the owner, the same Sylvia Bartlett. Perhaps James naming a tatty bear 'tatty' isn't that strange after all.

'Anyway, what do you mean?' James is asking. 'Who on earth would we give him to?'

His question refocuses me on what's important. The only thing that's important right now. 'A baby.' I wait until he meets my eye. 'Our baby.'

'I'm glad you want kids too one day, Cass.' It was something we had talked about before. 'What do you think our baby will look like?'

'They'd be beautiful. All babies are.'

'I wasn't.'

'Weren't you?'

'I dunno. Mum said my baby albums were lost during a house move. Perhaps she hid them because I was so hideous.' He pulls a face. 'Couldn't bear to keep a picture of me until I was around four, not like your dad with your baby photos plastered all over the walls but then you were cute.'

I laugh. 'I don't believe you were ever anything other than gorgeous. Anyway, you'll be able to tell exactly what our baby will be like, in about six or seven months.' Under the table, my fingers are crossed.

It takes a second for the penny to drop.

'You're... you're pregnant?' James whispers. 'But... You're sure?'

'Yes. I realized that I haven't had a period in weeks – that isn't unusual.' I notice the surprise on his face. 'I've always been irregular.' I don't tell him I think the stress and the medication had messed up my cycle. 'I've been feeling sick a lot and my clothes are tighter. So I walked to the village to buy a test earlier and—'

James doesn't say anything. Instead he drops his head in his hands, despairing. The bottom falls out of my world. This is not what he wants.

'James?'

He raises his head. Tears are trickling down his cheeks. The expression on his face so raw, so vulnerable.

'Mum...' He swallows hard. 'Mum would have loved being a grandmother.'

I rush to his side, wrap my arms around him, cradle his head against my chest as though he is the child and I am already a parent.

His shoulders shake, his resurfaced grief raw. Does it ever really go away? That sense of loss? It has been twelve months now since James's mum passed away and yet, as I hold him, I can tell that, for him, it feels like only yesterday. I'm crying too now, not for James or his mum, but selfishly for me. How would my own mother have reacted? Would she have been the type to knit tiny cardigans in pastel colours? I'll never know.

'Sorry.' James gently removes my arms from around him and takes my hands. 'I'll make the best dad.'

His earnest eyes tell me that he is telling the truth. We both have troubled relationships with our fathers. Something silent passes between us. A promise.

We will do things differently.

Be better.

That was when I thought James and I knew all we needed to know about each other.

And perhaps in another place, another time, things would have turned out differently.

But not here, not at Newington.

When I'd arrived bright eyed and full of hope I didn't believe in evil.

But now, I've seen it.

Chapter Ten

Rose

THEN

Although she couldn't see anything out of the ordinary, Rose hovered uncertainly in her hallway, still tasting the alcohol on her breath, the lingering tingle from Gunner's lips on hers.

Something was wrong.

There wasn't anything specific Rose could pinpoint but she'd read the phrase 'the air felt thicker' in books and thought that it was stupid, air was air, but all at once she understood it. The sense of impending bad news pressing down, making it harder to breathe.

Something was wrong.

The house was quiet. Too quiet. But then she heard it, a soft weeping.

Her mother.

Rose hurried towards the sound, finding her mother sitting at the polished-to-perfection dining table, her head in her hands. They barely used this room, it was too formal, easier to eat at the breakfast table in the kitchen rather than trek plates through, the food growing colder in their hands. Still, as her father insisted, places were laid, cutlery polished, wine goblets glinting, waiting for guests that never came. It gave Rose the creeps. 'Mum?'

Mum hurriedly blew her nose, tried to pin on a smile which slipped almost immediately.

'I'm okay.'

'You're not.' Rose's sympathy was tinged with irritation. 'I'm not a child. You can talk to me, you know.'

'I know.' Mum twisted the wedding band round and round on her finger.

'So?' Rose prompted.

'We might have to move, that's all.'

'Move house? But we can't. We live *here*.' Even the thought of moving was painful. Sometimes when she came back for the holidays she felt more like a visitor and this was in the only home she had ever known, safe and familiar. How would it be somewhere new? Somewhere Mum, Dad and Roo lived in permanently, properly, but she'd be away at school. A perpetual guest. It would be like she didn't belong there. She wouldn't belong anywhere.

'It wouldn't be the end of the world.'

'It would. My world anyway. It would be the end of... *everything*.' Rose blinked back tears.

'Rose.' Her mum reached for her hand and Rose snatched hers away.

'Why do you want to live anywhere else? You love this house. You grew up in this house.'

'It's too big for us.'

'No it isn't. What's the real reason?'

'It was just a thought. We don't have to. Please don't cry.'

'You're crying,' Rose bit back and then they both smiled, wiped their eyes. 'Promise we can stay here?'

'I promise.' With her forefinger Mum drew an 'X' across her heart.

Reassured, because as far as she knew her mum had never lied to her, Rose enveloped her in a hug but when they drew apart her mother asked, 'Rose, is that alcohol I can smell on you?'

'No.'

'Have you been out?'

'Yeah. I went for a walk.'

Mum's eyes travelled over Rose and Rose felt the burn of shame begin at her toes and rise to her scalp.

'Why are you blushing? Have you been with a boy?'

'Mum! I went for a walk, that's all.' As she spoke the lie Rose felt the thrill of the illicit. The joy of having a secret, keeping it to herself.

She didn't know then that soon she would be full of secrets and she would never feel joy again.

The sound of her dad shouting roused Rose from sleep. Light from the hallway pooled onto her bedroom floor as her door was pushed open, Roo scuttling over to her bed. She flung back her covers and shifted over to make room for him.

'I'm scared,' he whispered.

'Don't be.' She soothed back his hair from his warm forehead. 'It's because Mum and Dad never argue that it sounds—'

'They shout *all* of the time.' Roo choked back tears.

Rose pulled him close to her, held him until he had stopped trembling. Was it true? Did her parents argue? She cast her mind back to last time she had been home. Her dad seemed quieter, tense, but Mum seemed happy, didn't she?

'Do you think they'll get 'vorced?' Roo asked, his voice small. 'Ben who's my best friend at preschool, well, my second-best friend next to Daniel. Well, third next to Amy. His parents got 'vorced and instead of getting one big present for Christmas he got lots of little horrible ones.'

'They won't get divorced.'

'Promise?'

Rose hesitated. Her mother had been crying at the table, talking about moving house.

'Rosy Posy?'

But then Mum had promised her that everything would stay the same so she offers Roo the same assurance.

'They won't get divorced.'

It was an argument. Nothing more.

The summer was a tight ball of heat. Plants withered, leaves brown and curling, soil scorched. Weather warnings were given on the news. Everyone was irritable, especially Dad.

Rose had been observing her parents carefully. Even if Roo hadn't told her that they had been fighting while she'd been at school, she would have known. Something was very wrong. Her mum, still adoring of her father, made every effort. Painting on lipstick and a smile when he arrived home after work like a Fifties housewife, fussing around him, pouring a drink, serving a meal, single-handedly setting feminism back. Blinking away tears as he criticized *everything*.

One balmy evening she had dropped Roo off with Daniel's parents – he was having a sleepover. As soon as she walked back into the house she sensed the anger, heard her mother pleading.

'I can get a job.'

'I won't have my wife working. What will people think?'

'Does it matter what they think?'

'They'll think that I can't keep you—'

'I'm not a pet.'

'You are my *wife*. You have my child to look after.'

Child not children.

In the hallway, Rose covered her stomach with her arms, feeling sick. Most of the time she forgot David was only her stepdad, that Roo was her half-brother, because together, as a family, they felt like a whole.

Mum was pleading, 'There are after-school clubs and—'

'You don't need a job.'

'I do. We need the money. You're not—'

There was a crack. A cry. A thud.

'I can provide—'

'Dad!' Rose ran into the room. Mum was on the floor, hand over her cheek. 'Did you just hit Mum?'

'How dare—'

'How fucking dare you.' Rose stood, jabbed her finger into his chest.

'Rose.' Mum pulled herself up. 'It wasn't anybody's fault. I slipped.'

'On what? His bullshit?' she said as scathingly as she could.

'Rose.' His voice a warning. 'Don't. Or I will—'

'What? You'll hit me too?'

'Stop it, you two. Everything's fine. I'm fine. Just a silly accident. I hit my cheek on the corner of the table.'

'Really? It looks like a handprint to me.' Rose turned to glare at her father once more but he was already leaving the room.

'Is this why you want to move? To get away from him?' Rose asked.

'No. Of course not. He's my husband.'

'And you're his wife, not a punchbag.'

'He doesn't hit me. Honestly. Things have just been a little fraught lately and they got out of hand today. Dad has a lot of work stress.'

'That doesn't give him the right—'

'Look, your father—'

'David,' Rose said, his name full of venom. 'He's not my real father and I won't call him that ever again.'

Red hot anger flowed through her veins as she thought of the way she had welcomed him in, calling him 'Dad' almost as soon as Mum asked if she would mind if David moved into their home. She had been desperate for a father, never knowing her own. How seamlessly they had fitted together at first, David lifting her onto his hip when he came home from work. Carrying her through to the kitchen. Resting his briefcase on the table, letting Rose play with the combination lock.

If you figure it out I'll give you £5.

Her delight when she had, eventually, opened it after multiple hints and realized that the combination had been her birthday all along.

It was bittersweet to think of this now. But how well had Rose known him really? He had packed her off to boarding school within two years of meeting Mum. It was easy to be nice for the few weeks a year she was around. What was he like when she wasn't? If Roo was right, there had been problems for a long time. Problems she was unaware of.

Part of Rose wished that her mum had never met him. They had been happy when it was just the two of them. Rose was closer to her mum than any of the girls at school seemed to be to theirs. They'd snuggle together under the soft blue blanket which draped over the back of the sofa, watching Disney films. Hands dipping into a bowl of crisps, licking salt and vinegar off of their fingers. But then Roo wouldn't be here and really, she never thought of him as a half-brother, he was whole, entirely hers and she loved him deeply.

Later, over a strained dinner, David said, 'Rose. Your grades aren't what I hoped for. I'm afraid I can no longer justify the cost of sending you back to boarding school.' He didn't even look at her as he said it. He thought it would hurt her, thought it was a punishment, but she was glad she wasn't going back to boarding school. Glad she'd be here to look after Mum and Roo, keep an eye on David. He had struck her mum for the first time and the last time.

She glared at him.

'And don't think because you're here your mother will wait on you hand and foot. You can clear up your mess in the kitchen after dinner.'

'My mess?' Rose was momentarily confused. 'You meant the book I was reading in there earlier?'

'A place for everything, and everything in its place.'

'Christ, can't I even—'

'And don't take the Lord's name in vain. What have you become?' He took a slow sip of his red wine and stared at her. 'I'll pray for you.'

He wasn't even religious. She hated him.

Hated him.

Why did Mum love him so much? Forgive so much?

Rose vowed that if he ever laid a hand on her mum again, she'd kill him.

Chapter Eleven

Cass

NOW

It sounded like Dad was dying as he grappled for breath. My fingers tighten around the mobile James insisted I must have 'just in case' now that I'm pregnant. I listen to the scrape of a chair leg on the kitchen floor as he sits down heavily, as though the shock might kill him.

'I thought you'd be pleased.' The lie catches in my throat. I swallow it down. 'A grandchild…' I trail off, my voice cracking. It isn't the pregnancy hormones making me emotional but a desperate need for Dad to be happy for me.

Despite our complicated relationship, I need him.

There's the spark of a lighter, a deep draw. I can almost smell the smoke. Picture his nicotine-stained fingers tapping the end of his cigarette. Ash sprinkling over the table.

'Dad?'

'I'll ring you later, Cass. There's someone at the door.'

I hadn't heard the bell or a knock, but he hangs up just the same.

It's after lunch and Dad still hasn't called me back. I can't focus on painting and oddly the brushes I'd been using aren't on the table where I'd left them so I think I'll carry on with the inventory. Not the basement though. I still tremble when thinking of the bulb shattering, plunging me into darkness. The sense I was not alone.

I hadn't mentioned it to James, all we've talked about for the past couple of days is the baby, but as I climb the stairs towards the chapel I wonder if he's sensed anything too.

The chapel was once a bedroom and yet it holds a calmness, a serenity I often feel in places of worship even though I wasn't raised in any particular religion.

It's small. There isn't enough room for rows of pews but there are prayer stools and a pulpit. A sense of light and space despite the dark panelling. Deep burgundy velvet curtains frame the windows , their hems trailing across the floorboards and I wonder whether past generations had drawn them shut to keep out prying eyes in the days when Catholics were persecuted. When was that? I cast my mind back to school, recalling that it was Henry VIII who initiated the reformation of English religion. I vaguely remember that he declared himself the head of the English church so he could marry Anne after the Pope refused to grant him a divorce from Catherine. That must have been around fifteen something. Some of the portraits hanging around the house are probably from around that period.

By the door is a table with shelves. There is a row of white candles and a box of matches. I take a candle and try to light it, expecting the matches to be damp, but one sparks to life and I hold it against the wick until it flames.

On top of the table is a wooden box with a slot in the lid. Perhaps this was for collections? I pick it up and turn it over in my hands. There's a latch on the bottom and I release it.

Inside the box is a single piece of yellowing paper. Scrawled in large capital letters, ROSE.

So the girl who lived here *was* called Rose. Why is her name in this box? Did she put it there herself?

Suddenly I have the urge to pray for her, to pray for all of the Madleys.

My lips move, forming the words I do not speak aloud. Hoping that in the face of such brutality they didn't suffer too much. That they are at peace now.

When I've finished I sit back on my heels.

What would you have prayed for, Rose? I whisper.

Health?

Happiness?

Safety?

An icy chill spider-crawls across the back of my neck, light and fast, but the change in temperature is enough to startle me. I open my eyes and spin around, trying to locate where the sudden breeze can have come from.

I'm not near any open windows and on the small table to my left the candle flame still glows and flickers.

Uneasy, I pull myself to my feet, hurry out of the room, but on the back of my neck, I can still feel it, the lingering touch of the lightest finger.

'Is everything okay?' James asks. 'How did you get on with the inventory today?'

I'm pushing fat chunks of tofu around my plate. Grease from my curry pooling on top of my congealing korma sauce.

'OK.' I pause. 'James, have you noticed anything... odd about the house?'

'You mean other than the stuffed animals everywhere we

turn, the portraits whose eyes follow you around the room, the weird noises.' James heaps mango chutney on top of his poppadom.

'Yes. Other than those things.'

'Like what?'

'I don't know. Sometimes I get the feeling I'm being watched.'

'Umm, yeah.' James gestures at the paintings on the wall with his fork.

'I'm serious. The other day I was in the basement when the lightbulb exploded. I think that Rose—'

'Rose?'

'The teenage girl who lived here, I found out her name, I think...' I trail off. Not sure what I think. What I believe. 'I can't stop thinking about her. About all the Madley family.'

'What happened in this house was tragic.' James puts down his cutlery and takes my hand between his. 'And when we moved in that's all it was to me, a sad event in the past that had no bearing on our present but...' His brows knit together. 'Learning I'm going to become a father has made me... I dunno... dads are supposed to protect their kids, aren't they? I can't imagine how Mr Madley must have felt knowing that he couldn't save his wife and child.'

'Perhaps he didn't know, if he were killed first.'

We fall into silence, gazing at the crackling fire.

'I went to the graveyard,' I say softly. 'I found him but I couldn't find Rose or Mrs Madley.'

'Cass.' James looks at me helplessly. 'Please don't be so fixated on the past, not when we've got such a lot to look forward to.'

'I know but... What do you think about the lightbulb?'

'It isn't unheard of that they can just explode. It's an old house. Old wiring. There could have been a surge of electricity.'

'I... I've heard the swing creaking when there isn't any wind, as though... It moves on its own.' I blurt it out, realizing how it sounds but saying it anyway.

'It wouldn't take much of a breeze to catch it and then if it's gathered momentum I guess it could keep going for a few seconds.'

It's been moving for more than a few seconds, as though someone is playing on it.

'The window—'

'Has a faulty catch. Every time we walk around and create a vibration it could force it open, or the wind.'

'The clock—'

'Is ancient. We're lucky it works at all.'

'But it always seems to be 8.30 when it stops.'

'That's because there are only a set number of hours in every wind.'

'But we wind it up at different times of the day so surely that doesn't make sense.'

'Perhaps there's a fault on the face that stops the hands at that time.'

'My paintbrushes keep moving.' It's my last-ditch attempt to get James to take me seriously. 'And don't blame pregnancy brain.'

'I wasn't going to. You were absent-minded enough before.' He grins and I know he will continue to bat away with logic every single concern I have about this house.

Before I can say anything else, my phone rings. Dad's name on the screen. James tells me he's going for a shower.

'Cass!' Dad says loudly and before I can say hello he launches into a barrage of questions. When am I due? Have I seen a doctor? A midwife? How am I feeling? It's as though he has a list and he's working through it, saying the things he ought to say rather than the things he actually feels.

I've told him I've registered with the local doctor today and booked my first appointment with the midwife. Yes, I'm eating well. Feeling fine.

He's asking too many questions so I don't ask my own because I can tell from the slur in his words that he's been drinking. My stomach twists with anxiety because I don't think he's been toasting happy news. Rather trying to block out that his only daughter is at the other end of the country having a baby with a man he does not like.

But I cannot bear the thought that he is miserable and hurting and so I cut in.

'Dad? You're not drinking again, are you?' It's a rhetorical question really. I can almost smell sour whisky on his breath.

'No.'

'Promise me?'

He changes the subject, not wanting to talk about himself. 'Are you still taking your medication?'

'I'm fine.' There are things I don't want to talk about either. As we say goodbye he sounds so lonely, so sad, and long after we've hung up I sit, still clutching my phone, berating myself for not telling him that I love him, because I do.

I hadn't told him that I missed him either but I'm not sure if that's true. When I think of him, of home, I think of Leon and so I try not to think of him at all.

Leon.

I still haven't told James about him.

The darkness is absolute. The sense of panic overwhelming. I'm sitting on the cold, hard floor. My knees to my chest, my arms wrapped around them.

Rocking.

Rocking.

Rocking.

Someone will come soon.

There's a pressure on my chest and I can hardly breathe. It's as though a heavy weight is pushing down on me but it isn't.

It's fear.

My heart is loud in my ears.

Why doesn't anyone come?

I can't get out. I'm trapped.

I'm going to die here.

Sobbing, I begin to claw at the walls, trying to find a way out.

Help me.

Help me.

Help me.

Then there's a knocking. A banging. Someone is out there.

My eyes spring open. I'm coated in a thin film of cold sweat, the duvet sticking to my body. The knocking I heard in my nightmare is still there.

In my head?

Shaking, I sit up, reassuring myself it was just my childhood nightmare. Nothing more. I hadn't had it for years and it was probably hearing Dad drunk again that brought it back. I rub the sleep from my eyes and when I breathe in it is lemons that I smell. Confused, I sniff my fingers, nothing. The scent has vanished as quickly as it appears.

What is happening to me?

I reach for my slippers and it is then I notice.

My fingernails. Torn and bloody as though I've been clawing at something, trying to get out.

I cover my ears, blocking out the knocking.

'Are you still taking your medication?' Dad had asked.

I can't. For the baby's sake I can't. I know Dad will tell me it is safe, and perhaps it is, but I don't want to take even the smallest risk. It's my decision and I'm sticking to it, but...

What's happening to me?

The banging stops and gradually my heart rate returns to normal.

I am fine. I'm not trapped in a cupboard. Not reliant on Dad to come and save me.

Not questioning whether Dad was the one who put me there.

I hold out my hands, they're shaking. My nails such a mess. I must have been sleepwalking last night.

'James?' I call, even though I'm pretty sure he's already left for work. The sun is high in the sky. The pregnancy exhausting me.

He doesn't answer. Instead, the sound of children laughing.

Shivering, I cross to the window, scoop back the curtain. The air is still, there's no breeze ruffling the leaves on the tree.

But I can hear the creak of the swing moving back and forth.

There's laughing again.

And then a shadowy figure moving along the driveway, next to the cover of the bushes.

Someone is out there.

I rush downstairs and fling open the door, on the step a bouquet.

Roses.

It's dusk. James still isn't home. He's taken a client out to dinner and won't be back until late. My stomach lurches as I scrape the wet meat, glistening with jelly, from the tin of dog food into a saucer.

I'd spent the afternoon fashioning a hedgehog house out of old crates and bricks. The hedgehogs need all the help they can get this time of year.

On the stove, I'm gently melting lard to make fat balls for the birds.

I can't help but glance to the roses I had found on the step just this morning. It's a shame they are already beginning to die, their petals turning crisp and brown. I still don't know who sent them.

My latest painting is of a single white rose. I don't remember starting it, but that's how it is with art sometimes. Once you're in the zone, creativity takes over conscious thinking.

My subconscious has obviously turned into a neat freak as well because rather than leaving my paintbrushes on the table, as I normally do when I work, I'm finding them neatly put away in their case, the case tucked out of sight in various places.

Perhaps I'm nesting.

Thoughts turn to the birds once again and I tip seeds and scraps into the saucepan, remove it from the heat as I stir them in. When it begins to cool I'll fashion the mixture into balls.

My phone rings.

Dad video-calling.

'Hello,' I say as he comes into focus. 'This is nice. You don't usually like video.'

'Is this a good time?' he asks uncertainly. His eyes dart around, partly I think because he's never seen Newington before, partly because he's nervous. Things have been tense between us lately.

'Yes, James is out for the next few hours. I'm making fat balls for the birds.' It was something he taught me to do. Because we lived in a flat he used to dangle precariously over our balcony to tie them. At least I won't have to do that. 'The grounds here are a haven for wildlife.'

'You always were such an animal lover. I remember many a time you'd come home from school leading a stray dog you'd found and wanted to keep, or holding a cat because they looked sad.'

'Remember when one of the "strays" turned out to be Mrs Cooper's Yorkshire terrier?'

'She was furious. Her face looked like a beetroot.'

We both laugh. Of all the versions of Dad, this is the one I love the best. I keep the conversation light.

'I'm going to make an insect hotel tomorrow. I've found some old crates and I've been gathering twigs.'

'Get you. So posh now you're a southerner the insects need a hotel.'

'We all need spoiling sometimes.'

'And James, is he spoiling you?'

'Yes.'

'Not coming home then?'

'No.' My spirit dips as his face falls.

He opens his mouth to say something but then he's looking over my shoulder.

'I thought you said you were alone?'

'I am.'

'Then who is that behind you?'

Chapter Twelve

James

Cass had been a mess when James arrived home last night. Babbling that her dad had seen someone behind her during their video call.

A woman.

Asking whether James thought it could be the ghost of Rose.

James did not.

Secretly he wondered whether Adrian had been drinking, letting his imagination get the better of him or – a terrible thought, he knows – but could he have made it up to scare Cass? He's desperate for her to return home.

Could Cass's erratic and worrying behaviour be down to stress? Since Cass had told him she is pregnant they have been thrust onto a new and terrifying path that he's not entirely sure they're ready for. It's so much responsibility and he worries constantly that he will end up like his father – cold and distant.

Cass probably has the same worries regarding her own father which could have resulted in her seeing things, hearing things, convinced that her paintbrushes are being moved. He'd tried to lighten the mood during their conversation last night but he had been worried. Could it be related to pregnancy hormones?

But there is another possibility. Adrian might actually have seen a woman outside the window. And so today, he makes a phone call he doesn't want to make.

'Let me guess? She's dumped you and you thought you'd come crawling back—'

'That's not why I'm ringing.' James cuts Angelica off. She is silent. Waiting.

'I…' He clears his throat. Grips the handset a little tighter. 'I'm going to become… Cass and I… we're going to be parents.'

'You're going to be a father?' She gasps. There's a beat. He waits for her to either scream and shout or break down in tears but she does neither.

'I could kill you, James. I mean literally kill you,' Angelica eventually says but there is no anger or malice in her voice, only an incredible sadness. He can picture her on the other end of the phone. Her eyes glistening with tears, hand covering her heart the way it would when she watched the latest John Lewis Christmas ad. Three Christmases they had spent together.

Three.

He hasn't even had one with Cass and yet they are having a baby.

'You're going to be a father.' She repeats.

'Yes.'

'You're having a baby with *her*.'

'Yes.'

The unspoken, *and not me*, hangs between them.

He reminds himself why he is calling and pushes away his sympathy for her.

'It's really important Cass remains stress free. Have you… have you been to the house?'

'The murder house?' She sounds incredulous.

'Don't call it that. It's our home.'

'For now. It's not even yours. What are you going to do when the baby comes, James? Where are you going to live?'

'That's not your concern,' he says, although he's been asking himself the same thing.

What *are* they going to do?

Focus.

'Why would I go to the house?'

'You were asking lots of questions about Cass. What she looks like. If she's pretty. If she looks like you. I thought you might have got curious and—'

'Did *she* tell you I was there? Because I wasn't.'

'Cass thought someone was outside the window last night. Earlier that morning she had seen someone in the garden. They hammered at the door. When she went outside there was a bouquet of roses on the doorstep.'

'Lucky her.' Bitterness dripped from her words. Spoken out loud it doesn't sound like a big deal but Cass had been upset when she had told him, babbling about roses and Rose being the girl who had lived here.

'We both know I wouldn't have sent her roses,' he says. Roses were their flowers, his and Angelica's. Every anniversary, every special occasion and sometimes just because.

'So she has a secret admirer. Seems she has everything.' Angelica's voice cracks and James doesn't know what to say so he says nothing at all, staying on the phone the way he had when they began dating and she couldn't sleep without him. Listening to her breath deepen while she drifted off.

'Sorry,' he whispers at last, not entirely sure what he is apologizing for. Accusing her of trying to frighten Cass. For leaving her. Building the life she wanted with someone else.

All of it.

Fran is waiting for him when he leaves the office that night. Bright red scarf wound around her neck. Hands stuffed into her pockets.

'James.' Her breath billows out in front of her as she calls him.

'Hey.' He jogs across the road to her.

'Coffee?' She tilts her head towards the café behind her. He hesitates. He really should get home to Cass but it's been a tough day at work, he's lost one of his clients. The phone call with Angelica hadn't improved his stress levels any.

He opens the door, stepping aside so Fran can enter first. The hiss of the coffee machine, the smell of cappuccinos instantly relaxes him.

Fran waves away his offer to buy the drinks and tells him to take a seat. He studies her while she stands at the counter, trying to read her. Has she come with bad news?

He's pulled out of his thoughts by Fran clattering coffee down on the table. Sliding a packet of ginger biscuits towards him. 'You look like you could do with a sugar hit.'

'I used to love these when I was younger.' He rips open the packet and takes a bite and ridiculously, unexpectedly, tears spring to his eyes. They remind him of his mother. Everything reminds him of his mother and he misses her.

Fran covers his hand with hers and if anyone other than Cass made the same gesture he would have pulled away, uncomfortable. As it is, he takes comfort in it. In her. She's gazing at him with such genuine concern in her eyes.

'Sorry. I had some news and...' He's too choked to continue but then he notices the way she squeezes his fingers, the concern in her eyes is now worry. 'It's okay, nothing terrible.' He forces the words out before taking a minute to compose himself. 'Cass is pregnant,' he says.

Fran grips both his hands between hers, a bright, wide smile spread across her face. 'A baby?' She's overcome and he wonders whether it's something she wants, whether it's something she can never have. But there doesn't seem to be any envy in her expression, more wonder and excitement, and he lets himself be lifted by her mood.

'A baby.' He is smiling too now. 'And I am happy about it it's just… it's brought up some emotions surrounding my own childhood. My own mother.'

'Did you have a happy childhood?'

Fran hasn't let go of his hands yet and he gently pulls away, stirs his coffee.

'Mostly.'

'Mostly?' Fran's eyes narrow.

'My dad was… working a lot. He wanted peace and quiet at home. I think I irritated him.' Even now remembering is sharp and painful. 'My mum though…' Again that fracture in his heart. 'She was amazing and she… she died almost a year ago.'

'And learning you're going to become a father has made you think of her as a grandmother?' Fran reads him easily.

'Yeah.'

'Your mother…' Fran's voice is low as she gazes out of the window at the multicoloured umbrellas bobbing past. 'Your mum would be overjoyed. And she'd be so, so proud of you.' She turns back to him. Her eyes are coated with a film of tears and he thinks this is about more than him and Cass. Fran has known loss too. He can feel it.

'We never really lose those closest to us, do we?' He covers his heart, his eyes briefly looking upwards. 'They're always here with us.'

'They really are.' Fran lowers her eyes, and this time it is he who takes her hands and holds them.

It is several minutes before they both inhale deeply, simultaneously, leaning back in their chairs, picking up their coffee cups.

'So.' James wipes the froth he can feel coating his upper lip. 'I didn't expect to see you today. Is there a problem?'

'Not at all. You sounded quite fraught when you called to ask if I'd sent Cass a bouquet earlier. I was wondering how you're finding the house?'

James doesn't know quite what to say. He's unsettled. Grappling for rational explanations in everything Cass tells him.

Why the swing seems to be moving of its own accord.

The shattered lightbulb in the basement.

The smell of lemons.

Cass hearing Rose's name.

Seeing her?

Her paintbrushes being hidden.

The clock always stopping at half past eight.

The same landing window opening on its own.

Yes, he has offered rational explanations for some of those things, most of those things, in fact, but not everything.

It's as though the house holds a mystery to be solved. Everything a clue to something but he can't figure out what.

'Do you know much about the Madleys?'

'There isn't much to know. They kept themselves to themselves. Nobody in the village knew them, or admits to knowing them. The youngest child was too little for school. The eldest didn't go to the local secondary, maybe she was home-schooled or she went away to boarding school.'

'I've googled but I can't find out much.'

'No. Obviously it was long before social media and every news story being online and it wasn't as though there were killers at large. They were both caught. One died, as I told you, and the other went to jail. You might be able to find out more about the Madleys from the house. Have you had a good look around?'

'Not really.' He doesn't tell Fran that there is a small part of him that is scared of what he'll find.

He knew where the nursery was before he had opened the door.

He knew the name of the bear.

Nothing is making sense and he's so very, very tired.

James plasters on a bright smile as he opens the front door.

The hands on the grandfather clock are motionless, 8.30.

He walks past it. It's faulty, that's all. He's sick of winding the bloody thing.

But... it always stops at the same time.

Christ, Cass's paranoia is starting to get to him. The wind probably only lasts a set number of hours or there's something wrong with the face. There's a rational explanation for everything.

Isn't there?

'Hello?'

'In the kitchen.'

'I'm just going to get changed. Be down soon.'

He tries not to think of the times he'd seen Cass before they'd lived together. They'd meet at the train station, their lips instantly pressing together. Hands under clothes. Barely able to control themselves, hand on knee all the way home, touching. Always touching.

Unbuttoning jeans, tugging T-shirts over heads. Trails of clothes leading to the bedroom.

And now…

It isn't that he doesn't fancy Cass anymore it's just that now she's carrying his baby she's changing, physically and emotionally. It isn't solely the thickening of her waist, the swell of her belly, she'll always be beautiful to him, but … she's edgy. Emotional.

Frightened.

Is it the hormones or is it just Cass? The bits he never got to see before. They've gone from zero to everything in such a short space of time. He can't help feeling that she's hiding a dark secret from him.

Once he's changed, he pops into the room Cass is using as a study.

On the easel a canvas, a half-finished painting of another rose.

He shivers, although it isn't cold. The wind must have got up though because, through the gaps in the window drifts the creak, creak, creak of the swing.

He hurries back downstairs. The kitchen smells of garlicky roast potatoes. Tongs in hand, Cass carefully turns them in the sizzling oil so that they brown evenly. Cass is barefoot, paint smudged over her denim shirt. He nuzzles into her neck, all at once feeling incredibly lucky. He's coming home to someone who loves him and he loves her.

'Good day?' She turns to him but her eyes are drawn to the window.

'Yeah.' He doesn't want to worry her with work stuff. He doesn't want to worry her at all. 'Nice to see you're painting again.'

'I've been working on a sunset. I think it's going really well.'

'A sunset? I thought you were painting another rose?'

'No.'

His shoulders stiffen, the memory of his telephone conversation with her father rattling round his mind. Was Adrian right?

'James? Is everything okay?' she asks.

Now is the time to say something.

To tell her what he knows.

Chapter Thirteen

Rose

Rose should say something. Although she hadn't seen it happen, she knew for certain that David had hit her mum.

After the strained dinner when David had told Rose that she couldn't return to boarding school she had cleared the plates away without being asked. When the kitchen was tidy she had found Mum sitting on the sofa, her eyes trained on the TV, her gaze blank. She hadn't heard Rose come into the room and Rose knew that if she switched off the programme and asked her what she had been watching, Mum would have no idea. Rose studied her. What was she seeing? The angry face of her husband? His fist coming towards her?

'Where's David?' she asked, suddenly fearful.

'Rose, please call him Dad again—'

'I can't. He—'

'Can you do it for me? It *was* an accident.'

'Roo says you've been arguing a lot. He's worried you're going to get divorced. You mentioned moving house and—'

Mum covered her heart with her hand as though Rose's words had hurt her.

'We can't.'

'Can't what? Divorce or move?' Whichever, it seemed an odd choice of phrase.

'Neither. Because… because we love each other. Everything's fine. Really. Do you want to talk about boarding school?'

'There doesn't seem much to say.'

'Dad pays the fees and…' Mum swallowed hard. 'But I can talk to him—'

'I don't need any favours from him.'

'Education isn't a favour and I want what's best for you. We both do. Your grades are fine. I'm proud of you.'

'I do try,' Rose said in a small voice.

'I know.' Her mother chewed her thumbnail, brows knitted together. 'It's an important year with your exams and—'

'Honestly.' Rose shifted closer to Mum, rested her head on her shoulder. 'It's okay if I go to the secondary here. Roo is growing so fast and I feel I'm missing so much. And… you know' – she sighed – 'you're not so bad, you know.'

'You're not so bad yourself.' Her mum dropped a kiss on Rose's head. 'But you must be honest with me. Don't tell me what you think I want to hear.'

'Okay.' Rose straightened up and tucked her legs under her and placed a cushion on her lap, wrapping her arms around it. 'I dunno. If I leave it kind of seems like the last four years have been a waste. I'll have to start again, making friends.'

'You'll soon make friends. You could reconnect with some of the girls from primary?'

'Yeah.' But it wasn't the girls Rose was thinking of. It was the boys.

One boy.

Gunner.

She touched her lips with her fingertips, feeling the tingle. The longing to be kissed again.

'Don't ask David – Dad – to change his mind. I think it'll be fine.'

'I *know* you'll be fine.' Her mum sounded relieved. 'And you have your whole life ahead of you. Endless opportunities.'

Of course, neither of them knew, then, that this wasn't true.

Her life would be cut short. Both of theirs would.

Rose kicked at the gravel as she headed down the driveway, a cloud of dust rising. Mum had gone for a bath. Dad – *David* – was still in his study, *working*. The house was quiet, empty, without Roo in it. Even when he was asleep he still filled the space. At least he had a friend to have a sleepover with. Rose had no one.

She was alone.

Despite her assurances to Mum earlier, she wasn't confident about starting again. She had spent the rest of the evening in panic. Imagining Gunner rejecting her. Laughing at her. She was a fool for pinning her hopes, her future, on one person but at that moment she felt that he was all she had.

Did one kiss mean anything?

She had no one to ask.

She hesitated at the park gates. She'd told Mum that she was going for a walk to clear her head and she had tried to pretend to herself that this was what she was doing but she knew that this had been her destination all along.

Gunner.

'See you soon, Rosie,' he had said. But he hadn't said when 'soon' was. Where it would be.

Now she was at the park. The same place at the same time. He had to be here waiting for her.

Had to be.

He wasn't.

The spot where he had sat with Kamal was empty. Grass flattened, dog ends scattered.

She was alone.

Her loneliness was a lump in her throat that she just couldn't swallow down. She remembered the warmth of the cider, the fuzzy feeling. She wanted that again. Craved it. She rummaged through her pockets and found a five pound note – was that enough? Even if it was, she wasn't eighteen, but she wasn't familiar to the shop assistant like the other school kids would be. Perhaps there was a chance, if she acted confident, that she would be served.

And if not, they could only say no, couldn't they?

What's the worst that could happen?

They were there, on the bench where Rose had sat drinking water last night, Gunner and Kamal.

'It's the posh bird,' Kamal shouted but Rose didn't answer him, barely noticed him. All she could see was Gunner.

Her heart hopped and skipped inside her chest, her head full of nothing but him.

'Hey,' she said as casually as she could.

'Hey yourself.' He grinned but didn't stand, didn't even move, hands still stuffed into pockets. Hands she wished he would…

'What you doing?' she asked.

'Talking about business,' Kamal said.

God he was a twat.

'I was just going to get some cider.' She jerked her head towards the shop. 'Want anything?'

'They'll never serve you. They don't serve school kids.'

'I'm not a school kid,' she said. 'Not from round here anyway. I haven't been in this shop regularly since I was eleven. I've changed a lot since then.'

'I bet you have.' Gunner's eyes travelled over her and Rose let them. Ignoring the instinct to cross her arms in front of her chest.

She flashed him a smile and strode into the shop, slinking out five minutes later, empty-handed.

'Sorry.' Her face was flaming.

'It's okay. Give me your cash.'

Rose pushed the note into Gunner's hand.

Minutes ticked by. 'Where is he?' she asked Kamal, scanning the entrance. 'Do you think something's gone wrong?'

'Nah. He's biding his time.'

Eventually Gunner sauntered out of the shop, past the bench, Kamal falling into step beside him.

'You coming?' Gunner called over his shoulder, and she trotted after him the way Roo trotted after her. Obedient. Adoring.

At the park they sat cross-legged in their spot. Rose already thought of it as that. Already thought of herself as Gunner's girl. He pulled a bottle of cider from his rucksack along with a bag of Doritos, the new snacks she had wanted to try. Then he gave her back her £5.

'How did you… oh.' She shook her head at her own stupidity.

He passed her a drink, their hands brushed and Rose felt… she felt *everything*.

She drank deeply from the bottle, feeling the fizz in her nose, in her throat. The warm bloom of alcohol caressing her stomach.

A girl sauntered by. 'Hey, Gunner,' she called. She had a short skirt and cropped top and Rose realized how out of touch with fashion she was. At school she wore a uniform and in their free time there was a dress code. When she came home for holidays she spent most of her time with Roo. She lowered her eyes, feeling ridiculous in her long skirt and baggy T-shirt but then, a weight on her shoulder, Gunner's arm around her. She snuggled in to him, placing her hand on his knee. Claiming him in the way he was claiming her.

'Hey, Tamsin,' Gunner said but he didn't invite her to join them, instead passing Rose the bottle. She drank deeply, forgetting about her ugly clothes. Her lack of confidence.

She was enough and the more she drank the more beautiful she felt.

Dusk painted the sky shades of violet and grey. The moon rising above the swings.

'Do you think it's a good idea, then?' Kamal asked.

Rose tried to focus, his face fuzzy, everything fuzzy.

'Umm, yeah.'

'We just need some cash to get started.' Gunner's hand was under her T-shirt, fingers pushing beneath her bra strap. Warm. Soft.

'Tamsin's family is minted.' Kamal shot Rose a sly look.

She felt sick. Remembering Tamsin's tanned midriff, long legs. 'How much do you need? I've got some savings from birthday and Christmas presents.'

'Not much. A couple of thou.'

Rose didn't have enough, she couldn't ask David for anything, or Mum.

'I don't have that.'

'That's okay.' Was it her imagination or did Gunner shift

away from her slightly? His thigh had been pressing against hers and now there was a gap, a coolness. 'Tamsin—'

'We've got some valuable art.'

'I don't think I can shift paintings, especially if they're originals. Something that can be pawned that aren't one-offs are better?'

'My dad collects military medals. Some of them are really rare. I think they're worth a lot of money.'

'Can you nick a couple?' Kamal asked.

'I dunno. Dad works from home when he's not with clients. They're in his study which he keeps locked when he's not in there. Anyway, Mum's always around, and my little brother.'

'I don't want you to put yourself at risk.' Gunner cupped her face between his hands and kissed her softly. He cared about her! She felt herself surrendering under his touch, her body melting until she was liquid, he was liquid, they were melding into one. His hands under her T-shirt, her nipples stiff and—

Kamal cleared his throat and Rose pulled back. She'd forgotten he was there, but she felt no shame. Only loved, and desired, and more than a little drunk. She swiped for the bottle and drained it.

'You're so cool.' Gunner grinned. She grinned back.

'I want to help you,' she said sincerely. Wanting to give him everything she had. Everything she was.

'It's better if I ask Tamsin.'

'What if...' She searched her mind, desperate for a solution.

'There might be a way.' Kamal crossed his legs, plucked a handful of parched grass from the ground. 'Then we wouldn't have to involve Tamsin. You know how clingy she can be, Gunner. Rose, have you got any days out planned?'

'Not that I know of but Roo wants to go to a farm. He's obsessed with animals. He's so cute when he's—'

'So you could arrange for your family to be out and leave the back door unlocked?'

'Umm...' Rose's head and heart raged against each other.

Again, that press of a thigh. Gunner's mouth on her neck.

'Yeah. I guess I could.'

'I can drive up to yours and—'

'Drive? I thought you were sixteen? At the secondary?'

'I am but I've borrowed my dad's car before.'

'He's ace behind the wheel,' Kamal said.

Gunner was trouble. She recognized that but on some level she welcomed it. She didn't have anyone else and if she could saunter into her new school in September as someone's girlfriend, one of them, not the ex-private-school snob, then there was no harm in it, was there?

No harm in letting him kiss her.

Run his hands under her T-shirt, slipping into her bra.

No harm in him and Kamal making plans that would never happen because they were only kids. All mouth, weren't they?

What's the worst that could happen?

Chapter Fourteen

Cass

What's the worst that can happen if I tell James the truth?

Immediately, my mind conjures a list because that's what my mind does. Jumps to the worst-case scenario. It's why I'm on medication in the first place.

Was.

Was on medication.

There's a roaring in my ears, the edges of my peripheral vision darken and momentarily I am trapped, screaming, hammering to be set free.

I am fine. I am safe. I am normal.

'Cass?' James gently takes my hands and lays them flat on the kitchen table and I realize I've been picking the torn skin around my nails. A drop of blood trickles down my finger and James gently wipes it away.

'What exactly did my dad tell you?' I'm shaking, feeling in this moment small and vulnerable in this huge house that doesn't, that probably never will, feel like home. I try to compose myself, drawing a deep, shaky breath.

Lemons.

I can smell lemons again, fresh and zesty, not the garlicky

potatoes roasting in the oven. I shake my head and the scent has gone.

'Your dad told me...' James glances towards the floor, he's choosing his words carefully I can tell, as though I am as delicate as china and the wrong ones might break me. 'He told me that you'd had a really tough time and you take medication.'

His eyes find mine and I search them for signs that he knows more than that. That he finds me less, because that's how I feel. Diminished. Not the Cass he fell in love with but the one who can't cope. I have tried to put months and years and miles between me and the woman I once was.

'Why didn't you tell me you're on medication? There's no shame in it.'

Instead of answering I stare forlornly at the scratched pine table, the dents in the soft wood, the marks of a family.

Were they happy? Did they feel safe? Loved? All of the things I want to feel.

'I'm not going anywhere, you know.' James reads me. 'Whatever you tell me. I love you and that will never change.'

'When I was a child...' I take a moment. Breathe in, garlic and roast potatoes once more. Not lemons. Is everything in my mind? Is everything in my mind again? 'I used to have this recurring nightmare. I was trapped. Trying to get out. My dad would wake me and I'd throw my arms around his neck, grateful that it was only a bad dream but... sometimes I'd wake and find myself in a cupboard, with no recollection how I'd got there. Dad would come and take me back to bed and tell me I'd been sleepwalking but...' I close my eyes, shake my head. It's too horrible.

'But?' James rubs his fingertips over my forearms.

'Sometimes...' My voice a whisper. 'I wonder whether Dad

put me there. He used to drink. A lot. More than now and… It was perhaps too much for him. Trying to hold down a full-time job. Raising a daughter alone, and I was difficult. Always asking about my mother. It was so painful for him.'

'I'd say that's natural curiosity rather than being difficult. Every child wants to know where they've come from.'

'Maybe, but I was so anxious. Always anxious that Dad would disappear. That I'd be alone. Dad started giving me these pills.' I notice James frown. 'He was a GP. He knew what he was doing. He wanted to calm me down and I guess it worked. I stopped asking questions.' I stopped caring, if I'm honest, but I don't tell James that, not wanting him to think I'm incapable of feeling.

'So the tablets were a good thing? Were you ever properly diagnosed with a specific condition?'

'No, but Dad said I didn't need to see anyone else. He called them "night terrors", said lots of children experience them.'

'Nightmares can be terrifying.'

It was more than nightmares. James is trying to understand but there is no way I can convey even a fraction of the horror I experienced.

'And you're still taking the tablets? Your dad said they are perfectly safe with the baby but I think when we see the midwife for our first appointment tomorrow we should—'

'I'm not taking them. I stopped when I realized I was pregnant.'

'And you feel…?' James is worried. Overly so.

He knows.

Dad must have told him that I stopped taking them once before.

Does he know what happened then?

'I feel fine. It's not like I've taken them constantly since I was a child. I came off them completely but then I went through a bit of a bad time' – *Leon* – 'and I began taking them again. It really wasn't – isn't – a big deal.'

It's ridiculous. I've moved across the UK to be with James. I'm having a baby with him and yet I'm keeping part of myself hidden, the deepest, darkest part which brings me shame.

'I've been thinking…' I'm crying now. Unable to contain my emotions, my fears. 'What if mental health issues run in my family?'

James tenderly strokes my cheek with the back of his fingers. 'Look, we know from his drinking that your dad has an addiction.'

'But I don't know about my mum. What if she had psychological problems? Or an illness? What if there's something genetic?' My breath is shallow, my head spinning.

'Shh, it's okay.' James pushes back his chair and rushes to my side. He pulls me close to him, my head against his chest. I feel the rhythm of his heart. Strong and steady. Dependable.

Still, I can't seem to pull myself together. It isn't just the fear of my child inheriting a disease; thoughts of nature versus nurture spin around my mind. Without knowing what sort of mum I had, I don't know what sort of mum I'll be.

'You are going to make an amazing mother.' Again, James reads my doubts and my fears, and his kindness, his faith in me makes me cry even harder. 'And if our child faces any challenges we will deal with them, together.' He takes my hand and kisses each fingertip in turn.

'I love you,' I tell him fiercely because it is all I can feel right now, everything else slipping away. There's no confusion as he kisses me. No turmoil as he unbuttons my shirt. No uncertainty as he lays me gently on the kitchen table. I have been lost but now I am found and his completely.

It is only afterwards as he rests his forehead against mine that I hear it. The creak, creak, creak of the swing. Smell the lemons. I rub my arms. James buttons my shirt up again thinking I am cold but the temperature is not the reason for the gooseflesh on my skin.

He pulls his own jumper over his head.

'You feel it too?' I whisper.

'It?'

'The house.'

Our eyes meet.

We live in this house, James and I, but I know we are not alone.

Chapter Fifteen

James

They're going to be largely alone when the baby is born. James worries about this as he eats his breakfast. Cass's dad is too far away. Too unreliable with his whisky breath.

James's family isn't much better. His dad has barely spoken to him, not even a congratulations when James told him he was to become a grandfather.

He misses his mum. He wants that support network. He doesn't feel ready to be a father. He's never even changed a nappy. What if he gets everything wrong? What if Cass can't cope either? She says she's okay without her medication but is she really?

She'd gone to the graveyard to find the Madley family because...

Because she believes that Rose is still here.

At least it's their appointment with the midwife later this afternoon. He has a list of questions on his phone that he wants to ask her.

The rain is hammering down outside. He needs to leave for work, traffic will be slower today.

He grabs the pad from the kitchen drawer to leave Cass her daily note but it is full. He smiles as he notices her lists – cot, pram, car seat – but his smile slips when he realizes how much it will all cost. He wonders if he can restore the cot bed upstairs? He will ask Fran. She'd already texted first thing with a cheery 'Morning, Daddy!'

He can't see Richardson's Retreats wanting the crib. He thinks of the youngest Madley child. What happened to them? They'd be too young to remember and that's a blessing but did they go on to have happy life? A fulfilled life?

He rummages around for another pad but can't find one.

Instinctively, without conscious thought, he hurries to the chapel. Reaches under the pulpit where he finds a pile of paper. He takes it back into the kitchen, unsettled now.

How did he know the paper was there?

He rationalizes that he must have explored the chapel more thoroughly than he'd thought, or perhaps he'd read it in the inventory, but he was sure he hadn't.

Cass would tell him the ghosts had led him there but there's no such thing as ghosts.

Is there?

Chapter Sixteen

Cass

There's a ghost of a smile on my lips as I wake to the feeling of a soft hand against my head, fingers gently stroking my hair. The sensation of someone sitting on my bed.

Outside, I can hear the rain hurling itself against the window panes, a chill breeze pushing its way through the cracks. The creak of the swing as the wind furiously tosses it from side to side. But here, I am warm and cosy in my cocoon. I keep my eyes closed, the pillowcase soft against my cheek. I snuggle deeper and stretch out my arm towards James.

But instead I'm met with air and then...

Singing?

Twinkle, twinkle, little star...

A girl's voice.

Simultaneously I open my eyes, flail my arms to ward off whoever is touching me. See that there isn't anyone there but still not believing it.

I had *felt* them.

With both hands I frantically ruffle my hair, in case there is anything crawling around in it that might have mimicked fingers.

Suddenly, footsteps on the landing.

The slap of bare feet against wood.

Giggling.

No.

I press my palms tightly over my ears.

No.

It's not real. I can't catch my breath. I force myself to think of the baby, this tiny life inside me that will be flooded with stress hormones, and I try to calm myself but I can't.

Ladybird, ladybird, fly away home.

No.

I cannot. Will not. Go through *this* again.

I am fine. I am safe. I am normal.

I lower my arms, the house is silent.

Still.

It's cold when I climb out of bed, a layer of cooling sweat sticking my pyjamas to me.

I edge out into the hallway, tell myself I'm being ridiculous, but I can't help feeling afraid.

In the bathroom, the ancient pipes gurgle and splutter, the shower head spitting out lukewarm water. The cubicle is more modern than the rest of the room. Normally I'm instantly cheered in here. The rolltop bath, so inviting, with its aged bronze taps, standing proudly on the grey and white chequered floor. From the tub there's an amazing view of the courtyard, the woods beyond. As I strip off my clothes and dump them on the ornate carved wooden armchair in the corner, I wonder whether the baby will like baths and thoughts of my future son or daughter lift my mood. But then I think of the Madley children. Did they bathe before they went to bed? Did the teenager experiment with face masks and conditioning treatments? Did the little one have rubber ducks or plastic whales?

I know it's not healthy but I cannot stop thinking of them.

Testing the water with my hand I find it's hot now and so I step under the jets. Wet my hair before reaching for my shampoo.

Lemons.

This isn't my usual shampoo. I rub the water from my eyes and check the bottle. It's clearly the lavender one I prefer. I sniff it again.

Lemons.

I am fine. I am safe. I am normal.

In my rush to get out of the shower I almost slip. I wrap myself in a rough white towel. The bathroom is steamy now. I'm heading for the door when I notice it on the mirror.

One word.

Three letters.

RUN

Frantically I wipe it away until I question whether it was ever really there at all.

Fran pops in at lunchtime. She thrusts two salads towards me. Layers of crispy green leaves, scattered with cubes of creamy feta.

'I know what you artists are like, forgetting to eat.' She stamps her feet on the mat, before shrugging off her raincoat and hanging it over the banister.

'Is everything okay?' I can't complain she's dropped in unexpectedly because, technically, she is my boss.

'Yes, fine. Just thought I'd pop in and as it's noon I've brought us some food.'

I follow her into the kitchen, feeling like a visitor. Reluctantly sitting at the table after she insists on fetching the plates. The cutlery.

We begin to eat. I hadn't realized how hungry I was. I'd been so unsettled after this morning's shower I'd skipped breakfast.

'So...' She forks a cherry tomato, the middle oozes out, bright red, and all at once I have a shocking vision.

Blood.

I push my plate away.

'Not hungry?' she asks. 'Or don't you like feta?'

'I love all cheese. Stilton is my favourite.'

'I'm not sure you should eat blue cheese.' Her eyes flicker to my stomach. 'I mean... It's...' She flounders, a pink flush creeping around her neck.

'James told you our news then?' I feel a flicker of annoyance. We hadn't discussed telling her but she's smiling so brightly I smile back, my hand resting on the swell of my stomach.

'I'm so happy for you both. A baby!' She reaches over and rubs my arm. 'How are you feeling? Any nausea?'

'There was but it seems to be going now. There are... other things though.' I bite my lip. I should save my questions for the midwife, it's not like Fran has even had a child of her own, but she's here and friendly and suddenly I realize just how lonely I am.

'What things?' she prompts.

'Just a weird sense of smell.' I don't share anything else. I don't want her to think I'm irrational, incapable of looking after myself, the house.

'You can get a heightened sense of smell in the first trimester. How far along are you?'

'I'm not sure. The midwife should tell us today.'

'There you go then. Everything's fine.'

She looks encouragingly at my food. I pick up an olive and bite into it knowing that everything isn't fine. It's one thing to have a heightened sense of smell but what about smelling things that aren't actually there?

The conversation moves to the house. She asks if I've explored properly. If I have any concerns.

I answer no to both.

'But' – I filter my words – 'I sometimes think about the children who lived here.' I don't tell her I hear them, playing.

Laughing.

Singing.

She fixes me with a look of sympathy. 'It's hard not to think about them all the time. It's so tragic. A family is the most important thing of all, isn't it?'

I think of the family I'll have with James.

The family I thought I'd have with Leon.

My dad.

I don't answer.

Once Fran has gone I lie on the couch in the drawing room, staring at the ornate screen in front of the fire, wondering who painstakingly embroidered the peacocks. I know it's purely decorative and not there for safety but I'm glad the inglenook fireplace is covered. There's still something about fireplaces that creeps me out. They seem so dangerous. Give me a radiator any day.

I refocus my attention, pulling the itchy wool blanket closer to my chin as I catch sight of the portraits. The beady eyes staring down at me. There are paintings everywhere but as yet I haven't found any photos. There is only one portrait that I think was the last Madley family. Their clothes are more modern. The styling different. The woman is smiling. Baby on her lap, swamped in an elaborate frilly christening gown. Eldest daughter, pigtails hanging over her shoulders, is stroking the baby's cheek, a look of wonder on her face. Behind his wife, hand on her shoulder, is Mr Madley. Spine straight, cheeks ruddy. With his tweed jacket he looks every inch the country gentleman.

It's too high for me to study the portrait properly but in that moment, frozen in time, they look happy. And that is my last thought before I drift off to sleep.

Something startles me awake. A shadow passes outside the window. My heart leaps into my mouth. Who could be in the back garden?

Leon.

Does he know where I am? Dad had told James about my breakdown, my medication. Could he somehow have let slip to Leon in a drunken stupor where I now live if Leon had turned up, demanding to see me?

I rush to the window. Both wanting and not wanting to see who is there. There's no one to be seen. I look down. There are footprints in the flowerbed.

Somebody was out there.

Somebody was watching me.

Who could it be if not Leon?

Peggy? The woman on the train who has my key? James had said the address of Newington wasn't on the contract but had I scribbled it down? I can't quite remember. But James is probably right. She was an opportunist.

Footsteps.

Footsteps coming from the great hall, slow and steady. I'm so, so scared as I head towards them. My hand protectively on my stomach wanting to shield my baby from whatever, whoever is out there. I reach the door. Hear giggles.

A banging.

It's someone knocking on the front door.

I rush towards it, my fingers on the key, not sure what to do. If it's safer out there than in here.

'Cass?' a voice calls from outside. A knock on the door again. I pull it open.

'Hi, remember me?' the man in front of me asks.

It takes me a second to place him.

'Robin, of course.' The man who had helped on the train.

I'm about to invite him in when suspicion crawls slowly down my spine. Is he the one who's been watching me? I glance down at his shoes, They aren't coated in mud the way they would be if he'd been standing in the flower bed. That means whoever it was could still be out there.

Leon?

I'd feel safer if someone was here with me. 'Come in.' I usher him in, he wipes the rain from his face. 'Coffee?'

'Please. I called around a couple of days ago but I don't think you were here. I left you some flowers anyway.'

'The roses? They were from you?' I ask as I make our drinks, relief and disappointment flooding through me. I'd thought they were a sign. A gift from Rose, the girl who lived here before. But that would be crazy, wouldn't it?

I am fine. I am safe. I am normal

'Yeah. I didn't have any paper to leave a note.'

'I'm so sorry I haven't been in touch. I've been—' I stop myself from talking about myself, the house, remembering what he'd told me on the train. 'Have you had the funeral yet? For your father?'

'Yes. It still doesn't seem real. We were planning a big celebration for his sixtieth birthday next year.'

'I'm so sorry. Fifty-nine is no age at all.'

'I think stress played a big part in it.' Robin heaps sugar into his coffee, stirring it carefully before his eyes meet mine again. 'He had an obsession.'

'An obsession?' My voice is light but a sense of foreboding crawls across my skin.

Robin takes a deep breath. 'There's something you should probably know. My dad was a police officer. He was on duty, that night.'

'That night?' But even as I ask, I know.

'My mum said he was never the same afterwards. Seeing the bodies, the slaughter of the Madley family. She won't talk about it. It was all so horrific. I was only nine but I remember it being literally the day the laughter stopped in our house.'

'I can't imagine.' I really don't know what to say.

'Neither can I. The girl, she was so young. A teenager with her whole life ahead of her.'

'Do you know anything about her? I've been googling but...' I shrug.

'There isn't much online.'

'Do you think her name was Rose?'

There's a shift in Robin's expression.

'I think I heard Dad mention that name before. It was around that time.' He frowns. 'It might be?'

'Don't you think it's odd there aren't hundreds of mentions online?'

'Not really. It was so long ago, and cut and dried, I guess. One of the intruders killed and the other convicted. But there was... something. Dad never really spoke about it, not in front of me, but one night I heard them in the kitchen...'

'Could that be when you heard the name – Rose?'

'It might be.' He screws up his forehead, trying to remember. 'There's one thing I did overhear that stuck with me though.'

'What?'

'Dad never believed it was a burglary.'

He must have been the officer who gave the quote to the newspaper.

It wasn't indicative of a robbery.

'Why did he think that?'

'Because, and this was never released to the papers, but "tell me where it is" was written on the wall. In blood.'

It's too horrible. 'Which wall?' My eyes scan the room as though I might see it now.

'I don't know but Dad says the whole thing was too brutal. Too specific. Targeted. And nothing was stolen. The jewellery box wasn't even touched. Mum said once that's why Dad could never let it go.' He leans back on his chair. '"Tell me where it is". They were looking for something. It tortured him.'

'I can't imagine.' But I know all too well about the guilt surrounding a loss of life.

Leon.

'I guess seeing those bodies, a family, that teenage girl with everything to live for, it seemed so senseless and Dad wanted to make sense of it.'

'It's so weird. And the surviving child?'

'I don't know. A few years back I looked up the house to see who might have inherited it but deeds weren't put online thirty years ago.'

'If it was sold five years after the tragedy then the youngest child can't have inherited it. I wonder if they got the money from the sale? I hope they are okay.' Being pregnant has brought out a maternal side to me.

'Me too. It's like after 8.30 that night they ceased to exist.'

'Eight thirty?' A thick slab of dread uncurls in my stomach.

'That's when Dad said it happened.'

Eight thirty – the time the clock in the entrance always stops.

The time of the murders.

'Holy fuck, there's a chapel!'

I'm showing Robin around the house and although the history has impacted his childhood, although Newington is not mine, I can't help feeling a sense of pride.

We come to the room I paint in – Rose's room.

'It's got a nice energy.' Robin looks around.

'I find it calming. I spend most of my time here.'

Robin crouches to tie his shoelace.

He's just straightening up when he says, 'Have you seen this?' He's pointing to something underneath the window sill.

I drop to my haunches. Trace my finger over the word that has been roughly carved below the window.

The warning.

Those three letters again.

Three letters that fill me with dread.

Run

The same word that I thought had been written in steam in the bathroom mirror.

What can have happened to the family who lived here? The girl whose bedroom I am in?

It wasn't indicative of a robbery.

What did they need to run from?

Or who?

And has that person ever returned?

141

I think of the footsteps outside the window, the person who's been watching me.

If the intruders didn't come to burgle the house, what did they come for, and has the surviving killer come back to find it?

Run.

Chapter Seventeen

Rose

THEN

'Run.' Rose clawed her hands. 'I've got my tickling fingers ready.'

'I don't need to run, I can fly. Guess what I am?' Roo tucked his elbows into his sides, clucking as he strutted around the room.

'A dinosaur.'

'No. Silly.'

'A monkey.'

'No! I'm a chicken. What am I now?' He dropped to all fours and made a bleating sound.

'A cat.'

'You're a stupid head.'

'No, you're a stupid head.' Rose tickled him until he squealed for mercy.

Red-cheeked and breathless he scrambled onto the sofa, this time mooing.

'You're a pig.'

'I'm a cow. Do you think we will see cows today? And donkeys? And chickens? And—'

'Fruit cake and hot chocolate.' Mum stepped into the lounge holding Roo's coat. 'That's what I want to see.'

'Yay! It's time to go to the farm!' Roo rocketed over to Mum and stuffed his arms into the sleeves of his jacket.

Rose knelt before him, guiding his feet into his trainers. She couldn't look Mum in the eye, knowing what she'd planned. For the millionth time she thought about calling it off but each time she had doubts she remembered the feel of Gunner's arms around her. His mouth on her neck. His thigh pressed against hers. He was all she had here.

Except he wasn't, was he? Not really.

Roo's small hands rested on the top of her head, steadying himself, as she tugged his laces tight. Mum promising he could buy a bag of feed for the goats.

She was betraying them.

Her blood was hot, heart racing. Nerves or fear? Perhaps both.

She couldn't do this to them. She just couldn't.

But then the memory of the red mark on her mum's face, the sound of her weeping. She wasn't doing anything to Mum. It was her stepdad's military medal collection. It would serve him right.

But still…

It was wrong. She knew it was wrong.

But she knew she was going to do it anyway.

She made a pantomime of coughing, her sleeve over her mouth.

'Sorry, I'll just get some water before we go.' She scuttled towards the kitchen to unlock the back door. She passed David's study where he was sitting at his desk, hunched over some papers.

She hesitated. They had barely spoken to each other since she'd accused him of hitting Mum.

'We're ready to go,' she said.

'I'm not coming, Rose. I've a lot to catch up on.'

Her stomach writhed with anxiety. 'But you *have* to come.'

'Have to?' He raised his eyebrows.

'I meant… I want you to… Dad.' She thought about what she had to lose – Gunner – if the house wasn't empty as promised, but when she thought of what she had to gain, Gunner wasn't the first thing that sprang to mind. Whatever had happened in that room Mum had forgiven David and Rose knew that life would be easier if she could too. If things could go back to a time when she felt safe and happy.

Loved.

He softened. 'Look, I know things have been difficult lately.'

'You've been difficult lately,' she muttered under her breath.

He pushed back his chair and stepped towards her. She flinched, afraid, and this fear was accompanied by an overwhelming sadness. This was the man she had regarded as a father. Who she had trusted with her heart, her mother's heart. Who was now a stranger to her.

But instead of striking her, he said softly, 'I know. And I'm sorry.' He wrapped her in a hug and she was stiff, unyielding in his arms, but then she breathed in the familiar scent of him, musk and spice, and then she was hugging him back.

'I wanted you to come to the farm with us,' she whispered into his chest, finding that this was true. That the trip she had begged for wasn't solely to get them out of the house for Gunner and Kamal to sneak in. It wasn't just for Roo and his obsession with animals. It was almost wholly for her because she wanted them to feel like a family again, the way they used to.

'Rosy Posy.' He hadn't called her this for a long time and she felt the burn of tears behind her eyes. 'I have to stay and work but soon I'll be on top of things and then we can all go on holiday perhaps?'

'Yeah. Yes. I'd like that,' and she found that despite everything, she would.

'Rose?' Mum called from outside the front door. 'We're getting in the car.'

'Just a sec.' Her T-shirt stuck to her back with sweat. What was she going to do? Gunner and Kamal were expecting the house to be empty.

In the hallway, she picked up the landline, Gunner's number imprinted on her brain.

It was his mum who answered. Gunner wasn't home.

'Please give him a message,' she whispered urgently into the handset. 'Tell him that my stepdad isn't coming to the farm.'

She hung up the phone, close to tears. What if he didn't get the message? What if they came and panicked, hurt David?

But no. The way Gunner gently caressed her cheek before he kissed her was not the touch of a violent man.

But then she never thought David would be violent man.

She ran to the kitchen, rattled the back door, tugging at the handle, checking again and again that it was secure.

'You okay, Rose?'

'Yeah, Mum asked me to make sure it was locked.' The lie tripped easily from her tongue. She didn't know who she was anymore.

'Don't worry, I've got to open it to take the rubbish out. You have a nice time.'

Rose slowly, reluctantly, trudged outside.

'I'm feeling a bit sick,' she said as she climbed into the back seat of the car.

'The fresh air might do you good?' Mum said.

'Please, Rose, you've got to come.' Roo slipped his hand inside hers. 'Please.'

'Of course I'm coming, stupid head.'

David would lock the door again once he'd put the bin out, wouldn't he?

Roo filled the fifteen minute drive to the farm with impersonations of all the animals he hoped to see. He'd gone from donkeys and horses to bears and tigers. He chattered to himself, fingers curved into claws, teeth bared, growls coming from deep inside his stomach. Rose could barely focus, panic tight around her throat.

What if, what if, what if...

Mum appeared equally distracted.

They bumped across the field that doubled as a car park and once they'd parked, Roo raced ahead, grabbing one of the white paper bags stuffed with animal feed by the entrance.

'Come on, slowcoaches.'

They wandered slowly around the farm. Roo talking to every animal, giving them a name.

'Which ones do you want to feed then?' Rose checked her watch constantly, the hands ticking both too fast and too slowly towards two o'clock. The moment when everything could change.

'I don't know yet. I have to meet them all first before I decide.'

The decision was snatched from him when they walked through the goat enclosure. A butt of the head, a demanding mouth.

'Hey.' Roo tried to pull the bag away from the goat but it was too late. The goat had snatched it, munching both the food and the paper wrapped around it. Roo burst into tears.

'I'll get you another,' Mum said. She hurried off towards the entrance. Rose crouched and hugged her brother, willing her mum to hurry.

But she wasn't the only one watching her mother.

There was a man dressed in black, leaning against a tree. There was something about him that made Rose uneasy. Perhaps it was the way he was alone, on a children's farm. She glanced around; his family must be somewhere but everyone seemed to belong to someone.

But not to him.

She pulled Roo closer to her, telling herself that she was on edge because of the plans Gunner and Kamal had made. Not everyone was a criminal. But still, there were bad people around. People who took children.

Mum jogged back towards them, two bags of feed in her hand.

They set off again, winding through the enclosures, Rose throwing glances over her shoulder.

The man was definitely alone.

Definitely following them.

'I'm just nipping to the loo,' Mum said.

Rose took Roo's hand, held it tightly.

She checked her watch again. Almost two.

Almost time.

Her mouth dried, her throat closed. She swallowed hard.

One minute.

Thirty seconds.

Ten.

Five.

She closed her eyes, felt herself sway.

Had Gunner got the message or was he at her house? She

thought of David, his temper. She didn't know who she was scared for. Both of them. Everyone.

Herself.

She opened her eyes and looked around. The man had disappeared.

But then Mum hurried out of the toilets, and seconds later the man sauntered out, lighting a cigarette.

'Come on, it's time to go.' Mum's face as white as the clouds that drifted across the brilliant blue sky.

'But I've still got some feed left,' Roo protested.

'You can give it to the rabbits at the exit.'

'Mum, what's wrong?' Rose asked in a low voice.

'Nothing.'

'I saw that man come out of the ladies.'

'*Nothing.*'

That was the last word anybody said until they got home.

Rose held her breath as she walked through the front door. Dizziness setting in as David strolled into the hallway.

'Have fun?'

She exhaled, relieved. Gunner and Kamal hadn't shown up. Everything was okay.

'I need to talk to you.' Mum took his arm and dragged him back towards his study. 'Take your brother upstairs, Rose.'

The door shut.

'Roo, if you go and play in your room for a little while I'll do anything you want later.'

'Can you be a horse?'

'Yes.'

'Can I sit on your back and say giddy-up?'

'Yes, now skedaddle.'

As he pounded upstairs, Rose crept toward the study, pressed her ear against the door. Listened to the frightened voice of her mum. The agitated tone of David.

'David, I was scared. I don't think you understand. He followed us to the farm.'

'Perhaps it was coincidence—'

'A man visiting a farm without any kids?' Her mum's voice rose in pitch. 'He knows what I look like. Who the children are. He threatened us.'

'He wouldn't hurt you. I know it was scary and I'm sorry but—'

'I'm going to call the police.'

'No.' David's tone was sharp. 'You can't. They won't be able to do anything and you'll make everything worse.'

'How can they be worse? He followed me into the toilets. He wasn't bothered that someone might have seen him. He said... he said that if you didn't pay him back immediately, he'd hurt me. The children. He's dangerous.'

'I know.'

'Then what—'

'I'm thinking,' David snapped.

'He knows where we live. It won't be hard to find out where Roo is going to school. Rose. Perhaps she could go back to boarding—'

'And how are we going to pay for that?' His words dripped with sarcasm.

'David...' Her mum's voice was shaky. 'We have to do *something*.'

'I know. Look, I'm sorry. I thought I'd be able to pay back the loan within a few weeks. If I'd known that—'

'You should have accepted when the bank refused to lend you the money that it was a bad investment.'

Silence.

'I'm sorry, I can get a job.' Mum talking too fast. Was David raising his fist to her? Rose's jaw clenched.

'No. You're not skilled and anything you earn will be a drop in the ocean.' His frustration was palpable.

'But it's better than nothing?'

'Not really. It won't look good to clients if you're out there working in a supermarket or something and if the clients I do have left lose faith and stop investing we'll lose far more than you'll bring in. Appearances are everything.'

'So then what do we do? Sell something? The art?'

Again, a beat.

'No. We can't have gaps on the walls.'

'What about your medals? You're always saying they're valuable.'

'Everyone knows I love them. It would look odd if I sold them. Word would get out, but... if some things went missing and we had to claim on the insurance, that would be different.'

'Missing? How?'

'Leave it with me. I need to think.'

'Don't take too long, David. He meant it when he said he'd hurt me. The kids. We *have* to protect them.'

Chapter Eighteen

Cass

My desire to protect my child is overwhelming. During my introductory visit to the midwife high levels of glucose were found in my urine so I've been booked in for an OGTT to test my blood glucose levels. In the meantime I've read up on gestational diabetes and followed all the advice I've been given. I'm not a bad cook but I tend to stick to the same few meals on rotation – Dad's favourite dinners, pie and mash, pasta – never realizing before how much sugar these dishes contain. How bad our weekly takeaway is for my health, for the baby.

Today, a week later, I'm lying on the bed, with the waistband of my yoga pants rolled down and a cold gel over my belly. I'm apprehensive. There's so much that can go wrong.

'Don't worry,' Robin had said when I'd confided my concerns. In the two weeks since I met him he's become a good friend, dropping around most days. 'It'll be fine.' He had hugged me but he doesn't know everything will be okay, does he? Nobody does except the sonographer and she's not saying anything.

'Is there a problem?' I ask her. Why isn't she speaking?

Instead, she's studying the screen with such intensity, gently moving the probe.

Something isn't right with the baby?

Have I caused it? I feel a rush of anxiety. I'd been so careful with my diet, but in those first few weeks before I knew I was pregnant I'd had the odd glass of wine. Taken my medication.

Although the midwife had said SSRIs were prescribed during pregnancy and 'seemed' safe I decided not to restart them. 'Seemed' wasn't enough for me. And besides, I am fine. I'd googled the strange experiences I am having and sudden changes in body temperature is normal. Senses can be sharper too. Tinnitus is common and perhaps it is this causing the occasional strange sound in my ears rather than whispers, singing, laughing.

I am fine. I am safe. I am normal.

James is quiet. I am frozen with fear. I want to press her to find out what's wrong with my child but I'm yo-yoing between wanting and not wanting to know. To pretending everything is fine the way I thought that it was before I came here.

I link my fingers through James's because I've such a desire to run away from this room, from the impending news, I'm afraid I might act on it.

'Everything looks great.' She turns the screen around so we can see. 'You're twenty-one weeks.'

'But I've only just begun showing.' Although that's a strong word. I don't exactly have a huge bump. It's more that I can't do my jeans up anymore and my bras are tight across my back.

'The worst thing you can do during pregnancy is compare yourself to other prospective mums. Your experience will be as individual as you are. All of baby's measurements are fine. There's no cause for concern.'

We marvel at the squirming mass on the screen, vague and

amorphous at first but then becoming clearer as the sonographer points out the head, the heart, the spine.

'It's a baby,' whispers James.

I turn to make a joke, ask him what he'd thought it might be, but then notice the tears in his eyes and so I squeeze his hand.

'Can you tell the sex?' he asks.

'I can. Although just so you know we can never 100 per cent guarantee we're right. Do you want to know?'

'I don't know, do we?' It's something we hadn't discussed partly because, until the moment, it hadn't felt real.

'It's up to you,' James says but there's such a look of hope on his face.

'Let's go for it.' I grin.

'As far as I can tell right now I'm convinced enough to tell you it's a girl.'

'A daughter.' A tear trickles down James's cheek.

'We can call her Isobel after your mother.' I know he's thinking of her right now.

'Hello, Isobel.' His voice cracks. 'What about your mum's name though?'

'Maybe for our next child'. I smile. For now, Isobel Rose, I think, perhaps in tribute not only to James's mum but also to the girl from Newington who never got the chance to live her best life. Perhaps Isobel can live it for her.

In the week since my scan I've been on a high, but today I've come crashing back down.

'But I've followed the diet sheet you gave me,' I say to the midwife. I'm behaving like a petulant child as she tells me that there hasn't been enough drop in my blood sugar levels and I'll need to take insulin.

'It's not something you've caused,' she says flicking back through my notes, studying my results. 'Did one of your parents have diabetes?'

'Dad doesn't. I don't know much about my mum.' I say miserably. 'She died and dad doesn't like talking about her but I'll ask him about her medical history.'

I so wish she was here.

Now more than ever I need a mother figure. Someone to share their own experience with me, to guide me through mine. I thought it was impossible to miss her any more than I did as a child, but I do. That longing for something I've never had is all consuming. When I wonder whether Isobel will take after me, I question whether I'm like my mother. Where did my artistic flare come from? Dad has no interest in art. Was my mother a painter? Will my daughter be? Her absence shouldn't matter so much. I'm being looked after. Fran has been dropping off daily fresh food parcels. My mother's absence *shouldn't* matter so much, but it does.

I'm in my second trimester and should have endless energy according to Google but I don't. When Saturday rolls around James offers to cook.

'Go take a bath or something,' he had said when I had offered to help so now I am in the tub, sinking into frothy coconut bubbles, trying not to look at the mirror. Trying not to think about the word that had been drawn into the steam before.

Run

The lights flicker.

Footsteps outside the bathroom.

Suddenly the room is plunged into darkness.

'James?' I call but all that comes back is a giggle. Something brushes against the back of my neck. I swipe at it and realize it is my hair coming loose from my bun.

Run.

Run.

Run.

The words are sung, soft and melodic, but the sound is not soothing. It's terrifying.

'James?' I scream now, thinking he is too far away to hear me but needing him as I slosh out of the bath, my foot skidding across the floor. I grab for my towel but it isn't where I left it on the rail.

All around me I hear singing, laughter, footsteps.

Ladybird, ladybird, fly away home.

The darkness is all encompassing, disorientating, I think I'm heading for the door but instead I stub my toe against the stand of the basin.

I sink to the floor, clutching at my toes.

'James!' I am sobbing now.

The door handle squeaks, the door begins to creak open.

'Cass?' All at once the lights burst into life, James rushing towards me.

'The lights went out and my towel had gone and—'

'Here it is. It must have slipped onto the floor.' James picks up my towel from where it is bundled under the rail.

He crouches and wraps it around my shoulders. 'Are you hurt, did you slip?'

'No. I stubbed my toe that's all.' But I am trembling. 'Someone turned the lights off – or something and…' I swallow the rest of my words as I catch the expression on James's face. 'Sorry. I'm fine. I thought… I don't know. I must have got confused in the dark.' I don't want to worry him. Don't want him to insist I go back on my medication.

SSRIs seem to be safe.

But what if they're not?

'It's just, the lights…' I gesture towards the ceiling.

'They were on in the kitchen,' James says. 'But they could be on a different circuit up here. Old wiring. I'll give Fran a call. Ask if they can send an electrician around. I came up to ask you if you like parsnips? I bought some with the shopping but realise that we've never had them together?'

I hate them.

His question brings home to me how much we don't know about each other. I stare at him. Could he have turned the lights off? Want me to think I'm going mad?

Of course he wouldn't.

What about Peggy who stole my bag on the train, who has a key? Even as I think this I know it's ridiculous. As though an elderly woman would want to play tricks on me. But someone is. Robin? Fran? Leon?

I want it to be *someone*.

Because the alternative, that everything I'm seeing, hearing, feeling is real, is even more terrifying. I'm no longer finding comfort in Rose's presence. It's gone beyond spotting the odd flower, hearing an occasional whisper. The singing, the giggling, the warnings to run. It all seems so sinister now.

I sit on the edge of the bath while James crouches before me, softly patting at my skin with the towel, absorbing the moisture, taking care to dry in between my fingers, my toes, and I see a glimpse of the father he will be.

He is a good man. Kind.

When he's finished he stands and offers me his hand. 'My lady.'

'My lord.' Our fingers touch and something I can't quite identify passes between us. An acknowledgement of something.

Love.

I think it's love.

'Dinner will be ready at 8.30.'

All at once I drop his hand and eye him suspiciously.

8.30.

The time of the murders. The time of the stopped clock. Is he the one stopping it? Is he messing with me?

My old anxiety rears with pointed teeth and sharpened claws. *Run.*

By the time I'm sitting at the dining table, Simon and Garfunkel singing about bridges over troubled water, the flicker of the candle casting a long shadow on the wall as James brings in the dinner, I am calm again. My moods swings are exhausting. I can almost feel the hormones milling around inside me, creating havoc.

'It smells delicious.'

James has cooked my favourite curry, 'Without all the sugar of a takeaway, and it's cauliflower rice and only a small portion so it's fine. I've checked.'

We chat about the changes we'll make to our lifestyle as James tops up our wine glasses with water.

'I can't wait to have a beer again though,' he says.

'I don't mind if you drink.'

'No. We're in this together.'

'I'm sorry about… you know. My diabetes affecting your diet too.'

'Cass, please don't apologize. It isn't your fault.'

'Maybe, but I feel terrible. I… I don't want anyone to know about it yet.'

'It isn't something to be ashamed of.'

'I know but… can we keep it to ourselves, just for now? Fran already fusses around me too much and Robin keeps sharing the experience of his sister's pregnancy as though mine will be exactly the same. They mean well but it's stifling.'

'Yeah, I noticed that about Robin when he came over for dinner.'

'I can't take any more well-meaning advice. Do you think it is genetic?' I ask him the impossible question. 'Do you think my mother was diabetic?'

'I don't know.'

'Perhaps there was a reason she fell from the ladder. What if she was dizzy because of a health condition we don't know about? We should really know the medical histories of our families. I did ask dad and he said she was healthy but what if there was something she didn't know? Or something he didn't want to tell me? At least your dad said that he and your mum were fine.'

'Yeah, but I forgot to ask about my grandparents.'

'Oh god. What abut great-grandparents? Could there be something genetic that skips generations?' My eyes well with tears. I put down my knife and fork.

'Dance with me. . .' James is pushing his chair back, walking towards me with his hand outstretched. 'My lady.'

I swallow the lump in my throat. 'My lord.' His fingers brush mine and there is such familiarity there, such a feeling that we are meant to be that I can't believe I ever doubted him, not for a second.

He wraps his arms around me, holding me loosely.

'It's okay,' I whisper, resting my head on his shoulder, pressing my body against his. I know he is worried about hurting Isobel, our daughter.

'I don't want to—'

'Shh.' I kiss his neck. 'Nothing will hurt her. *Nothing.*' My lips find his and our kiss is soft and tender, growing more urgent, and by the time we reach the bedroom we're not thinking of Isobel, only each other. This moment. And it's perfect.

At first, when I wake, I don't know where I am. I'd been trapped in the nightmare, trapped in the cupboard. My head feels fuzzy, heavy.

Becoming aware of my surroundings is like resurfacing. Taking a gasping breath of air after being underwater for too long. My chest is tight and I'm disorientated.

Confused.

I'm on the landing but the last thing I can remember is going to bed, the feel of James's touch, his skin, his smell. The way he'd made love to me, so tenderly, as though it was my first time. I'd drifted off in his arms. Happy content. Aware of him spooning against me, his body warming mine. Now my feet are bare. My pyjamas no defence against the chilly night air.

How did I get here?

Outside, the hoot of an owl. The creamy moon pooling through the window which, again, is open. Unnerved, I close it. James had said he thinks that the latch is loose and any vibrations in the house will cause the window to open but I'm not convinced.

I become aware of a stinging sensation. Just like before, my nails are dirty, torn, as though I've been clawing at something, trying to get out.

This time though, I hadn't had the nightmare.

I hurry back towards our bedroom. As I pass the room I paint in I see it. The rocking chair, moving of its own accord. Rocking as though someone is sitting in it. I cover my mouth to stifle my scream.

There is something very wrong with this house.

Or something very wrong with me.

I have to know which.

If there's some sort of mental illness in my family, don't I deserve to know? Not just for me but for Isobel too? There are so many genetic diseases that can be passed down and I don't know whether my wider family had any of them.

Tomorrow I'm going to go back up north. To see my dad. To find out my entire family history.

I need answers.

And I'm determined to get them.

Chapter Nineteen

Rose

THEN

Rose needed answers. She couldn't sleep. She couldn't stop turning over the things she had overheard.

They were in debt.

A man had followed them to the farm.

He had threatened them.

How much did they owe? And why? Mum inherited this house and some money from her grandparents. Had she given it to David? Is he now trying to persuade her to sell the house so she can bail him out? Mum would never want to move otherwise, never.

Rose's scalp was tight with a tension which ran all the way to her toes, her body rigid with it. She had had to leave boarding school because of *him*. She might lose her home because of *him*. She was angry and scared, not just for her future but also for Roo's. A memory, the day he came home from the hospital, swaddled in a soft cream blanket, eyes wide, focusing on nothing, and yet somehow Rose knew that he was seeing everything. His bedroom, the mobile suspended over the crib, slowly rotating in the breeze that pushed through the open window. Mum had gently laid him down and Rose stood watching him scrunch up his tiny fist, mouth gaping open into a yawn before he drifted off to sleep and Rose knew that he felt safe and secure.

She wouldn't let him lose that.

What could she do to help? She had some birthday and Christmas money left but she wasn't naive enough to think that her savings could make a difference. Did they owe hundreds? Thousands?

David said Mum getting a job wouldn't save them but perhaps Rose could be the one to turn things around.

'If some things went missing', David had said. Gunner and Kamal obviously hadn't been able to gain access to the house before but if they collaborated. . . If David was aware they were coming then it would be easier. David could claim on the insurance and perhaps the boys would also give them a share of whatever they made selling the medals.

It could work?

But first she needed to know all the facts. She needed to get into his study.

She slipped out of bed, her feet lightly treading down the landing. Her parents' door was ajar. She pushed it open. David always left his keys on the dressing table.

Quietly, quietly she reached for them. Wincing as they chinked together.

David mumbled, rolled over.

Rose froze, her breath stuck in her chest. Heat climbing through her.

David settled once more. Rose's fingers closed around the keys, she drew them to her and hurried away, down the stairs, avoiding the one that always creaked.

Her heart was racing as she unlocked David's study. He'd be furious if he caught her. She shut the door behind her before she switched the light on. She scanned the room. The desk was tidy, a stack of papers resting neatly in the middle. She rifled through them. Paperwork belonging to clients, investments they had made, investments David was recommending. She didn't really understand them. What she needed was a bank statement. She crossed to the mahogany chest of drawers and slid the top one open. The files were labelled, again with client names. The bottom drawer held household bills and a bank statement for David and Mum's joint account. They had a large overdraft and they were up to their limit. There were demands to pay it back.

Her stomach sank. It was eight thousand pounds. She looked at the military medals in their glass cases. Were they worth eight thousand? Something in this house must be. It was a lot of money, but it didn't seem too much.

She was putting the bank statements back when she saw it.

The briefcase.

The locked briefcase.

She knelt before it. Set the numbers to her birthday, experiencing a pang of nostalgia as she did so. Recalling the time she had sat on David's lap.

If you can open it I'll give you five pounds.

Her delight when she realized it was her birthday, how special she had felt.

How loved.

Now, the case wouldn't open, the code changed.

Rose felt rejected. Tried again.

Mum's birthday.

Roo's.

This time the catch sprang open.

Inside were papers from a different bank, a solicitor.

Details of a mortgage, this house, this address.

The signature shaky, similar to her mum's but Rose knew that it wasn't authentic. He had forged Mum's signature, mortgaged this house – their house. Did she know?

She worked her way through the rest of the paperwork. Another bank account, solely in David's name. A huge deposit made a few months ago – the money from the remortgage? She wasn't sure how it worked. And then large sums withdrawn.

Empty. Everything gone.

Even if the medals were worth thousands it wouldn't be enough. They owed hundreds of thousands. It was hopeless.

She was helpless.

Sitting at the kitchen table, Roo pushed his toy car in circles around Trip the T-rex, making loud brum-brum noises, ignoring his toast, the honey solidifying.

'Mum?' Rose spooned cornflakes onto her spoon before letting them drop back into her bowl, stirring them into the milk until they were soggy. 'You know you mentioned moving the other day?'

'And I told you—'

'We can't. That's what you said. *Can't*.' The odd choice of phrase was making sense now. Mum had broached moving at a time she probably thought they could sell the house, pay off the debts. Then there had been that awful argument with David where Rose was certain that he hit her and after that Mum had said they couldn't move, couldn't divorce 'because they loved each other'. But the truth, in Rose's mind, was that Mum had realized that they couldn't do either of those things because David had had to tell her about remortgaging the house.

But if he'd forged her signature surely that was fraud? Illegal.

Why didn't she go to the police? But even as she asked herself this question she knew the answer.

Because she loved him.

And because of Roo.

What was going to happen to them all? Rose felt sick with it. When her mum didn't explain what she meant by 'can't' Rose clattered her spoon into her bowl and scraped back her chair. 'I'm going for a walk.'

'You can't.'

'Can't?' That word again.

Mum's face was pinched; she chewed her thumbnail as she glanced at Roo. Rose could almost see the excuses whirring around her brain, as she waited for Mum to pluck a suitable one out, because she wouldn't say that Rose couldn't go out because there was a violent debt collector watching the family, would she?

Although she was frightened, Rose wouldn't stay in for the rest of her life because of David, waiting, waiting, waiting for something, for the worst to happen. Besides, school would start soon and then what?

Their eyes met. *I know*, Rose conveyed with hers. *I'm so sorry*, Mum silently replied.

'I'll be walking to school and back soon,' Rose reminded her. She could keep her in today, tomorrow, but not once the new term started. 'I promise I'll be careful.' She kissed her mother on her cheek. 'And if I get worried about anything, *anyone*, I'll come straight home.'

Still, Rose couldn't help checking over her shoulder as she hurried towards the village, past the green, the shop. Slowing as she approached the bench. It was empty. So was the park.

She wandered down to the disused railway track. She loved the view here, unspoilt.

She shielded her eyes against the sun and gazed out over the fields, remembering when it had been just her and Mum and they would run through the maze fashioned from maize, laughing at each dead end, never feeling scared or stuck because they had each other.

A noise.

Uneasy, Rose turned. The old waiting room was decrepit, a hole in the roof. Rose never ventured in there because other than the patch of light that shone through it was gloomy, dank. It smelled of urine and cigarettes.

A shuffling sound.

Rats? Or something else? Something worse?

The man from yesterday?

A clearing of the throat.

Run.

Rose began to sprint towards the exit, arms pumping by her sides, heart hammering out of her ribcage. Footsteps behind her.

Faster.

A hand grabbing her shoulder, pulling her back.

She twisted around, kicked out, her foot landing on a shin.

'What the fuck, Rose!'

'Gunner. You scared the life out of me. I thought you were…' Rose was shaking.

'Hey.' Gunner pulled her close to him. She relaxed against the solidity of his chest, her cheek against his soft cotton shirt which was damp with her tears. He led her to the edge of the platform where they sat on a weathered bench. Neither spoke. Gunner holding her hand, his thumb caressing her wrist, her lower arm. Fingers travelling up, up, lightly across her collar bone.

She swallowed hard. Enjoying the sensation but not quite ready for what was coming next. His palm brushed against her breast, moved over the flat of her stomach before his fingers slipped under her T-shirt.

'Gunner—'

'Shh.' He kissed her, kneeling on the floor and pushing her backwards until she was lying flat, the slats of the bench hard against her spine. Uncomfortable. He climbed on top of her. His hands everywhere, in her hair, in her bra and then his fingers tugging at the zip of her jeans.

She moved her head to one side. 'Stop, somebody will see.'

'There's nobody here.' He was relentless, his hand inside her jeans now. She felt herself losing control and the feeling was unfamiliar, unsettling.

'Stop.'

He kissed her again, her lips were moving against his, their tongues meeting, her protests lodged in her throat.

He pinched her nipple and her eyes snapped open.

'I don't want to.' She tried to push him off her.

'I think you do.' His weight was pressing down on her, his fingers inside her knickers. 'I can feel that you—'

'Stop.' Her voice sharp with panic. She wriggled onto her side, palms pushing against his chest. 'I'm not ready.'

He held her with his eyes, his pupils dilated, his breath hard and fast. There was a second when she thought he wasn't going to move but then he shifted until he was sitting at the end of the bench. Rose zipped up her jeans and tugged down her top, miserable. Wondering whether that girl who liked him, Tamsin, would have stopped him. Whether anyone her age who hadn't been to an all girls' school would have stopped him.

In her peripheral vision she could see him pull something out of his pocket. The spark of a lighter. The smell of weed.

'Want a drag?' He offered the joint to her and she shook her head. He sighed.

'What went wrong yesterday then? The door was locked so we scarpered.'

'My stepdad decided to stay home.'

'So when can you get everyone out of the house?'

On the bench beside her somebody had spray painted that Lynsey was a slag. She picked at the white paint with her thumbnail as she tried to find the right words.

'We don't have any money,' she said at last.

'What do you mean?'

'My stepdad's business is in trouble. He's spent everything. Taken out a mortgage on the house. I think we might have to move. I don't know where we'll go. How far away.'

She was testing him. Wanting him to tell her that he wouldn't let her leave, that he'd miss her too much.

'What about the medals?'

'They're still in the house.'

'There you go then. It doesn't matter about the fucking mortgage or anything else.' He took a deep drag on the joint.

'But my family need them now. We might have to sell them. I think David might be planning to—'

'I don't give a fuck what David is planning.'

'But if I offered to stage a robbery and introduced you so that he could claim on the insurance then—'

'Are you fucking insane? That wasn't the plan. Look, just get everyone out, leave the back door unlocked and—'

'I can't.'

'Can't or won't?'

'Is there a difference?' Rose shrugged. 'I'm sorry but—'

'Are you?' Gunner said bitterly. 'Rose, if your stepdad has got himself into trouble then…'

'But it's not just himself, is it? It's all of us and I've got my little brother to protect.'

'It isn't your job to protect him.'

'Somebody has to. And it isn't really my job as your girlfriend to let you in to my house—'

'Girlfriend? Ha. You are not my girlfriend, because if you were, if you loved me, you would put me first.'

'I do…' Rose tailed off. Was it love? This desperation to see him? This happy skip in her belly when his eye caught hers? The tingle that ran down her spine whenever he touched her? Were those things love or loneliness? She had been so certain of her feelings but now as she looked at him, the disdain on his face, the way his mouth twisted cruelly, she just wasn't sure.

'I… I do really like you, Gunner.'

'But you won't help me? You won't have sex with me? You won't get high with me? What exactly will you do, Rose?'

She shrugged miserably because she knew that whatever she said wasn't enough.

That she wasn't enough.

Chapter Twenty

Cass

'Am I not enough?' Agitated, Dad jumps to his feet, spreading his arms wide, a pained expression on his face. 'I've tried to be both a mother and a father...'

'I know and you've been great, really. I haven't come here to ask questions about Mum because you're lacking somehow but because... Dad...' I take his hands and tug him until he sits back down on the brown threadbare sofa next to me. I explain about the gestational diabetes. The fact that I'm worried it's genetic, that there are numerous diseases that can be inherited. I don't tell him I'm worried about my mental health. That I had told James I had seen the rocking chair moving on its own, wanting him to offer me one of his rational explanations, but instead he had looked at me with worry, pity, unable to offer me a thread of hope to cling on to. 'I know I've asked and you said that Mum was healthy but is there anything you can tell me about her family. Your parents and grandparents, anything would be really helpful.' I stifle a yawn. The train journey has wiped me out.

'You look shattered.' I'm not sure whether Dad is purposefully changing the subject but he isn't wrong.

'I am. Perhaps we can pick this up in the morning?'

The relief that spreads over Dad's face sends a spike of irritation through me. I'm not going to let this drop. 'I do need to eat something before bed. I've brought some mushroom soup with me. I'll just heat it up.'

'I'll do that, love. Why don't you go and have a shower and get all snuggly. I'll bring it up and tuck you in.'

He speaks as though I am three, not thirty-three but ridiculously this makes me want to weep. I had worried that when the baby arrives I haven't got a support network but as I gaze around the room at the photos – me, in a hospital crib hours after birth in a pink hat that has slipped down over one eye; first bath; first steps; learning to crawl; attempting to ride a bike, Dad hanging on to the back of the seat; playing Mary in the primary school nativity. I may not have a mum but Dad has done it all and he had done his best.

'You are enough.' I hug him tightly.

The smell of hot food wakes me, the sound of Dad running water in the kitchen. I can imagine him filling the kettle, cracking eggs into sizzling oil, the whites running over hash browns.

'Morning.' I rub the sleep from my eyes.

Dad dries his hands on the red-and-white-checked tea-towel draped over his shoulder before he carries a coffee over to the table.

'Are you still drinking caffeine?' he asks.

'Only one a day.'

'That's okay. The odd—'

'Frying isn't fine, not with diabetes.' I look pointedly towards the stove.

'I'm grilling yours and it's only a small portion. I am capable of looking after you, Cass.' The unsaid 'I've done it for years' hangs between us.

'Is that what you were doing when you called James and told him I was a nutter?'

'Is that what he told you I said?' Dad fixes me with that look. The one that tells me he knows I've sneaked biscuits before dinner, that he knows I wait until I'm on the corner of the street before I slick on glossy lipstick. The one he always gives me when he knows that I'm lying.

'No.' I cradle my hands around my mug, elbows on the table where I've eaten countless meals, done my homework, got ready for my first date, mirror angled towards the kitchen window where the light is better than it is in my bedroom.

We make awkward small talk as we eat. Dad filling the silence so there is no room for my questions. He tells me that they're building a Lidl on the retail park, that the pub has a new landlord again, that Mrs Willis down the hall with the Westie that constantly barks has had a hip replacement.

Details about his life that are inconsequential. That don't tell me how he is, but I notice he looks drawn, tired.

Sad.

When our plates are clear he waves off my offer of help and squirts washing-up liquid into the bowl and as bubbles froth in the sink I take a quick shower and get dressed, not wanting to remain in my old forest print pyjamas with squirrels and foxes. If I want Dad to treat me like an adult, I can at least look like one.

Back in the kitchen Dad is squeaking a cloth across the already sparkling worktop.

'Come and sit down,' I say.

Slowly, reluctantly, he trudges across the kitchen and lowers himself into his chair. We've always sat opposite each other. Empty spaces either side of us. Chairs I'd wished we could fill with a mum or a brother or a sister.

'Dad.' I stretch out my hands and he does the same, our fingers meeting in the middle. 'I love you dearly and I don't want to upset you but since I've been pregnant I can't stop thinking about Mum. Her parents. Yours. If there's anything genetic that might—'

'Cass, I'm so sorry you've developed gestational diabetes but really, it's something I saw a lot in my practice and your midwife will—'

'It isn't just the health stuff, Dad. It's …' Tears thicken my throat. 'I don't know where I came from and I want to know. I want Isobel to know. I might have stopped badgering you about Mum when I was younger because I could see how much it upset you but that didn't stop me thinking about her. Did she paint? Did I get my love of folk music from her? I want to be able to tell my daughter who she takes after and I… I…' I pull my hands away from Dad's and cover my face while I take a deep breath to compose myself because all I want to do is dissolve into tears and say it isn't fair, but I am going to be a parent and I need to act like one. 'I have all the photos you gave me of Mum before she had me, but I only have the Polaroids from the hospital of me and her together and they aren't the best quality.'

'I'm so sorry, Cass.' Dad's eyes are bright with tears. 'I wish we had had smartphones to record every memory. But I should have included her in our lives. I was wrong and I can see that now. When you were younger I didn't think you were ready and then you stopped asking and…' He pinches the bridge of his nose between two fingers. 'Your mum was healthy. Kind.

174

I adored her. When she died it… it broke me. I felt such an enormous guilt. You're supposed to look after the ones you love, aren't you? Protect them? I let her down. I let you down. You were motherless and I… I was completely out of my depth.' Dad takes a breath. I've never seen him like this before. Vulnerable. He's opening up to me in a way he never has before and I don't want to push him. In truth I just want to hug him but instead I let him talk. 'I should have told you about her but it was… is… so painful to think about still.'

'It was an accident, Dad. It wasn't your fault.'

'But everything that came after was. I should have filled the house with pictures and memories but I thought we'd feel her absence more.' He wipes tears from his cheeks and looks at me with such tenderness. 'You get your love of animals from her. She was always feeding the stray cats, the birds. It was her who taught me how to make fat balls.'

It's such a small thing but I feel something has been passed down and I hold on to it tightly.

'She didn't paint like you but she was creative.' He fetches a small clay pot from the window sill. 'She made this.' He hands it to me and I cradle it as though it is the most precious thing in the world, and to me, it is.

'What about music?'

'I can't explain your love of folk, I'm afraid.'

'Perhaps it came from my grandparents?' I rest my fingers lightly on my bump, wondering whether Isobel will have inherited my taste in music too. 'Did you stay in touch with them?'

'Your grandparents were killed in a car accident before you were even born.'

'And you lost your own parents when you were young?'

'I was twenty-one, so not as young as your mother but…'

'It was something you had in common with her. I get that. It's the same for me and James. His mum died and… I don't know. Right from when I met him I felt as though we had a bond. Some sort of connection. I wish you'd give him a chance.'

'It isn't that I don't like him. I haven't really had the opportunity to get to know him. Why don't you move back here? Both of you, I mean? With the baby coming…'

'You know why I don't want to be here.' I lower my eyes. I don't want to say his name but I don't have to, Dad knows.

Leon.

'Have you… have you seen him since he was released?' I ask.

'Haven't seen him. Haven't heard from him. I don't have anything to do with him. Cass, don't let him put you off coming home—'

'Dad.' I stop myself. He already looks so small and alone. If I tell him that my home is where James is then that won't help them bond and, more than anything, I want my father and my boyfriend to be friends.

He sighs and massages the sides of his temples as though he has a headache coming.

'I'm going to get some shopping in,' he says.

'But…' We're communicating for the first time in what feels like forever but because I mentioned Leon, Dad has closed off. I know he blames himself for what I went through. Blames himself for not protecting me.

'If I'd known you were coming, Cass, I would have stocked up before you arrived.' He stalks towards the door and I know the conversation is over.

Dad won't be in any rush to return to pick up where we left off. I can imagine him strolling towards the Tesco two miles away rather than the small Co-op a couple of streets down. I pace the cramped flat, frustrated. When he'd opened up about my mother he'd shown real emotion. I'd learned a lot today but not enough. The information I have received has made me hungry for more.

There must be something here to tell me about my past. Some clue I'd missed as a child when I'd rummage through cupboards hoping to find photos, letters to me, anything.

There isn't a lot of space to store things. Dad isn't a hoarder.

It's uncomfortable rummaging through his drawers. His greying vests, and socks, thin at the heels. I really wish he could meet someone, fall in love, be looked after.

There's nothing in the bedroom, or in the lounge. I even go through the bathroom cabinet, not that I think there'll be any clues in among Dad's razor and boxes of plasters and paracetamol but because I'm avoiding the hall cupboard where I'd find myself as a child. Trapped.

Sometimes silent.

Sometimes screaming to be free.

Always, always, scared.

I steel myself before I open the door, half expecting to see myself as a small child, cowering, crying for my father, but of course, there is nobody there.

I switch on the light. On the doorframe, scratches, and I splay out my fingers, examine my own ragged nails, torn and bleeding from the nightmares I am now having again since I moved into Newington House.

Since I stopped taking my medication.

But I don't need it anymore, do I? I am far away where Leon cannot find me. Cannot hurt me. And yet, I think of all the times I've felt somebody watching me, the footprints in the mud outside the window, my paintbrushes always disappearing.

Could it be him or is it only in my head?

I hear things that don't exist.

I see things I can't possibly be seeing.

I smell things that aren't there.

But more than all of that, I sense things.

Am I going crazy? Is everything a manifestation of my relentless remorse now that my emotions are not dulled by medication?

Leon might have served his time but I am locked in my own eternal guilt for what he did.

For what we did.

The cupboard is full of coats and shoes, the hoover, a mop and bucket, a clothes horse – it's a wonder I ever fitted in here. On the shelves are boxes, neatly labelled:

Bills

Bank

Cass. I lift out the box with my name on it. It's full of mementos from my childhood that I had no idea Dad ever kept. There are Father's Day cards, a terrible painting of a castle, four stick figures in front of it – I'd signed my name at the bottom, always the artist – swimming certificates, school photos. I'm emotional as I sift through them. Soon I'll have a similar box for Isobel. Will I, too, feel a quiet pride? Will I be an embarrassing parent? Cheering her on loudly at every given opportunity. Will I be heartbroken when she grows up and leaves home? Suddenly I feel awful – I hadn't given Dad time to get used to the idea and it isn't like I've only moved around the corner.

I stuff everything back into the box, vowing to persuade him to come to Newington. He could make an occasion of it. Travel first class. My eyes flicker towards the box labelled

Bank Statements and although I shouldn't, although it isn't any of my business, I can't help looking.

These are neat, filed in month order. There is little money in Dad's current account. How does he manage? Where did his income go? His pension? I never went without, not really, but there was never an excess. He was a single parent with only one wage coming in, but still, our home is perhaps more modest than you'd expect for someone on a GP's salary. There were no exotic holidays. I've never been abroad.

I rifle through them, looking for clues, and when I find them, I wish I hadn't. On the first of every month, a direct debit payment leaves Dad's account.

It goes to Leon.

My head spins as I try to make sense of it. I go back months, years, it's always there. Always to Leon.

Suddenly, there's noise in the corridor outside. The slap of shoes on the concrete floor.

There are feelings I can't quite identify as a shadow passes across the privacy glass of the front door. Anger that Dad has lied to me – *I never have anything to do with him.* Confusion that he has, and that gut-curling fear I get whenever I think of Leon. About the things we did.

I have blood on my hands.

Three slow knocks on the front door.

I don't want to open it but the knocking comes again, more insistent this time, and I am sick of running, sick of feeling scared.

I open the door; in front of me stands a policeman.

I was a fool for thinking moving to Newington would give me a fresh start.

The past always comes back to haunt us, doesn't it?

Chapter Twenty-One

James

Cass thinks the house is haunted by the past but James doesn't get that sense. All he feels is a warmth and a familiarity, a sense of home, but now he is here alone, since Cass has been with her father, it feels colder somehow.

Emptier.

He realizes that it is not Newington that has evoked the feeling of warmth and safety but Cass. It's clear that since the death of his mother, he hasn't felt settled. Instead, he'd been poised for something else terrible to happen, for another loss.

Those anxieties had dissipated since he'd met Cass. During their initial meeting in the bar it was the first time in months it had felt like he could breathe again. It was as though he'd been waiting his entire life to meet her. As though he'd always loved her.

He wonders how she's getting on with her dad, whether she is getting the information she so desperately needs. Everyone deserves to know where they've come from, don't they?

Their history.

Especially when her history might affect their daughter. He winds his scarf around his neck and pulls on his gloves. He's going to clear the leaves from the driveway. They are slippery when damp and the last thing he wants is Cass coming home in the dark and tumbling over.

While he picks up handfuls of soggy leaves, still a gorgeous hue of reds and oranges, he thinks about genetics. About nature versus nurture.

Could Cass's anxieties have come from her mother? Is it inevitable to develop traits of a parent even if that parent has been absent?

He thinks of his own father, the scowl that always creases his brow whenever James walks into a room. His mother's bright smile and optimism. He doesn't look like them, with differences in eye colour and his hair as dark as theirs is white blond. But is he like them in personality? He thinks he's probably a blend of them both. Cautiously optimistic?

He feels hopeful now about the future, the driveway clear, three bin bags stacked together. He shakes open a fourth, crouches under the window and begins to scoop up the leaves. There's something soothing about the ritual. He digs too deep, his gloves pulling up soft earth.

Finds something hard.

He pulls it out, brushes off the soil and holds it up to examine it.

A dinosaur.

A plastic T-rex. Its green colour faded with age.

He goes to stuff it into the sack but it is solid and secure in his fist and he doesn't want to let it go. It's only a toy but it's representative of so many things.

The innocence and hope of the child who once played with it.

The promise of a family.

James thinks of his family, his mum and dad, and then of

Cass and Isobel as he rests back on his haunches, staring up at the house, dinosaur in hand.

A strong sense of déjà vu engulfs him.

Chapter Twenty-Two

Cass

There's a strong sense of déjà vu as the policeman stands before me, asks me to confirm my name.

'I believe this belongs to you.' He holds out the bag which had been stolen on the train and my heart begins to slow. 'I was passing so thought I'd drop it in.'

I take it with one hand, the other hand is holding on to the doorframe, my legs shaking.

Of course he isn't here for me.

But I can't help studying his face, wondering if he's one of the policemen I talked to after everything with Leon when it was all such a blur. Wondering what he thinks of me if he is. But he's nothing but friendly as he smiles at me.

'Sorry, there isn't any money left inside but your empty purse is there and some papers and a key. It is yours, isn't it?'

'Yes. Thank you.' I force myself to speak.

I am fine.

I am safe.

I am normal.

'I wasn't expecting to see it again and I don't live here any-more.' I had automatically given the police Dad's address when

I'd reported the theft, not yet living at Newington. 'Anyway, thanks again.'

I close the door and stumble into the kitchen, run the tap and gulp water from my scooped hands. Seeing the police brings it all back again.

Leon.

Water dribbles down my chin as I wipe my mouth with my sleeve, remembering with clarity the day I first met him. It was my seventh birthday, Dad had lit the candles on the cake when the doorbell rang.

'Wait here,' he had said and I'd watched the pink wax melt, dripping onto the white icing blanketed over the sponge. Impatient to blow my candles out and make a wish I'd run into the hallway. Dad was talking in a low, angry voice to a man I did not recognize but I didn't really register anything except the gift-wrapped parcel he was holding out.

'You must be Cass. Happy birthday.'

Dad was trying to bundle the man out of the flat, but the man had held the doorframe with one hand, thrusting the present towards me with the other.

'I'm your uncle Leon. Your dad's brother.'

Dad said something. I can remember that his voice was cold and hard but I was too engrossed in the gift to take any notice of what he was actually saying.

I ripped the wrapping paper off, right there in the hallway. 'Old Maid?'

'It's a card game. I can teach you to play if you'd like?'

'Okay, but come and have some of my party food first.'

'No, Cass.' Dad was firm. 'Leon, you're not wanted here.'

'Why?' I had asked and when an answer didn't immediately come I had taken Leon's hand and dragged him into the kitchen not caring why I'd never met him, never even heard of him. Only pleased to fill one of the empty chairs. Happy to discover I had an uncle I never knew about. I blew out the candles.

'Make a wish,' Leon had said and I didn't tell him that my wish had already come true. I wanted a bigger family and he was right there.

'Do you want some cake?' I asked him.

'Leon can't stay,' Dad said.

'I'm in no rush, if Cass wants a game of Old Maid?'

It wasn't until we were on our third round, the cards fanned in my hand, that I asked, 'How come I've never met you before?'

'He's been away,' Dad answered.

'Did you know my mum?'

'Yeah, I did.'

Dad glared at him. There was an undercurrent of... something. A friction between him and Dad I couldn't quite decipher.

'You look a little like her, kiddo.'

My heart lifted as Leon said this. It really was my best birthday ever.

After that, Dad sent me to have a bath and when I came out, Leon was gone. I didn't see him again for a long time.

Years.

I bumped into him again by chance. I was leaving art college, canvas tucked under my arm, when I heard my name being called.

I spun around. It took me moments to place him, not knowing how I felt when I realized who it was. All those years ago when Leon first came to our door, when all I could think about was the family I had desperately craved, the family I thought we could be. But then he'd disappeared, left me like my mother, and although I knew that wasn't fair to think of my mother as leaving me when she had no choice, I felt abandoned by him.

'Hello.' I carried on walking past him.

'Wait. Can I buy you a coffee?' he asked. I was cold and tired and as he manoeuvred my possessions into his arms I thought, what harm could it do?

I was such a fool.

By the time Dad returns home laden with bags, I have put everything I found back into the hall cupboard and I am sitting at the kitchen table, a mug of tea in front of me which has grown cool, scum forming on the surface.

My stomach churns violently. I don't move to help Dad unpack the shopping, I don't even offer. I just... sit. Not answering him as he chatters away about vegetables and nutrients and did I know that carrots were originally purple?

Eventually, he switches on the kettle and makes me a fresh drink, one for himself too. He uses the mug I bought him one Father's Day with 'World's Best Dad' on it and my jaw tightens.

'The police came while you were out,' I say. A flicker of something passes across his face. The expression of someone with something to hide.

'I thought they were here for me.'

'Why would they be? You're not still thinking about the past, are you, love?'

But the past is all I can think about because in the present I am sitting with a stranger and I do not know what the future holds.

All I know is that someone died, because of me.

Over coffee that day, when I bumped into Leon outside my college, he had offered me a job.

'I've set up a new company. Financial advice. You could help out part-time, fit it around your course.'

The thought of extra cash was enticing.

Dad was so against it that it made me want it more. Leon was family, a link to Mum. He'd know all of my parents' secrets and I hoped he'd share them with me.

Mr Peters was one of the first clients Leon introduced me to. We sat on a shabby brown velour sofa, a plate of custard creams on the table in front of us while he poured us tea from an old-fashioned pot. His hand wrinkled, speckled with liver spots.

'You have a gorgeous family.' I gestured to the photograph on the mantelpiece of a family beaming under a beating sun, aquamarine sea glistening behind them.

'That's my Christopher. My only child. He moved out to Australia for a year when he was twenty-two and then fell in love. Never came back.' Mr Peters smiles but there's a sadness in his eyes. 'Since I lost my Eileen I've been feeling very lonely. Let me show you her. Now she was a beauty.' He gently placed a heavy photo album on my lap. Tissue paper crinkled between the pages and when I carefully leafed through it I was met with a sepia wedding photo that was somehow full of colour and life. The young couple outside the church, confetti fluttering around them, her gazing adoringly at him while he clutched the hand of his new bride as though he never wanted to let her go.

I looked up at Mr Peters as he stooped over my chair and wanted to tell him how sorry I was that he lost her and how happy I was that he found that once-in-a-lifetime love, how I wished that I could find that too, but his eyes met mine and I knew he was feeling everything I felt without me voicing it.

'It's worth waiting for,' he whispered, patting my shoulder before returning to his chair. 'Christopher has invited me to go out there and live with them now I'm on me own. That's where you come in. Need to invest me savings to pay for it.'

We visited several times. Mr Peters squinting as he read the paperwork from over the top of his wire-rimmed glasses. Asking Leon to explain and then looking at me in bewilderment and, not wanting to tell him I didn't fully understand it either, I reassured him it was okay because that was my job and Leon was family and I trusted him.

'You'll have to come out for a holiday, Cass,' Mr Peters said as he signed on the dotted line and I felt a surge of affection for this man I barely knew. If I'd had a grandparent I'd want him to be just like Mr Peters. Always a warm smile and a sweet in his pocket. Once I'd sneezed and he'd whipped out a handkerchief. I'd no doubt, when I looked at the faded photographs of him and Eileen, that when they'd courted he'd walk on the pavement nearest to the traffic, open doors for her. He was a gentleman in the truest sense of the word. I would miss him.

One day my phone rang, it was him. I had given him my personal number after the first time we'd met, telling him, 'If there's anything you ever need, even if it's only a pint of milk fetching, please ring me.'

'Are you okay?'

He'd never rung me before.

'Cass? I can't seem to...' His breath was shallow, panic in his voice. 'The bank have written. The house. Is it still mine? They say it isn't. And my money. I can't... I don't know where it is.'

I soothed him, promising him I'd talk to Leon straight away and we'd get it sorted out but I had a knot in my stomach tightening with every reassurance I uttered.

I think I knew then.

Leon had taken everything. Duped a lonely old man. I sat with Mr Peters while I explained, apologized. We had both cried and when I'd finished I went to the police station and told them everything. Leon denied it, stating that Mr Peters had known what was happening. He'd signed willingly.

Mr Peters was discovered the next day. Surrounded by the paperwork he'd been trying to make sense of. Surrounded by photographs of Australia where he longed to visit but now never could.

His heart had given out. His death was recorded as natural causes but I knew losing everything had killed him.

The fraud had killed him.

Leon had killed him.

I felt I had too. I played my own part but the police didn't see it that way. I was never charged but I've never let go of the feeling that I should have been.

I remained strong and steely during the court case but as soon as Leon was convicted I broke down.

Dad stepped up, stepped in. He built me back up with love and tablets until it seemed that love *was* tablets and I was a junkie craving a fix. I bumped into Shobna, my old friend from art college, and saw the shock on her face as she registered my sallow skin, my thin frame, and that was my turning point. It turned out she had a spare room to rent in her flat and there was a job going in her office. It wasn't creative, but it was something. Dad didn't think I was ready.

'You just want to keep me here for ever, dependent on you for prescriptions and—'

'Cass. That couldn't be further from the truth.'

'Really? I think you like me like... like this. Needy and—'

'I was wrong,' he said quietly. 'The way you're standing up for yourself now. You're ready to stand on your own two feet. I'll help you pack.'

And so I left with hugs and tears and an underlying excitement blended with fear but I needn't have worried. I thrived. Until almost a year ago when Dad rang and told me that he thought I should know Leon had been released.

I fell apart again. Became scared, paranoid. Everywhere I went I imagined I saw him and then, one day, I actually did.

'You reported me,' he said. 'You testified against me. Cass?' he called as I ran, not to my flat, but without consciously thinking, my mind tumultuous… I don't remember arriving at Dad's. I don't remember letting myself in with a key but I do remember him opening the door of the hall cupboard to find me curled into a ball, sobbing.

I didn't go to work that day. Or the next. I couldn't face anything. It wasn't solely the fear that Leon would want revenge because I was the one who sent him to prison, but also because my guilt was, once again, paralysing. Seeing Leon had stirred up all of my shameful thoughts and as well as feeling scared of him I had felt envious. He'd served his time and that gave him permission to put it behind him in a way that I never would.

Within days Dad had restarted my medication, cleared my things out of my flat and into my childhood bedroom where I'd pull the duvet up to my chin, breathing in the overpowering fabric softener Dad had always used, wishing I was small again.

Wishing I had a mother to comfort me.

But then came the phone call from Shobna inviting me to her hen night. She had given me a roof over my head and a job when I desperately needed one and so, reluctantly, I went along, and had met James.

Now, Dad shakes his head, despairingly. 'Cass. You have to let Mr Peters go. He wouldn't want—'

'How do you know what he'd want? You never met him.'

'No, but Leon—'

'Leon? Oh you want to talk about him now do you? Tell me this, Dad. Why do you give him money?'

'What? I don't—'

'Don't lie to me. I saw your bank statements.'

'You have no right to—'

'Why do you pay him?'

'To help him out. He *is* my brother.'

'But you don't... you don't love him! You don't even like him.'

'He's still family, and—'

'Did you invest in his business? Did you know what he was doing?'

'Of course not. You know I'd never hurt anyone.'

He reaches for me but I move my hand out of the way. 'I don't know who you are.' It is the sad truth but, worse than that, I don't know who I am. I'd come here for answers but all I have is more questions but I don't ask them because I have felt something inside me break.

Dad's lies have broken me.

And I won't let him stuff me with medication to put me back together this time.

Chapter Twenty-Three

Rose

THEN

'Please stop with your questions,' Mum begged Rose.

Rose could tell her mum was at breaking point so instead she focused on the food.

It was pizza for dinner. Not something they generally ate but David was out with clients and Mum was too exhausted to cook.

They were eating on their laps, the doors to the TV cabinet wide open, a quiz show firing out questions that were too hard. Often in this room Mum turned off the main light, clicked on the lamps, the soft yellow light pooling on the rugs. Lit the candles that flickered on the mantelpiece. Not tonight though. The big light glared, the room bright.

Eating on their laps was rare and it crossed Rose's mind that they might be tucked away in this room because it was round the back of the house. All of the lights were switched on to make Mum feel safer. Still she could imagine the debt collector creeping around the perimeter. Cupping his hands as he peered in the window.

Tap.

Tap.

Tap.

Rose saw the stiffening of Mum's shoulders, felt it in her own, but it was only the branch of the tree outside.

The heat of the jalapeños and the tang of garlic swirled around in Rose's stomach along with her nerves and her misery.

Since Gunner had stalked away from her at the railway station earlier she had felt an emptiness deep inside that she knew no amount of pizza could fill.

'You'll regret this,' he had said, his voice low and even, chilling.

Should she have said yes to sex?

Yes to everything?

He thought that she didn't love him and although she didn't know whether she did, she needed him. Needed someone.

'Look at me, Rose.' Roo pulled a string of mozzarella from his mouth. It stretched and stretched until it snapped and that was how Rose felt. Pulled in a direction she didn't want to go in but unable to prevent the inevitable.

Tomorrow.

Tomorrow she would wear the black top that cinched in her waist. Coat her lips with gloss.

Give Gunner everything he wanted because he was the one.

The one who could save her from loneliness, save them from the debt collector.

The answer to everything.

She only hoped that he'd forgive her for today, that he wouldn't hold a grudge.

'You'll regret this,' he had said. But it wasn't too late to fix it, was it? Fix everything?

Rose woke, a prickling sensation crawling over her skin.

Something was wrong.

She moved the book from her chest – she had fallen asleep reading – and sat up.

A creak.

David coming home?

She held her breath as she listened for his tread on the landing, the opening of her parents' bedroom door.

Nothing.

From downstairs she thought she heard a thump.

Something was wrong.

She was hot and cold and at a loss to know what to do. A childish instinct to pull the covers over her head and pretend that everything was okay was overwhelming but she was no longer the child in the house.

Roo.

She slid out of bed and pulled on her dressing gown, wrapping the belt tightly around her waist.

Her door was open a crack and she waited, eyes adjusting to the gloom.

The tick-tick-tick of the clock from downstairs was loud, her heart marching to the same rhythm.

Thud.

Thud.

Thud.

She swallowed hard. There was no other sound. No movement. No cause for alarm and yet a sense of foreboding pressed down on her, driving her towards Roo's bedroom. He was fast asleep, the glow of his nightlight warm and comforting. Trip, the T-rex watching over him from his bedside cabinet. Rose passed her parents' room, hesitated. Was David home? Was that what had woken her?

Silence.

She chided herself for her overactive imagination.

And then, when she was halfway down the stairs, she smelled the smoke.

Rose didn't know how quickly the fire might spread. She didn't know if she raced back upstairs whether she would be able to get down again or whether the flames might be licking at the banisters, burning through the treads, but she didn't care. She was driven by love for Roo, the desire to protect him. She pounded upstairs.

'Mum? Dad?' she screamed. 'Fire.'

She pushed open her parents' door. 'Get up.' The urgency in her words yanked Mum from sleep.

'What's—'

'Fire!'

Mum was scrambling out of bed before Rose had even left the room.

'Have you—'

'No.' Rose predicted her mother's question. 'I haven't called for help. You do that. I'll get Roo.'

She rocketed into Roo's room. Scooped him into her arms. 'It's okay.' She dropped a kiss on his face as, confused, he began to wriggle. 'We're going outside but everything is okay.' Rose could feel the shake in her limbs, her whole body flooded with adrenaline.

'Trip!' Her brother stretched out his arms towards his dinosaur as they headed towards the door. Rose knew they didn't have time to waste but on some level she also knew Roo could lose everything tonight, his home, his toys, and whatever happened Trip would be something he could hold on to. She dashed back towards the bed, Roo swiped the dinosaur into his hands and then they were running.

Running.

Running.

Mum already in the hallway, the front door blocked by flames, garbling into the phone. The smoke was acrid, thick and black, catching the back of Rose's throat. Roo pressed his face against her chest and began to cry. She hesitated for a moment, torn, flooded with love for her mum, her feet stuck to the floor, not wanting to leave her but then aware once more of the weight of Roo in her arms. He began to cough. Her heart was heavy in her chest, a sick feeling in her stomach as she headed towards the back door, raising her knee and balancing Roo on it as she twisted the key.

The air was cold and sharp in her chest. She set Roo down as she breathed in deeply and doubled over as she began to cough and cough.

'Mummy.' Immediately he began to run back into the house.

'No!' Rose grabbed him, her throat raw. She had only been near the fire for minutes, her mum was still in there.

'Wait here. Promise me you won't move.' Rose grabbed him by the upper arms as she stared at him. 'Promise me.' She gave him a shake.

'Promise.' His voice small, Trip clutched tightly in his hand.

Rose pelted back inside the house. It was the rug that was ablaze, her mum beating at the flames with the blanket, the ends ignited. Mum whipped it higher, brought it down harder.

'Mum,' Rose said urgently, 'we've got to get out.'

'No. We need to put this out. I don't know if Dad is home, sleeping on the sofa.' Mum was hysterical.

Since they'd been arguing, is that where he'd been sleeping? There were so many things Rose didn't know.

The smoke was swallowing her up but the flames were growing smaller and smaller. Rose began to stamp on them.

Eventually, the fire was out.

Rose told her mum to wait while she ran through the house to check the sofa – it was empty. Back in the hallway, they clung to each other, crying, lungs burning, eyes streaming from the smoke. They staggered out into the night. Roo was sitting on the ground, his knees to his chest, rocking back and forth, Trip pressed to his chest, and then the flash of blue lights.

The emergency services.

Thinking that the worst was over but then learning that the fire had likely been started by a candle falling onto the large rug that had covered the entrance hall. It was an antique, highly flammable.

'There will be a full report,' the fireman said. 'You should never go to bed and leave candles lit.'

Mum stared at the ground, her eyes glistening with tears. Rose waited for her to say that they hadn't lit any candles that night. That the house had been bright with electric light.

That the only way a candle could have ignited the rug was if someone had pushed one through the letter box.

But her mother didn't speak.

'I know it's a shock. But really it looks worse than it was. Even a small fire can cause a huge amount of smoke,' the fireman said gently. 'Other than the rug and the telephone table everything is intact but there will be soot and smoke damage to deal with.'

The purr of a car.

Her stepdad finally home.

'Oh my god.' David jogged towards them. Swept Roo onto his hip, Mum into his arms. 'Are you okay? What happened?'

'Rose woke and came downstairs for a glass of water. She found the fire and woke us up. If she hadn't then we... we...' Mum collapsed into tears.

'Can I wear a fireman's hat, Daddy?' Roo asked, seemingly unaffected, his earlier panic forgotten.

'Where were you?' Rose cut in.

'I had a meeting and—'

'At eleven o'clock at night?' Rose crossed her arms over her chest to hold herself together. Every part of her was shaking. Her teeth clattering together in her skull.

They could have died.

If Rose hadn't woken and come downstairs and discovered the fire in its infancy.

They could have died.

'I was entertaining clients.'

Rose glared at him, wanting to ask if he had paid someone to set the fire, whether he intended on claiming on the insurance, but there was genuine worry on his face and as much as she mistrusted him she didn't think he would do that.

But someone had started the fire.

The debt collector?

Gunner?

'The important thing is that no one was hurt,' David said and Rose knew that he was right.

Miraculously, they were all still alive.

Then.

Four hearts beating.

But not for much longer.

Chapter Twenty-Four

James

NOW

They won't be here for much longer. That's all James can think about as Fran gives him the news. He's glad Cass is in the drawing room, on the phone to Robin, oblivious.

'We've received permission to start work on phase one.' She doesn't look excited or happy as she relays this.

James takes a sip of coffee while he thinks, wanting to sound calm and together and not as worried as he feels.

'Does this mean we need to move out?' His voice is steady, his mind whirring – where are they going to go? They don't yet have enough saved for a deposit on a house and he really doesn't want to rent again.

'Yes. I'm sorry. This hasn't quite worked out as I'd hoped.'

'It's not your fault. We knew this was only temporary.'

He should have insisted the contract was for a fixed term rather than on a rolling month-by-month basis but Fran had seemed so certain they'd be here for quite a while. The disruption is the last thing Cass needs with her pregnancy.

'How is Cass?' Fran reads him.

'She's...' He swallows back the 'okay' he'd been about to say because he can see that Fran cares. 'She's tired. She got back a couple of days ago after visiting her father to try and find out about her family history on her mother's side.'

Rather than relieving her anxieties the visit seems to have made them worse. He hoped she'd be able to lose herself in painting, work through her feelings, but when he suggested it she had said, 'My brushes have gone missing again.' She said this so matter-of-factly, he wondered whether she'd been hiding them herself, either consciously or subconsciously, so that she didn't have to paint. He knows how much she'd wanted to make a career out of art when she was younger, and how excited she was for the chance to move into Newington and focus on her work. Perhaps it is too much pressure.

He's glad she has Robin, a friend close by while he's away.

'The journey must have exhausted her,' Fran says.

'Yes.' He doesn't expand. He doesn't tell Fran that last night he'd woken to find Cass's side of the bed empty. He'd padded down the hallway and found the window open again. He'd definitely closed it before bed. For the first time he wonders whether Cass is the one opening it, but then it had opened when she was at her dad's, hadn't it?

Nothing is making sense.

As he had tried to find her he had felt apprehensive. The bathroom was empty. Where was she?

Creak.

Creak.

Creak.

He'd followed the sound, both wanting and not wanting to know what it was.

It was the rocking chair, not moving on its own as Cass claimed it had done. She was sitting in it, gazing ahead but focused on nothing.

'Cass?'

She muttered something and James strained to hear, was about to ask her to repeat it, when she laughed. Muttered something else and paused for a reply, before nodding. Agreeing with whatever she had thought she had heard.

Moonlight pooled through the window, her skin translucent. The creak-creak-creak of the chair speeding up his heart.

He had felt... scared seems too dramatic, in the cold light of day, but definitely uneasy. Unnerved.

Back in the present, he shakes himself from his thoughts, aware that Fran has asked him another question.

'Everything okay with the pregnancy?'

'Yes, but she's worried about genetic diseases, that sort of thing.'

'I'm sure it's natural. Every pregnant woman probably does.'

'Yes, but...' He's promised Cass he won't tell anyone about her diabetes until she's ready. 'I guess you begin thinking about your own bloodline when you're about to become a parent,' he says.

'That's understandable. And what about your bloodline?'

James shrugs. 'I don't really know much about my health history, not when it comes to my grandparents anyway. I need to ask my dad but he's never really forthcoming when it comes to talking. We've always had a strained relationship.'

'That's such a shame,' Fran says. 'You might have had a rubbish dad but you know your mum loved you very much.'

'Yeah. I can't believe she won't be here when Isobel is born.'

He feels overcome. He rummages in his pocket for a tissue, fingers finding the plastic T-rex. He takes comfort from it.

'Isobel? That's a pretty name.'

'Cass chose it. Isobel is after my mum, and then Rose.'

'Rose?' She leans forward. 'Who chose that?'

'Cass again. She thinks the teenager who lived in Newington was called Rose.'

'Isobel Rose. It's beautiful. It's… it's something very special to name a child after a member of the family,' she says quietly.

'Yeah. I really should tell Dad we're naming her after Mum.' James drains the last of his coffee.

'When do we need to be out by? I'd better make a move. I'm going away with work for a few days.'

'Probably at the end of the month.'

James zips up his overnight bag. Pats his pocket. He knows his passport is there, the dinosaur too.

He makes the bed, sits Mr Tatty on Cass's pillow. 'Look after her while I'm away,' he says to the bear before shaking his head. He's a mad as… he stops himself thinking the rest of that sentence. Nobody here is mad.

They're all under pressure.

From downstairs a chilling scream.

'Cass?' He's running down the stairs, two at a time. 'Cass?' The house is too big. Too quiet.

He can't find her.

Chapter Twenty-Five

Cass

James finds me at the window. I'd heard his voice calling me. Felt his arms holding me, but I couldn't answer, can't move.

Somebody is out there.

I can't tear my gaze away from the window. Rain patters against the glass, zigzagging in fat droplets down the panes.

'Cass?' James turns me around so I'm facing him.

'Somebody is out there.' I crane my neck to stare back outside. 'I saw them. Behind the bushes, near the trees.'

James follows my finger as I point. 'I don't see anything.'

'Robin said his dad was always convinced that the intruders came for something specific. Not the jewellery or antiques but something they didn't find.'

'Just because nothing was taken doesn't mean—'

'It isn't only that. Apparently, written in blood on the wall was "tell me where it is". And out there I've just seen two men. Two. Just like that night of the murders. What if they've come back to find "it", whatever "it" is?'

'Well that's impossible – one of them is dead.' James looks at me again, with concern this time. He thinks I'm imagining the ghost of Rose. He thinks I'm imagining this too.

But he doesn't voice any of this, instead he says, 'You stay here. I'll go and have a look around.'

He runs outside. Still in slippers, he isn't wearing a coat. He disappears from view and I am so, so scared that something will happen to him.

He disappears behind the shrubbery.

Where is he?

My whole body is tense. Hands formed into fists, fingernails carving grooves on the soft skin of my palms.

Where is he?

Time passes, long and slow.

Eventually, James jogs back towards me. His hair wet, plastered to his scalp. Cheeks pink.

'There's no sign of anyone.' He's breathless and he joins me at the window. 'But I'm going to call the office. Postpone my trip.'

His eyes are fixed on me. I don't know what to tell him.

Tell me where it is.

There's a sense of inevitability that somebody would return one day to find whatever is so precious it was worth slaughtering a family for.

I don't want to be alone but I don't have to be because I can call Robin and he will come.

James can go on his trip because the last thing I need is someone here who doesn't believe me. Because I know there is somebody out there.

I know, because, over James's shoulder, through the hedge, I can still see them.

Chapter Twenty-Six

James

James can't see what Cass is staring so intently at as he turns back towards the window. Their breath mists the glass, he rubs it with his sleeve.

'What are you staring at?' He's unnerved. This is the Cass that worries him. The Cass he is standing right next to, but can't reach.

He pulls his mobile from his pocket.

'Wait.' She leans forward, cupping her hands against the pane above her eyes.

There's a beat.

Slowly, slowly, the swing begins to move.

'It's okay.' Cass nods as though convincing herself. 'Go on your trip.'

'I don't want to leave you like this.'

'I'll be fine.'

But it isn't just Cass he's worried about. It's their daughter. So small and vulnerable, growing. Stress can't be good for the baby.

'Honestly.' She gives him a gentle push. 'You'll only be gone a few days. Robin can come and keep me company. I'll take my insulin and eat healthily and if I'm worried about anything I'll call Fran.'

'Me.' James pulls her to him. 'Call me. I might be in Paris but... hey...' He tilts her chin, their eyes lock. 'Why don't you come with me?' He's suddenly excited. 'We've never had a holiday. Not that this would be much of a break, I've meetings lined up. But you could explore and we'll go to dinner at night and—'

'We're paid to look after the house,' she says gently. 'And I don't have a passport. But I'd love a romantic weekend away when we've finished here.'

'Then you shall have one.' He kisses her deeply. A faint taste of minty toothpaste. 'I love you.' And he does.

His flight isn't for several hours but James isn't going straight to the airport. He sits in the taxi, the T-rex in his hands. Ever since he found it there's a memory he can't quite put his finger on.

A ghost.

He is on his way to ask his father, not only about his childhood, but about his family history. Cass's talk of genetic diseases, of nature versus nurture, has made him realize that he doesn't know enough about his own family. His world was mainly his mother; other relatives hovered on the periphery, names in Christmas cards, a voucher every birthday.

He's about to become a father and he wants to know everything. He wants to trace his relatives. To repair his relationship with his dad. He wants to take Cass on that romantic weekend away, but without a support network, someone they can trust to look after Isobel when she's born, it will be, not impossible – James doesn't believe anything is insurmountable – but difficult.

James still has his door key but he feels uncomfortable using it and so he rings the doorbell.

'This is unexpected.' His dad leans against the doorframe, not ushering him in, fussing around him, making him tea, food, the way Mum used to do. 'But timely. I've something for you.' He hands James an envelope, probably junk mail. He folds it and puts it into his pocket.

'Can I come in?' James steps forward and it's this movement that forces his father back, rather than a willingness to invite his son inside.

The hallway smells different.

He'd never really thought about the scent of home before, where it came from, what it was, but now he realizes that Mum must have used a particular brand of air freshener or cleaning product which gave it that freshness, that consistency. Now she's gone James will never know what it was, how to recreate the smell, and ridiculously a lump swells in his throat because if feels like another loss. So many things he'll never know the answer to, but if anything it makes him more determined to wheedle the information he has come here for from his father.

His father heads down the hallway towards the kitchen but James can't bear it. There, he'd picture Mum grating Cheddar for a sandwich, slicing fat, juicy tomatoes, even if he'd told her he'd already eaten. Or perhaps he'd find his mind wandering further back than that. After school chats, his legs swinging from the stool at the breakfast bar, too short to reach the floor. Licking the pad of his finger before pressing it onto his plate to gather every single crumb of cinnamon-spiced home-made fruitcake.

James swerves left, into the lounge. This too makes up the fabric of his history. The towering Christmas tree that would stand in the corner, coloured lights and golden tinsel twisted around its middle. Curling on the sofa with Mum, her stroking his forehead, him believing she enjoyed *Power Rangers* as much as he did.

But this room also evokes painful memories. Dad in his armchair by the window, making a pantomime of shaking *The Times* before turning the pages – *look at me reading a broadsheet, aren't I clever.* Snapping at James because he was too loud, too disruptive, too… disappointing.

'Dad?' James freezes as he crosses the threshold. Notices the packing boxes. The dark rectangles on the wall where the family photos used to hang.

'I'm moving.' Dad doesn't offer any sort of apology or explanation.

'You've sold the house?'

'Probate has come through and it's time for a fresh start.'

The green carpet has faded around the sheepskin rug which is now rolled up and tied with string. James remembers when they bought that rug for the space in front of the fire. He had hoped that, come his birthday, there'd be a puppy snoozing on it but Dad had forbidden it.

James sinks down onto the sofa. Not on the end, where Mum used to sit, her mug of peppermint tea resting on the table beside her, but in the middle.

'Why…' James looks at his father, bewildered.

Why didn't you tell me?

Why are you moving?

But what actually tumbles out of his mouth is, 'Why don't you like me?'

'James.' Dad perches on his own chair, spine straight, knees together, no slouching for him. 'You're… perfectly fine.'

It is a knife to his heart. He knows that of all the hundreds, the thousands of words in the English language he will use in the future to describe his daughter, 'perfectly fine' will never be the ones he'll choose.

In the corner, the grandfather clock tick-tick-ticks and James is reminded of the clock in Newington that's forever stopping, and then he thinks of Cass and remembers why he is here.

'I've some questions for you.'

Irritation passes across Dad's face and all at once James is furious.

'There are things I need to know. For the baby.' His fingers roll into his palms and he tightens his fists despite knowing that he will never use them. 'Not that you seem very excited about becoming a grandfather. We're calling her Isobel, by the way, after Mum. Isobel Rose.'

He'd expected something from Dad at this revelation. A 'she'd have liked that' or 'what a lovely tribute' or something, but it's as if he hadn't heard it.

'I'm not sure I can help with questions.'

'You can at least try. You don't even know what I want to ask.'

'I'm hardly an expert on babies.'

'Oh, I know *that*,' James spits. 'If I wanted fathering advice, believe me, you'd be the last person I'd ask.'

James waits. He's never spoken this way to his father before. Would never have dared to. Any rough edges of an argument were always quickly smoothed over by his mother before they could escalate. Now she isn't here and all the pain James feels at that he directs towards his dad who just... sits. There's no reaction. No outrage.

Nothing.

As though James isn't worth summoning any emotion for, good or bad.

'Cass isn't doing so well,' James says, again his father's face impassive. 'Gestational diabetes. The midwife has been asking about our family medical history. You've said you and mum were healthy but beyond that I don't know what to tell her.'

'I don't know either.'

'You must know *something*? I need to know about your parents? Grandparents? Or didn't you show an interest in them either, the way you've never shown an interest in me? You really are fucking useless.'

James swallows hard. He's gone too far.

For a moment there is a perfect silence. James waits for an explosion but instead, in a cold voice, Dad says, 'You. Are. Not. My. Son.'

James feels as though he's been punched. There's a ringing in his ears.

A lightness in his head. He cannot make sense of it. He wonders whether his father shouted that to hurt him, made it up, but as he looks at his face, he wonders if it might actually be true.

This man in front of him, this man he has feared and loathed and so desperately tried to win love and affection from, might not be his father.

'Was...' James clears his throat. 'Was Mum married before—'

'No.' Dad shakes his head, calmer now. 'Mum... Isobel, she wasn't your mother. We adopted you when you were four.'

'No. No you didn't.' James does not believe this because he doesn't want to believe it. He looks at the patches on the walls where the photos used to hang and recalls the earliest one of him.

First day of primary school, when he was nearly five. Hair shaped into a bowl, grin on face. On Cass's father's wall there are photos of her in the hospital hours after being born, learning to crawl, her first steps, learning to ride a bike, chubby toddler legs pedalling furiously, a whole history. Here, it is as though his life began at the age of four.

'But… I'd know. I have a passport. A driving licence.'

'We applied for your passport when you were a teenager using your adoption certificate. It's been renewed since then. The driving licence took the information from your passport. I thought that you should know. We'd planned to tell you but Isobel kept putting it off, and putting it off. She was scared that you'd look at her differently, that you'd want to trace your biological family and she… she loved you very much.'

Bile rises in his throat.

Over the past few years he's been through so many changes but the one constant has always been his mother's love. Now it's wrapped up in lies and deceit and he doesn't know how he feels about her anymore and, worse than that, he can never ask her to explain.

'I know she loved me very much. Now I also know why you didn't.' He's close to tears, he can feel them in his throat.

'James.' Dad holds his hands out helplessly. 'It wasn't – isn't…' He sighs long and hard. 'I'm sorry I blurted it out like that. It must be a shock.'

'If you never wanted me then…' James can't get the rest of the sentence out.

'When I met your mum I knew she couldn't have children and it didn't matter because I'd never felt that longing. She told me that I was enough for her and I knew she was enough for me. But then, all of our friends began to have families and she wanted that too.'

'But you didn't?'

'I wanted her to be happy. I told myself that once we were approved for adoption, once we had a child I'd feel, I don't know, however you're meant to feel but… Here's the thing. You never really know if you're cut out to be a parent until you become a parent and by then it's too late. It wasn't your fault. It wasn't mine. It just…wasn't how either of us would have liked it to be. I… I did try. I know it probably doesn't seem like that but…' He shrugs helplessly.

For a moment neither of them speak. James has so many things he wants to know he doesn't know where to start.

'So…' He is the one who straightens his spine now, presses his knees together, trying to keep himself together. 'Who am I?'

Three little words that mean so much. He grips on to the soft fabric of his seat because without the anchor of his mother he is floating away from everything he thought he knew, everything he was.

'We weren't told much about your history. Your case was classed as sensitive. Nowadays there might be more information provided, I don't know, but then it was thought the less we knew the better. We did glean, from something the woman at the agency let slip, that you had a sister. She wouldn't tell us anything else.'

A sister.

Family.

He has many, many, more questions. He wants to know why his parents couldn't have children of their own, why they chose him, but his head is reeling from all he has learned today and honestly, he doesn't think it matters. He knows there will be organizations that will help him trace his family.

Slowly, unsteadily, James rises to his feet and makes his way over to the door. His father – Nick – doesn't try to stop him from leaving.

James realizes he has been wrong. There are some things that are insurmountable.

Irreparable.

His relationship with this man is over.

James leaves, knowing that he will never see him again.

He is left with one overriding thought that he pushes away.

He can't be... can he?

It's one relentless, dangerous thought.

Chapter Twenty-Seven

Cass

Danger.

I felt it before when I found myself curled up in the cupboard, shaking with fear.

I feel it now.

Someone is outside the house.

As I'm looking down into the garden, I can see the shadows move through the trees. But it's not just seeing them, it's sensing them.

Run.

Run.

Run.

The words whisper in my ear.

A movement. I crouch down, run my fingers over the rough carving in the wall.

Run.

Robin hasn't picked up my calls so I am alone but I'm weirdly okay with that. I've been brought here for a purpose and although I don't know what that purpose is I've been waiting, endlessly waiting. The air is suffocating, as though the thing I've been waiting for is close.

Breath on my neck.

'You'll look after me, won't you, Rose?' I think the words are only in my head but I feel a hand smoothing my hair. And it's comforting. I can't rely on Dad. Ever since I discovered the bank statements I've lost my grip on reality. Not seeing him as Dad anymore. He's a stranger. Someone who can't be trusted.

Laughter.

The rocking chair creaks. It's moving again but when I reach out and touch it, it is still.

My heart is pounding out of my chest.

Lemons.

I smell it again and it calms me.

Rose.

Rose.

Rose. I sing.

Run.

Run.

Run.

Echoed back to me.

I don't know if I'm losing my mind. I don't know if I've already lost it. There's a banging. The front door? Real or imagined? I can no longer tell.

Quiet.

The chair is still. No one is stroking my hair. The air smells of musty old house.

Rose?

Nothing comes back to me, but then... footsteps. Footsteps from the hallway.

Heavy. Solid.

No one is outside the house anymore.

They're inside.

Downstairs.

Hide.

Chapter Twenty-Eight

James

James wants to hide from everything he has learned, everything he has heard. He feels vulnerable, exposed as he clips on his seatbelt. As though everyone is staring at him. Everyone knowing who he is.

He stares out at the wings of the plane. That dangerous thought beating at him again and again.

Is he the missing Madley child?

A sister.

He has a sister.

Rose?

But he can't be a Madley. He'd know.

You were classed as a sensitive case. They couldn't release information about your background.

Mum.

More than anything, he wants his mum to hold him and tell him it was all a mistake, of course he isn't adopted, but he knows that his dad spoke honestly. It wasn't contempt on his face after he'd revealed the truth but relief. Relief that he no longer had to pretend to be James's father. No longer had to pretend to care.

But Mum did care, didn't she?

James finds himself doubting her. Searching through the fabric of his history, looking for loose threads to pick at, wanting to unravel it all so he can piece it back together again.

But there's nothing. She loved him. She really did.

Why couldn't she have told him? He wouldn't have wanted to trace his biological parents, would he?

Sensitive background.

Would he?

He just doesn't know. He is empty inside.

Mum.

He closes his eyes to contain the tears that threaten to spill.

There's a squeeze of his arm. 'Take-off is always the worst,' says the elderly lady next to him, obviously thinking he is scared of flying.

He is thrust back in his seat as the nose rises but he barely notices because he has felt unsteady, unbalanced ever since he'd left Dad's house.

Dad? He can't call him that anymore.

His world had spun off its axis and he has no idea how to right it.

Should he look into his past? Who he really is?

The missing Madley child.

The thought prods again. James shakes his head, trying to dislodge it. The woman next to him makes soothing noises and he wants to tell her that he isn't scared but that would be a lie. He is terrified right now but not of flying, of what comes after. Telling Cass he has no idea who he is.

What if his family carry some sort of terrible disease and that's why he'd been given up for adoption? What if that disease is passed on to their daughter?

He moans.

217

'It's okay now,' the woman next to him says. 'We're in the air.'

But it isn't okay. It isn't okay at all.

Would health reasons be classed as a 'sensitive background'?

Or is it something else? Something worse?

The missing Madley child.

That first time, looking around the house, he'd instinctively known where the nursery was before he'd opened the door. He'd known where to find writing paper. He'd known the bear was called Mr Tatty. There had always been a sense he'd been there before. A familiarity. He takes the T-rex out of his pocket. Was this his? Is that why he can't let it go?

Trip. The name pops into his head the way Mr Tatty's name had.

They are over the ocean now. Wisps of white clouds in the clear blue sky, and below them a dark and choppy sea.

He can't stop thinking about the house. Cass.

Then, he sits bolt upright, sweat instantly prickling his armpits.

What if…

What if the things she is seeing are real? What if there has been somebody watching the house? Somebody in the house?

If he is the surviving child, had he seen something he wasn't supposed to see that night?

Tell me where it is, was written on the wall in blood, Robin had said.

Has somebody come back to find it?

To force James to tell him where it is even though he has no conscious recollection of that night?

Fuck.

He hopes Robin is with Cass.

Otherwise she's alone.

Chapter Twenty-Nine

Cass

I am alone and there are two of them. Standing in my hallway as though they have every right to be there.

Chapter Thirty

James

James has such a lot to live for: Cass, his baby, but all he can think of is the past.

Who his biological parents might be.

The second they land he is fumbling for his phone. Trying to call Cass to make sure she is okay but it goes straight through to her answer service.

He redials. If she picks up this time, will she notice a difference in his voice? He doesn't want to worry her if everything is fine.

But he feels different.

How could he feel the same?

He is not who he thought he was.

Chapter Thirty-One

Cass

My whole body is trembling. My hands rest lightly on my bump and I imagine that my palms are covering Isobel's tiny ears because I do not want her to hear what is coming next.

'Why are you here?'

Unannounced. Uninvited.

My eyes flicker between the two men. Dad and Leon both look as uncomfortable as I am.

Dad gazes at me imploringly. 'The way we left things was awful, Cass, and—'

'We're here to explain,' Leon says simply.

'We didn't mean to frighten you,' Dad says. 'We did knock and then thought we'd try the door and it was open.'

'I'm not frightened.' I'm experiencing myriad emotions and I can't decipher exactly how I feel. With Dad here Leon cannot take revenge and hurt me, but why is he here? Why are they both here?

I lead them into the kitchen, my held head high, and wordlessly make tea. When we are sitting at the table, hands clasped around mugs, Dad begins.

'Cass, I've something, several things actually, to tell you, and they won't be easy to hear.'

'Why should I believe anything you say?' I'm defensive because I am scared. I instinctively know that whatever Dad is about to tell me will cause irrevocable damage. He has travelled a long way to speak to me and he looks worse than I feel. Dark shadows under his eyes, unshaven. Thinning hair uncombed.

I lower my eyes because I can't bear to see him looking so dishevelled. I can't bear to look at Leon at all.

'Leon and I grew up in a family that was… normal, I guess? Loving. If anything, too loving.'

I swallow a gulp of tea, feeling the scald in my throat burning away the sarcastic remarks that were rising.

Poor you, imagine feeling too loved.

I had never felt that.

Never.

'Leon was the eldest and then me.'

'You're not telling me anything I don't already know.'

'And then there was our younger sister.'

'You have a sister?'

'Had. Had a sister.' The pain in Dad's voice is cutting and instinctively I reach for him but his hands remain clasped around his mug, the tremble in them causing coffee to slosh over the rim. Drip over his fingers. He doesn't seem to notice.

'She was the baby and very much doted on by our parents.'

Dad looks helplessly at Leon as though he doesn't know how to carry on.

'In the meantime, I'd gone off the rails a bit,' Leon says. 'Got in with a bad crowd. Rebelled, I suppose. So much was expected of me. Being the eldest… well, it seemed my parents had planned out my entire life before I was even born.'

I cover my bump again, a flush of embarrassment heating my face. Is this what we've done? James and I? In sharing our hopes and dreams for our daughter have we inadvertently mapped out her path? Written her story before it's even begun?

'And then…' This time it is Leon who struggles to continue.

'And then they were killed, in a car accident,' Dad says. 'I was twenty-one, Leon was twenty-five and our sister, just seventeen. We muddled through at first, I was still at university and attempting to study while trying to act as a parent to a hurt and confused teenager, but then she met a man.' Dad's tone changed. He releases his grip on his mug and balls his hands into fists before furiously rubbing at the spilt coffee with his sleeve. 'Married him very quickly. Neither of us went to the wedding.'

'He was twenty years older than her and already had a child. We didn't…' Leon sighs. 'Adrian didn't approve.'

Dad nodded. 'I didn't. It wasn't only his age although that was a big factor. She was a grieving child searching for security and he… he…'

Over the years I'd witnessed my father in various moods, but this is a new one to me. Pure rage.

'I didn't care,' Leon says. 'And… that will always be a regret of mine but…' He shrugs. 'I didn't want the responsibility and as the eldest… If I could go back.'

They fall into silence. Both of them lost in their own thoughts, their own regrets. I still don't understand why Dad has been paying Leon every month for all of these years but I wait, not wanting to rush them, trying to digest all I have learned. I have an aunt.

Had. Had an aunt.

It might be the hormones but my tears well. How I'd longed for a large family over the years. I might have had cousins.

Dad clears his throat and I turn my attention back to him. Push my selfish thoughts away. I didn't know her. Dad had lost his sister. He's obviously still carrying guilt and grief and perhaps that accounts for his drinking over the years. Already, I feel I understand him a little better.

'What happened to her?' I ask.

'She became pregnant – little more than a girl herself – and I was furious with her. Furious with *him* for stealing her life. Taking advantage. She sent me a letter when she'd given birth, and regular photos and... I was an uncle but I couldn't separate the baby from the circumstances. Couldn't quite bring myself to visit. I wasn't ready to make peace and accept she was a married woman. I wasn't ready then but... I always thought there'd be time.'

'You always think there'll be more time, don't you?' Leon mutters and I see real emotion on his face.

'What happened?'

'One night she called me. She was so distressed. Said she needed me to come. Her voice was... she was terrified. I left home immediately and by the time I got to her she... she...'

Dad is crying now and so am I because although what comes next blindsides me, perhaps on some level I already knew.

'It took such a long time to get to her house.' A beat. 'This house.' Dad takes my hand. His is cold but his skin isn't as chilling as his words.

'Cass. My sister...' Leon takes Dad's other hand as he falteringly carries on. 'Our sister, Marina, married Sylvester Madley and moved here to Newington House.' He pauses but I can't fill the silence, waiting with dread. 'You were her baby, Cass. I took you in after she died.' I'm shaking my head as he says, 'You... you are the missing Madley child. The only one who survived.'

Chapter Thirty-Two

Cass

I am the missing Madley child.

I'm numb.

Swallowing down the vomit that rises in my throat only to feel the burn again. Stuck in a perpetual nightmare.

I am not who I thought I was.

I'm aware of Dad speaking to me, but his voice sounds distorted and echoey as though he is underwater.

My fingers are wrapped around something cold and hard.

Leon says something this time but all I can hear is a whooshing in my ears.

Dad's hand circles mine and together we raise the glass I didn't know that I was holding to my lips. Water dribbles down my chin. I've forgotten how to drink.

My lungs are burning, my chest heaving.

I have forgotten how to breathe.

'Cass?' Dad is shaking my shoulders now, his face close to mine. 'Calm down, for the sake of the baby. For Isobel.'

It is my little girl's name that reaches through the panic.

I am fine.

I am safe.

I am normal.

My mantra spins around in my mind but I know I am not any of those things and I want to weep but I do not have enough air to do so.

I am dying.

Everything fading away. My body jerks backwards as my chair is dragged away from the table. Dad's hand is on the back of my head gently easing it down towards my knees, not forcing it, conscious of my bump.

He rubs my back in circular motions.

I am fine.

I am safe.

I am normal.

Eventually, my breathing regulates, my senses sharpen but I don't sit up because I don't want to face Dad or Leon.

The truth.

It is the cramp in my belly that jerks me upright, a puppet on a string, and that's what I feel like. A marionette with no control over anything.

I finish my water and when Leon refills my glass, I drain that too. Still my mouth is dry.

'You must have a lot of questions.' Dad's nervous, chewing on his thumbnail in the way he used to when he was fighting the urge to drink. No wonder he used to get drunk. I've a strong urge for a vodka myself. 'Please ask anything.'

There is so much that doesn't make sense to me but I don't know where to begin.

'You're not my father?' The first question I ask almost breaks me.

I am not who I thought I was.

'No. I'm your uncle.'

'But you let me believe I was your daughter? Those photos

on the wall, me at the hospital hours after birth, crawling, first steps...'

'They're all you. Marina sent them to me. She sent them to me...' His voice thick with fresh tears. 'After I'd turned my back on her.'

'Not just you...' Leon tried to cut in but Dad waved him away. Carried on talking. 'Marina and I were so close and instead of supporting her I came here to try and talk her out of marrying Sylvester but she went ahead with the wedding and I felt... hurt. Rejected. She rang me after they were married, and I said... I said, "You've made your bed and now you must lie in it." What sort of brother does that make me?'

'She knew you loved her. That's why she sent you pictures. She didn't send any to me. If anyone failed her it's me. I failed you both. Cass.' Leon crouches and looks me in the eye. 'I know I've done some terrible things but what I did to Mr Peters was unforgivable and I had a lot of time to think in prison. I came out determined to make amends. I wanted to talk to you but you were so scared you ran away from me. I am sorry—'

'I don't fucking care if you're sorry.' I jab him in the chest.

'It really isn't the time for this, Leon,' Dad says sharply.

Leon paces over to the window.

'When she... Mum. When she died. What... Why...' I fall silent. I do not know what I am asking. What I want to know.

Everything.

Nothing.

'You were three and your stepsister was fifteen. Marina had turned twenty-one and I'd been thinking of her more and more, wanting to get in touch. She called me... that night. She asked me to come and I knew... I knew from the fear in her voice that something terrible was going to happen. I came straight away but by the time I got here... There were police cars and officers and tape around the house and... oh god.' Dad drops his face into hands.

The fridge thrums, outside a bird sings. Life goes on but it feels that here, in this kitchen, the life as I knew it has ended.

I am the missing Madley child.

'I explained to the police who I was, that Marina had telephoned me and they said there had been an incident. They asked me to sit down... here.' Dad looks around the room, eyes wide, and I know he is seeing what he saw that night. 'They brought me in this room because in the drawing room' – he gestures to the doorway – 'she was, my beautiful sister was...' He swallows hard. Composes himself. 'The officer told me that Marina and Sylvester were dead. That a child... oh god, I thought it was you at first, but you were missing.'

'Missing?'

'Yes. They'd seen your room but didn't know where you were. They were trying to trace any relatives who might be looking after you, but—'

'Where was I?'

'Hiding.' Dad wipes his nose. 'The police said they'd searched the house thoroughly but I remember when Marina had showed me around when I came to try and talk her out of marrying him she had shown me a priest hole. I just had a feeling...'

'I was in the priest hole,' I finish.

'I lifted you out,' he says quietly.

Suddenly, I know that is my earliest memory. Feeling trapped, Dad lifting me out, my arms around his neck.

'I think you felt safe there. After, when you had nightmares or were really scared, you'd hide in the hall cupboard. I think it felt the same to you. A small, enclosed space. Safe.'

228

'I can't believe I didn't know any of this.'

'I thought... I didn't want you growing up known as the Madley murder child. I changed your name.'

'I knew someone who got you a new birth certificate,' Leon says. 'And then I made Adrian pay me every month to keep it quiet. I promised never to tell you, tell anyone, who you really were.'

'What was my name?' So much of my identity is wrapped up in Cassie.

'It's Cassandra, Cassandra Madley. I didn't want to confuse you any more by changing it completely. Cassie was close and Freeman is my name so it was Marina's maiden name. It isn't too far from the truth.'

'But it isn't the truth. And you thought it was okay to lie to me too, Leon?'

'I... I didn't really care.' He has the grace to look ashamed. 'I know that's terrible but when I helped Adrian all I thought of was that I could use it against him. He'd have done anything to protect you.'

'So that's why he paid you all that money over the years.'

'Yes.'

'From my wages. The money didn't come from this house,' Dad says but I don't care if it did. Money is the last thing on my mind but he takes my silence for curiosity.

'The house was left to me,' Dad says. 'Sylvester didn't have any relatives. I put it up for sale, couldn't bear to come here and didn't think you'd want to either. It didn't sell for ages until the building company bought it. It was tainted by its reputation, by ghosts. It didn't fetch even half as much as I'd hoped but I thought it would be enough for your future. I was going to give it to you when you turned eighteen, tell you everything but… you'd always been so fragile. The nightmares, the anxiety medication, so I put it off until you were twenty-one but by then…' He glances at Leon.

'I felt responsible for Mr Peters and had a breakdown.' It is a day for honesty, there's no point sugar-coating anything now.

'I kept putting it off and putting it off and I was going to. Really. The money is safe, it's in a trust. Once I knew I was going to be a grandfather I wanted you to know everything. It makes you think, doesn't it? The bloodline living on.'

'So why didn't you tell me when I came to stay and was asking about my past?'

'You arriving unexpectedly was such a shock, a surprise really, a lovely one, but after you'd told me you were so worn out from the journey you went to bed. I sat up all night, thinking. I'd bought some veggie steak at Tesco, was going to cook a special meal and tell you everything but when I came home you'd found the bank statements and asked why I'd been paying Leon and…' Dad shrugs. 'I'm so sorry. I didn't know what the right thing to do was. I've tried to be a mother and a father to you when all I really am is a terrible uncle who is so far out of his depth…' He is broken. I see pieces of him shattering, falling to the floor.

'Didn't I ever ask about them after you took me in? Mum? Dad?' It feels odd saying that word. I have another father. 'My sister?'

'At first you'd call out for them in your sleep. That's when I'd find you in the cupboard and then… you were so young. Had suffered such trauma.'

Dad and Leon exchange a look.

'What?'

'We think perhaps you saw everything that happened that

night. You were hurt, your arm. The scar… You never cut yourself on my glass. I made that up because how could I tell you that the people who murdered your parents did it to you? If you were a witness it could be why you've always been… troubled. Cass, when you told me you were moving to Newington I was horrified. I thought it might all come flooding back.'

'And that's why you tried to stop me? Pretended you hated James?'

'I… I did resent him. He was taking you to somewhere I'd tried so hard to forget. It seemed too coincidental.'

'You once told me that coincidences mean we're on the right path, but then you said a lot of things that weren't true, didn't you? That night we video-called and you said you saw a woman behind me. Did you make that up to scare me?'

'No. Not consciously. It was the first time I'd seen the kitchen since that night and I was thinking of Marina and… I don't know. I thought I saw something but I probably didn't.'

'So you didn't actually see my dead mother who didn't actually fall off a ladder. That was some story.'

'You needed to know she had died but I thought if I said she had died doing something for you it might… bring a little comfort. I was protecting you.'

'Stop.' I hold out my hand to deflect his words. 'I can't… I can't hear any more, not now. I can't take it all in. I want you to go.'

'Cass.'

'No, Dad. You've ripped my world apart and I don't know how I feel about it. How I feel about you.' I don't include Leon, he is the least of my worries.

'Come back home…'

'Home?' I give a hollow laugh. Where is home? I'd asked

myself that weeks ago when I'd moved in here and told myself that it was at Newington because that's where James was, where my heart was. But perhaps my heart had been here long before that.

'Dad.' The word still feels natural on my tongue and I know that whatever the future holds there will be a future for us, as a family, although it will take on another shape but I don't know what that looks like yet. 'I will have more questions and I will talk to you another time but please, just stop.'

Exhaustion drips from every pore and he must see this because he says, 'I promise I'll wait until you're ready to talk but surely you can't want to stay here? At Newington? Not now you know it was your childhood home.'

But that's precisely why I want to stay.

When I woke this morning I was Cass Freeman. I had one father. One uncle. James and the baby. Now I know I had two parents who loved me. A sister. Here, I feel close to them. I want to go to my sister's room and process my thoughts. There are so many of them spinning around my mind.

'They're buried near my flat,' Dad says quietly. 'I took them home. Your mum and stepsister.'

'Did you ever meet Rose?'

Dad frowns. 'Rose?'

'Your niece. Step-niece?'

'Cass.' It is Leon who replies. 'Your half-sister was called Tamsin.'

I feel myself deflate, my body sag as I realize I don't know her at all. The girl whose room I'd been painting in. Had felt so comfortable in.

Tamsin.

I don't know who she was any more than I know who I am.

My family was slaughtered and I possibly saw it all.

What did the intruders want?

What did they kill for?

Why can't I remember?

Dad and Leon leave and I head into the drawing room. Stand under the portrait of the Madley family – my family. I pull out my mobile, swiping past all of James's missed call alerts and take a photo before pinching the screen. Zoomed in, I can see what I couldn't with my naked eye. The pendant of the swan around Mrs Madley's, Marina's, Mum's neck.

The pendant I am wearing now.

Suddenly I am full of fury.

Someone murdered my mum and I want to know why.

I decide to visit each room of the house. I'm going to jog my memories.

I'm going to remember it all.

Chapter Thirty-Three

Rose

THEN

Rose wished she couldn't remember the fire but she kept having terrifying flashbacks. The skin on her hands was red and raw. She'd spent yesterday scrubbing the front door, the walls, Mum balanced on a stepladder using a mop on the ceiling, David painting the hall a brilliant white once the walls and ceiling had dried. The smoke damage was no longer visible but Rose could still feel the burn in her chest, the terror she had felt as she had pounded back upstairs to save her brother, not knowing what she would find when she tried to come back down.

In the two nights since the fire she hadn't slept. Every little noise signalled danger. The hoot of an owl, the rain pattering against the window, even the hum of the fridge.

She ran over everything in her mind again and again. Hopping from theory to theory.

Gunner had started the fire to pay her back.

The debt collector had carried out his threat to hurt them.

David had paid someone to start the fire to claim on the insurance.

David had lit it himself.

It was this theory that Rose kept pushing away – no matter

what trouble he was in, his business was in, surely he wouldn't risk the lives of his family?

Would he?

But as she watched him paint, she focused on the tremor in his hands, the tightness of his jaw, his silence and she just didn't know what to think.

How to feel.

Roo ran around the house making siren noises, a rolled-up towel serving as a makeshift hose.

'I'm going to be a fireman when I am big,' he said. Rose shuddered. She never wanted to see, smell, another fire again.

The remains of the rug had been taken to the tip, the exposed floor cold and hard and that was how the entire house seemed to Rose now.

Cold and hard. No longer a home. Not somewhere she felt safe and secure.

They could have died.

Now, David was out at a breakfast meeting. It was the first time that Rose had been alone with Mum.

'Who do you think started the fire?' Rose asked, anxiously picking the skin around her fingernails.

'Rose' – her mum hugged her – 'have you been worried? Nobody started the fire.'

'Of course they did. I'm not a child. Do you think it was the man from the farm?'

'I don't know what you're talking about.'

'Yes, you do. Have you told the investigating officer?'

'Our business is our business.' The phrase slipped out of her mother's mouth but it didn't sound like anything she would say.

'Mum. Somebody tried to kill us.'

'We're fine. It was… Rose, I know it was frightening but—'

'Was it David?'

'Of course not. How could you—'

'The only way you wouldn't be scared this would happen again is if you knew who—'

'David wouldn't endanger us. Look, he's sorting everything out right now.'

'So, you're not scared?'

A beat. 'No.'

'So why have you taped up the letter box?'

'I'm nipping out to get something for lunch. Keep an eye on Roo.' Mum grabbed her purse from her bag and strode towards the door.

Rose mopped up splashes of milk and dumped the soggy corn-flakes that Roo had left at the bottom of his bowl in the bin. She sat back down and tried to focus on the jigsaw of a donkey that she was helping Roo with but she frequently checked the doors were locked, the windows, letter box still taped shut. She didn't think she would ever feel relaxed again.

They could have died.

Mum was smiling when she arrived home. She pulled out a pack of Roo's favourite biscuits, biscuits they certainly couldn't afford, and gave him one. He scuttled off. Holding the ginger snap tightly in his hands.

'Has David sorted everything out?' Rose's mood lifted.

'I don't know but I met a homeless woman outside the shop—'

'And that's made you happy?' Rose bristled. 'Seeing what our life will be like and—'

'No. We chatted. Her name is Dorothea and I gave her some money and—'

'Great, so according to Dad we're about to lose everything and you're giving away what little we do have.'

'Rose.' Mum frowned. 'That's not like you. What happened to kindness? Compassion?'

'Sorry,' Rose mumbled, ashamed. The truth was, she was on edge. Scared.

'Anyway, she told me, this Dorothea, that she'd literally just been offered some work. That there is another job going.'

'Doing what?'

'Waitressing. She was really nervous because she doesn't have any experience but the woman who offered it to her had reassured her that she was going to get someone else too. That she wouldn't be on her own. Anyway, I'm going to go and check it out. If they haven't found anyone else yet then…'

'But you said there was no need to worry. That David is sorting everything out?'

'He is. It's just…' Mum plucked out the milk from the shopping bag and shoved it into the door of the fridge. Crammed a bag of frozen peas into the freezer. She turned to Rose and raised her hands helplessly. 'I have to try and do *something*.'

'Right. And what happens if this job has already gone?' Rose began to stack cans of beans in the cupboard. A cheap white loaf.

'Then something else will come up,' Mum said quietly. 'Rose, I know you're scared and, in truth, I am too. The fire. It could have been catastrophic, fatal. I see it every time I close my eyes, not as it was, but as it could have been. Flames swallowing the house. Us.' She pinched the bridge of her nose and Rose knew that she was trying to stem her tears. 'Please. Can you watch Roo again while I nip and check this job out?'

Rose deliberated. David really didn't want Mum getting a job and Rose didn't want David to have any reason to get angry. To hurt Mum again. Besides, she wanted to talk to Gunner. She no longer believed he had started the fire but she wanted to be sure.

'I can't babysit. I have plans. Sorry.'

'Okay.' Her mum chewed her bottom lip, thinking. 'I'll take Roo with me. He's so cute, he's bound to win them over.'

'Are you sure you should—'

'Just wish me luck, Rose.'

'But—'

'Please. It'll be fine. I'll be back for lunch.'

Rose swallowed hard, tasting smoke at the back of her throat. Everything was changing again. Perhaps she should be more supportive? Mum was being proactive for the first time in a long time. She needed to know that Rose was on her side.

'I can watch Roo,' she said.

'It's okay. I think I will take him. He'll be my secret weapon.'

'Okay. Good luck.' Rose kissed her mum on the cheek. 'They'll love you both.'

'I hope so.' Mum smoothed her hair, ran a finger around her lips, checking for lipstick bleeds. 'Right.' She took a deep breath. 'You must be on your best behaviour, Roo. We need to impress these people.'

'Okay.' He nodded solemnly.

'We'll use your actual name today.' Her mother held out her hand and her brother slipped his small one inside of hers. 'Ready to meet the Madley family, James?' She smiled, excited. 'Newington House is going to change our lives. I just know it.'

PART TWO

Chapter Thirty-Four

Marina

THEN
THIRTY YEARS AGO

The doorbell of Newington House chimed, loud and imposing.

Marina Madley felt like a child playing dress-up as she hurried down the corridor in her ridiculous shoes, high and polished, each step threatening to turn her ankle. She thought if she could make herself taller, she'd be filled with confidence but the faces from the portraits of those who had trodden before her glared at her with such cold, hard eyes and she knew she wasn't enough.

After four years of living here, she knew that she'd never be enough.

She'd never be happy.

To outsiders looking in she and Sylvester had it all – a beautiful home, two gorgeous girls: Tamsin and Cassandra – not that they let strangers look in, of course.

Sylvester was *very* careful to keep everyone out.

'Is it so wrong to want you all to myself?' he had said, nuzzling into her neck, when she had asked whether she could invite her brothers, Adrian and Leon, for her first Christmas in her new home.

She had felt both special and disappointed.

'But I haven't seen them for such a long time.' Neither had come to the wedding. Neither had approved of her marrying a man twenty years older than herself who already had an eleven-year-old daughter.

'Marina.' Sylvester had cupped her cheeks between his warm palms with such tenderness it made her want to weep. 'We're your family now. Tamsin and I. I want you to feel settled here. Complete. I couldn't bear it if you... if you... walked out like Jane, Tamsin's mum.'

The crack in his voice made Marina's heart swell. 'I won't leave you. Never.' Tears pricked. She knew what it was like to be left. Her parents had been killed in a car crash and she had felt so alone, abandoned, even though it wasn't their fault. Sylvester had found her when she had been lost, when they had both been alone and directionless and grieving for loss in different ways. They could save each other, she had thought.

Then.

As much as she wanted to pick up her three-year-old daughter, Cassandra, and leave this dark, brooding house that had never, would never, feel like home, Sylvester had made it impossible. Not only that, but she wouldn't leave Tamsin.

Because Jane hadn't voluntarily left Tamsin, had she?

She—

A rattle. A shout. 'Hello?' Two eyes peeked through the letter box.

'Coming.' Marina reached the front door and pulled it open, tucking her hair behind her ears, wishing she had swept it up into a French pleat, at least tried to look sophisticated.

'Can I help you?' Marina was confused.

She had been expecting Penelope, the wife of Gerald, one of

Sylvester's 'Gentlemen's Club' associates. She can't say they're friends, despite the fact that Penelope reminds her of herself in many ways, although she's loath to admit it. They're both Stepford Wives. A couple of times a year Penelope picks the children up and takes them out of the house for a few hours while she and Sylvester attend to his 'business'. Today was one of those days.

The lady standing on the doorstep wasn't Penelope. She wasn't Dorothea either, the young, foreign woman Marina had met begging in town that morning. Marina had crouched down to push a crumpled five-pound note into the woman's hand as she told her in a low voice that if she came to Newington later she would find her work. Pay a decent wage. She needed help for the event to run smoothly or Sylvester would be cross.

'But I can't... I don't have the right...' Dorothea had bitten her lip as though she'd already said too much.

'Don't worry about tax and paperwork and all of that. It can be cash in hand if you don't tell anyone.' Marina knew she was doing the right thing and the wrong thing.

'A secret?'

'A secret.' Marina knew all about those but what she didn't know right now was who was standing before her.

'I'm looking for Mrs Madley?'

'I'm Mrs Madley.' Marina straightened her spine, glad of her heels, steeling herself for the 'But you're so young', but it didn't come.

'Hello. It's lovely to meet you. I'm Zeta. Zeta Harvey. I know you've some work going and I—'

'How? How do you know that?'

'There was this woman, outside the shop. I asked if she was

okay. If she needed anything. She said she had found a job. She was so excited. Is she here yet?'

'No, she isn't due yet.'

'She said that you were looking for someone else to help. I'm used to catering. I have a family I wait on hand and foot. This is my son, James.' She thrust forward a small child who flashed a toothy grin, a green plastic dinosaur clutched in his hand.

'Hello,' Marina said to him before looking expectantly at Zeta who carried on talking.

'I have a family to support and… and…' Zeta's eyes filled with tears and Marina recognized something in her. Something she had felt herself.

Longing.

Desperation.

Zeta was also the first person she had met with a child of a similar age to Cassandra. She felt a kinship. She glanced over her shoulder; Sylvester had gone to the city for a couple of hours to his Gentlemen's Club.

He wasn't a gentleman.

'It'll give you time to organize my birthday surprise, my dear,' he had said, running his finger across Marina's cheek. She had tried not to show her revulsion, but with Zeta here and Dorothea absent she might have to rethink her plans anyway. Bile rose in her throat. If she let Sylvester down there would be a price to pay.

There was *always* a price to pay.

'Mummy, I need a wee,' James whispered loudly, tugging his mum's hand.

'Sorry.' Zeta looked at her apologetically.

'Come in.' Marina ushered them both inside, grateful for the distraction from her tumultuous thoughts.

'Thank you.' Zeta smiled as they came out. 'He's doing really well at staying dry but it can all be a bit last minute.' She gazed around the entrance hall in wonder. 'You have such a beautiful home.'

'Thank you.' The compliment warmed Marina. She didn't have any friends, didn't have anyone she could invite around. 'I could give you a quick tour, if you'd like?'

'I'd love that. It looks like just the place lords and ladies would live, doesn't it, James? Do you remember when we went to the castle that time and watched the battle re-enactment?'

Once James had used the bathroom, Marina showed them the chapel. The eagle pulpit, wings spread.

James was enthralled. 'I wish we lived here,' he said.

'We're lucky we have a nice home too.' Zeta looked so downcast that Marina beckoned James over to the pulpit. 'Look.' She pulled out slips of paper and a pen. 'This is a Madley family tradition that dates back years and years. We write on the paper something we're grateful for and pop it in that wooden box by the door.'

'Kind of like giving thanks to God?' Zeta asks.

Marina smiled but she didn't answer. She couldn't. She didn't believe in God anymore. Not since she married Sylvester.

'What are you thankful for, James? I'll write yours for you.' Marina had her pen poised.

'My sister, Rose,' he said immediately and Marina wrote the name down and popped it into the box.

Upstairs they poked their head into what they still called the nursery although at three Cassandra was growing out of the ducks marching around the walls. Her cot bed. Marina and Zeta chatted as they ambled down the hallway, James racing ahead.

There was a cry as he collided with Cassandra who was coming out of her sister's bedroom, knocking her to the floor. Her beloved teddy bear tumbling beside her.

Cassandra's eyes welled with tears. James picked up the bear. 'What's his name?'

'Mr Tatty,' Cassandra whispered.

Tucking Mr Tatty under his arm, James offered her his hand and helped her up, before he gently kissed the back of it. 'My lady,' he said grandly. Marina and Zeta laughed.

'He's a charmer,' Zeta said. 'He saw that at the castle.'

'You're supposed to say "My lord",' Marina called to her daughter. 'I think they've definitely got a spark,' she said to Zeta, never knowing her daughter so still, James continuing to hold her hand. 'You okay, Cassandra?'

Her words broke the spell, Cassandra scuttling off to Tamsin's room. James gazing forlornly after her.

'Where's she gone?'

'To find her older sister, Tamsin. She's…' Marina stopped herself. If she mentioned the age gap she'd have to tell Zeta that Tamsin was her stepdaughter. That she'd married a man so much older and she was scared that if she began to talk she wouldn't be able to stop.

'It's lovely they're so close.'

'Oh, they have their moments, believe me. Cass is a terror for hiding Tamsin's paintbrushes when she wants her attention. Sometimes Tamsin will play along with the game, sit Cassandra on her lap in her rocking chair and tell her stories. Sometimes she shouts at her for taking them. Then all I hear is slamming doors. It usually ends in tears. But Cassandra's so sweet she has all of us wrapped around her little finger.'

'Mummy, I'm hungry,' James said.

'I can probably find you a biscuit. Is that okay?' She turned her attention back to Zeta. 'And… do you… do you fancy a coffee?'

Sylvester was out for the morning, the girls were occupied.

A hot drink. Two mums chatting. Something so normal was tantalizingly in reach and Marina was desperate for it.

What harm could it do?

Marina didn't realize at that time that a simple act of kindness would have such far-reaching consequences.

Be so devastating.

Chapter Thirty-Five

Rose

It was devastating.

'James. I think it was because of James that I didn't get the job.' Rose's mum kept her voice low even though James was upstairs in his room building a dinosaur park out of Lego and wouldn't be able to hear her. 'I should never have taken him to the interview.' She looked desolate as she flopped onto the sofa next to Rose.

'What did he do?'

'Nothing. He was adorable. She, Mrs Madley, had a little girl, probably a year or so younger than James, and they were so sweet together. They held hands and it looked so natural. I had a vision of him in the future, all grown up, with a girlfriend.'

'Trying to marry him into the rich family.' Rose tried to lighten the mood.

'It wouldn't be Cassandra, obviously. They're very unlikely to see each other ever again unless fate brings them back together. But one day there will be somebody. Another woman will be centre of his world instead of me.' Mum's eyes glassed with tears.

'Now, you're trying to make yourself feel worse.' Rose stepped into the role of the parent. 'James thinks girls are stinky. He's never going to leave you. I probably won't either so you'll be stuck with us both, forever.'

'I'd love to be stuck with you both, forever.' Mum rested her head on Rose's shoulder. 'But one day—'

'Shall we just focus on today?' Rose said gently. 'What went wrong at the house?'

'Mrs Madley – Marina – said that she needed somebody flexible, without family, somebody that didn't mind being called on during weekends, in the evenings.'

'Sounds like she wants a slave.'

'No, I don't think it was that, she was really friendly but, I guess she knows what it's like with small children. Always picking up bugs. She probably thinks I wouldn't be reliable.'

'She sounds like a bitch.'

'She wasn't. You know, in another life I think we would have been friends. I found out a lot about her over coffee. Despite our differences we had a lot in common. Two children with large age gaps. Both married young.'

'What about Mr Madley? Did you get to meet him?'

'No. I saw a picture of him, Sylvester, well, a portrait I guess you'd call it, in the drawing room. There were all these paintings lining the walls, of the family going back generations. It was so posh. And I thought our house was big.'

'It is. It's lovely.'

'You know… I hadn't wanted you to find out but… we're having a few… *difficulties*. Financially, I mean. We might not be able to stay here.'

It was the first time her mother had vocalized the financial problems they were having. She stared into her lap, picking at a stray thread hanging from the hem of her shirt. Her shame written all over her face. Rose didn't have the heart to tell her that she already knew. That it was impossible not to have heard the rows, picked up on the atmosphere. Christ, the neighbours probably knew. The entire village.

'Home is where the heart is,' Rose said softly but inside there was a hard ball of dread. Despite the words falling from her tongue she felt her home was here. In her bedroom with the jungle print wallpaper that Mum said Rose must have grown out of by now. But Rose loved it, it made her feel camouflaged. Invisible. The animals peeking out from behind the trees her friends. She had given them all names: Malcolm the monkey, Lulu the lion, Graham the giraffe. If they left here she would have to leave them all.

Leave Gunner. She still hoped she could sort things out with him.

'As long as you, me and James are together that's the most important thing.' Rose purposely didn't mention her stepdad. 'But…' her selfish side pushed her kindness aside, 'there must be something we can do? To stay? Other jobs to apply for?'

'Maybe, but my CV has a huge blank space on it where I haven't done anything.'

'You've raised two children!'

'I know, and there are transferable skills from that, valuable skills, time management, organization, budgeting, but employers won't see that. They don't care. I'm underqualified for everything. Lacking in experience. Too old.'

'Mum, you're not—'

She stiffened at the sound of a key jabbing into the lock, sensing her mum doing the same beside her. Her stepdad stormed into the house.

'That meeting was a waste of fucking time.'

'It's okay,' her mum said. 'I was just explaining to Rose that we might have to move.'

'And I was just telling Mum that as long as we are together as a family, it doesn't matter.'

'Oh, it might not matter to you, *Rose*.'

'But it does to you, *David*.'

There was a beat before he turned his attention back to her mother. 'This place is a pigsty. How can I bring clients here when—'

'I tried to get a job this morning,' Mum said quietly. Bravely.

He stepped forward confrontationally. Mum leaned back, pushing herself into the cushions, trying to make herself smaller.

'At least she tried,' Rose said.

'Did you get it?' David asked, and Rose couldn't read whether he hoped that she did or didn't.

'No, but I can try again.'

'But what can you actually do?' David said but not nastily, more bewildered, and Rose was suddenly saddened that David did not know her mum at all. Didn't know she was capable of so much.

Everything.

'Mum can do anything she sets her mind to and in the meantime why don't you follow her example and try and find a job?' Rose spoke quietly, placing her hand on her mum's knee, feeling the tremble in her fingers, knowing that Mum would feel it too but wanting her to know that she wasn't alone.

'My business—'

'Is a *joke*.'

David raised his hand at Rose's harsh words. Rose tilted her chin defiantly, steeled herself for the slap, wanted it almost, but it didn't come. Mum babbling apologies on her behalf, trying to fill the cracks in their relationships with carefully chosen words, but the crevices were now chasms. Too deep and too wide to repair.

David nodded, soothed, and Rose seethed, wishing he *had* hit her. Knowing that Mum had been pushed to her limits, and beyond, but also knowing there was a line and that she, Rose was that line. If David hurt her physically, Mum would leave him, of that she had no doubt. She just wished that Mum could see that it wasn't only punches and kicks that hurt. Witnessing the slow disintegration of her mum's self-esteem, her self-worth, had been an altogether different kind of pain, inconceivably cruel. But worse than that was the knowledge that although Rose was almost sixteen, almost free to leave, she wouldn't because she couldn't leave her mother or her brother with this monster.

Rose didn't speak throughout lunch. She couldn't. The toast sticking in her throat despite being softened by baked beans.

'I went to a castle and met a princess today, Daddy,' Roo said taking a huge bite from his toast which was dripping with honey.

A shadow passed across the window.

'Under the table,' David snapped and they all ducked out of view as fists thumped against the glass outside.

Roo pressed himself against Rose, his small body shaking with fear, picking up that something was very wrong, even if he was too young to understand what.

Eventually the shadow fell away, the midday sun, high in the sky, once again flooding the room.

'I'm going out.' David pulled himself to his feet.

'But what if he comes back? Starts another fire?' Rose said.

'Don't like fire.' Roo began to cry.

'I can't sort things out if I stay here. *Hiding*,' he said scathingly as though it hadn't been his idea to huddle under the table.

Rose, Mum and Roo held hands, watched him leave.

'Mum?' Rose was scared of so many things in that moment.

David coming back. David never coming back. The debt collector returning when they were alone. Vulnerable.

'Don't worry,' Mum said in a shaky voice after the front door had slammed. 'I'm going to sort it out. It isn't fair that the Madleys have so much when we have so little and she liked me, I know she did. She wouldn't have made me coffee otherwise, would she? If she'd let Roo use the toilet and then told us to leave it would be different but… No, there was a friendliness there. Definitely. I'm going back to the house. My wages may be a drop in the ocean compared to what we owe but it will be something to offer our creditors.'

'Okay.' That one word was all that Rose could force out of her constricted throat. Her eyes burned with tears.

Later, she would look back and wish she had told her mother that she loved her.

Wish she had never let her leave at all.

If Rose had known how her mum would try to sort it out, what the consequences would be, then she would never have let her go.

Never.

It isn't always possible to identify the definitive moment when everything changes but for Rose it was at that moment when her mother made the decision to return to Newington House. When she closed the door and left.

For when she came back, she would never be the same again.

Nothing would.

Chapter Thirty-Six

Marina

Marina hadn't been the same since she'd married. She didn't feel the same. She didn't act the same. She didn't even look the same, she thought, as she painted on a baby pink smile. She stretched her mouth upwards, the skin on her pale face taut and uncomfortable. She'd lost so much weight. She was shrinking, skin and bones, but she couldn't disappear entirely.

She couldn't remember the last time she had felt like herself. It was probably when Sylvester slipped that thin, gold band onto her seventeen-year-old finger and promised to love her while she promised to obey.

What was she going to do?

She couldn't do *this*.

Not again.

Dorothea had turned up shortly after lunch and Marina had prepped her but it wasn't enough for Sylvester.

It would *never* be enough.

She clung to the edge of the dressing table, bile rising in her throat, sharp and sour. In the mirror she could see the outfit Sylvester had chosen laid out on the bed.

'I want something extra special,' he had said.

'But... but...' Despair sapped her strength. 'I told you I can't. Please.'

'Don't you want to be a good wife? A loyal wife?' Sylvester had wrapped his fingers around her neck and squeezed gently. 'Jane wasn't a good wife. A loyal wife.'

He left the unspoken hanging between them.

'If you make today extra special for me then perhaps that can be it.'

'Do you mean that?' she had asked but knowing even if he did, she would still hate him. Still be forced to stay with him.

Till death do us part.

She stared so intently at the tight black dress that it began to blur, shift, slithering across the duvet towards her.

She wouldn't wear it.

She couldn't.

She couldn't.

She couldn't.

Marina began to cry, huge wracking sobs that tore through her body, She didn't want Cass to hear her so she stuffed her fist into her mouth, biting on her knuckles, welcoming the pain, knowing it wouldn't hurt as much as Sylvester's plans.

He'd be waiting.

Impatient.

Angry.

With shaking hands, she pulled on the dress, the stockings. Her hair fell long and loose over her shoulders the way he liked it and she dragged a brush through it.

He'd be waiting.

She felt sick.

Where was the babysitter? Penelope was late picking up the children. They couldn't both disappear while the girls were here.

She took one last glance at the mirror, her dress, her lipstick – she couldn't look herself in the eye. She pulled on a long cardigan over her dress to cover up her shame and went downstairs to wait.

The phone trilled, breaking through Marina's thoughts.

'Hello?'

'Marina, it's Penelope. I'm sorry but I can't take the children after all.'

'But… you must. Sylvester will be furious.'

'I know. Gerald will hate that I've let him down but I've got food poisoning. I've tried to get to you but I've had to rush back to the bathroom and… please, if there's a way Gerald doesn't have to know. I'm sorry.' She hung up.

Adrenaline rushed through Marina. What was she going to do? She didn't have any real friends. Didn't know anyone from the village she could ask. These events took so much planning. If it wasn't Sylvester's birthday it wouldn't be quite so bad but…

She couldn't make the decision on her own.

Sylvester would know what to do.

Lost in thought she didn't make the usual checks as she entered the kitchen, the pantry. Didn't make sure that she was alone as she pressed the button and waited while the false wall slid back, revealing the hidden scullery beyond.

Old houses often had them as a place for keeping food and all of the clutter out of sight.

She hurried towards the thick butcher's block against the back wall that held a lifetime of criss-cross knife marks and all of her secrets.

The drawer was closed, as it should be. Gripping the handles with both hands she pushed it in further and then yanked it to the right where it slid on its tracks, before pushing it forward even more, compressing the spring until she heard the click as the spring released the catch at the back. It was basic mechanics but really quite clever for its time. You'd never be able to trigger the release mechanism by accident, in the unlikely event you discovered the scullery in the first place. Once the catch was released Marina pulled the block towards her, the wall opening up, revealing the vestibule behind.

It was an ingenious space. Sylvester had only known about it because the knowledge had been passed down through generations. There was a way to close the entrance once you were on the other side of it and as long as the drawer in the kitchen remained closed it could be released with a hidden catch. At first she had panicked that the drawer would somehow open and she and Sylvester would be trapped inside but Sylvester had laughed at her. Trailing his finger across her cheek.

'There's no one here but us to open it, my dear. Unless you believe in ghosts?'

Marina forced a smile. Feeling foolish. Too young. Too unsure to voice her opinion and say that yes, since she had moved into this house she did believe in ghosts. She thought she heard them sometimes whispering to her in her sleep.

Run.

Run.

Run.

Footsteps behind her yanked her from her thoughts.

'Cass?' Marina felt hot and cold, fear and shame as her daughter ran towards her. What if Cass had followed her into the hidden room? Seen her father like... that?

She hurriedly swung the panel closed, pushed the drawer back inside the block.

'Hide and seek!' Cass clapped with delight.

'No, darling.' Marina hoisted Cass onto her hip. 'This isn't like the priest holes.' The house had two and Cass hid in them constantly. It was common for houses from this era to have several hidden rooms. Obvious ones the priest hunters could find, sliding back a fake wall, a bookcase, then the real ones, virtually impossible to uncover no matter how hard you searched.

'You must never come in here on your own, understand?' There was a harshness to her voice, a warning. Even though she thought Cass was too young to be able to copy what she'd seen, she was still horrified. Cass shrank in her arms and she wanted to tell her daughter that she hadn't done anything wrong but she couldn't.

'Want a story.' Cassandra stuck her thumb into her mouth.

'Mummy's busy but I bet Tamsin has time.' Marina hurriedly carried her over the other side of the house to Tamsin's bedroom.

'Tamsin—'

'I told you to bloody knock before barging in here.'

Cassandra wriggled to the floor and ran to her sister while Marina took a step back, pushed by Tamsin's anger, burned by the glare that came from under her stepdaughter's lowered lashes, lashes that Tamsin had begun coating with mascara lately. Her downturned lips often slick with gloss. Liberally spraying her neck and wrists with a lemon perfume that Marina secretly thought smelled like toilet cleaner.

Marina suspected there was perhaps a boy on the scene, knew he'd be unsuitable, but she hadn't broached this with Sylvester. He'd forbid Tamsin from leaving the house for a walk around the grounds in between her home-schooling lessons if he thought that she was sneaking off to the village. Let her have some fun.

He wasn't the one who had to put up with Tamsin's endless, awkward questions. Why couldn't she go to school? Why was she kept a prisoner?

Marina had shaken her head at this. She knew all about prisons, being trapped. This was not the same.

'We just want to protect you. You and Cassandra. There are bad people out there,' Marina would always say, not telling Tamsin that her father was one of them but she felt that somehow she suspected anyway.

'Sorry,' Marina says now, because she was always apologizing to somebody for something. 'I should have knocked but I…' She hesitated, knowing that if he were there, Sylvester would scoff at her inadequacies.

'No wonder Tamsin doesn't respect you,' he often said. 'She needs a mother, not a friend.'

But Marina was neither.

Tamsin was angry and confused that her beloved mum had left. Angry and confused that Marina had moved in a year later.

She was *still* angry and confused.

Marina had tried, she had, but she was only a few years older than Tamsin and didn't know how to handle her, how to comfort her.

But she did love her.

Then she found she was going to have a baby of her own. Her pregnancy had been a shock but Sylvester was delighted, longing for an heir. A boy. He had no family of his own, he had inherited Newington Hall, and there was an age-old tradition that only a male could inherit it after they had passed. As it stood, Marina's brother, Adrian, was the sole benefactor with

259

the proviso he provided for Tamsin should anything happen to her and Sylvester – Leon, although older, couldn't be trusted – but that could change if they had a boy.

A son!

It wasn't to be, though. Cassandra had made her noisy appearance into the world all doe-eyed and pink-cheeked and Sylvester had swallowed his disappointment and fallen in love with her. They both had. Cass was placed in her arms, face wrinkled and red, mouth roaring her displeasure. Marina was filled with a love like no other. A deep knowing that she wanted to protect her child, nurture her, and she had. Delighting in each stage. Spooning baby porridge into a gaping mouth, finger painting in bright blue and red and yellow, walking, talking. The feel of Cass in her arms, the smell of her. She was everything.

Tamsin became a doting big sister. She played the little mother, bathing the baby, dressing her, pushing her around the grounds in her pram. Later, playing hide-and-seek, Simon says. Rearranging the furniture before draping old sheets over it to build a tent.

Now she was growing up. Developing interests outside of this family.

Boys.

They were the beginning and the end of everything, weren't they? When she had first met Sylvester she'd been innocent, inexperienced. He had forced her into the unspeakable, the unimaginable.

'So?' Tamsin asked now, her confrontational tone at odds with the way she gently began plaiting Cassandra's hair.

Marina had a thought. If Tamsin and Cass could stay upstairs then Sylvester needn't know that Penelope had let them down. Then perhaps Gerald wouldn't find out either. Neither of the women would be in trouble.

'It's Dad's birthday—'

'I know. When's Penelope coming?'

'That's the thing, she isn't well.'

'Good.'

'Good?'

'I don't need a babysitter. I'm not a child.'

'I know. It's just that I have a… a surprise for Dad.'

'A surprise?'

Tamsin's eyes penetrated deep into Marina's dirty, tainted soul and Marina felt something dark and heavy flood through her.

She tried to maintain eye contact with her stepdaughter, but she couldn't. Did Tamsin know? She couldn't. They had been so, so, careful.

Marina gazed out of the window, over the grounds, wondering what life might have been like if she'd never become Mrs Madley. Didn't live in Newington Hall. What life might be like in the future.

'Can you watch Cassandra please; can you both stay upstairs while I give it to him?'

'"It"?'

'Tamsin…' Marina began but she didn't follow it up. What could she say? She lowered her eyes, spotting, carved into the wood beneath the window sill, a word. Just three letters that chilled her, pulled her.

Unbidden, she crossed to it and ran her thumb over the small word with the huge connotation.

A command.

A desire.

Run.

Her eyes met Tamsin's.

Had she carved it, wishing she could escape what she called a prison, go and find her mother?

'Where do you think Mum is? I still don't believe she would have chosen to leave me,' Tamsin whispered.

Marina looked at the carving again.

Had Jane written it, dreaming of one day being free?

Or perhaps it was a message for her.

Jane wasn't a good wife. A loyal wife.

Marina had to get out while she could.

Run.

Chapter Thirty-Seven

James

*R*un.

James checks for messages from Cass again as he jogs across the airport.

There aren't any.

Panic rises and he tells himself he's overreacting. He's unnerved because his entire childhood has been built on a lie. Unsettled because he is an ocean away from his partner and unborn child and from here he cannot protect them.

He calls once more. Exhaustion is a heavy weight on his shoulders, as well as guilt. He shouldn't have come. He'd put his career before his family.

She doesn't pick up.

Something is wrong, he knows it.

He sits on a hard metal bench, his head in his hands. Should he book a flight back to the UK? What would his boss say if he's flown all this way and doesn't take the meetings? How can he explain he'd left because of a 'feeling'?

He tries to calm himself. Eyes scanning the airport for familiar sights that can ground him.

A luggage trolley with squeaky wheels.

A battered green suitcase.

He slows his breathing, inhaling deeply, pausing before exhaling. Counting his breaths.

One.

Two.

Three.

He's being ridiculous. Even if he *is* the missing Madley child it doesn't mean he witnessed anything, doesn't mean whoever killed his family will come back, does it?

He's understandably anxious because his world has been tipped on its axis.

To set his mind at rest, he tries to call Fran and Robin. When neither of them answer he fires off texts to them both.

In Paris. Cass is alone & not answering calls. I'm worried about her. Pls check & let me know all ok.

He slips his phone back into his pocket but still he can't relax. Moving across the airport with urgency.

Run.

Chapter Thirty-Eight

Marina

*R*un.

Marina's pace was fast, urgent as she rushed from Tamsin's room.

Run.

She broke into a jog but could still feel her shame snapping at her heels.

Cass had almost discovered the room today. Her darling baby who was curious and growing.

Tamsin sad and confused.

I still don't believe she would have chosen to leave me.

Sylvester, terrifying.

Jane wasn't a good wife. A loyal wife.

Oh god. What was she going to do?

She fiddled with the silver swan pendant she always wore around her neck, chosen partly because of her love of wildlife, birds, but partly because that's how she felt. Serene on the surface, paddling furiously to get away underneath.

Her mind turned to Penelope, petrified of Gerald's reaction if he found out she had let Sylvester down.

She thought of Zeta who had come for a job earlier. Her

financial stress dragging down the skin on her face, her mouth, the fine lines that spidered from her eyes and yet, despite her desperation, she had such a glow of happiness as she'd gazed at her son.

There were more important things than money and a big house.

Love.

There was love.

But then Marina wasn't here for the money or the big house. She was here because she had no choice. Because Sylvester had proof that—

The doorbell chimed.

She hesitated. Knowing if she didn't answer it then it would likely ring again and she didn't want Tamsin coming downstairs.

She opened the door.

As though she had conjured her with her thoughts it was Zeta, this time without James, her little boy.

'Can I help you?' Marina was guarded. Her earlier warmth gone. Why had she come back?

'I hope so. My son, James, he lost his toy dinosaur, Trip. You know how attached kids get to their favourite toys.'

'I'll keep an eye out for it.' She began to close the door but Zeta stretched out her hand, her fingertips resting lightly on the wood. 'Look. I thought we got on well today?' Marina didn't fill the pause. 'You invited me for coffee and we had a lot in common. And... I know that being a mum comes first, you know that being a mum comes first, but I can promise you if you give me a chance I won't let you down.'

'I am sorry, Zeta.' Marina noticed the desperation in her eyes, she felt it herself right now.

'If I can just come in.'

Marina hesitated. She liked Zeta. She didn't want to expose her to Sylvester. He was not a nice man. But there was a flicker of possibility.

She pushed it away.

No.

She leaned heavily on the door, fearing that she would fall without it.

Her thoughts wrestling with each other.

No.

Her throat swelled and tears burned behind her eyes. She could not. Would not.

And yet Sylvester had said, 'If you make today *extra special* for me then perhaps that can be it.'

No.

She was nauseous at just the thought, saliva pooled in her mouth. She swallowed it down.

They could get through this quicker with an extra pair of hands. She was painfully aware that her children were in the house.

Her eyes met Zeta's. She could feel the despair in them.

'Please... I need help,' Marina said desperately.

'Perfect. I can help.' Zeta pushed her way in quickly as though worried Marina might change her mind. 'I can begin right now. Cooking, cleaning, anything.'

Marina tried to tell her that wasn't the sort of help she needed.

'I'm in no rush to get back. My husband doesn't even know I'm begging for work, because that's what I'm doing. Begging.'

'Where does he think you are?'

'He's at work so he'll assume I'm at home.'

'But your children know you're here?'

Zeta hesitated. 'No. I told them I was just popping out. Nobody will think you're taking advantage of me if that's what you're worried about. Look, my car wouldn't start and I had to walk all the way here and...' She kept her voice low but Marina could detect the crack in it. The crack in her. This woman was broken like a spider with seven legs, a moth with one wing.

'I don't know.' Marina swayed, faint. Leaned against the grandfather clock.

If you make today extra special for me then perhaps that can be it.

Had Sylvester meant that? She didn't trust him but if there was even a smidgen of a chance that this really could be the last time, then didn't she have to grasp that chance and take it? For the sake of the girls? For one, brief, glorious moment, she imagined herself strolling out of the front door with her belongings. Cass on her hip, Tamsin by her side. Sylvester waving them off.

It was stupid and fanciful but she wanted it more than anything she had ever wanted in her entire life.

'Quietly then.' She couldn't look Zeta in the eye. 'Cassandra is having a nap.' But even as she said it she wanted to yank open the door, tell Zeta to get as far away from the house as possible.

Run.

Zeta's face lit up with an expression of gratitude and Marina dropped her eyes to the floor, unable to bear it because she knew.

She knew what was to come.

Chapter Thirty-Nine

Cass

NOW

What will become of me if I run? I want to leave Newington. Flee from the house I'd moved into knowing there had been a tragedy but having no idea that it was *my* tragedy.

That I am a Madley.

I also want to stay here to be closer to my sister, Tamsin, my parents, even though I cannot remember them.

Really, I have no idea what I want. My phone is switched off but its weight in my pocket reminds me it is there, that Dad will be bombarding me with messages, but I don't want to speak to anyone while I try and process the way I feel.

But I don't feel anything.

I want to cry but tears won't come. I want to rage, the way the storm is raging outside. To scream at the unfairness of it all.

I have felt unsettled my entire life.

What did I see that night?

Something terrified me enough to drive me into the priest hole, to make me stay there for hours, long after the police had arrived and had searched for me.

Why can't I remember?

Since I fell pregnant I've researched when children first form memories they can retain, wondering when Isobel will remember the love we will shower on her, the fun we will have. Although the subject is complex, and dependent on various factors, in the most recent research experts believe that children can recall events that happen from around the age of two and a half. I had been three the night of the murders.

Why can't I remember?

It isn't like a birthday gift, or a visit to Santa. My entire family were killed. What did I see? What did I endure?

My scar throbs and I trace my fingers lightly over it. Dad told me it was a result of that night but he couldn't tell me exactly how I'd been hurt.

Had someone tried to kill me too?

I was only a child, is that what saved me? But so was Tamsin. My sweet, sweet, sister who I can't recall and yet somehow can. The feel of fingers lightly brushing my hair. A whispered story as we rock-rock-rocked on the chair in her room.

Are these memories or wishful thinking?

I just don't know.

It's all too much. I can feel my mind fracturing. Shattering into tiny pieces. On each fragment, an emotion, too many to bear. Sadness for my family, gratitude I am alive, guilt that I survived, fear that there is something irreparable inside me. Something that broke that night that can never be fixed.

There's a banging, banging, banging inside my head.

Why can't I remember?

I am slipping away from myself. It is a strange and confusing feeling. I've dissociated from myself. From my body.

I find myself in front of the mirror. Stare at the pale face reflected back at me. The same eyes. The same hair. The same bone structure.

Me, and yet not.

'I am Cassandra Madley,' I whisper and there is a sudden, violent sound of breaking glass.

Chapter Forty

Marina

The sound of Marina's heart breaking was violent and loud and she was surprised that Zeta could not hear it.

'You're okay with kitchen work?' Marina led Zeta through the house, hating herself.

'Yes. I sometimes feel like a scullery maid at home.'

Marina took Zeta's words and tried to hold them tightly against her chest as proof that this woman's life was miserable but she wasn't convinced.

She couldn't do this.

'Actually, I don't think—'

'Please.' Zeta grabbed her arm. 'I need this. I feel… So worthless. So useless. I need to contribute because sometimes I… I feel that my children, my family, are better off without me.'

Was this confirmation?

On autopilot, Marina retrieved a black dress, tights and white apron from the dresser, closing the door on the row of identical uniforms that would, from this day forward, if she got her way, remain unworn.

If you make today extra special for me then perhaps that can be it.

272

She waited outside the room, her stomach churning, legs shaking, while Zeta got changed.

'Ready,' Zeta called. When Marina stepped back inside she was tugging down the hem of the dress, her cheeks flushed pink.

'It's a bit tight, short.'

Marina didn't speak, because if she did she feared she would say the word she could not say.

Run.

She led Zeta over to the far wall where she pressed a button, glancing at Zeta as the wooden panel slid back, revealing the hidden room beyond.

'What on earth?' Zeta looked in wonder.

'It's a scullery.' Marina explained the original purpose. 'There's a butler's pantry too which is where we're heading. Somewhere all the silverware is stored.'

'It's like a kitchen within a kitchen.' Zeta spun a slow 360. 'What an amazing idea. Somewhere to stash all the mess.'

Marina approached the butcher's block. Her palms slick with sweat. Once she pushed against the drawer that would be it. No turning back. Zeta would have seen the room, seen too much.

She took a long, slow breath.

Sylvester would be waiting, furious at the delay.

Zeta would make him happy.

Then they could stop.

But however she tried to rationalize it, she couldn't. Zeta was not like the others. She had a family.

She couldn't do this.

'I don't know what I'd have done without you,' Zeta garbled as though sensing Marina's hesitation, her second thoughts. 'Life's been so... difficult. I've been very...'

Unhappy.

Marina could anonymously send Zeta's family money when this was all over.

She told herself this to make herself feel better.

She told herself lies. Veering between believing Sylvester could stop, to knowing full well that he wouldn't. But she wanted so very much to believe and that little bit of hope was all she had so she held it tightly within her grasp as she forced the drawer in, pushed it to the right, shoved it forward again, swung the panel out. Heard the breath hitch in Zeta's throat as the tunnel beyond was revealed.

'That's so cool. A little... creepy though.'

'It's fine. Follow me.'

'But where... What exactly is it I'll be doing?' Doubt had crept into Zeta's voice.

Marina swallowed hard, the words she'd used before dry on her tongue. What was it about this woman? She felt something she had never felt before. The possibility of a friend. She conjured an image of Cass.

She *had* to come first.

If there was any other way she would not be doing this.

'You'll be fetching the china and silverware. We store it somewhere secure. Old houses are often targets for burglars. Then you'll lay the table in the dining room and when the chef arrives you can help with the prep and then serve. Is that okay?' She tripped out the words she'd used before, almost wanting Zeta to say no, but instead she took a step forward and peered into the tunnel, but she didn't go any further, crossing her arms over her chest, her thin shirt no protection against the coldness of the stone walls.

'Is £250 for the night okay?' Marina asked.

Zeta turned to her, eyes wide. 'Two hundred and fifty pounds?'

'Five hundred?'

'I...' Zeta covered her heart with both hands in gratitude. 'I was happy with £250. Really. It'll make an enormous difference.'

Marina lowered her eyes, conflicted. She was straddling the invisible line between the pantry and the tunnel. Between the person she wanted to be and the person she had become.

Run.

'Are you all right?' Zeta touched her arm and a lump formed in Marina's throat.

One. Last. Time.

'Let's go.' Marina let Zeta lead the way, unaware that Marina was the dog and she was the sheep. She would not be allowed to change direction, change her mind.

Marina closed the entrance behind her. The latch clicked. The light sucked from the space. A dull light ahead beckoned them forward.

'This tunnel was apparently made when the priest holes that I showed you earlier on the tour were fashioned.' Marina distracted Zeta, gently pushing between her shoulder blades so she began to walk on. 'So if persecutors found the first priest hole and believed it was empty, they would leave the family alone, not knowing about the second. But more and more houses had priest holes and they became easier to find and it became known there'd always be a second so some properties had a third.'

'And if they found the priest he would be killed?'

'Not just the priest but the family who had hidden him as

well. It was a great risk. Using this space instead minimized the chances of being caught.'

'The family must have been very scared. Very brave.'

Marina nodded, thinking of the imposing portraits that lined the hallway like soldiers, cold eyes and stiff smiles. When she had first moved in she hadn't felt good enough for the family but now she wondered what they would think if they knew what Sylvester had become. All along it had been he who wasn't good enough for her.

Run.

They walked stooped through the narrow tunnel, the change of temperature startling, but Marina barely noticed the cold anymore, her blood was adrenaline hot.

Marina and Zeta had reached the end.

Really, they could turn back now before Sylvester saw them but in her heart Marina knew that she had passed the point of no return many years back. When Sylvester had brought her here as his seventeen-year-old bride. She had compared herself to Cinderella, whisked away to an entirely new life by her prince.

But her life wasn't a fairy tale and she was still waiting for her happy ending. The difference was now it seemed within her grasp.

One last time.

Perhaps she could repair her relationship with Adrian. Her beloved brother had refused to come to the wedding and she hadn't seen him since. She'd sent a picture of Cassandra when she'd been born, photos since, hoping that a niece would change his mind, that he'd come to visit, but he never did. Her other brother, Leon, she didn't care about. He'd always been a bad penny, the black sheep, but Adrian was different.

Kind.

Good.

Things that Marina used to be, things that she wanted to be again.

The ceiling sloped upwards, giving them space to straighten up. 'You'll be working with Dorothea tonight. The homeless woman you met earlier who led you here today,' Marina told Zeta.

'Great. Hey, this is really cool. I feel like I'm on a film set.' Zeta stopped and raised her face to the battery-powered torches hanging from wrought-iron brackets on the walls. They mimicked flickering flames, casting an orangey glow across her face.

Marina didn't answer. Didn't tell her that she wasn't on a film set yet, but she would be very, very soon.

The tunnel expanded and suddenly they were through a door and inside a small room.

'This is my husband, Sylvester.'

It was difficult to see Sylvester's expression from under his mask but Marina could read his body language. Knew he was angry with the interruption, the unexpected visitor. He didn't like surprises. He stalked over to the record player and lifted the needle off the record.

'I... I don't understand. What is this?' Zeta asked in a panicked voice, backing away, but Marina was blocking the door. Even if she got out and reached the end of the tunnel she would never find the catch to open the exit.

Marina felt sick as she watched Zeta's jaw hanging open as she took in the camera. The equipment. Dorothea suspended from the ceiling by chains. Her terrified eyes met Zeta's. Her muffled cries frantic as she jerked her body, trying to free herself. Blood dripped from the slashes on her arms onto the flagstone floor.

'Are you... Is she okay?' Zeta turned to Marina, 'What the fuck is going on?' then glanced to Sylvester. 'This is fake, right?'

'This' – Sylvester approached Zeta, knife in his hand – 'is about as real as you get.'

'What the fuck?' Zeta covered her mouth with her hands. 'What are you doing?'

'It's called a snuff movie, my dear,' Sylvester said. 'And it looks like you'll be the star of the show.'

Chapter Forty-One

Marina

'The star of the…. Marina?' Zeta turned to her.

Marina slipped on her mask, hiding her face, her feelings. Transformed herself into someone else. Someone numb. The masks had been her idea. After that first time, that godawful first time where Marina had cried and vomited and begged Sylvester to let the poor woman free, she couldn't bear to see her face in the mirror afterwards. Her shame. She had been in a state of shock throughout. Thought that because Sylvester had arranged for Penelope to collect Tamsin they'd be having a romantic meal.

It had all been so traumatic.

There were so many things that she could have done, should have done, after Sylvester had struck her again and again as she'd tried to make him stop, so in the end she had stood mutely and watched her husband, the monster she had married, hurt that woman. A part of her was relieved that if he was hurting someone else then he wasn't hurting her because she knew then what he was capable of.

Everything.

Afterwards, Sylvester had told Marina that she too was on

camera, complicit. Did she really want to leave? Risk going to jail if she reported him? Wasn't he good to her?

'This is a small part of my life,' he had told her. 'It satisfies some... some need in me and it... it's a job. Not a conventional one but I make good money selling these films. Gerald, from the Gentlemen's Club takes the original footage away, copies them and distributes them to a select few for a hefty price tag. Sometimes I make a film specifically for one person, tailored to what they want to see. When you have that much money you can buy anything.'

'But I'm on that ... my face.' Marina had touched her cheeks.

'And I won't let anything happen to you, my darling.' He had stroked her hair the way you would a frightened pet but she was beyond frightened. Terrified. Shaking so hard her teeth rattled in her head.

Later that night she had called Adrian. Although her brother had been absent from her life for the past few years, she needed him now.

'Please...' was all she could say when he picked up. Her tears trapping the words she wanted to say in her throat.

'You've made your bed, now lie in it,' he said gently before hanging up on her.

Although she had nowhere to go she had thrown her things into the small, battered suitcase she had arrived here with nine months ago.

'Where are you going?' Sylvester had wandered into the bedroom, an amused look on his face.

'I... I'm sorry...' Ridiculously, she was the one apologizing.

'I can't let you leave, Marina,' he said, gently taking out a blouse she had balled into the case and smoothing out the creases before hanging it back up.

'I won't tell anyone—'

'But you will. So you can't leave me,' he said matter-of-factly. 'And you can't kill me because the tape with your face on it is somewhere safe and if anything happens to me then it'll be sent to the police.'

I don't care. Marina thought being in a cell was better than being married and perhaps no more than she deserved. Could she have stopped him, fought harder? Her fingers fluttered to her bruised cheek.

'You may think you don't care about going to jail but there isn't just you to think about.' Sylvester covered her stomach with his hand.

Marina batted it away, repulsed, confused.

'You're pregnant, my dear. Didn't you know?'

Marina shook her head. The thought had never occurred to her even though she hadn't had much of an appetite, had been feeling sick, but she had put those things down to adjusting to her new life. How could this have happened? She had been taking the contraceptive pill although she'd noticed they'd changed in size, shape. Sylvester, who picked up her prescriptions, had told her it was a different brand as he popped them out of their foil cocoon into a days-of-the-week tablet holder, as though she might forget to take one.

When had she last had a period? Couldn't stress affect the menstrual style? But even as she asked herself this she knew, she could suddenly sense it, the life within, and so she covered her belly with her palms and vowed to protect it.

'If you go to prison they will take your baby away. Put it into care. You'll never see it.'

Could she give up her child? The thought tore her in two but she knew she would have to, if that's what it took to take Sylvester down with her. To stop him hurting anyone else.

'I wanted to share my…. hobby with you from the beginning.' Sylvester said. 'I didn't do that with Jane and unfortunately she didn't take it too well when she found out.'

'And…' Fear crawled up Marina's throat. 'That's why she left?' Her voice was small, full of doubt, of question.

'Left?' Sylvester smiled. 'Unpack your things, my dear. Think of the baby. There isn't anywhere you could go where I couldn't find you. You could ask Jane, except… well, she'd find it difficult to answer.'

Marina's knees buckled and she sat down heavily on the bed. *He had killed Jane.*

And if she didn't stay, keep quiet, she'd be next and although she felt in that moment she'd rather be dead than with him, than watch him ever make another of his films, he was right. It wasn't only her life she had to think about now.

There was the baby. If he killed her, her child died too.

And so she stayed, vowing to find a way to escape once the baby was safely born.

Sylvester tried to rationalize it.

'It's the women no one will miss. No homes. No families. A drain on society. Really, I'm doing the world a favour and it's not as though I'm a monster who needs to do this to feel happy. It's only a few times a year.'

And this didn't make it okay, nothing made it okay, but Sylvester didn't make another film the whole time she was pregnant. Marina had almost convinced herself it was nothing but a bad dream, but then when Cass was six months old, Sylvester's birthday rolled around and he told her he wanted a special treat. That he'd arranged with Gerald for Penelope to come and collect the children.

As he said this he had been holding a knife, carving a joint of beef. He leaned over Cass and stroked her cheek, the blade close to her tender neck.

That time she had slipped on a mask and tried to pretend she was dressing up the way she had as a child and that it was all make-believe.

But the screams, the screams were real.

And the blood…

Marina couldn't bear it. She had lunged for the knife, forgetting the consequences, determined to kill her husband. He had wrapped his thick fingers around her throat and breathed his cigar breath close to her face as he whispered, 'Your priority should be your child,' while he squeezed and squeezed until she had passed out. When she came to, on the stone-cold floor, the woman had gone. Marina had waited every day for a knock at the door, a report on the news, but Sylvester had been right. It was the women who wouldn't be missed.

It had happened a few times since. She hadn't tried to stop it, full of the diazepam her doctor had given her for her nerves, and she knew that was unforgivable. That she was a terrible person.

She felt this more than ever now as she waited for the shock to wear off and Zeta to react. This was a woman people would miss. That gorgeous little boy she had brought with her earlier, James. Her other daughter, Rose. And then it was overwhelming, the realization that all of the women probably had somebody who missed them even if they lived alone, on the streets. Isn't everybody loved by somebody at least once in their lives?

There was a beat.

Two.

And then Zeta sprang into action.

Chapter Forty-Two

Marina

Zeta sprang forward, trembling fingers running over the chains, searching for a way to free Dorothea who was quietly moaning now. Shock had set in, her pain immense.

'Who is this woman?' asked Sylvester, amused.

'Zeta. She came for an interview earlier.'

'And you thought you'd give her to me as a gift.' Sylvester patted Marina on the head as though she were a pet and she realized that was exactly what she was to him. An animal he had owned from a young age, trained.

What had she done?

She should never have brought Zeta here.

Panic clawed at her. What should she do? Sylvester wouldn't let Zeta leave, she had seen too much and so Marina did what she did best.

Nothing.

She felt her mask for reassurance. Straightened her spine. Felt her mind begin to drift away from her body, or was it her soul? If Marina still had a soul it would be black. Damaged.

'I'll come back for you,' Zeta said to Dorothea before she sprinted towards the tunnel, hands fumbling to slide back the door.

'How do I get out? Let me out!' Her voice rose in pitch.

'But then you'd miss all the fun,' Sylvester said.

'*Fun?* Fun for who?' Zeta held her hands out in front of her as though that might be enough to keep her safe.

Nothing would keep her safe.

'Fun for us. Fun for those who watch.'

'But snuff movies aren't real.' Zeta shook her head. 'They're just, they're not real.'

'But they are, my dear.'

'But... But that means...'

'She dies. You die.'

'You sick—'

'I'm not the sick one. We're the suppliers and we can only supply because there is a demand. People who are willing to pay—'

'But you have *children*. What are they going to do when you're in prison because you can't get away with this?'

'I've got away with this for many years, my dear. The room is undetectable. Soundproofed. I pick up hitchhikers. The waifs and strays. Young. Stupid. Nobody knows who they are, where they are. Nobody misses them.'

'Marina? You can't... surely... You know this is wrong. You can stop this. Please stop this.'

Marina didn't answer because in this room she was never Marina.

Zeta put up a decent fight. Sylvester restrained her, bound her to a chair, tied a gag tightly around her mouth, not because anyone could hear her from outside, but because he didn't want her ruining the audio for Dorothea's movie.

He clapped his hands with glee. 'Right. Back to it,' he said brightly and in that moment Marina wanted to kill him but even if she did, that wouldn't bring back the women he had already hurt, wouldn't stop her going to jail once she had let Zeta and Dorothea go. She had been a fool to think that providing an extra woman would satisfy his appetite, make him content to stop, go out on a high.

As she watched the lightness in his step she was sickened, knowing that she had fuelled his hunger. That he would never stop.

He restarted the record, Flanagan and Allen's 'Run, Rabbit, Run'. It was their signature tune on their films and then he turned his attention back to Dorothea.

Ten minutes later he held up his hand. Removed Zeta's gag. She began to garble, terrified, as she should be.

'Please. My family will be worried about me. Looking for me.'

'You said that you didn't tell them you were coming here.'

'I lied. I did. My daughter, Rose, she knows.'

'Does she?' Sylvester tries to force amusement into his voice but Marina knew him too well. He was worried. 'Perhaps I should pay a visit to, *Rose*, is it?'

'No. No, please. She doesn't know anything, she—'

'You need to make your mind up. Either somebody knows where you are or they don't.' Sylvester curled his hand and ran the back of his fingers gently over Zeta's cheek.

Marina noticed her swallow, hard. Observed how slender her throat was. How fragile.

'They… they don't know,' Zeta whispered, tears rolling off her chin. 'But. Please,' she turned her pleading gaze on Marina, 'you're a mother. How would you feel if Cassandra was left without a mum—'

Behind her mask, Marina began to weep.

Flanagan and Allen began to sing again.

Run.

Run.

Run.

Half an hour later and Zeta was no longer screaming. No longer crying. Begging. She was mute. Slumped on a chair. No fight left in her.

The only sound was the song replaying again and again until Dorothea finally, probably thankfully, drew her last, juddering breath.

But then, to Marina's horror, small hands tugged at her skirt, Cassandra saying in a small, scared voice, 'Mummy?'

'Cassandra?' Marina felt her heart actually skip a beat as she pulled her daughter into her, shielding her eyes. Why hadn't Tamsin kept her upstairs as she'd promised? Through her panic and her fear there was a smidgeon of pride that Cassandra had remembered how to slide back the false wall, operate the butcher's block. She knew her daughter was clever, destined for great things if she could only get her away from Newington.

'There's a storm and I'm scared.' Cassandra patted Marina's thigh to get her attention.

'Why isn't Cassandra with Penelope?' Sylvester's words a growl.

'She wasn't well and I—'

Cassie swung her head around at the sound of her father's voice. 'Mummy, why is that lady bleeding?'

It took an effort for Zeta to raise her head. Stretch out her hand. 'Cass. Help me. Please. You have to—'

'Marina, get Cassandra out of here.' Sylvester cut Zeta off, sweeping Cass up and handing her to Marina who settled her daughter on her hip.

287

Those few seconds while their attention was on Cassandra was all it took. Suddenly there was a weight pushing past her.

'Zeta!'

Marina put Cassandra down and pelted after Zeta, confident of catching her. The house was like a maze and Zeta was hurt, bleeding. But terror propelled her forward, faster and faster, Marina trailing behind.

'Zeta. Stop. Let's talk,' Marina called but there was nothing she wanted to say. She was filled with a deep shame that Cassandra – her baby – had witnessed *that*.

Her only hope was that she was too young to remember. That Cassandra could pass it off as a bad dream.

Zeta rattled at the front door but it was locked. She carried on into the great hall, up the stairs.

Marina lost sight of her but then she heard it.

The squeak of the window opening on the landing.

Felt the sudden gust of cold breeze.

Marina rounded the corner. Zeta had one leg over the window sill.

'Don't.' In that moment Marina felt more than she could have imagined. Fear that Zeta would escape and tell everyone what they had done, who they were. Shock that Zeta would risk death rather than stay in this house for one second longer. Shame that she had driven this woman, this mother, to the brink.

Before this, the chosen women were young. Homeless. No ties. No family, not that Marina chose to think about anyway, but Zeta was different. Perhaps it was because she had met James. Laughed at his cheeky grin as he had bowed in front of Cassandra, kissing her hand, 'My lady.'

Their eyes met. Zeta's filled with desperation. Marina's full of apology and regret.

'How many? How many women have there been?' Zeta asked quietly.

Marina swallowed hard. Dorothea was the fifth that she had seen but she knew that Jane had been one of them and god knew how many more over the years.

'Too many,' she whispered.

Zeta swung her other leg over the frame. 'I won't tell anyone. I don't want my children hurt. And... I... I don't want anyone to see me like... *that*.' Her voice was small, broken. She was small and broken. 'Will you destroy the tape before he makes any copies or is it too late?'

Zeta looked at Marina as though she was a monster but she wasn't, was she? She hadn't always been anyway. She didn't want to be anymore.

'The tape won't reach Gerald today.' Usually she sent the original with Penelope when she dropped the children off. 'There's only one copy.'

'You'll destroy it?'

Marina gave a simple nod and something deep and wordless passed between the two women. An unspoken agreement, an understanding. Marina wouldn't share the video. Wouldn't make any more whatever the consequences.

A muffled cry.

A smacking sound.

Then, there was a space where Zeta had been. Marina hurried over to the window, watched as Zeta struggled to her feet. Limped towards the trees.

Run.

Run.

Run.

Marina was going to make sure that Sylvester could never hurt anyone else.

She had a plan.

She was glad Zeta was free.

Chapter Forty-Three

Cass

Am I free?

For a split second I had thought the sound of shattering glass was the mirror. That somehow, me speaking my birth name had caused the glass to fracture. Releasing me from myself. From my past.

But then, 'Cass?'

It's Fran.

I have a ridiculous urge to run and hide. To climb inside the priest hole with my eyes screwed shut and my hands over my ears. Because, more than anything, I want to feel safe. Instead, I am draped with a heaviness, a foreboding as I slowly walk down the stairs, wondering what Fran will see when she looks at me. Who she will see.

I am Cassandra Madley.

But I do not want to be her.

I want to be carefree Cass. Already I am looking through rose-coloured spectacles at the girl I thought I was because I have never been carefree. The difference in me is that now I know why.

I am the carrier of secrets. The witness to something so

unthinkable, so unimaginable that my mind has kept it hidden from me.

'Cass?' Fran sounds frantic.

'Coming.' I cover my mouth as soon as I speak, surprised that I still have the ability to talk. Surprised that my voice sounds the same.

'There you are. Are you okay? You look' – *like someone else* – 'upset?'

'I'm fine.'

'James is worried. He's been trying to reach you. He messaged me from Paris. I rang him straight away and told him I'd come and check on you.' She leads me into the drawing room.

There is blood on the rug, crimson and dark.

When I blink and look again it's gone. Am I remembering what I saw that night?

I moan. 'I can't be in here.'

Fran leads me to the kitchen, settles me on a chair. The rain batters the windowpanes. Thunder rumbles low.

'Cass? What's going on? I was knocking on the door for ages and you didn't answer. I haven't got my key so I had to break a window to get in.'

'I'm…' I flounder for the right words. Any words. I cannot speak.

'I'm going to fetch you a drink.' Fran hurries to the sink and by the time she comes back, glass in hand, I am a little more together. I sip at the water.

'Thank you.'

'What's happened? Are you sick?'

I shake my head.

'What then? Has something here frightened you?'

The past.

'Cass,' she continues, 'you look really freaked out and, if I'm honest, there's something about this house that gives me the creeps. You can tell me. Really. Anything. No matter how silly you think it sounds.' She is on her haunches before me, hand on my knee, and I so desperately want to tell her everything but I can't. I can't because I know the look of sympathy in her eyes will increase tenfold. I do not want to be the girl that everyone pities.

I do not want to be Cassandra Madley.

But I am and for the first time I think about all the implications that might bring. What if I witnessed something I shouldn't?

It wasn't indicative of a robbery.

Tell me where it is.

What if I know something? What if there really has been somebody watching the house? Watching me?

'Can you stay with me?' I feel small and scared and I do not want to be alone.

'Of course.'

'Are you sure? If you need to work I can ask Robin?'

'Robin?'

'Robin Fletcher. I met him on the train a few weeks ago. He grew up here.'

'I know that name,' Fran says, frowning.

'His dad was the leading officer in the Madley murder investigation. Apparently, he never got over it. Never stopped thinking about it.'

'That must be tough for Robin, his dad being so obsessed with the Madleys.'

I think of the way Robin is whenever he comes, his eagerness

293

to explore every inch of the property. What if he doesn't visit because he wants to see me?

Tell me where it is.

It's hard to comprehend, but what if he's looking for some-thing?

Chapter Forty-Four

Rose

THEN

Rose couldn't comprehend what she was seeing at all. This half-broken woman in front of her dressed in a black dress that she didn't recognize was her mother. Hair dishevelled. Carefully applied make-up streaked across her face. She was limping.

'Mum?' Rose rushed to help her, slowing as she noticed the way Mum flinched from her touch. 'Are you okay?' she asked tentatively, knowing in that moment that her mum was many things, but okay wasn't one of them. She was in shock, that much was apparent. She looked like one of those people you saw on the news sometimes who had witnessed something so terrible that the trauma had sucked all of the emotion, all of the tears, out of them, leaving behind an empty shell.

Mum trudged into the kitchen, not glancing up the stairs or asking after James as she usually would.

'Roo is asleep. I read him two stories,' Rose said as though normal facts about normal life would somehow bring her mother back. She crouched down, rested her palms lightly on Mum's knees; again that flinch, feeling the tremble in them, hearing the rattle of her teeth in her skull as the tremble became a shake, her whole body sounding as though it were about to split into fragments.

'Mum. Please. You're scaring me.'

Mum raised her eyes, dark and haunted, and tried to speak but nothing came out of her mouth.

'I'll get you some water.' Rose hurried over to the cupboard and pulled out a glass but before she could reach the tap she changed her mind, instead unscrewing the lid from a bottle of brandy. She slugged some into the tumbler before she pushed it into Mum's hand, keeping her own fingers over her mother's so she didn't drop it. The liquid sloshed over the edge but despite the tremor Mum managed a small sip, and then a larger swallow and then the glass was empty. Rose refilled it.

'What's happened? Are you hurt? Do you need me to call anyone?'

Mum took a long, juddering breath before asking, 'Dad?'

'I can try and find him. I think—'

'No.' Her mother's voice suddenly loud. 'No. No. I don't want him to see me... I don't want *anyone* to see me. I'm so... I'm so...'

It was as though the release of her words was a release of all of her pent-up emotion because suddenly she was keening, a primal sound that Rose had never heard before. A sound that terrified her. All she could do was hold her mother, stooped uncomfortably, Mum's face against her chest, trying to calm her, quieten her, sure that at any moment her brother would wake.

It seemed to take for ever for Mum to become still and silent in Rose's arms, Rose stroking her hair the way you would a frightened animal.

Eventually, Rose let her go, crouching again while Mum

poured another drink. She knocked it back in one before her eyes began to focus on Rose.

'She's dead.'

Rose's heart flip-flopped in her chest.

'Who? Who's dead?'

'The homeless woman I met earlier.'

'Was there an accident? How do you know?'

'There wasn't an accident and I know because... because I helped kill her.'

Rose inhaled sharply. Automatically she knew that Mum, her sweet, gentle mum, was telling the truth. Rose slowly stood. Her body swaying as she staggered to the sink, swallowing back the horrible taste that had risen in her mouth, reaching for a second glass which she filled with brandy. Mum didn't tell her that she was too young to drink because there were far worse crimes. Apparently, her mother had committed one tonight.

Rose sank into a chair, raised the glass to her lips and felt the burn in her throat, her nose, her stomach as she gulped it down. She choked. Eyes streaming with tears that had not only been brought on by the sharp sting of alcohol but also by knowing that after tonight everything would change.

'Do you want to talk about it?' Rose asked, not wanting to hear but knowing that somebody had to listen to Mum, to help her, and in the absence of David she was all that there was.

Mum's hands were rotating her glass, eyes fixed on the brandy, watching intently as the amber liquid swirled around the glass, mini whirlpools. Perhaps she was wishing she could jump into it, be sucked away, disappear.

'Mum?'

'You can't...' Mum cleared her throat. 'You can't tell anyone.'

'I won't.'

'Promise me.'

Rose hesitated, already understanding that so many things had been broken tonight, her promise could not become another. Yet she also knew that whatever Mum was about to reveal was big. Bigger than her, this house, this family. What if the weight of it was too much to bear?

The air stilled around them. Mum's hand over her heart as she waited for an answer. Rose could feel her own heart in her chest, faster than usual, and she wondered if it was synchronized with her mother's. Their hearts had beaten together when she was in her mother's womb and once Rose had been born she knew that Mum felt her pain. That the umbilical cord may have been cut but the bond between them, invisible and strong, was indestructible. Indescribable. Her mother had always, would always be there for Rose and Rose would not let her down now.

'I promise.' Her voice clear and strong.

'On James's life?'

Momentarily Rose could feel the warmth of her brother's body, his pudgy arms around her neck, soft cheek against her face. 'I promise, on Roo's... on James's life that I will never tell anyone.' Her words were fierce, full of truth. Brimming with love. Whatever Mum had done Rose could, Rose would, forgive her. Rose drained her glass and steeled herself for the words she did not want to hear.

'I killed her,' is all Mum said again, softly, sadly.

'How?' Rose asked because the word was practical, detached. The only other question she could think of was 'why' and she was not yet ready for the complexities of that answer.

'I tortured her.'

Rose lurched towards the sink, vomit splattering the white washing up bowl. She had been wrong. The 'how' was not the easiest question. None of the answers tonight would be easy. A childish urge to pound up the stairs to her bedroom, to throw herself into her bed and tug the duvet over her head overwhelmed her. She could feel the twitch in her feet, the impulse to run away was so strong, but she looked at Mum, diminished somehow, smaller, and she knew that for her sake, for James, she had to unpick what had happened tonight. Figure out what they would do if – when – the police came as they surely would.

Her mother had killed someone.

It felt horribly real and yet not. Rose could see them both from high above as though she was watching a soap opera and they were the actors. Mum sobbing into her hands, Rose wiping her mouth on her sleeve as she straightened up. Perhaps it wasn't too late to change the script. Stop Mum going to prison.

She returned to her seat, elbows on the table, chin in hands and looked directly at her mother.

'Tell me *everything.*'

Mum's head snapped up as though the urgency in Rose's command had dragged her back to the present.

'Oh god, James. I'm going to go to jail. Rose, I'm so sorry. I'm so scared—'

'Tell me what happened,' Rose said sharply. 'We don't know how long we've got before…'

Before Dad comes.

Before the police come.

Before their lives are irrevocably ruined.

'At Newington House I pleaded with Marina Madley to reconsider. I told her that no one knew where I was, begging for work, but… She said she could offer me a few hours. That they were having guests for dinner and… she gave me a dress.'

Mum stared into her lap in horror as though she had only just remembered she was still wearing it, perhaps seeing in her mind what she did when she wore it.

'Mum?'

'She led me to a hidden room, and... oh god.' Mum shook her head. 'I can't talk about it.' Her voice hoarse with the memory.

'You *have* to.'

Mum nodded. Began to recount her story in monotone, without emotion, although Rose could tell from her glazed expression, from the way she constantly twisted her hands round and round, that she was feeling it all.

'I knew something wasn't right the moment I stepped inside. It was so cold. These dull red lights on the wall. Sylvester was there, the husband, in a mask and... and... Dorothea the homeless woman who had first told me about the job. She... she was draped in chains and suspended from the ceiling. Crying. Bleeding.'

'Fuck.' Rose linked her fingers together, fighting the desire to clamp her hands over her ears. She did not want to hear this.

'I tried to help her. I *tried*. They were... they were making a snuff film. The Madleys.'

'What's that?'

'It's a movie where women are sexually degraded and then murdered on screen.'

'What the actual... why?'

'Sylvester said it's a lucrative market. He knows lots of wealthy people who will pay to watch. Apparently there are a lot of fake ones around. You can tell a real one from the eyes, from the screams, he said.'

'Bastard.'

'He takes orders and...' Mum shrugged helplessly. 'Supply

and demand, he said. It isn't always sexual, apparently but… the death… that's the… that's the…'

'I can't believe there are people who pay…' Rose could not begin to comprehend. She knew about porn; although she hadn't seen any she was aware there were sick people who got off on children, animals, degradation and humiliation, but watching a life slip away? That… that was something else entirely. 'They've done this before?'

'Yes.'

'But… then there are women going missing. Where are their families? Their bodies?'

'Sylvester said that sometimes as many as 200,000 people are flagged as missing each year in the UK and they are only the ones who are reported. He finds people like Dorothea. Homeless, nobody to notice, nobody to care. I don't know what he does with them… after. But they've so much land I guess he buries them?'

'How many women?' Rose didn't know why this was important right now, but it was.

'I really don't know but I…' Rose leaned forward so she could properly hear her. 'I… I was nearly one of them.'

Rose scraped back her chair and rushed to her mother's side, sitting on her lap as she had when she was small, enveloping her in one giant hug in which their tears merged together, their arms entwined.

'I didn't want to…' Mum buried her face in Rose's hair as she spoke. 'I tried to save her but… they know where I live. They know about you. Had met James. They said if I didn't… if I didn't do what they asked then the next person they filmed would be you, Rose. I told them to do what they wanted to me, to leave you alone but they said… they said… all the time I was hurting her I kept apologizing over and over. I was crying. She was screaming. The Madleys kept playing the same song over and over. *Run. Run. Run.* And I remember thinking that if I could I would run. I would leave her there. Save myself. How awful is that? I always thought I was a good person. A kind person.'

'You are both of those things. Nobody knows what they would do, how they would act in a situation like that. If someone threatened you or James I would do whatever it took to save you.'

'What if whatever it took meant the death of someone? Her eyes.' Mum lets out a deep, distressing cry. 'I'll never forget the terror in them. Do you know what her last words were?'

'What?'

'She said… she said, "Do it. I can't take anymore." I said I couldn't. I wouldn't. She… she whispered, "If I were you I would do the same, for my babies."' Mum sobbed noisily. 'She was a mother.'

Rose held her tighter. 'She might have meant *if* she had children, not that she did.'

'Even if she didn't, I have killed someone, Rose,' Mum said quietly before she stiffened, winced, as though in pain.

'Are you hurt?' Rose climbed off her lap, knelt before her. 'Did they…'

'What am I going to do? I'm so… I'm a monster.'

'*You* are not the monster, Mum.'

'But the things I have done. If anyone ever saw… James. Your dad.'

'Nobody will ever see,' Rose said determinedly, as though the steel in her statement would make it so.

'But how? The police have to be told. The Madleys need to

be stopped. There was a moment before I escaped when Marina looked at me and I thought… I thought that she was sorry… but she'll do it again. She needs to be in jail. They both need to be in jail. Her poor children. They won't have any parents. That poor woman, Dorothea.' Hysteria takes over. 'What's going to happen to us? To me? It's selfish when somebody has died to think of myself but—'

'It is *not* selfish. You won't go to jail. You were *forced*.'

'Nobody can see the footage. He won't have copied it yet but if I report him the police will seize it. I can't let it be taken into evidence. Played in a court. I just can't.' Mum's face, already pale, takes on a strange hue. 'I'll know. Even if the Madleys end up in jail I'll know that the video will be out there somewhere. That one day James might stumble across it somehow. See it. Me. Doing… those unimaginable… unspeakable things. That will be what I become, in everyone's minds. What everyone will remember about me.'

'I won't let him see it. I won't let anyone see it.'

'Promise me, Rose.' Mum is clutching at her chest now, swaying in her seat. Sweat pearling on her brow, on her upper lip.

'Mum?'

'Promise me,' a whisper.

'I promise you, Mum, that the film with you on it will be destroyed. That the Madleys won't hurt anyone again.'

'Don't.' Her mum grappled for breath. 'Tell.' Her face screwed up in pain. 'Anyone.'

'Mum?'

But she didn't answer, eyes wide, hands covering her heart. Rose raced for the phone. Called 999.

Dad arrived home shortly after the ambulance. Rose was still holding her mother's hand as she was loaded onto a stretcher, wheeled towards the door.

'Zeta?' Dad pushed past Rose. Cupped her mother's face gently in his palms.

'Sir, we need to get to hospital.'

'This is my wife.'

'You can ride with us.'

'I'm coming too,' Rose said.

'We can only take one passenger,' the paramedic said apologetically.

'Somebody needs to stay with James.' Dad didn't even look at her.

'We need to go now.' The paramedics began to move again. Rose felt her mother's fingers slip through her own. She pressed her fingertips against her lips, lips which mouthed a silent promise. She would never tell anyone what her mother had done.

She would somehow retrieve that video.

Chapter Forty-Five

Cass

A crack of lightning and the room illuminates, Fran's face pale.

'Did you hear that?' she whispers.

I shake my head, my eyes locked on her frightened ones.

'I think there's somebody in the house,' she mouths.

My heart accelerates. My sense on high alert. Fran had broken a window to get in and now anybody could have access.

Not that this is a house you can just stumble across. Whoever is here, is here for a purpose.

'Wait here.' Fran slowly stands and creeps towards the door. My first instinct is to go with her but then I think of Isobel.

I pace.

Thunder growls. The panes shake with the force of the raindrops.

Then, there's the sound of a struggle, a blood-curdling scream.

'Fran?' I call instinctively before clamping my hands over my mouth.

She doesn't reply.

There's silence.

And then footsteps.

Chapter Forty-Six

Marina

Sylvester was furious that Zeta had escaped.

'I'm going to clear up your mess,' he snarled. Which meant he was going to bury Dorothea. 'Make sure the girls stay inside the house and thanks for ruining my birthday.'

So what? He'd ruined her life. Zeta's life. The lives of so many women.

She wouldn't let there be any more.

She sat in Cassandra's room with Tamsin while Cassandra assembled a tea party. Tamsin, too old for the game but wanting to please her sister, brought the grotesque-looking doll she kept at the bottom of the wardrobe.

Marina was lost inside her own mind, weighing up her options, dismissing each one.

If she killed Sylvester then his solicitor who had the tape with her face on it would release it to the police. She'd go to prison – which was no more than she deserved – but the girls would be left alone, would be taken into care, and one day they'd hear what she had done, potentially see the tape.

If she left, Sylvester would find her, of that she had no doubt.

He had connections in his wretched Gentlemen's Club. He'd kill her and take the girls.

If she took her own life, she'd be leaving the girls to him.

There was only one possible solution.

She'd kill them both.

Her and Sylvester.

If she was also dead the solicitor would have no reason to release the tape. No one would ever find the hidden room with the original tapes. The girls would never know who or what their parents were.

But...

She buried her face into Mr Tatty who Cassandra had placed on her lap.

Her girls.

Her beautiful Cassandra, and Tamsin who had already lost so much.

'Drink.' Cassandra thrust a toy teacup into Marina's hand.

She took a pretend sip of the pretend tea because that was what she had been doing for years.

Pretending her heart wasn't breaking.

Marina fed Mr Tatty an imaginary slice of cake.

Should she poison herself and Sylvester? Make it look like an accident? Hire somebody to kill them? Where might she find such a person?

She turned it over and over, wiping away her tears before they properly fell. Trying to relish this last tea party with the girls.

Knowing this might be one of the last memories they ever had of her.

Sad.

Broken.

Crying.

She pulled them both to her. Kissed their heads.

She loved them more than life itself.

Her mind was made up.

Later, when Sylvester was back and the girls were playing tag in the hallway, she phoned her brother.

'Hello.' Adrian's voice was warm and familiar and it sounded like home. Marina opened her mouth but she couldn't speak, emotion had swollen her throat, trapping the words she wanted to say inside.

Hello.

It's me.

Can you forgive me?

Will you help me?

'Is there anyone there?' Adrian asked and the question tore another strip from Marina's heart. He did not know it was her. He could not sense her. Despite the years and the miles between them she had always felt a connection to him, an invisible cord that had been stretched to its limit but still held strong. Now she felt the snap.

She remembered the bond they used to share.

The times he had found her crying in the garden when a baby bird had fallen from its nest.

'I'm so sorry, Marina, but even if I put it back in its nest the mother will reject her now.'

'Can't you do something?' For she had absolute faith in her big brother.

'It's too small. Too weak.'

Marina had swiped at the tears rolling down her cheeks with the back of her sleeve.

'I can try though.'

He had lined an old shoebox with hay and set his alarm to

wake him every couple of hours during the night. Tenderly, he'd fed the bird using a pipette and slowly it regained its strength. Eventually they set it back in the wild but it never flew off to pastures new, instead, staying close to the ones who had showed it such kindness.

She needed Adrian to show her the same kindness now for she was that injured bird and although she was broken beyond repair he could save Cass. Save her daughter, and Tamsin too.

His breath accelerated, synchronizing with her own. She gripped the receiver tightly as he whispered, 'Marina?'

It was still there, that bond.

'Don't hang up.' She swallowed hard, trying to rearrange her words into the right order.

'I won't. I'm… I'm sorry I did before. I miss you.'

Her shoulders shook with silent tears. More than anything she wanted to see him one last time. She closed her eyes. He was there, in her mind. Aged eight with scraped knees and a gap-toothed smile chasing her around the garden. At nine holding on to the back of her bike the first time she rode without stabilizers. At twenty-one holding her while she cried herself to sleep after her parents had died. He'd make a good father.

He'd be a far better parent than her, than Sylvester.

'I need you.'

All that she was, everything she felt, she packed inside those three words and when they reached him he felt the desperation in them for he said, 'I'll be there.'

Grateful, she began to replace the handset before she completely fell apart but then raised it to her ear again.

'I love you, Adrian,' she said, but he was already gone.

She toyed with the idea of leaving a note for Cass, to Tamsin too, but what could she possibly say that would explain why she was doing this? That she was voluntarily choosing to leave them? They'll never find out about the videos so they'll never really understand. Sorry doesn't seem enough and I love you more than life itself would be too confusing.

Best to quietly slip away and trust that her brother will be able to fabricate some story to comfort them.

By the time he got here it would all be over.

Chapter Forty-Seven

Rose

Rose was on edge, unable to settle, waiting. Checking the phone to see if it still worked before hanging up quickly so Dad would be able to get through from the hospital. She both wanted and didn't want him to ring, knowing that the news could tear her world apart. Not only hers, but Roo's too.

She stood by his bed now, watching him sleep. The steady rise and fall of his bare chest, his cheeks pink and still stained with tears. He hadn't gone to bed easily tonight, not without his beloved Trip the T-rex. If he'd had such a meltdown after losing a plastic dinosaur, how would he cope with the loss of their mother?

Stop it.

How would Rose cope? Roo was so young Mum would fade from his memory, but Rose would never forget her, forget the promise that she had made.

Stop it.

Mum would be fine, she had to be. She was their mother. She was strong, capable. Rose tried to summon up an image of her mother like that but all she saw was how she had been tonight – sad and broken. The doctors might be able to repair her body but they could never repair her mind, erase the terrible things that she had seen, that she had done.

Rose was determined to get that video. To be able to visit Mum and tell her that the only copy had been destroyed, that no one would ever see it. That she had burned it and then called the police and reported the Madleys anonymously. She would tell them where the rest of the films were. They would uncover the bodies. Give the women a proper funeral, give frantic families the news, not the news they would be hoping to hear, but some closure at least.

Mum would never be implicated. Humiliated. James would never, ever know. Rose smooths his hair from his face, feeling a wave of love, a fierce desire to protect him.

She would get the video.

She would.

Rose headed back downstairs and picked up the phone, not to check it this time, but to make a call.

'Gunner? It's Rose.'

'What do you want?'

'I need your help.'

'What's in it for me?'

'Money,' she said simply because it was all he cared about. 'Can you get your dad's car? Come to mine? It has to be now.'

'How much money?'

'A lot.' She replaced the handset, going to get ready, knowing that he was on his way.

By the time Gunner pulled up outside the house, Rose was waiting outside, dressed in black. In her hands were the two sheep masks that she and Roo had bought when they visited the farm. Hidden in her sleeve, two knives. After a quick glance at

Roo's window, she climbed into the passenger seat. She hated to leave him alone but he shouldn't wake. They wouldn't be long.

She plucked the smouldering cigarette from Gunner's fingers and took a deep drag on it. She didn't usually smoke but she thought it might calm her. Instead, it made her choke. Still, she took another drag.

'Where are we going?'

'Newington House. Know it?'

'Yeah. It's Tamsin's house.'

Tamsin. Rose remembered the pretty girl from the park. How jealous she'd been of her. She wasn't jealous anymore.

Gunner drove erratically. She wasn't sure if that was inexperience, adrenaline, but when he pulled up outside the gates and turned to her she noticed how wide his pupils were.

'Are you high?'

'Does it matter?'

She bit her bottom lip. She needed him to be clear-headed but then perhaps if he was, he would never agree to this.

'Nobody is to get hurt.' She stated this emphatically as she carefully removed the knives, passed one to Gunner, its blade glinting under the moonlight. 'This is just to threaten them.'

'We're robbing them?'

'We're here to... there's a hidden room. There's something in it that I want.'

'Diamonds?' His teeth bright, smile wide.

'No. Nothing of any monetary value but when we've got it I will give you all of my stepdad's military medals for helping me.'

'There's got to be loads of valuable antiques and shit in there.'

'No. We are not criminals.'

'But breaking into someone's home with a knife is okay?'

'Yes. No.' Rose's voice cracked. 'I don't think any of this is okay but... but... These are *not* good people and... and...' She felt her heart race painfully, wondered if her mum's heart was still beating.

'Hey, Rosie. I believe you but... a house like this... do they hunt? Have they got guns?'

'I don't know.'

'Security of any kind?'

'I don't *know*,' she said desperately, fighting back tears.

'I can scope it out. We can come back.'

'No.' She gazed at him imploringly. 'It *has* to be tonight.' Before Mr Madley could arrange to get the tape copied. She needed to tell her mum that the video no longer existed. She needed to be able to report the Madleys so they couldn't hurt anyone else.

'I don't wanna get nicked.'

'They won't want the police involved in this. Believe me.'

There was a beat.

'Yeah, okay. Whatever.' Gunner plucked a tablet from his pocket and swallowed it. Rose didn't ask what it was, she didn't want to know.

'Nobody needs to get hurt,' she said again as they left the warmth and safety of the car. She raised her face to the endless velvet sky which was speckled with stars and thought about how small she was. How insignificant.

She couldn't do this.

She thought of Roo, tucked up in bed, warm and safe.

She *had* to do this. For James. For Mum.

'Ready?' Gunner's excitement was palpable but all she felt was dizzy with nerves as she trudged behind him, keeping to the shadows, wishing all of this could be over soon.

Gunner had circled the house, appraised the windows, the doors. He had obviously done this before. 'Right.' He returned to where she stood shaking in the shadow of an oak tree. 'There is a woman downstairs, there are lights on upstairs. I'm not sure who else is in the house.'

'Shit.' In Rose's mind it had all been so... not easy, but doable. The Madleys would be sitting on the sofa together. She and Gunner would wave their knives, threaten them and they'd lead them to the room. Give up the video and all of their secrets. Then Rose would leave, call the police and go straight to the hospital where Mum would wake and smile and thank her for sorting everything out.

But life wasn't a fucking fairy tale and she wasn't a fucking child.

'Right...' She thought carefully. 'I'll go to the woman, you find the man. We're asking where the secret room is. You can threaten him with a knife, threaten his kids if that's what it takes.' She felt sick saying this but wasn't that what the Madleys did? Threatened her and Roo so Mum would be compliant. 'Don't let the kids see you, I don't want to upset them. In and out as quickly as we can. Okay?'

'Okay.'

Everything happened so quickly after that.

Everything got out of control.

Chapter Forty-Eight

Cass

NOW

'Fran?' I call her name. I shouldn't have let her check out the noise alone.

What's happened to her?

The scuffle.

The scream.

The footsteps.

My mind is in overdrive. I pull my mobile from my pocket and switch it on wondering whether to stay here while it boots up or whether to get out of the house. If I do, where will I go? There aren't any neighbours and it's a good fifteen-minute walk into the village. I want to help Fran but I have to think of Isobel.

Myself.

But didn't I think of myself all of those years ago? My family were killed and I hid. Rationally, I know I was a small child and couldn't have faced an adult but I could have tried to fetch help that night but I don't think that I did.

I am not a child anymore. I can't leave Fran, I just can't.

Music.

A song, something old, something chilling. The hairs stand

up on my arms. Almost of their own accord my feet move towards it.

Somewhere, deep in the recesses of my mind, I have heard this song before about running and rabbits and although I cannot place it I am shaking, sweating, but still I find myself stuffing my phone back into my pocket, moving towards the music.

The record spins in the drawing room, crackles and hisses as though it's trying to tell me something.

Run.

Run.

Run.

A shadow in my peripheral vision.

I turn and my knees buckle with fright.

Someone standing in front of the window wearing a sheep's head mask.

Holding a knife.

Chapter Forty-Nine

Marina

THEN

Somebody was trying to break into the house.

It was almost inaudible, the sound of the front door handle being lowered, slowly, slowly, but on her way back from the fridge with a bottle of wine, Marina heard the squeak.

Saw the movement.

Her heart pounded painfully in her chest.

Think.

Could this be connected with earlier? Zeta?

She thought they had come to an understanding. An unspoken agreement. Surely she wouldn't dare come back here – but what if she had? What if she had brought reinforcements, but who?

Not the police.

She was terrified of anyone seeing the video. Ashamed. She wouldn't risk it being seized, used as evidence.

Would she?

No. Above anything else Zeta might feel right now, her maternal instinct must surely override all of her other conflicting emotions.

I won't tell anyone. I don't want my children hurt. And...

I… I don't want anyone to see me like… that. Will you destroy it?

To protect herself, protect her dignity Marina was confident that Zeta would not have reported her.

But she was sure there was somebody out there.

A burglar?

A house like this, big, isolated, an easy target? Times were changing. Criminals no longer waiting until properties were empty. She'd read about the rise in home invasions over the past six months and each time it made her shudder.

Sylvester was upstairs taking a shower – all of her family were upstairs. Their youngest child already in bed, the eldest supposedly reading.

Marina's eyes were locked on the handle but it did not move again – had she imagined it? There was a raging storm battering the house. Could the ferocious wind have rattled the door? She checked that it was locked.

She crept past the grandfather clock, into the great hall to look out of the window. It was only just gone 8.15 but the nights were already lengthening. On the record player Flanagan and Allen sang 'Run, Rabbit, Run'. She was playing the song because she wanted to stay in the memory with Dorothea and Zeta so she didn't take the coward's way out.

She was going to drug herself and Sylvester tonight. Kill them both.

She needed it to be over by the time Adrian got here. He'd take the girls, she knew it.

Run.

Run.

Run.

Outside, the sky was inky black, the moon casting a creamy

319

light. In the darkness the window was a mirror, all she could see was her own worried face peeking back at her. Rain lashing against the pane, a cold breeze pushing through the cracks in the frames. The beech tree creaked and bent, a branch tap-tap-tapped against the glass.

Let me in.

Let me in.

Let me in.

She was just berating her overactive imagination, allowing herself to relax, heading back to the drawing room, to the battered leather armchair that moulded around her body, when she heard the crunch of gravel from the courtyard.

A throaty cough.

Oh, god.

That was not a storm or a tree or anything innocuous.

Somebody was out there.

There was a sudden whip of lightning. Startled by the flash she whimpered, her fingers tightening around the neck of the wine bottle. What was to be her last ever drink, the source of her nightly pleasure, had now become a weapon.

Thunder rumbled, low and loud.

Remembering the back door she hurried through the kitchen to double check it was locked, feet cold against the flagstone floor. She ground to a halt, terrified.

A face outside the kitchen window.

Eyes staring in.

Hot breath misting the glass.

She pressed herself against the wall, trying to make herself invisible. The lingering scent of mince and onions from the children's dinner turned her stomach.

The shadow lifted. The figure gone.

Hurry.

Should she call the police? Knowing what lay in her secret room? The terrible, terrible things that have taken place inside this house?

Yes.

This had to be a coincidence and it wasn't as though the police would be able to locate the room. Nobody could, unless they knew it was there.

Zeta knew it was there.

No. This was not her. She would not come back here.

She had to protect her children from whoever was out there. Marina rushed back to the entrance hall, picked up the phone with a shaking hand. Her fingers trembled so violently she had to jab at the numbers several times until she got it right.

999.

As soon as she was connected she whispered urgently, her name, that she lived in Newington House. That she was scared.

Somebody was trying to break in.

She garbled that she was downstairs, by the front door... That, no, she was not safe.

When she first moved in she loved the solitude here, it was beautiful when the buttery sun melted over the woodlands. Peaceful. Often the only sound was the rustling of leaves, or birds singing loud and clear, the bubbling of the brook.

Now she felt too isolated.

Aside from her family, there was nobody to hear her scream.

'Mrs Madley, help is on the way,' the operator said in a calm voice. 'Who else is in the house with you?'

'My family.' She ran through them even though it was painful to think of her youngest child, Cassandra, starfished in the cot bed that had been passed down through generations, in the pale yellow nursery where cheerful ducks marched endlessly around the border.

Her eldest child, Tamsin, a teenager, concentrating on her book, forehead creased as she absorbed herself in a world which, right now, was very preferable to this one. Why oh why couldn't she be out chasing some unsuitable boy tonight?

'How long will the police take to get here?' Marina asked. What should she do in the meantime?

There were precious things under this roof she needed to protect.

The shatter of glass from the kitchen.

A creak.

The back door?

The phone thudded from her hand. Dizziness engulfed her. Ridiculously she was still clutching the bottle of wine. Sweat trickled from her upper lip into her mouth which hung open as she drew in quick shallow breaths.

Think.

She heard the sound of a low voice muttering, the dull thud of footsteps, slow, leaden.

Somebody was inside the house.

Terror beat at her chest with clenched fists.

Run.

She darted into the great hall. The wooden panelling Marina had once thought so elegant was now dark and oppressive, closing in on her. The ceiling with its ornate carvings and crystal chandelier pressing down.

There was nowhere to hide, and upstairs...

She had to warn her family, *had* to.

She raised the bottle. Could she really smash it into some-body's face?

Yes.

Yes, she could do whatever it took for the girls, her fight or flight response had kicked in, and she was not running away.

But she had never, ever, felt so scared.

From upstairs, the groan of a floorboard. Her daughter moving around her room.

Don't come downstairs.

Don't come downstairs.

Don't come downstairs.

She sprints, had almost made it to the bottom of the stairs, when an arm snaked around her neck, a hand clamped across her mouth. The wine bottle smashed as it hit the floor, liquid splattering her legs.

She writhed and kicked and tried to bite the fingers that smelled of nicotine and that was when she noticed.

There was somebody approaching her.

Two.

There were two people in her house. Possibly more.

Hysteria rose.

The intruder was wearing a mask, a sheep's head, and she had never seen anything more terrifying.

Tears leaked from her eyes as she watched helplessly as he took the stairs two at a time. She was still fighting to be free.

Her children.

Marina was bundled roughly into the drawing room. Shards of glass from the broken bottle pierced the tender skin on the soles of her feet leaving a trail of bloodied footprints behind her. She tried to resist, knocking over a side table with her elbow as she scrabbled for traction on the oak floors. The china bowl smashed, the scent of floral potpourri cloying. It had always been her favourite but after tonight she would forever associate the smell with this.

If there was an after.

She felt a momentary rise of hope that Sylvester might have heard the bowl smash but this was dashed when she heard the water gurgling in the ancient pipes.

He was still in the shower.

She imagined him naked, vulnerable. And although she hated him with all of her heart she wanted to weep that he could not protect them.

The intruder threw her onto the sofa. She scurried into the corner and folded in on herself, crossing her arms over her chest both forming a barrier and trying to hold herself together.

'Help,' she screamed, her throat almost closed with panic.

There was the stinging crack of a hand across her cheek. She began to cry.

'Please, don't hurt me. I can give you money.'

'Money is not what I'm here for.' The voice was sharp from behind the mask.

Terror was a heavy pressure building in her lungs.

Breathe.

She couldn't.

'Where is the secret room?'

She shook her head – *I don't understand who you are, how you know* – and the intruder advanced towards her, eyes blank behind the sheep mask. She cowered. Her cheek still throbbing with pain, fearing there was more to come.

'Please. Take what you want. The candleholders are solid silver. You could sell them. I've got jewellery upstairs.'

'This is not a robbery.'

'But there are antiques, you could—'

'I am not here for money. Where are the videos?'

Marina was shaking so violently her teeth rattled together.

'I called the police.' Her voice trembled. 'They're on their way. If you leave now you can get away. I won't tell them anything. I haven't seen your face.'

Almost in slow motion, the intruder raised their hands either side of their head and lifted off the mask.

And grinned.

Marina stared into the face, the face of the teenage girl, and saw courage, a sense of invincibility, immortality. Eyes that she recognized.

'You're Zeta's daughter aren't you? Rose?'

'So? I know what you did to my mum. That other woman. Probably other women before that.'

Rose didn't even try to hide who she was. And that's when Marina knew, she was going to die tonight.

But not in the way she thought.

Not by her own hand.

There was a chilling scream. Her daughter. What was the man upstairs doing to her?

'No!' She staggered to her feet. 'Tamsin.' She charged towards the door. Feet stinging. Felt a burning pain in her skull. Instantly there were fingers wrapped around her hair, she felt a clump being yanked from her scalp.

'Please, Rose,' she begged. Her arms above her head, hands holding Rose's wrists, digging her nails sharply into skin, clawing at it.

'Bitch,' Rose said. Her voice full of venom.

Marina was roughly pushed away, landing heavily onto her

hands and knees. A foot stamped on her back so she was sprawled flat on the floor. Rockets of pain shot through her spine.

'Gunner.' Rose screamed. 'Don't hurt anyone.'

'Please.' She began to crawl. Begging, not just for her life, but for her family's. How could a teenage girl have overpowered her? But Marina knew how. The love for her mother, the desire for revenge had given her a strength that Marina just couldn't match.

From upstairs, her husband roared in pain.

'Please!' Somehow she staggered to her feet. Hands held out in front of her. 'Please stop.' Every cell in her body buzzed with panic. Willing for someone to save her. For the sound of sirens. For anything.

Lightning whipped. Thunder grumbled.

'Mummy?' The sound of a small voice. 'I'm scared.'

'Don't hurt my baby,' Marina begged.

Her Cassandra.

Chapter Fifty

Cass

NOW

'Robin?'

As I back away from the figure in the sheep mask, eyes fixed on the knife, my confused mind sifts and discards theories. His father was obsessed with the house. He is obsessed with the house.

Is he the surviving intruder? Is there no record of his name online because his father was a police officer?

What does he want?

But even as I think these thoughts I know.

I know it isn't Robin because, although I can't quite process it, the person advancing towards me, brandishing that blade, is wearing Fran's clothes. Has Fran's build.

I glance towards the door. I could run but would I make it? Would she catch me and if she did would she hurt my baby?

I am so, so scared.

'Fran?' There is so much desperation in that one word. It's a question. A plea. It's all my dry mouth can come out with.

'My name isn't Fran, it's Rose.' Her tone is cold, chilling.

It's as though the breath has been knocked out of me. Before my father had told me my stepsister was called Tamsin I had believed Rose was the name of the girl who lived here before.

The name I'd heard whispered, the flowers I had found. The name that Robin had overheard his father mention.

For a brief second I close my eyes, wishing I could feel Tamsin's fingers in my hair, her arms around me as we rock in the chair. For I believe she is here in some form, has been present, trying to tell me something.

Trying to warn me of the name of the killer. That she was back.

Rose.

I open my eyes.

The music stops and there is a moment of perfect silence before the needle lifts and whirrs to the beginning of the record before it begins to play again.

Fran lunges forward, eyes blank behind the mask. She grabs my wrist and instinctively I cover my belly with my other hand.

'Please don't hurt my baby.'

Chapter Fifty-One

Rose

'Please don't hurt my baby,' Cass begs, using exactly the same words her mother had used thirty years ago and instantly Rose is back there.

'Please don't hurt my baby,' Marina had begged. Rose had released Marina the second she heard the child's voice.

Oh god, oh god, she was trying to act all tough but it was all getting out of hand.

She had been certain that the second she was inside the house, the moment that Marina saw the knife, she would give up her secrets, the videos and then... Rose wasn't entirely sure what she thought would happen then. It wasn't just her mum she wanted to protect, but other women who might be enticed here.

She *really* hadn't thought this through properly.

The noises coming from upstairs were unbearable.

The shouts.

The screams.

Gunner had promised he wouldn't hurt anybody. She had made it clear that they were to frighten the family, that was all, but the cries of pain from the second floor told a different story. She should never have brought him along, knowing he was high, dangerous, but she could not have done this alone.

She turned and stalked towards the little girl, Cassandra. Mum had said how sweet she was earlier with James. Her hair was damp, she was wearing hedgehog pyjamas. Her brother had some similar and Rose felt bile rising in her throat.

What was she going to do?

Leave, was the obvious answer. The fucking song urging her on.

Run.

Run.

Run.

But she had removed her mask to show that she meant business. That she wasn't afraid of Marina. In truth she was so very, very scared.

Suddenly, a weight descended on her. Marina on her back, arms around her neck.

Somehow, as she twisted, she threw Marina off, on to the floor, but before Rose could catch her breath Marina was coming for her again.

Rose put out her hands to protect herself, forgetting about the knife until she felt the press of it against Marina's flesh. Heard the soft pop. The give. The slick sensation as it slid into flesh. Smelt the metallic tang of blood.

Rose was flooded with a panic unlike anything she had ever felt before. Marina was going to die. From the silence coming from upstairs the others were seriously hurt. She would never find the video. It would come out one day, when the police searched the house or when new owners moved in.

She had to find it.

Had to.

'Marina.' She grabbed Cassandra and pressed the knife

against her arm. 'Tell me how to get into the room or I'll hurt her.'

Marina stared at her with wide eyes, moaned. 'I... I can't.'

'Don't make me do this.' Rose could feel the tears in her throat, felt the wriggle of the child in her arms, so like James. 'Tell me where the videos are.'

'I... I won't.'

Rose was crying now because she knew she had to do something to get Marina to take her seriously. Something she didn't want to do.

'Then I'll carve a "Z" into Cassandra's arm as a reminder of my mother before I kill you both.'

Rose tried to keep her voice steady but she heard the tremor in it. She had no intention of killing anyone, she just didn't have it in her, but she wanted Rose to believe that she would. Surely she would give up her secrets for her daughter's sake?

Rose sobbed as the tip of the blade zigzagged across Cassandra's forearm, blood springing to the surface. Cassandra howled. Rose closed her eyes.

'Sorry. Sorry,' Rose tried to soothe the little girl. 'Do you know where the secret room is? Then I won't have to hurt you again. Hurt Mummy.'

'Yes.' Cassandra nodded, her cheeks blotchy with tears.

'Can you show me?'

Cassandra ran.

'Wait!' Rose sprinted after the child, looking wildly around the great hall, seeing a flash of yellow pyjamas at the top of the stairs. She pounded up to the next floor, slowing as she passed the master bedroom. Her stomach churned as she saw the lifeless body of Sylvester sprawled on the bed.

Tell me where it is written on the wall in blood.

One of Sylvester's arms hung over the mattress as though he had been reaching for help. His eyes, lifeless, skin waxy. Rose felt the vomit sting her throat along with hysteria.

Gunner had killed him.

He'd murdered someone. Taken a life.

He was no better than Mr and Mrs Madley. Had Cassandra seen her daddy like this? It would scar her for life.

'Cassandra?' Rose tiptoed out into the corridor. Afraid of what she'd find next.

She discovered Gunner sitting in the corner of a bedroom, knees drawn up to his chest, rocking back and forth, softly singing that song.

That fucking song that was still playing downstairs.

Run.

Run.

Run.

On the floor a girl, Tamsin, the one from the park, the one she thought fancied Gunner. A similar age to her. Eyes staring at nothing.

Dead.

It was then that Rose began to cry, for Tamsin, for Cassandra hiding, too scared to come out. For her mum who she cannot help and for herself who she can, but she doesn't want to. She'd come to the house for the video. She would not leave without it.

With one, last, sorrowful look at Tamsin she headed towards the doorway.

Felt a hand around her ankle.

She sprawled onto the floor. Gunner on top of her, shaking her.

'They're dead. They're all dead.' His spittle dripped onto Rose's face. 'This is all your fucking fault.'

From outside she heard the sirens. Through the window, the flash of blue lights.

Gunner raised the knife towards her. She grabbed at his wrist to stop him. The knife slipped to the floor and she grabbed it, too late realizing that her fingerprints were now on it.

The murder weapon.

She pushed Gunner's chest and to her surprise he rolled off. Why wasn't he putting up a fight?

But then she saw the blood, pumping out of a wound on his side. One of the Madleys must have fought hard, injured him.

Her eyes met his, she knew he was dying, knew she should apply pressure to his wound but all she could think about was helping her mum.

In front of her, Gunner took his last breath but her mum's face was all she saw.

Chapter Fifty-Two

Cass

NOW

All I can see is the face of my mother lying on the floor, blood pooling on the rug next to her. It comes in flashes. My fragmented memories trying to piece themselves back together.

The song begins again. That bloody song.

Fran – Rose – is watching me, waiting for me to make my move but I am frozen in time, the past holding me in place.

Outside, the sky blackens, the rain lashing against the panes.

The room illuminates and then darkens.

Run.

Run.

Run.

A rumble of thunder. I feel it coursing through me, deep and low, vibrating every single cell in my body. Shaking-shaking-shaking my muddled mind.

The storm.

The knife.

The music.

The mask.

All of it.

It is all of it that brings it back in a rush of clarity.

I remember.

That night, the storm had raged outside; they had always scared me. I was curled up in bed in my favourite hedgehog pyjamas but I didn't want to be alone.

'Tamsin?'

I liked it when she came and got in my bed. She would hold me and I would tell her she smelled like lemons and she'd tell me I'd understand about perfume when I liked boys, but I would never like boys. They're yucky.

'Mummy?'

She didn't answer either.

Slowly I had slipped out of bed and opened my door.

From down the corridor I could hear shouting. I thought it might be Daddy on the phone but then lightning cracked and I pelted down the stairs as fast as I could before the thunder came.

Mummy would give me a biscuit and a cuddle.

That song was playing, the one about rabbits running that always made me laugh and hop around as though I were a bunny. I could jump *really* high.

The thunder rumbled and I shot in the drawing room.

'Mummy? I'm scared.'

But then I saw Mummy on the floor. The blood. The sheep mask. The girl with a knife. I was even more scared.

The girl who I'd got to know as Fran the last few months while I've been living with James at Newington, not dreaming she was the cause of my nightmares.

Who I now know as Rose.

Thirty years ago, Rose had grabbed me around the wrist and it had hurt. I'd tried to pull away but I was only three. When

335

she yanked my arm and I thought she was going to pull it off. Pain seared through my shoulder.

'Marina,' she said. 'Tell me how to get into the room or I'll hurt her.'

Mummy didn't tell her. She just said, 'I... I can't...'

'Don't make me do this.' Rose had been almost crying and I knew that she hadn't wanted to hurt me then.

Does she really want to hurt me now?

But then I remember what came next, all of those years ago. The tip of the knife against my skin. Her carving a Z into my arm.

The zigzag scar I had grown up believing was the result of an accident where Dad had dropped a glass.

It was Rose.

Now, it throbs, and I rub at it with my fingers, remembering doing the same thing all those years ago. The feel of blood, the smell of blood, not being able to tear my eyes away from my mum, dying in front of me.

'Do you know where the secret room is?' Rose had asked. 'Then I won't have to hurt you again. Hurt Mummy.'

I had told her I did know and I ran upstairs towards the priest hole. Was that the room she meant? I hesitated, suddenly unsure, because I had seen another secret room, hadn't I? In the kitchen, and that one had made Mummy cross.

But then...

It's too much to remember. I can't cope with the memories that are flooding back. The sight of my father, sprawled on his bed.

Dead.

My beloved Tamsin.

Dead.

A boy rocking on the floor next to her.

I had felt a warm stream of urine run down my leg and I thought of my lovely hedgehog pyjamas and whether Mummy would be cross and then I began to cry because Mummy would be dead too if I didn't show Rose the room.

I carried on running until I reached the priest hole. I had turned around but Rose wasn't behind me.

All I could hear was screaming, screaming, screaming and so I climbed into the hole and I stayed there. Even when I heard my name being called.

'Cassandra? This is the police. Where are you, sweetheart? You're safe now.'

I hid for hours and hours until a man who said he was called Uncle Adrian lifted me out. I didn't even know I had an uncle but I had wrapped my arms around his neck.

My fingers were bleeding and nails torn from scratching at the walls but I hadn't made a sound. I had been brave. A big girl. I hoped Mummy would be proud.

But I had never seen my mother again, had I?

Because of Rose.

She has changed immeasurably over the years but I have no doubt this is her, the same person who is once again standing in front of me.

Once again holding a knife.

Chapter Fifty-Three

Rose

The feel of the knife in Rose's hand brings it all back. The horror and revulsion she had felt that night. The horror and revulsion she feels right now.

She didn't know what she was doing then.

She doesn't know what she is doing now.

All she is certain of is that both times she had acted out of fear and desperation. Last time it had gone so horribly wrong, ended in tragedy.

She cannot, will not, let that happen again because this time there is so much more at stake.

Cass is carrying her niece.

Standing in front of her is the family she has longed for during those long, lonely days when she served out her punishment for her crime. But Cass does not know that because she does not know who Rose really is.

Or does she?

Rose had never thought she'd see Cass again, never thought she'd see her brother, James, again. Now it all seems so inevitable, as though they'd always been destined to be reunited.

When Rose had been released she'd expected conditions attached but there hadn't been. Nobody said she couldn't come back to the area so she had because she wanted to be close to her childhood home. Even though it had been repossessed after that night, it was where she had lived with her mother and James.

Where she had been happy.

She had stood in front of her former house, at first throwing glances over her shoulder, on edge, certain that one of the neighbours would recognize her, but she had changed over the years. She didn't think anyone in the village would know what she'd done anyway. Due to her tender age when she was convicted the press weren't allowed to name her. Now she had a new name. She had chosen Fran because of the Fran in the 'Dinosaurs' programme James had loved so much. It made her feel closer to him somehow. Her eyes had been drawn to his former bedroom. Memories of tucking him in, reading him stories, Trip the T-rex clutched tightly in his fist until his eyelids began to droop.

Her little Roo. Who had he grown to be? Did he miss her the way she missed him? She had thought about him every single day.

Was he happy?

She had been drip fed certain information by the police and by the prison wardens in the weeks and months following her arrest. She knew that James had been found alone that night and had, at first, been fostered. Later, he had been adopted because who was there to look after him with her stuck inside? Her beloved mum had died. Her stepfather, David, had been sentenced for fraud and arson within the year. He'd bled mum dry and there was nothing left for her or James to inherit.

Rose hoped she'd be able to find her brother, not to build a relationship – because how could she ever explain the terrible things she had done – but just to check he was okay. But there was no trace of him. Not on Facebook, not anywhere. His name must have been changed when he was adopted.

Eventually she had found a job at Longridge estate agents. Familiarizing herself with the listings, a cold chill had crept down her spine when she recognized Newington House.

'That's been for sale for ever,' her manager said. 'Creepy as fuck and you can't get planning for sod all. A building company tried. It's overpriced and with its history...'

'Excuse me.' Rose had run to the toilet, dropped to her knees on the cold, hard floor and retched and retched.

Newington.

But over the next few days, she began to wonder if she could fulfil her mother's dying wish. Find the tape. If she could find proof that there were other women taken there, likely buried on the property, she could tell the police. Their families deserved to know what had happened to them. They deserved a proper burial.

But not until she'd destroyed the tape with her mum on. She owed her memory that much.

Rose had spent hours and hours at Newington. Carefully examining every inch of the house and grounds. Tapping on the walls like they did in the films, not sure what she was listening for. Ghosts?

The house wouldn't give up its secrets.

When she wasn't at work or at the house she googled older properties. Learning how many have hidden rooms, priest holes. Where they might be located.

Hour after hour she scoured Newington, crying with relief when she found the priest hole but there was nothing there except scratches in the stone as though someone had been trapped there once.

Stalking around the perimeter, she thought she'd found an anomaly in the footprint of the house. A discrepancy between the inside and the outside of the kitchen but she hadn't been able to figure it out.

It seemed fruitless but almost as she had given up she had made a discovery.

One that made her heart sing.

Chapter Fifty-Four

Cass

My heart is ricocheting around in my chest.

I cannot make sense of this.

How has Rose ended up back here?

How have I?

The past may bind us together but there is one common link in the present.

James.

Chapter Fifty-Five

Rose

James.

Meeting him again was serendipitous.

Rose had been sent to value a flat in town.

'The landlord is selling it – don't think the tenants are too happy.' Her boss had given her the keys.

The flat was a state, pizza boxes and scrunched-up beer cans strewn over the lounge floor – a typical lads' pad. Two of the bedrooms were littered with clothes but the third was neat and tidy. Bed made, bookcase crammed full of books. She had run her fingers down the spines, until she came across one so familiar she was instantly transported back to her childhood.

Roartastic Dinosaur Adventures

Roo clambering on her lap. 'This one, this one.'

Gently, she moved the book from the shelf, opened up the cover. Inside, 'Happy Christmas, James' in her mother's handwriting.

It was impossible.

And yet, it was real and solid and part of her past.

She began to look around the room. Strode over to the photograph on the bedside table.

A man and a woman, tanned in sundress, her arm around his neck, laughing into the camera.

As she looked into his eyes she knew undoubtedly that this was James and she raised her eyes upwards and thanked a god she had never believed in for leading her to him.

She placed the photo on the bed and opened the drawer of the cabinet, wanting to know more about adult James. There were some bank statements addressed to James Chapman. Whoever adopted him must have changed his surname but kept his first name for familiarity. Rose was glad.

She rummaged through the other papers. Wage slips for Pinkus Pharmaceuticals. Also, a note.

You're right, your flatmates are pigs but I still had the best time this weekend. Hope to see you soon. Cass xxx

Cass.

A common name, it couldn't possibly be Cassandra Madley, but Rose went back to the photo. Noticed that the sun had tanned Cass's arm, making her scar stand out.

The zigzag scar that was supposed to be a 'Z'.

The scar Rose had given her.

How had James and Cass found each other?

It seemed impossible.

She was determined to find out.

Rose quickly completed her valuation and left.

For the next few days, each lunchtime, she waited outside the building of Pinkus Pharmaceuticals, imagining James inside, at his desk, eating a sandwich. Knowing she would recognize him from his photo.

She was despairing that he'd ever come out but then, one day, he did.

The feeling of utter joy was indescribable and she held it close to her chest as she hurried after him. Trailing him into a café. It was lunchtime busy.

He grabbed the last table and she asked if she could join him.

He said yes as he perused the menu and she wanted to ask him if he still liked honey on toast and ginger biscuits.

If he was happy.

Instead, she ordered herself a tea and wanted to weep in it. How could he not realize it was her?

He ordered a slab of cake, 'not a balanced meal but I'm trying to cheer myself up,' he said apologetically.

'Bad day?' Her eyes connected with his.

You can tell me.

I'm your sister.

I love you.

'My bastard landlord is selling the flat I'm living in.'

'I'm so sorry.' She stopped herself touching his hand just in time, reminding herself that she was a stranger to him. 'Do you have any family that can help?'

His face clouded. 'My mum died last year and I don't have a great relationship with my dad. I don't have anyone else.'

Me, she wanted to say, *you have me,* but she couldn't.

They chatted about inconsequential things while he quickly ate his cake and when he walked away he took another piece of Rose with him.

She couldn't lose him again.

For the rest of the week she wondered how she could help him and then she thought of a way she could help them both.

No one had looked around Newington House for years. The company didn't even advertise it anymore.

Could James somehow live there? It wasn't solely because she wanted to get to know him again but James had been in the house earlier that day with Mum.

What if he'd seen something and it triggered his memory?

What if he took Cassandra with him?

Is it possible Cassandra could lead her to the tape of her mum and somehow Rose could forge a relationship with her brother?

She couldn't figure out a way to get him to Newington, though, until she was curled up on her sofa that weekend watching *The Shining*.

A caretaker.

What if there was a job as a caretaker? No one from the office would check the house. The utilities were still connected. The house was out of sight from the road so it wasn't as though anyone could just drive past and see any lights on.

Rose had googled until she came across Richardson's Retreats. A real company if James ever checked them out, not that he would need to. She would be his contact with them and she would always be available.

She had some money saved. She could pay his and Cassandra's wages for a few weeks. It probably wouldn't be long until her memory was triggered, and then she'd think of an excuse to move them but find them something else affordable and close to her.

It was perfect.

Well, maybe not perfect but it was the best idea she had. She'd figure it out as she went along.

The following Wednesday James had returned to the café. Rose was already there.

'Hello.' She waved him over. 'You sorted out your housing problem yet?'

'No.'

'I work for a company called Richardson's Retreats. We've acquired a new property in the area, it's a gorgeous listed building. We're looking for a short-term caretaker.' She crossed her fingers in her lap, under the table. 'The thing is, we only want couples. No wild parties. I didn't know if you lived with a girlfriend?'

'No, Cass is up north but I want to move in with her. I've been saving for a house deposit, which I've only been able to do because my current rent is cheap. I can't find anything similar. This could be the answer. What exactly will we have to do?'

He leant forward, trusting her, as he had always trusted her.

Cass had trusted her too.

She doesn't anymore though, now, warily eyeing the knife in Rose's hand. The expression on her face has changed. Cass knows who she is.

A Madley.

She knows who Rose is too.

Rose can tell that she has remembered and that's what this has all been for, the sheep mask, the knife, the song, because she is running out of time. She is running out of money. She can't keep paying their wages.

Just as Cass has remembered who she is, James thinks he knows too.

He had told her today on the phone, in a panicked call from the airport.

Only he'd got it so very wrong.

'Fran.' His voice had been shaky when she had called him after receiving his frantic text. 'I'm so worried about Cass.'

'Is something wrong with the baby?' Rose had quickly asked because ever since she found out about the pregnancy she'd been daydreaming about her future role as an auntie. Painting orange tiger stripes on her niece's face before she took her to the zoo. Later, teaching her to apply make-up of a different kind when she discovered boys.

'The baby is fine it's just...' She hears the quickness in his breath. The airport announcer in the background. 'Nothing really. Cass isn't replying to her texts though. Can you check on her please?'

But it wasn't nothing. Rose knew him. He was her brother, her little Roo, and she felt what he felt and right now it was confusion tinged with fear.

'Talk to me,' she had urged in a soft voice.

'It sounds mad.'

'I won't judge you.'

'I... I've found out I'm adopted.'

This time it was Rose's breath who quickened. Did he remember her?

'Dad couldn't tell me much about my family, other than I had a sister.'

Rose's heart lifted. She held on to the banister with one hand to stop herself floating away.

He remembered her.

But no, he didn't; that became clear when he said, 'Dad told me that my background was sensitive so he and Mum hadn't been told anything and I think it's because' – a beat – 'because I'm the surviving Madley child.'

'What?' Her hope drained, a balloon deflated, she sank down onto the stair.

'I told you it sounds mad, but I know things about the house.

348

It's so familiar. I've been there before, I'm certain. And if I'm right then I can't help thinking that Cass might really have noticed someone hanging around. What if—'

'It's okay.' She didn't want to hear his speculations and his theories about the intruder, not when she *was* the intruder. 'I'm on my way.'

It was all coming to a head. She had to make Cass remember. *Had to.*

And now, it seems, she has.

'What do you want?' Cass asks, staring at her determinedly, one hand over her bump, a wobble in her voice.

'There's a secret room here and I need you to show me where it is.'

'Why?'

'Because… because I promised I'd get it.' Rose's voice shakes, she's close to tears.

'Get what?'

Rose sees some of the fear slip away from Cass's face, replaced instead with sympathy so she raises the knife as a reminder. She cannot lose the upper hand.

'If you don't show me where the room is I'll slice that baby out of you.'

'You wouldn't.' Cass shakes her head, her eyes bright with tears, but her face is pale, the fear returned.

'Wouldn't I? Have you forgotten what I did to your mother? What I did to you?'

Cass's fingers flutter to her scar.

'Please don't hurt my baby.'

Those same five words again.

Spoken that night. Spoken today.

They're enough to push Rose over the edge.

349

Chapter Fifty-Six

Cass

Rose is on the edge.

I can tell from her eyes, wide and frightened. The way she's gripping so hard onto the handle of the knife, her knuckles are white.

She can't keep still. She's agitated, shifting from foot to foot. Chest heaving.

I really don't know if she doesn't want to hurt me.

Or whether she does.

She reminds me of a trapped animal, scared and ready to attack.

'Can I sit down?' I rub my bump, reminding her that I am pregnant. I try to smile, feel the grotesqueness of my face, my mouth twisted up at one side. I let it drop. We're past the point of pretending to be friends.

She swallows hard. Glancing at the sofa, at me, at the door. Back to me again. The faintest of nods and I walk slowly across the room. Not wanting to make any sudden movements.

Startle her.

I don't know what I'm thinking. My head's a mess. But in every hostage situation I've ever seen on TV crime dramas I know the importance of keeping talking.

Keeping calm.

I'm going through the motions, acting how I think I ought to act, saying what I think I ought to say.

Behaving in a way that gives my child the highest chance of survival.

'Are you okay?' I ask her once I am seated. 'Do you want to sit?'

She shakes her head before edging towards the armchair. Perching on the edge of the cushion. Knife in front of her. Ready to spring forward if I give her reason to.

I will not give her reason to.

'Let's talk,' I say but neither of us speak. The record still restarting.

Run.

Run.

Run.

But I can't. She's faster than me and I have more at stake. Isobel shifts position as though she knows I am thinking of her. A sharp knee or elbow jabbing at my belly.

'I know you don't want to hurt me. Us.' Again, I stroke my bump.

'I just need you to show me the room,' she pleads.

She knows I am Cassandra Madley. I don't know how she knows this when I had no idea but it isn't important right now. What's important is getting out of here.

Living.

'What's in the room?'

A tear trickles down Rose's face and for a split second I feel another prod of sympathy towards her but then my eye catches the glint of the blade and I remind myself that she is not deserving of my sympathy.

'Tapes. A tape of my mum.'

Of all the things I thought she might say – money, gold, jewellery – this never crossed my mind.

'I don't understand.'

'My mum came for a job interview here. She thought... she thought that she was saving us. We were in trouble, in a lot of debt. My stepfather... he wasn't a good man.'

I wait for her to steady herself. 'She was...' She is shaking so violently I keep my eyes firmly on the knife, in case it slips from her grasp. 'There was a woman being tortured, in a secret room.'

I shake my head. 'No.'

She's got it wrong, she must have. She's mad.

'Yes. The Madleys made my mum take part. Told her if she didn't then they would kill me and my brother. Kill her. She didn't want to. She wasn't a bad person.' Rose wipes tears away. 'You're going to be a mum, Cass. Think about the protective instinct you feel now. How much stronger that will grow once your baby is here. Mum would have done anything to protect us, and she did. She was filmed. They made snuff movies, the Madleys. Enjoyed it.'

'I can't...' I won't believe it. My parents were murdered. They were the victims.

Weren't they?

'They killed women. For fun.'

No. I had seen women like that on the news. Myra Hindley. Rosemary West. They all had something in their eyes. Something cold and hard. My mother was soft and gentle. She had died trying to protect me.

She was not a monster.

Because if she was, what does that make me? Isobel?

Nature versus nurture.

'I don't believe you.' It's all I can say.

'It's true. Mum managed to escape the room. She had to jump out the landing window to get away.'

The window that's always open.

I feel sick. Light-headed.

'When she got home she was hurt. Hysterical. She begged me, made me promise I would get the tape and destroy it and then she... she...' A look of utter despair races across Rose's face. 'I thought she was having a heart attack but it was a panic attack. They took her to hospital because the paramedics couldn't calm her down. They were worried about her heart rate and blood pressure. She left A & E. Ran straight onto the dual carriageway.'

'She killed herself?' I can't imagine.

Rose shrugged, sadly. 'Part of me thinks she'd never leave me and Roo but she wasn't in her right mind. She was traumatized. She might have been trying to find her way back here, to get the tape. I'll never know. But I have to destroy the tape and then I can hand the other recordings over to the police. I think the women are probably buried here, in the grounds. They deserve to be laid to rest with dignity. They've suffered enough.'

'So have we.'

We listen to the rain battering the roof.

My eyes meet hers.

Please don't drag up the past, my past, I silently implore.

I have to, she replies.

I want her to leave and never come back. I want to scrub every single word she has said from my mind.

'Show me where the room is, Cass.'

'I can't.'

She's in front of me in three large strides. Yanking me up from the chair. Her fingers biting into my wrist.

'Fucking show me,' she roars, transforming the sobbing woman from moments ago into someone else entirely.

Someone terrifying.

She raises her other hand. The hand with the knife.

Chapter Fifty-Seven

Rose

The hand with the knife hovers over Cass's face but then her face morphs into an image of her mum.

Mum broken and bleeding, tight black dress torn.

The last time she had ever seen her.

The only thing that might ease the horror, the helplessness she still feels whenever she thinks about her mum – and she is always thinking about her mum – is to carry out her last wishes. To find that tape and destroy it.

For the police to locate the other bodies, for those poor women to finally be at rest.

And if getting peace, justice for all of the victims is only possible with one more fatality, so be it.

'If you don't show me the room, I'll kill your baby.' Rose doesn't mean it, but still she pushes the point of the knife into Cass's stomach.

Chapter Fifty-Eight

Cass

It's enough to push me into action, the threat against my child.

Because although the woman in front of me has been nothing but friendly towards me these past few weeks, she killed my mother in cold blood.

My father.

My sister.

Would she really hurt my unborn child?

I do not know what she is capable of but I cannot risk it.

I try to shake my wrist free but she holds it firm.

The secret room is there in the depths of my memory but I'm not sure, and if she's right, if my parents are the monsters she is making them out to be, do I really want to find out?

Perhaps I can buy some more time while I think.

'The priest hole—'

'I don't mean the priest hole. I'm not fucking around here.' She pushes the tip of the blade against my protruding belly button and immediately I feel the loosening in my bladder again.

'I've only seen it once I'm not sure...' My words come out in a garbled rush. What if my memory has it wrong? What if I can't get in the room? 'I think it's in the kitchen.'

But I do not think my shaking legs can carry me there. Somehow, though, I place one foot in front of the other.

As we pass through the entrance hall, I glance at the clock. It has stopped at 8.30 again.

In the kitchen my teeth are chattering together with fright. I can remember being scared for my mother, but today I am so, so, scared for my daughter.

I know how to open up the scullery. I push a button and the wall slides back. The tunnel, though, is a different matter.

'I think it's behind here.' I gesture to the wall.

'Open it.'

'I don't know how.'

'Then you'd better fucking remember.' The knife lurches towards my belly again but this time I'm expecting it. I bat it away, feeling the blade slice into the soft flesh of my palm. The warm blood trickling down my fingers.

The smell.

Oh, god, the godawful, familiar smell.

I hunch over and retch and retch.

When I straighten up Rose thrusts a large bottle of Evian towards me; she must have darted back and grabbed it from the kitchen. She's such a contradiction, I can't figure her out. On one hand she's threatening me with a knife but she seems to care about me and the baby. The bottle is almost too heavy to hold to my mouth but I tip it back, letting the cool water trickle down my throat, washing away the sharpness of the bile that had risen.

'Thank you,' I say as I screw the lid back on. It's the kindness of her act that gives me hope, but as though she can tell I think I've found a weakness she shoves me hard. The bottle falls to the ground, my head banging against the butcher's block. I'm steadying myself against it with the hand that isn't hurt when I remember.

Mum pushing the drawer in.

I do the same, think it hasn't worked when I meet resistance but then I push it harder. Something in me taking over. Thrusting it over to the right, forward again.

Hear the click.

Feel the give.

The entrance to the hall springs open.

The frigid air hits me, as does the smell of mustiness.

Suddenly there's a banging at the front door.

A knife in the back of my neck.

'Quiet,' Rose whispers. 'They'll go away.'

The knocking stops and I think she is right but then my name again, coming from the hallway.

'Cass?'

I open my mouth to scream.

Chapter Fifty-Nine

Rose

Before Cass can scream, Rose shoves her hard into the tunnel. There's the slap of bone on concrete as she falls onto her hands and knees.

Cass is scrambling to her feet so Rose kicks the bottle of Evian at her to slow her down. She slams closed the entrance, fumbles to push the drawer back to its original position and just like that, the wall is intact. You'd never guess there was a hidden passageway behind it.

Rose holds her breath, listening for Cass, but either she is silent or the passageway is soundproof. Judging by what went on in the room and the thickness of the walls of the house, Rose guesses it is the latter.

'Cass?' the voice calls again.

Rose puts the knife down and rushes out into the hallway. 'Robin?'

'Where's Cass? Is everything okay? James texted and asked me to—'

'Check on her.' Rose forces a smile. 'Me too. She's okay but feeling a bit nauseous. Morning sickness is back, you know. She's having a nap. I was just making her some soup for later.'

'What happened to the window? It's broken.'

'Yes.' Rose had been recreating that night as best she could. 'I've a glazier on the way, don't worry. Richardson's Retreats will cover the cost.'

'Right.' Robin is still staring at her. Rose second-guesses what he's seeing. Flushed cheeks? Guilt? Panic?

'You can let James know everything is okay. I've texted him too. I'll tell Cass you called around when she wakes up.' Rose steps forward, edging Robin backwards.

'Okay. Tell her to let me know if she needs anything. Dry crackers are good for sickness.'

'Will do.' Rose unlocks the front door and stands back so he can leave and when he has she leans back against the door and breathes a sigh of relief.

But it isn't over yet.

She still has to deal with Cass.

With the tapes.

Chapter Sixty

Cass

The darkness is absolute.

Horrifying.

Chilling.

'Help!' My fists already feel tender and bruised as I hammer them against the walls. 'Help.' My voice becomes a croak.

I press my ear against the wall. I can't hear anything.

Can't hear whoever came to the door so they likely can't hear me.

I slump against the wall. Something hard digs against my hip.

My phone!

Quickly I take it out of my pocket and switch it on. The screen lights up but there's no signal.

There's a torch though.

I light it and inch carefully down the tunnel, the blackness reaching out and stroking me with its dark fingers. The gap narrow. Ceiling low.

There isn't enough air.

I'm clawing at the neck of my jumper, pulling it down, trying to catch my breath.

There isn't enough air.

The walls are closing in, crushing.

I'm going to die.

My knees buckle at the thought. I sway, falling against the wall. It's cold and slimy and grazes my cheek. I'm so unsteady on my feet I feel I might fall but the only thing keeping me upright is the thought that there are bound to be rats here.

Panic is overwhelming me.

I'm going to die.

Part of me wants to rush back to the entrance but I know from the lack of light, the silence, it is still closed. What if Rose never figures out how to open it?

I take a deep breath, the air damp, the smell of mildew catching in my throat. If I keep moving forward I might find another way out. I have to try, for Isobel at least.

I edge forward, carefully. The ground beneath my feet rough and uneven. Even if it were solid and flat I would still experience the sensation of falling because since learning I am the surviving Madley child the bottom has dropped out of my world and I am free-falling through time and space.

My memories are coming back to me in flashes but not the good ones. Visions of blood. The knife. The lifeless faces of my entire family. They come in a burst of torturous technicolour before fading to grey again. To nothing. Until all that's left is the feelings from that night. The fear I felt then merges with the fear I feel now. My legs are shaking so violently now I have to stop.

Where does this lead?

I'm scared to find out. Analysing everything Rose told me. It can't be true, can it? My parents can't have been evil people because I'd... I'd just know, wouldn't I?

I think of how obsessed I've been with genetics since finding out I was pregnant. Nature versus nurture. The genuine distress I felt when Leon conned Mr Peters out of his life savings.

I am not evil.

I am not my parents.

Although I don't know who I am, I know who I'm going to be.

A *mother*.

The thought tramples on the edges of my anxiety until my pulse begins to slow again.

I *can* breathe. I am *not* going to die.

Gripping my mobile in my hand I shine the light around the small space. I can't see too far ahead of me. Lining the walls are wooden torches like something you'd see in a medieval film.

The type an angry mob used to brandish before setting fire to a suspected witch.

My stomach turns. Is this where my fear of fire came from? Why I shake when I light a fire in the grate?

My teeth are chattering, both with cold and with dread. I don't know what I'll find ahead but I force myself to move on.

The tunnel widens. I find myself opening a door, entering a room. From the ceiling, rusting chains. On the floor, two black masks. There's a stack of equipment in the corner – I don't even want to think what it might have been used for. Because in front of me is a bookcase.

A shelf full of tapes. Tapes with women's names scrawled on the spine.

The shock of it is a punch to the gut. My knees buckle. I drop to my haunches, and then onto my knees. Not caring about rats now because there is only one single thought in my mind.

Rose was right.

I am the daughter of monsters.

Chapter Sixty-One

James

Monsters aren't real.

James tells himself this as he unpacks his case in his hotel room.

The dark thoughts he's been having are due to the shock of finding out he was adopted.

That his parents must be the Madleys.

It makes no sense that whoever killed them would have come back because Cass has searched the house while she has completed the inventory. She hasn't unearthed any hidden treasures. No pot of gold.

He sits on the bed when he's finished hanging his shirts and from his pocket hears the rustle of the envelope his father handed to him. When he opens it and reads the contents of the letter he weeps.

He places it carefully in his suitcase to deal with later. Right now, his priority is Cass.

It's natural that she has been unsettled. New house, new town, finding out she's pregnant.

It's been a lot to cope with.

She's bound to have experienced some side effects, some withdrawal after she stopped taking her medication. Being an artist – a creative – she has an overactive imagination and this is one of the many things James loves about her.

Her ability to see the world in a different light.

She's okay.

Isn't she?

He doesn't need to rush back.

Does he?

Still, there's a niggle of doubt.

He picks up the phone and makes another call.

Chapter Sixty-Two

Rose

Rose has spent the last ten minutes reassuring James that Cass is okay and he needn't rush home.

'If you like, I'll stay here until you get back?'

'Would you?'

She hears the relief in his voice, can see in her mind the way his mouth will be lifting at the sides, knows that he'll be nodding the way he always did when she reassured him when they were small.

'Yes, you've been good enough for Santa to come.'

'No, your teeth won't fall out because you forgot to brush them last night.'

Her little Roo. How is he going to feel when he finds out who she is? What happened to their mother?

He'll be devastated but will he forgive her? Understand at least that what happened that terrible night doesn't reflect on who she really is. That all she was trying to do was to scare the Madleys into giving up the tape. To protect their mother.

That she wanted to leave without anyone being hurt. That she wanted the other victims to be laid to rest with dignity.

She has no idea how James will react when he discovers the past or the present.

Cass, locked in a room.

Where will his loyalties lie? His sister, his mother, his blood, or his girlfriend?

She tries to tell herself that he will choose her but Cass isn't purely his girlfriend, is she? She is the mother of his child.

Perhaps there's a way she can ensure he'll never find out about this.

Cass is the only one who could tell him, but will she? Will she really want him to know who she is? What her parents did to their mother?

How can a relationship possibly survive that?

If Cass doesn't tell – and really, why would she want anyone to know about her heritage? – then the tape can be destroyed, the bodies discovered. Nobody needs to know Cass is a Madley. Who Rose really is. She can go on living as Fran, still in James's life, get to know her niece and perhaps, one day, somehow, James might learn that she is his sister.

And he might be happy.

Rose stands at the butcher's block, her fingers tight around the handle of the drawer, weighing up her options.

If she opens the door to speak to Cass, Cass could lunge at her, she might have found a weapon.

Didn't Gunner once say that old houses such as these often had shotguns?

She can't risk opening the door. Not yet.

Rose doesn't want any harm to come to her niece but could she leave Cass there until she is too weak to argue, too weak to fight?

James is away for five days.

Of course, she can't keep Cass there until he returns but perhaps until the day before or something. She doesn't know.

She's panicking. Throwing thoughts around and dismissing them just as quickly.

It's not as though you can starve to death in a few days, is it? She googles it to make sure. It seems that having access to water is more vital than food but Cass has that huge bottle of Evian, doesn't she?

If she keeps drinking then the baby will be fine.

What harm can it do?

Rose has no idea.

Chapter Sixty-Three

Cass

Without windows I have lost all sense of time as it bends and stretches and plays tricks on me. It's freezing. I could check the time on my mobile but I'm trying to preserve the battery, and really, it doesn't matter does it? It won't help me get out. I stuff my hands inside the sleeves of my jumper and rub my arms, feeling the goosebumps beneath my fingers. I'm lying on my side. The hard floor pressing into my hip.

This stone room is my tomb but I am not alone.

Scratch-scratch-scratch.

Two bright eyes.

A rat.

'Shoo. Get away.' My voice quiet. I don't have the strength to shout any longer. My throat is raging from all the screaming. I'm only taking small sips from the bottle of Evian that Rose kicked at me when I'd tried to lunge at her. I don't know how long it has to last me.

How long can I survive without food?

How long can Isobel survive without nutrients?

How long will I remain healthy without my insulin?

I draw my knees closer to me, not reaching my chest because

of my bump, trying to wrap my arms around them, to make myself smaller.

The glow of the eyes grows nearer.

I clap my hands, wincing with the stinging pain from my cut as my palms connect but it's worth the discomfort because the rat scuttles away.

It will be back.

Perhaps not alone this time. How many rats are down here? Is it their sharpened claws I've been hearing all along, or the desperate scraping of fingernails? The ghosts of the women trapped in this room by—

No.

I don't want to think it, I can't, but I know that it's true.

My parents owned this house.

My parents were monsters.

I try to curve my body into a tighter ball again, sick, dizzy, afraid.

It's so, so cold.

Eventually, thankfully, I drift into sleep.

When I wake nothing has changed except there is a stabbing pain behind my eyes that wasn't there before. I begin to softly weep, my shoulders shaking. My bladder is full despite barely drinking anything. It takes a gargantuan effort to stand, to pull down my jeans and pants and to urinate in the corner again like a dog. Feeling the hot splashes against my thighs. The pungent smell of ammonia. I am dehydrated but I dare not have too much of the Evian. What if I run out and I have to collect my urine in a container of some sort and drink it?

The thought turns my stomach, but anything would be better than dying.

Anything is better than this.

Ladybird, ladybird, fly away home. Your house is on fire, your children are gone.

Hands smoothing my hair, fingers deftly untangling the knots.

The smell of lemons.

Tamsin.

The sense of my sister being by my side is so vivid I reach for her, expecting to feel solidity but grasping at nothing but air.

Something warm against my cheek. A palm?

Fur.

I stumble to my feet, my head spinning, the room swimming. My legs fold in on themselves and I crash to the floor. Feel the burn of my knees, smell the coppery blood as its warmth drips down my legs.

Scratch, scratch, scratch.

'Somebody help me!' I scream over and over, my strength momentarily returned. 'James!' It's fruitless, I know it's fruitless but still I try until my throat is raw, voice a whisper.

Nobody can hear me.

Nobody ever heard them did they? The other women who were brought here.

Who died here.

The ghosts of my parents' victims crowd in on me, laughing, laughing, laughing.

We won't let you go.

Exhausted with it all, I close my eyes, clamp my hands over my ears, afraid of going mad.

Afraid I already am.

My bladder is uncomfortably full for the millionth time, the baby pressing down on it.

'Shh,' I soothe as she wriggles around, kicking to be free. Is she picking up on my panic? 'You'll be okay,' I promise. 'We'll be okay.' Because I cannot save her unless I save myself.

Tamsin.

If James and I are calling the baby Isobel after his mum then her second name will be Tamsin after my sister because the bond between sisters is unbreakable, it crosses oceans, worlds, lifetimes.

But then Rose is James's sister so where does that leave me? Whose side will he take?

Mine.

I have to believe he will take mine.

I have to believe he has come home and he is looking for me because this is all the hope I have left, and it is almost too much to bear.

Chapter Sixty-Four

Rose

Rose is losing hope. Losing time.

Cass has been in the room overnight and she cannot bear it.

She only has a few days left before James comes home. She had spoken to him on the phone at length.

'She's asleep again. She's still feeling a little under the weather.'

'But she hasn't even texted me.' James had been worried.

'Sorry. That's my fault. I hid her charger because she's constantly googling things that can go wrong with the baby. I'm so worried about her,' Rose had said.

'She's very... obsessed is perhaps too strong, but curious about nature versus nurture. Genetics. Fran' – a beat – 'do you think kids always take after their parents? Personality wise?'

'No.' Rose had been adamant. Because if they did then yes, she would be good and kind and trusting like her mother but she would also be a victim and Rose does not want that.

'Should I come home?' he asked.

'You don't have to. I brought some face masks and a manicure set. We could have a mini spa. A digital detox. It would really do her good.'

James had agreed, grateful to her for being here. Later that night Rose had texted him from her phone, pretending to be Cass.

Sorry lack of contact. Feeling rough. Can't find my charger so texting you from Fran's mobile. She's going to pamper me. See you when you get back. Love you xxx

She had sent the text, switching off her phone.

It hasn't yet been a full twenty-four hours without Cass eating but is that enough to weaken her so that she won't fight when Rose goes in or will it have made her more desperate?

More dangerous.

What if Rose never goes in?

No one would ever find Cass. It's impossible to find the room without knowing it's there.

The tapes would remain for ever hidden because nobody can get permission to knock down the house.

If Cass dies, perhaps all of her problems would disappear?

Chapter Sixty-Five

Cass

I'm disappearing. Fading away.

Dying.

The last thought comes to me, clear and sharp and painful.

I haven't been trapped for long but my blood sugar levels have plummeted. I feel so weak. So ill.

The rat is back. It has brought a friend this time. They stare at me, unblinking, unflinching.

The scratching amplifies. A thousand glowing, beady eyes filling the room. They advance and I retreat. Spine pressed against the hard wall, covering my bump with my hands to protect my baby.

Hundreds of tiny teeth sink into my skin. The pain is unbearable. But I do not once try to draw my arms away because they are a barrier protecting my unborn child. I feel the moistness of my flesh as blood and muscle and tissue spill out onto the flagstone floor. I hear the chink-chink-chink of teeth against bone, a searing agony as they claim me but still I cradle my bump even as they gnaw away at me.

I am crying, harder and harder, realizing that the rats will never be satisfied. That they will not stop. Once my arms are nothing but bloodied stumps they will eat through my belly. Devour my baby.

'No.' I try to push them away but there are too many of them. They clamber and climb and advance over and over again. 'No,' I scream and it is then that I wake. My eyes springing open to see one rat watching me, only one, but I can still feel the teeth, feel the fur, the sour stench they carry and my dream, as disturbing and horrific as it was, is nothing compared to the nightmare of waking.

Knowing I am still here.

Still trapped.

My stomach roils as I breathe in the smell of my own urine and my shame. There's a pain under my ribs. I vomit but there is nothing in my stomach to come up. The headlines of every article I've ever read on Google plays out on a cinema screen in my mind. All the terrible things that will happen to me and my baby if I do not eat. Do not take my insulin. I had been trying to preserve the battery in my phone but I switch on the torch and examine my hands. My fingers are swollen, my feet are too. I'm afraid pre-eclampsia is setting in.

I am going to die.

My hand over my bump.

We are going to die.

No. No. No.

It takes every ounce of energy I possess to crawl around the room for what feels like the thousandth time.

Ladybird, ladybird, fly away home.

Tamsin is with me, urging me on.

My resolve is steel because deep down I know if I do not get out of here right now, I might not get out of here at all.

Not alive, anyway.

Methodically I circle the room, hands slapping against the cold stone walls as I try to find something, anything, to help me. A light switch, a catch. My parents used to shut themselves in here to make their videos. Just like there was a way into the room from the kitchen, there has to be a way out.

There *has* to be.

I think about how I got in here. The drawer in the butcher's block was shut. Instinctively, because I had seen it done before, I was able to trigger the release catch. This was when the block could swing to one side so I could enter. If my parents wanted to leave the room how did they do it? There must be another release, another way to swing that part of the wall.

My heart sinks, sudden and heavy, as I realize. When my parents were in here the drawer would still have been shut, the catch still open. Now, if Rose has left the drawer open, even if I find the opening this side, I will never be able to escape.

My parents were a lot of things, cruel, reckless, irresponsible, criminals. But one thing I think that they weren't is stupid. There must be another way out of here. They wouldn't risk being stuck themselves.

Think.

What was this room used for originally? It wasn't a scullery. I remember the day I arrived, recalling the history I had learned at school. The Catholics that used to have to hide.

Ladybird, ladybird, fly away home. Your house is on fire.

Fire.

It all comes flooding back to me. I am not afraid of fire, I never was. I was afraid of the fireplace.

Crying on my mother's bed. Her sweeping me into her arms.

'It's eaten Daddy.' Pointing at the large inglenook in her bedroom that I had seen my father walk into but never walk out of.

I try to visualize where I am in this house of horror. Where the master bedroom would be. I concentrate on this corner of the room. There must be a staircase behind the wall somewhere. A second way into and out of the room. There has to be.

There are bookcases stacked with video tapes. I sweep them to the floor and press each shelf. Put my weight against them and try to shove them aside.

Run my fingers under the shelves; at the bottom, tucked in the corner, a button.

I press it.

There's a give. I push harder. A blast of air, but fresher. Warmer. I step forward and the bookcase slams back into position behind me.

Through the dying torchlight, a spiral staircase. Slowly, I begin to climb. My heart in my mouth.

The space tight but then wider. Lighter. A rectangle of light ahead.

And then I'm stepping out of the inglenook fireplace. Into the master bedroom.

My parents' bedroom.

Heading towards the doorway I had passed that night as a child and had seen my father prone on the bed.

Murdered.

And I think, perhaps, he deserved it.

Slowly, silently, I creep down the stairs. I can't hear Rose. I head into the kitchen. My priority is food, stabilizing my blood sugar, keeping my baby safe.

I see Rose in the pantry. She's fumbling with the butcher's block.

I make a split-second decision. A decision that could cost me everything.

Chapter Sixty-Six

Rose

What Rose is doing could cost her everything but she can't leave Cass in there to die. She just can't.

She knows she could go to prison for a very long time for what she has done but it will be worth it to finally destroy that tape.

For the other women to be acknowledged. Laid to rest respectfully.

'Cass?' Rose calls as the false wall opens. She steps into the blackness of the tunnel. The stench of urine is overpowering.

What has she done?

'Cass, I'm sorry. I've come to help. I've—'

Rose feels hands on her shoulder blades, the shove. Loses her footing on the uneven ground. Her head slaps against the concrete as she falls.

'Upsidaisy.' She is in the garden, helping a giggling Roo to his feet. They hold hands again, spin around and around under the bright midday sun. He smiles at her, her beloved brother, and she is truly happy.

Loved.

But her head hurts. Roo slipping away from her. Warm blood escaping from the gash in her skull.

Her eyes close and it's all over.

Chapter Sixty-Seven

James

'It's all over?' James asks. He had only been home five minutes before Cass had rushed into his arms, shaking.

Then she'd dropped her bombshell.

Cass nods, pale. Quiet.

'Richardson's Retreats aren't going ahead with the renovation?'

'No.' Cass can't look him in the eye and he knows she is scared. They will lose the first home they have ever known together.

'And Fran has just… gone?' James feels the loss keenly. He'd felt a friendship with Fran but to her, he must have been purely business.

What should he do now?

There is so much he wanted to tell Cass but now he is here, he can't. If he tells her he is adopted, she'll want him to trace his family, for genetics, for Isobel.

If he tells her that he believes he is the Madley child then what? She'll pity him? Worry that the tragedy will have damaged him somehow?

Nature versus nurture.

The Madleys were decent people.

Victims.

He is a decent person and he wants to shield her from everything unpleasant.

If she knew the truth, she'd definitely say no to the question that is sitting on the tip of his tongue.

'Cass.' Is he doing the right thing? Is it too much? Too soon?

Chapter Sixty-Eight

Cass

There is such intensity in the way James is looking at me. Such love. But also something else, something I can't identify. I feel my stomach plummet. Does he know?

Has Dad told him who I really am even though I made him promise not to?

I cannot bear for James to know I am the surviving Madley child. He'd look at me with such sympathy. And he can never, ever find out what my parents did to all those women.

To his mother.

Nature versus nurture.

There is evil in my genes.

'Cass,' he begins again, 'how would you feel about staying here?'

'Staying? How?' But even as I ask I feel my body sag with relief. The room can remain hidden. The tapes. The bodies.

If we stay it will never come out what my family did. Will never become known that I am part of that family.

'Mum's probate has come through. Dad gave me a letter from the solicitor. I've inherited quite a lot of money. What about if we made an offer to Richardson's Retreats? We could buy Newington? If you'd like?'

I begin to cry because that is what I'd like, more than anything. To bring Isobel up in the place where I spent my formative years. Where I played with my sister. Perhaps, in time, Isobel will have a sibling too.

A brush of cold air against the back of my neck.

Giggling.

I turn around but there's nobody there. Out in the hallway, without being wound, the clock begins to tick.

Epilogue

Time ticks on.

It's been almost five months now since that conversation with James and again, everything has changed.

James had been confused, of course, that Richardson's Retreats weren't the legal owners of Newington but it made it easier for us to buy the house at a good price.

The paperwork is complete, Newington is ours but we're not only homeowners.

We're parents.

Our daughter was born here, in the master bedroom. My labour progressing so quickly, faster than I'd been expecting from the books I had read. It was as though Isobel couldn't wait to be here, at Newington, where she belongs. Her middle name is Tamsin, of course.

She is a complete joy. Even my dad raised a smile when he came to visit after she was born although he couldn't understand why I'd chosen to stay here.

'It's where I feel closest to them,' I had whispered and he'd nodded. Understanding if not condoning. Of course he doesn't know about the room, the tapes, the bodies, and they are often on my mind, the victims of my parents. Sometimes

I wake in the night feeling ghostly fingers on my skin, hearing their screams.

Sometimes I hear them in the daytime too.

'It's just… Cass. Are you okay?' Dad had asked. 'You seem… now Isobel is here perhaps it's time to think about going back on your medication?'

I had shaken my head because for the first time in my life I felt like me. I know who I am. A mother. A partner. A daughter. A sister.

Dad's transferred the money that was in trust for me into Isobel's name. I can never explain it to James. I don't want to use it. It feels like blood money to me. By the time she turns thirty and it becomes hers, Dad won't be around anymore and I can feign ignorance when she inherits.

Isobel lies in her Moses basket, eyes trained on something I cannot see.

I like to think it's her Aunt Tamsin. Eventually her eyelids droop and close. Her mouth twitches as she sleeps. Although James had been able to offer a rational explanation to all the happenings I'd been convinced were supernatural, I know what I believe. We all have our own belief system, don't we? Things that bring us comfort. Believing my sister was, *is* still watching over me is mine.

Mr Tatty the bear stands guard over Isobel from his position on the bookcase.

I tuck the blanket in around her. It's warm and cosy here now. We never find the landing window open anymore. The clock never stops at 8.30.

James will be home in an hour. I make a start on dinner.

I prepare two vegetable pies. Cooking the smaller one first, and putting it on a plate.

Glancing at my daughter to check she is safely asleep I take the plate and open the wall to the scullery before setting it on the butcher's block while I open up the passageway.

Rose doesn't speak today. She doesn't cry. She doesn't beg. One hand is chained to the ceiling; the chain is long though, I don't want her to be uncomfortable. She picks up the fork as she glares at me as though she wants to stab me with it. It's only plastic, so even if she tries, it will not hurt me.

After I pushed her that day and she'd knocked herself out I fetched the sack trolley and somehow dragged her through the tunnel. It was only supposed to be temporary. I'd always intended on letting her go but then James came home and suggested buying the house and I thought about what would be uncovered if I told the truth. My family's history, those bodies, and it wasn't just my anonymity I was worried about. I didn't want Isobel growing up as a Madley. The subject of endless speculation. After all, the internet is here now and it is a powerful thing.

Part of me reasoned that by leaving Rose where she was I was protecting James from it all too.

It has been easier than I'd thought keeping her hidden. Pretending to be Rose, I'd text her boss from her phone and said that due to family complications she wouldn't be back. That's close to the truth, isn't it?

James doesn't know about the scullery and if, by chance, he managed to find the button that slides the wall back, he'd never be able to operate the butcher's block by accident. Would never guess what lies beyond it.

I'm careful to ensure he is out of the house when I take Rose her food. Empty her camping toilet. Take her a bowl of warm water so she can wash. Monday to Friday he's at work and on Saturday mornings he plays football now for the village team. We're making friends here.

On Sundays Rose is on her own all day and this isn't something I feel good about. I'm not my parents, after all. I'm not cruel.

Sometimes I daydream about letting her go. She's promised me over and over that she'll never tell. That all she wants to do is be a part of James's life, Isobel's life, however she can. That she's family. That we can put everything behind us. Start again with a fresh slate.

Sometimes I think this is what I want too. But I don't know. So much has passed between us. Can I ever trust her? She is family, that much is true, but she also killed my family. She has explained that my mother's death was accidental. About Gunner's part in my father's and my sister's murder. How she'd instructed him not to hurt anyone but he'd become out of control. I think she's telling the truth but the bottom line is that if she hadn't brought him here, Tamsin would still be alive.

Knowing what I know now about my parents, it pains me to admit that they deserved it, but Tamsin? Even if I could forgive Rose for my parents, how can I forgive her for the loss of my sister?

I don't know. Sometimes I believe that Rose and I are both victims. That perhaps it is possible for us both to heal, and it is during these times I stand by the butcher's block, fingers fiddling with the drawer, thinking, This time, this time I'll set her free. There is a huge part of me that wants to let her go.

But I never do.

My head is too muddled to make sense of it all. Thoughts

circling around and around like the yellow plastic ducks that I used to try and hook at the fairground, Dad behind me, his large hands over my small ones, holding the pole steady. I try to snatch some clarity but there is no space for rational thought among the guilt and the grief and the anger and the fear that I'll be the one sent to prison. That Isobel will grow up without me.

My daughter is the one who calms me. Reassures me in the times that I feel I've completely lost my mind, that there is something in my world that makes sense.

It is her I try to focus on, not Rose, but of course, my mind returns to her over and over.

There is so much I don't know.

I don't know how long I'll get away with this. Last week there was a report on the news of a girl who'd gone missing fifteen years ago being found in the basement of an American home.

Fifteen years. I can't imagine.

I don't want to be doing this.

Already, Rose is pale, weak. I'm bringing her vitamin d supplements but it isn't the same as being in natural light, I know.

I don't even know how I'll manage next week, or next month, or when Isobel is old enough to walk, talk, ask questions, but for now all I can do is look after Rose as best I can.

Anyway, it won't be forever. I will let her go soon. I really will. I'm not a monster. I promise you that. We'll come to some sort of agreement eventually, Rose and I. I'm sure.

I really don't want to be doing this.

I hope that one day, whatever the future holds, she might understand.

That she might even forgive me.

That you might forgive me too.

I didn't mean to hurt her but my family's reputation, mine and Isobel's anonymity, is precious and irreplaceable and I was desperate to get it back when Rose threatened to expose us. And now that I have it, I'll do anything to keep it.

Anything.

And now you've heard my story I hope you'll understand. Perhaps you'd do the same?

THE FOLLOWING LETTER
CONTAINS SPOILERS

Hello,

Thank you so much for spending time with Cass, James and Rose. I really hope you enjoyed their story. If you did, I would be very grateful if you could please pop a star rating or a short review on Amazon. It really makes a huge difference to the visibility of a book.

If you want to keep up to date with my news and special offers please sign up for my newsletter. You'll get two free short stories when you do and I promise you I won't bombard you. www.louisejensen.co.uk/mailing

The idea for this, my ninth psychological thriller, came about after my youngest son wanted to watch some classic old horror films. *Amityville* was one of the movies we chose. Afterwards, we became a little obsessed with the history of the house and what had happened to it since.

I thought much about the people who bought it after the alleged events took place. Would I have chosen to live in a home with such a supposed dark past? I wasn't sure if I would.

Cass and James came to mind straight away. Cass initially unaware that Newington was the scene of such horrific crime. James not being put off by the past.

But what was the story?

I had an idea that the perpetrators of a violent crime could come back, years later for... something. But what? It had to be something well hidden, something small. A key, I decided.

Then came three long years of trying to figure out what the key was for. While I usually launch into a story without knowing the end, if I couldn't figure out what the key fit, there was no story.

During meals, car rides, days out I'd ask my family what the key could be for. Nobody knew.

It was in the school holidays when I asked my youngest son again. He got a pad of Post-it notes and two pens and told me to sit at the table. 'We're not moving until we figure out what the key is for,' he said.

Once we started brainstorming ideas, it came to me and immediately, three years after the initial idea, I began writing.

I hope you think it was worth the wait.

Do join me next year when we'll meet Amy and Jen who, while trying to trace their missing mother, realize they don't know each other quite as well as they thought...

Louise x

Acknowledgements

As ever, it has taken a village to bring this book to life.

Huge thanks to my publisher, HQ stories. I really am living my dream and I'm very grateful. Special mention to my wonderful editors, Manpreet Grewal and Cat Camacho, our fearless leader, Lisa Milton. Marketing, PR, Production, Design and everyone who plays a part in the process.

Thanks to my literary agency, The Blair Partnership, in particular Rory Scarfe and Hattie Grunewald.

John Duller, who volunteers for the National Trust at Baddesley Clinton for answering my many questions on manor houses and priest holes. Your enthusiasm for history made researching this story a joy.

Of course, I wouldn't be writing books if it weren't for you, the readers. Thank you to everyone who has supported, recommended and reviewed my books. There are so many amazing bloggers and book groups online.

A special shout out to everyone who takes part in my Sunday Book Share on Facebook. It really is one of the highlights of my week although my TBR pile is groaning under the weight of the recommendations.

Love to my friends, particularly Sarah, Natalie and Hilary and to Sue who always reads my books (usually on a beach…).

My family, Pauline and Mike, and Jo and the gang. My daughter-in-law, Rebecca, Mum and sister, Karen. My husband Tim who has survived another bout of first-draft angst.

Callum, Kai and Finley who are EVERYTHING.

And Ian, of course.

Book Club Questions

1. Nature v nurture is something Cass and James think very deeply about when they find out they will become parents. What are your beliefs or experience?

2. At the beginning of the story Cass and James believe they know each other well enough to build a life together but at several points they begin to question whether they really know each other at all. How long do you think it takes to get to know someone, or do we ever really know anyone?

3. Did you have an idea at the start of the book who was 'good' and who was 'bad'? How had your opinions changed by the end?

4. Cassie heard children giggling. Do you believe this was her own childhood memories, her imagination or could it be a spirit trying to protect her?

5. In what way is Newington House a character in its own right?

6. Coincidences are referenced throughout the book (all of them are remarkably true). Have you ever experienced a strange coincidence? Adrian said, 'Coincidences mean you are on the right path'. What do you believe?

7. Both Cass's father and James's parents lied to them about their identities. Discuss why they did this. Do you think they were right?

8. Have you ever experienced anything supernatural? What do you believe?

9. What would you like to happen to Cass, James and Rose?

Turn the page for an exclusive extract of *The Fall*,
the pulse-pounding thriller from Louise Jensen

She promised not to tell. They
made sure she couldn't...

AVAILABLE TO BUY NOW!

PROLOGUE

The darkness is absolute.

A ragged breath.

The wait excruciating.

A whimper.

Light floods the stage.

Two little girls stand shoulder to shoulder, hands anxiously fiddling with their tutus, pink tulle stiff, before their fingers find each other, linking together.

The audience collectively sighs, hearts melting, as the girls edge forward, ballet shoes shuffling, chubby legs clad in cream tights. The hall smells like every other primary school – poster paints and lemon cleaner – but tonight it has been transformed into a theatre. Rows of grey plastic chairs stripe the shiny parquet flooring.

The girls look at each other for reassurance, so similar with their bright blue eyes and blonde, tightly wound buns that they could be mistaken for twins instead of the cousins they are.

They're the best of friends.

From the speakers, the first strains of Tchaikovsky's *The Nutcracker*. From the wings the frantic whisper of their teacher.

'Come on. Everyone's waiting.'

The lower lip on one of the girls juts out before it begins to tremble, her eyes filling with tears. On the front row, her mother grabs the arm of her sister.

The desire to go and rescue the girls is immense.

'Shall we go up there and—'

'Give them a minute,' her sister says in a low voice. Although she's concerned about her niece, she knows her own daughter will take care of her. 'They've got each other. They'll be okay.'

The first girl steps into position, raising one arm in a perfect arc above her head. The other stays by her side, still tightly gripping her cousin's hand. The first girl squeezes her cousin's fingers, three times in the way she knows her mum does to her aunt when she is stressed about something.

The second girl wipes her eyes, mimics the move.

They begin to dance, their moves clumsy at first because they never once let go of each other until beaming smiles replace worried frowns.

Then, they break apart, each spinning pirouettes that are only fractionally out of time. Even then you could see they had rhythm, talent. Too young to go on pointe, they run, graceful, circling the perimeter of the stage, arms outstretched as though they are flying, hair escaping their buns.

Their mothers relax. One sister placing her head on the shoulder of the other.

A family united. A family who love each other. Support each other.

A family full of secrets.

As cameras click and bright flashes fill the auditorium, no one could have ever guessed that ten years later one of those girls would be in a coma, fighting for her life. Everyone close to her hiding . . . something.

That the two sisters, so proud of their daughters, would be at war, trying to uncover the truth, conceal the truth.

Protect their children.

The entire family forced to take sides, torn apart.

It was impossible to predict as they sat watching the show.

But in the years to come, they wouldn't be the only ones watching those girls.

ONE PLACE. MANY STORIES

Bold, innovative and
empowering publishing.

FOLLOW US ON:

@HQStories